SARAH MOSS is the author of seven novels, *Cold Earth*, *Night Waking*, *Bodies of Light*, *Signs for Lost Children*, *The Tidal Zone*, *Ghost Wall* and *Summerwater*, as well as a memoir of her year living in Iceland, *Names for the Sea*. Her work has been shortlisted for the Women's Prize for Fiction, the RSL Ondaatje Prize, and the Wellcome Book Prize. Born in Glasgow, she lives in Dublin where she teaches at University College Dublin.

Signs for Lost Children

Sarah Moss

Typeset by M Rules

Printed and bound by CPI Group (UK) Ltd, Cro...

MIX
Paper from
responsible sources
FSC
www...
FSC C020471

GRANTA

Granta Publications, 12 Addison Avenue, London W11 4QR
First published in Great Britain by Granta Books 2015
Paperback edition published by Granta Books 2016
This paperback edition published by Granta Books 2021

1 3 5 7 9 10 8 6 4 2

ISBN 978 1 78378 769 2
eISBN 978 1 84708 912 0

Prologue

Home

There is a boy.

Through the leaves, the sun shines copper on his hair. He doesn't hear the sea meeting the shore behind the trees as he doesn't hear the wingbeat in the chambers of his heart. The trees make oxygen and the boy's lungs expand, his ribs rise, blood reddens in his arteries. There is a boy.

There is a bird near the boy. The bird is as big as the boy's hand and it's not brown but the colour of wet straw and its speckles look like indentations and there are two charcoal stripes on each wing, as if the bird has been drawn fast in oil pastel, and the boy has been still for so long that the bird doesn't know there is a boy.

The boy is waiting.

The red maple leaves are bright as blood against the greens of a Cornish garden. The rabbits don't take cover there, as if they know what's foreign. Sparrows and blue tits don't gather in the black bamboo. No fox footprints mar the ribbing of raked gravel, nor is a heron reflected beside the stepping stones leading only to the middle of the moon-watching pond.

Sometimes, at night, the owl lands on the roof of the tea-house and turns its head, looking for mice by moonlight.

Twigs break and a rustle comes through the leaves. Papa, humming. Then t'worms'll coom and eat 'ee oop. Not in front of the patients, please, my loves, *says Mamma.* Or at least not with such gusto. *Later, there will be proper tea in the house with the patients and Mamma at the head of the table, potted meat sandwiches, salad from the garden, a sponge cake made with eggs Laurence carried from the henhouse before he went to school this morning. Later there will be piano practice, arithmetic, hair-washing. Papa sits down on the edge of the veranda to take off his shoes. He has darned his socks with the wrong colour.*

They can't always get green tea but Papa has brought a new package from Bates across the water. A ship came in, he says. Papa kneels on the floor to lift the lid of the shiny wooden box of utensils Makoto sent him from Tokyo. He sets up the primus to boil water. He arranges the cups and the teapot, rough and heavy as grey pebbles, on a black tray that shines like ice and has gold birds painted on it. Laurence squats on the veranda and watches. Papa's trousers strain. Laurence can kneel like that, with his heels under his bottom, but his feet get squashed and he doesn't see why he should.

'A story?' Papa asks. 'The badgers and the bag of gold? The traveller and the fox cubs?'

Laurence smiles at Papa and shakes his head.

'The cat and the moon-watching pond?'

Papa likes to tell Japanese stories in which animals change shape and speak.

'Tell me how you made our house. Tell me about the garden.'

Papa smiles at him. 'Let me make the tea first. Gather my thoughts.'

a scatter of black hairpins

The white cottage feels different in Ally's absence. Like a factory with the machines lying idle, like a ship becalmed. The papers on his desk breathe as the breeze off the river passes over them and he moves his fingers in the sun to see his shadow-hand thicken and elongate on the half-written page. It is not a bad thing, for a house to lie at rest, for the hum of his thoughts and the scratch of his pen to be what happens. That was how it was before they married, before he brought her back here. *With all my worldly goods, I thee endow.* Shadows strengthen on the lawn as the cloud that has chilled the morning for the last few minutes passes across the sun and out over the water towards St Mawes. He holds up his hand in light strong enough to glow through his fingertips, to pass through the edges of himself. He turns his wrist to see the webs between his fingers translucent. Birds' feet, he thinks. Maybe he will bathe from the beach this afternoon. Can Ally swim, does she own a bathing dress? He imagines her wet, a brief gown clinging around her legs, her arms white against dark soaked cotton. Come now, if he is not going to work he might as well have accompanied her to the boats. He applies himself.

He is reading about the lighthouses of Japan. He rests the volume's spine against the desk and leans back in his chair. A person would think that lighthouses must be particularly vulnerable to earthquakes. His mind's eye sees a tower sway, sees cracks appearing in the brickwork as the structure twists like a wrung towel. Glass arches through the air, the reflector in perfect, glittering flight until it explodes on the rocks below as the tower shivers and falls, the land discarding buildings as a sleeper shrugs off a blanket. The waves below have turned around, running the wrong way because the Pacific Ocean itself is disturbed by upheavals in the ground on which it lies.

But a person would be wrong. If correctly built, tall, columnar structures can counteract seismic activity. Unlike the long, low buildings in which people tend to live, towers can be made to bend rather than break. It is already known, after all, that the best lighthouses are the more responsive to wind and waves. The base must move with the ground on which it stands, but with good masonry, the top, the light itself, can be a still point, axis and anchor.

The sun goes in again, and a seagull screams as if in protest. He closes *The Proceedings of the Asiatic Society of Japan*. The writer of this article, a Scottish engineer, does not like the Japanese. They lie, he says, sometimes because it is the easiest way of getting what they want and sometimes for no discernible reason. They are characterised by 'complete indifference to time and to the exigencies of circumstance'. They imprison and enslave their women, and have no idea what to do with a cruet. He wonders if this man knew what to do with the Japanese equivalent, whatever it might be. However inscrutable the natives, it is the sort of thing it ought to be possible to learn. The sort of thing he will try to learn.

He hears the front gate click, and stands, cranes forward, to see Ally cross the garden. She is foreshortened by the height

4

of the house, abbreviated to hat, skirt and basket. The basket drags on her arm; the boats must have come in. A seagull, sentinel on the roof of Greenbank House, announces her return, and is answered from the chimney of Symond's Hill and the ridgepole of Penwerris House. If he dies out there, he sometimes thinks, if his ship founders in the Bay of Biscay or off the Horn before he even glimpses the Inland Sea, the seagulls will cry his passing here weeks before the messenger comes up the path. The front door closes quietly. Trained in her father's house, she is scrupulous not to disturb his work. He will go down to her. Better to spend time with his new wife than in such morbid fantasies.

She can feel the heat of the flagstones through her shoes. All the captains' houses along Dunstanville have their blinds down to bar the sun flickering from the estuary and flashing from the windows across the water in Flushing. The Flushing houses are patent follies, with turrets stuck on the corners, crenellations in unlikely places and outbreaks of Gothic stone like carbuncles in modern red-brick walls. Papa would find them personally offensive, but Ally doesn't mind. Let rich men have their games: it is entertaining if not edifying for the rest of us to see how like the daydreams of little girls are the trappings of masculine wealth. The monkey-puzzle tree in front of a captain's white bay window bows over the pavement, embossing its dark limbs on the stucco of the Greenbank Hotel. Captain Motton is said to have brought it back from Africa, along with a monkey which died and is now stuffed in a glass case on his sideboard. She likes Falmouth.

She shifts the basket onto the other arm, smiling at what her aunt in London would say about her, Dr Moberley Cavendish, haggling over fish at the docks. This time of year, the neighbour's housekeeper told her yesterday, the boats go out at dawn and they're back by lunchtime, often enough. When the boat's full, it's full, and the quicker the catch is on the London train the better. If you want fish, you want to be there on the quay when they come in. Mrs Trevethan herself gets fish from her cousin, most people round here know someone on the boats and that's why there's no fish-shop, see? But as long as hotels haven't got there first, should be someone will sell her a couple of mackerel or a codling. Mrs Trevethan did not tell her that the fishing quay is upriver of the Packet Quay, the fishing boats having a shallower draught than the ocean-going ships, but although she was late there were still great coffin-sized caskets of dead fish lying in the sun. Hundreds, she thought, maybe thousands, and even at the top a few tails still flicking and silver faces mouthing outrage into the hot air. Some of the fish are still alive, she wanted to say to the men heaving wet nets around the stones, there is a medical emergency here.

Ally tugs her hat forward to shade her face. She has not cooked fish before. Mamma did not serve it. Perhaps fish was unavailable in Manchester twenty years ago. She should, perhaps, have been less cavalier in dismissing Aunt Mary's offer of lessons from her cook; it had not occurred to Ally that in rejecting the lessons she was condemning Tom to a domestic economy learnt from Mamma. But she has also learnt something from the years with Aunt Mary in London. She has not required Tom to choose between butter and marmalade at breakfast. She offers him cream in his coffee and sugar in his tea. And the cooking of fish cannot be especially complicated. It is necessary only to apply sufficient heat in one form or another to set the albumen, remaining mindful that boiled fish is inevitably abominable. Lighting the oven is difficult and anyway the warmth would be unwelcome in the house: let the soles, then, be fried. She enjoys the gleam and weight of her new copper pan. Boiled potatoes, with mint from the garden, and the rest of the plums for pudding. A meal of sorts. When he is gone – no, even in her own mind, even trying to make a thought about cooking, about how the cooking will be *easier*, she falters at those words. Time will pass, and he will leave. There will be endurance. There is always endurance as there is always air, because there is no alternative. She opens the gate. Now, anyway, she will put the fish in the pantry and write Annie a cheerful letter about sea-bathing and fishwives, reassure her friend that married life in Cornwall is not only exile from London work and London friends.

But Tom comes down, his tread heavy on the bare wooden staircase, puts his arms around her from behind as she transfers the fish to a plate. It has skin instead of scales, and the scar of an old wound below the dorsal fin. Its orange spots have dulled.

'I thought you were working,' she says.

'I stopped.' He kisses her neck above the high collar. 'It ought to be our honeymoon.'

She leans against him for a moment, feels his breath in her hair. They have so short a time. 'Yes. But it isn't. Don't make Mr Penvenick angry. If you have work to do—'

His hand touches her breast through the grey cotton and a response flickers through her body. But Mr Penvenick, she thinks, he will be annoyed if your report is not written, he will chide you, he will express disappointment when he has trusted you so far

He lifts her hair. 'There is always work to do. Put the fish down, Al.'

Her head bends as he unbuttons her collar.

The weight of her head in the hollow under his collarbone is making his arm numb but he doesn't want her to move. She

7

probably knows, he thinks, how much the human head weighs. She has probably lifted a human brain with her own hands and placed it on a scale. Before the wedding, there were jokes that were not jokes about how at least a doctor would know what to expect, at least he'd be able to get down to business on the wedding night without first having to explain what goes where. Almost, said his junior George, draining his fourth pint, as if you were to have all the advantages of marrying a widow *and* all the advantages – Charlie took him outside and when they came back in George apologised. George means no harm, can't hold his drink and doesn't think before he opens his mouth, but Tom hadn't been that close to hitting someone since his schooldays.

She moves her head onto the pillow and lifts her sticky hand from his belly to his chest. He strokes her hip bone, the curve of her waist. Her hair has come down on one side and there is a scatter of black hairpins across the sheet behind her.

'I forgot to tell you.' He picks up some of the pins. 'De Rivers has asked us to dinner.'

She raises her head, the expression of satisfaction he was enjoying gone as if wiped with a cloth. 'De Rivers? The big house at the top of the High Street?'

'Ludgate House. He said he wanted to welcome you to Falmouth.'

She sits up, sees his glance and hugs her knees to cover her breasts. 'Why would he feel a need to do that?'

'Maybe he's proud to have a prize-winning young doctor in town.'

She shakes her head. 'How on earth would he know about my prize? And why would he care anyway?'

He folds his hands behind his head. The crack in the ceiling probably isn't really any bigger than it was last time he saw it. 'He'd know because I told him. And it was in *The Times*, remember. Anyway, I accepted. For Thursday.'

But married men, he recalls too late, say that they must consult their wives. He has assumed both her availability and her consent. An oversight only, but he has heard her and Annie speak of men whose sympathy for women's suffrage lasts only until they find themselves obliged to pour their own tea. Perhaps he has not inspired trust enough to overlook such errors, perhaps she will fear that this is the first sign of his intention to dominate. If so, he supposes, he can only try to explain: it is not that I thought myself entitled to consent on your behalf but that – well – but that I forgot that I am now a married man. I forgot you. He waits. These sunny days have run golden lights through her sparrow-brown hair.

'Very well,' she says. 'I must air my grey dress. It will be something to tell Annie and Aunt Mary in my next letters.'

He reaches out to run his fingers down the fine carving of her vertebrae.

the inverse of Noah's Ark

The sun goes down behind the town, sunset hidden on the western side of the Lizard Peninsula. But over the estuary the hill above Flushing glows with refracted pink light. The masts around the harbour are cradled by a kaleidoscope of land and sky reflected in the waves, and there are two great ships winging around Pendennis Head, their sails slackening as they pass the castle at St Mawes and enter the shelter of the land. It is not very long until he will be going the other way, watching the sails belly as the ropes tauten and thrum and the ship leans on the wind. The sea will expand around him as Falmouth, Pendennis, the Lizard, Cornwall, diminish to the north-east; the stones beneath his feet, the gardens and trees, replaced by the slap and foam of waves on the hull. And then some weeks later, he will arrive in Japan. He tucks Ally's arm more tightly against his ribs.

'We should have a fine view from the dining room,' she says. 'I went along the quay yesterday to admire it from below.'

'Penvenick tells me it is a remarkable house, and apparently De Rivers is something of a collector. You will enjoy seeing fine pictures again.'

Her uncle's house was crowded with paintings and sculpture. He had never before seen a full-sized marble figure in a private house, and now he has brought her to a cottage most of whose walls would be too damp and uneven for pictures even if he owned any.

She rubs her cheek on his shoulder. 'I cannot say I have missed them. And somehow it seems unlikely that I will share Mr De Rivers' taste.'

Taste. There are worlds in her mind that he cannot enter, ways of categorising people and their possessions that are foreign to him.

'Ally?' he says. 'Ally, on Saturday, would you take me around the Art Gallery?'

The Gallery has been open all the time he has lived here. It is one of the Yarrow family's gifts to the town, municipal culture to improve the minds of sailors and tradesmen, and he has set foot in it only once, to deliver a public lecture on new developments in lighthouse design. There are also concerts he does not attend.

She looks at his face. 'Of course, with pleasure. They have a few interesting things. But I do not know that I can tell you much.'

'More than I know now.'

Her hand slides down his arm and takes his. She likes the insides of his wrists, not a part of his anatomy to which he had given a moment's thought until after the wedding.

'And you like to learn. Tell me, my love, shall I show you around the nervous system and the skeleton also?'

'Why not,' he says. 'A man cannot have too much knowledge. Or, of course, a woman. Perhaps the human spine offers a model for an aseismic lighthouse.'

'It is a weak point, the spine. And from what you have told me, perhaps prone to the same difficulties of physics as other columns.'

He kisses her hand.

They ascend the steps and he rings the bell.

She was right about the view. Mr De Rivers, a man who looks so much like a frog that it is almost a surprise to see him walk up the stairs, shows them all over the house before allowing them to sit. Dark oak panelling makes the square hall and shallow stairs cavernous, so the windows over the sea seem as radiant as the Canalettos she used to admire in the Manchester City Art Gallery. The bannisters are carved into barleycorns. The floorboards, bare ships' timbers as in all the buildings in this town, creak as they pass. The house was built, Mr De Rivers says, more than two hundred and fifty years ago. Mr De Rivers puts his hand on her elbow, bared by the grey dress's short sleeves, as if to guide her around the turn of the stairs. His hand is damp and she resists the urge to shake him off. Nine generations of births and deaths here, she thinks. His thumb presses against her triceps muscle. It may well be the oldest building in which she has set foot. Nonetheless, it feels familiar. She moves away from Mr De Rivers, across the landing. Papa's house was newly built for him and Mamma, with modern decorative brick coursing and bay windows, but like Papa's, Ludgate House is designed for display, to impress. Six people could come down the staircase abreast. The timber in the panelling would build a ship to cross the seven seas, the marble in the fireplaces suffice to memorialise a platoon of much-loved sons. Ally peers at a small glass dome on a side table and suppresses a gasp when there is something inside peering back. It is too dim to see clearly; a small mammal with a pointed nose and grey fur, frozen as it ducks under a stripped branch. Tom takes her hand. There are potted palms reaching from behind occasional tables and more of those glass cases, shiny in dark corners. An antlered head protrudes from the wall over the fireplace, as if on a pike. She doubts, some-how, that De Rivers personally oversaw these animals' deaths.

'My Central America case,' De Rivers says. They gather and peer. He reaches for her arm again but Ally sees his hand rising and moves to Tom's other side, as if for a better view. The birds inside are not bird-coloured but turquoise, violet, scarlet and so small it is hard to imagine how they were killed. They are not big enough for a bullet. Chloroform, probably, after catching them in a net. The panicky wing-beats would slow, and then stop, the heads drooping as the eyes filmed. The birds' hearts must be smaller than Ally's little finger-nail, must beat faster than one could count.

'You have been in Central America?' asks Tom.

Mr De Rivers inflates himself a little. Ally's fingers find the inside of Tom's wrist, above the pulse point where she can feel the muscle rising under tender white skin. She likes these places in him, the junctions of softness with strength alien to the female body. De Rivers is saying something. 'Oh, I have no time to gad around the globe. The mine does not run itself. But it is easy, here, when one knows the right people, to have almost anything brought from anywhere in the world. Why, Captain Polwarth has shrunken heads from Africa in his cab-inet!'

'Human heads?'

'Forgive me, Mrs Cavendish. It is not a subject for ladies. Here, let me show you my Chinese fans instead. Are they not exquisite? It is hard to conceive how such carving is done, is it not?'

In a carved cedar chest are silks from China, painted with dragons and tigers. The light is too dim to see colour properly but he encourages Ally to touch, pours them into her hands while he watches her face. She looks away from him and won-ders about the hands that made these. Papa would like them.

There is a glass cabinet crowded with porcelain figures and – De Rivers winks at Tom – more put by that are not quite the thing for public display. There is another chest made by having Chinese carved screens cut up and rearranged by a Cornish carpenter. The waste-paper baskets are made from elephants' feet and the candlesticks carved in ivory. It is a mausoleum, it is the inverse of Noah's Ark. She imagines the noise if all these eviscerated animals came to life, if in the depths of a winter's night their spirits returned fluttering bellowing squealing, oak panels splintering and bannisters broken off like trees in a storm—

When they reach the dining room, there is a woman bending over an embroidery frame in an armchair by the fireplace, set in the darkest corner of the room. The woman stands up, holding her work as if it were a handkerchief and she about to weep. She is taller than Ally, older, and wearing a limp rabbit-coloured evening gown that makes her the same sepia tint from fascinator to shoes and must pass barely half an inch above her nipples. Ally finds her gaze dropping as if to protect a patient's modesty; even she knows that such décolletage requires firmer upholstery beneath.

'My sister. Deborah, Mr and Mrs Cavendish. Mrs Cavendish, Miss De Rivers.'

Dr Moberley Cavendish, Ally thinks, but in the three months since graduation she has already understood that there are situations, many situations, in which there is nothing to be gained by saying this.

She holds out her hand. 'How do you do.'

'Mrs Cavendish. How do you find Falmouth?'

Mr De Rivers has placed his dining table, an expanse of mahogany with a surface area probably greater than her bedroom, in the window, and placed her, as newly-married guest of honour, on his right, where she can watch the hills and water darken towards the monochrome as the boats begin to prickle with light. As the soup is removed by a maid in white frills, outside the tide turns and the ships swing in the dark. Despite Tom's explanations, the turning of the tide still seems mysterious to Ally, and until she arrived here she had not known that it would be so plain. Yesterday, she saw the moment of pause at low water and then the first rivulet of the incoming tide trickling upstream. Seeing the turn of the tide is as definite as watching a patient's return to consciousness.

'Mrs Cavendish?'

She meets Tom's eyes.

'Forgive me, Mr De Rivers. I was distracted by your beautiful view.'

He smiles. He is the sort of man who cannot smile without resembling a crocodile. 'I dare say our little town is quite fascinating to one accustomed to London. And – Manchester, was it? I have not been there, and I cannot say I wish to return to London. I lived there, you know, as a young man.'

Ally sips her wine. Excellent wine, as good as anything in Uncle James's cellar. 'Manchester is an interesting city. In some ways it is in the vanguard of a social change that may take many years to reach more secluded parts of the country. And London was not my choice, but the only place in Britain where it was possible for me to train. I was happy there.'

His face tightens a little, as if she has mentioned something unmentionable, but the smile remains. 'As I hope you will be happy here, my dear.'

Tom puts down his fork. 'My wife will be working at the Truro Asylum. She takes a special interest in nervous cases.'

Mr De Rivers coughs. If he chokes, she thinks, he will be glad enough of her training. He takes water.

'In the asylum? Your wife? Cavendish, what are you thinking?'

Tom smiles. He can smile at anyone. 'Dr Moberley Cavendish is thinking that there is a great need for women mad-doctors. That, as we know, the majority of patients are female, and many of their troubles begin in exactly those crises of life where it is most desirable that women should be attended by women. Do I summarise correctly, Ally?'

She nods. They still do not know why this invitation has been issued, but Mr De Rivers is a powerful man who appears to take an interest in Tom. It is not necessary that he should sympathise with her cause.

'But I will not begin my work until Tom leaves. I wish to spend as much time as I can with him, and having no acquaintance here, naturally I will need occupation in his absence. Tell me, Mr De Rivers, what was your profession in London?'

Mr De Rivers' shirt front puffs out over his waistcoat. 'I would have thought that under such circumstances a young lady would return to her father's house, but I see you have a mind of your own. My father thought it best that I should spend some time in an exporter's office. The markets for much of our tin are overseas and he wanted me to understand that side of the business. I was glad enough to return to Cornwall, I must say.'

Ally nods. 'I can understand that. And that is when you found your beautiful house?'

She can do this, now. Mamma never understood the power of courtesy, or that not every battle needs to be fought every time. Feminine wiles, Mamma would say, the cowardly tactics of those who fear the judgements of fools and care more for worldliness than salvation. Did the Son of God depend on toadying and sweet words? Did he fear to offend the money-lenders in the temple?

*

He stands as the ladies leave, one of those gentleman's tricks learnt late. Ally's gaze is dropped, demure. The coils of her hair have softened and a strand trails on the pale curve of her neck. Miss De Rivers draws back to allow Ally to precede her into the drawing room, where the flock of humming-birds, the tiger-skin rug and the moose's head await them in the twilight. He cannot imagine what they will find to talk about.

Mr De Rivers keeps silence, sipping the last of his Burgundy, until the door closes behind the women. The maid removes two plates, leaving the dessert to accompany the port which Mr De Rivers takes from the sideboard behind him.

'Care for a cigar, Cavendish?'

Ally dislikes the smell. 'I won't, thank you. But another of these walnuts.'

De Rivers passes him the basket. 'Grow them myself, you know. And I've a fine fig tree. Doesn't fruit every year, mind.'

'It is a very gentle climate. I find it hard, sometimes, to believe myself in England when I see the palm trees and jumping jacks.'

'Ah. Not what you grew up with. Yorkshire, isn't it?' He pours port, generously. 'Never been there. Right, Cavendish, shall we talk business?'

'I thought you had something to say to me, Mr De Rivers.'

He wants Tom to bring him silks from Japan. Kimonos, yes, those too, perhaps one for Miss De Rivers, but he has seen a particularly fine hanging in James Poldoon's house, a mixture of applique and embroidery of a sort he believes to be previously unseen in Europe. Poldoon got his from a London dealer but he wants the real thing. Go to the workshops, young man. Watch the needles flash, see the dyes put on with your own eyes. Can't be too hard, can it, to watch those Oriental girls at work? He's heard a thing or two about Japanese women ... Anyway, he'll make it worth Tom's while. Bring him something really fine, something to cover a whole wall and make Poldoon's eyes pop, and Tom might be able to leave Ally on Florence Terrace instead of in that damp little cottage next time he goes to sea.

Tom swirls the port around his glass, centrifugal force working against gravity. The first movement tends to overthrow, the second to restore equilibrium. He had hoped to be back home within six months.

'Do you know where these workshops are, Mr De Rivers?'

Mr De Rivers blows smoke. 'That would be part of your business. There are doubtless guides. I believe there is a part of Osaka known as the textile district.'

'My commission would be to find these places, place an order and oversee its fulfilment? I might not depart until your hangings were finished, and you would wish me to bring them with me in my own luggage on my return?'

De Rivers taps ash onto a plate. Later, the scullery maid will clean it, probably cursing the thoughtlessness of gentlemen who have never had to see a woman scrub. 'Exactly the situation. And if you have an enterprising bone in your body, young man, you'll bring all you can to sell on your own account.'

The port swirls the other way. 'It is intended to be a brief trip. Mr Penvenick cannot spare me long.'

'Penvenick! Come, Tom, we are none of us irreplaceable. If Penvenick can do without you for six months I dare say he will contrive to get through a few more weeks. In any case, you have not asked me to name the sum.'

He puts the glass down and looks up. Enough, he thinks, enough. He owes this man no duty. 'That, Mr De Rivers, is because I am happily not in such a case that I must necessarily think of money before paying heed to my profession and indeed to my wife.'

18

De Rivers smiles. 'You have a temper indeed, like your wife. I foresee interesting times in your house, Cavendish. Take the girl with you if you cannot do without her. It is not as if you were going to Africa, Japan is a civilised country. Especially if her comparison is the Truro Asylum.'

Of course he has thought of it. Penvenick himself suggested it. The additional expense would be negligible. He has even tried to convince himself that Ally might practise in Japan, where there are several settlements including European women whose need for medical care is doubtless at least as acute as that of their sisters at home, or that she might observe the Japanese care of the insane, for there must, presumably, be madmen there as here. There were women doctors in India for many years before it was possible to qualify and practise in Britain. Japan is not India. The fact remains that she cannot accompany him on a tour of lighthouses and would, then, be left alone in some colony of expatriates for many weeks. The fact remains that she is eagerly anticipating her work in the asylum. There are stars out over the water.

'It is impossible. And I cannot think that Mr Penvenick would allow me to do as you ask.'

'Don't be a fool, Tom.'

De Rivers puts down his glass and names his figure.

Jacob's Ladder

The gulls are raucous. A ship's horn sounds low, three times, from the harbour, probably the big steamer that came in two days ago signalling its departure. Ally, curled away from him, doesn't stir. He watches the sheet move with her breathing. Her nightgown, which he unbuttoned sometime last night, has slipped over her shoulder. There is a pale mole he had not noticed before at the top of her shoulder blade. Perhaps everyone looks younger asleep than awake. She has tangled the sheet around her legs, her one bare calf shaded with gold fur in the morning sun, and left him with none. By the time he is accustomed to sharing his bed, he will be behind the guardrail on a wooden berth, rocked by the waves. He has always slept well at sea.

The room is not much changed by Ally's arrival. His two jackets now hang from the hook on the door, ousted from the mirrored wardrobe by her dresses. Her best shoes, too high for comfortable walking, lie under his chest of drawers, and the grey silk dress reclines as though faint in the hard-backed chair, but she will put them away this morning. Sunlight is strained by the striped curtain as it always was, and the counterpane his mother made for him when he first went to London is folded back over the foot-rail as it always was. He remembers Ally's accounts of her father's house, of the Briar Rose wallpaper her father designed especially for her and her sister May, the winter and summer curtains that changed the light and colours of the drawing room where the famous autumn wallpaper first hung. He has not seen the house, has not been invited, but even his mother recognised Alfred Moberley's name. Oh, the bird curtains, she said. Mrs Gummersall has them in the pink. Ally's Uncle James's house, where he met her, also had patterned papers and curtains, a profusion of lamps and soft chairs. Perhaps he should suggest that Ally redecorate the cottage, make it more like what she is used to. If he accepted De Rivers' commission, there would be enough for that and more.

Careful not to disturb her, he slides from under the covers, steps over the creaking board by the door. He used sometimes to creep out of his mother's house early on summer mornings, off to the river to fish or sometimes just for the pleasure of a secret outing, without the gaze of those who assume that a boy alone is up to no good. He has not had to move silently around this house before. Most of the garden is in the shade but there is sun on the roses at the gate and on the high brick wall between the cottage's ope and the garden of number two. The basement kitchen is cool and dim, the flagged floor cold to his bare feet. It always used to feel dusty, until Ally came. He removes the whistle so it won't wake Ally and sets the kettle to boil. She baked bread on Saturday, and there are eggs in the pantry and the special India smoked tea that was one of her Aunt Mary's lesser wedding gifts, just a small token, she said, a little luxury for the first days of their married life. They have no tray but a baking dish will do the job; he will make breakfast in bed for

21

his wife. For his bride. On the way up the stairs he pauses, balances the tray while he opens the front door and invites the day to come in.

The kitchen floor is washed, properly scrubbed as well as mopped. She has washed Tom's clothes for the first time, watching his sleeves and the legs of his drawers swim and entwine themselves with her shifts and blouses. Please, Tom said, I did not marry a doctor to have her wring my shirts. It is beneath your dignity, he says. Send it out, Al. He has always done so. What, she said, so I can sit idle as a fine lady while some other woman toils? Can you imagine what Mamma would say? She has rinsed everything, but Tom has no mangle. It is a bright day. The neighbour's housekeeper has given her some wooden pegs, and Ally has rigged a line between the holly tree and the fence. There is no reason why she should not sit down, even in the leaf-dappled garden, and re-read Professor Browne's book about asylums. Housework is never exactly done, for one might always wash the curtains or dust something, but her new status as a wife must not be allowed to prevent her real work. Idleness, says Mamma's voice in her mind, frittering away the afternoon in self-indulgence when there is misery and despair on your very doorstep. The voice has reason: there are back lanes in Falmouth as infernal as anywhere in Manchester, where Mamma labours day after day, month after month, teaching illiterate women to feed their children, clean their houses and wash their clothes for little thanks, showing despoiled girls and diseased prostitutes that there are still other ways for them to live. Here there are open sewers running down to the sea and malnourished children begging outside the baker's shop. Women in limp finery greet the arrival of every ship and frequent the bars around the harbour. Ally could be working like Mamma to save bodies and souls this very minute instead of arranging cushions for herself on the stone steps beside the camellia. She could be soliciting subscribers for a reformatory for those women, or at the very least offering medical care to them and their children. She remembers her eighteen-year-old self telling the inmates of Mamma's Home that when she qualified, she would attend women who had nowhere else to go, who could not pay doctors' fees and so died with their children for lack of the most elementary care. And now she devotes herself to the study of chimerical disorders of the mind, to the least respectable branch of medicine. From three hundred miles away, she can feel Mamma's disappointment. She opens the book.

The history of mental disease, writes Browne, reveals some awful truths. And one of these is that the mind may be trained to insanity, to destroy itself. It is the beginning of an essentially optimistic argument: if the mind may be led or pushed to insanity, if it is possible for a sane person to be driven mad, then the process must be reversible. There is no reason why anyone who has once been in full possession of his intellects should not be restored to that state. Browne commends 'the well-regulated efforts, the virtuous contentment, the settled principles, of a highly educated mind'. A seagull screams over Ally's head. The leaves of the camellia are almost as dark as the holly's prickles, and both gleam white in the sun. It is not her experience, not the experience of any woman she knows, that a highly educated mind brings either virtuous contentment or settled principles. A trained intelligence, she would go so far as to suggest, is likely to unsettle the virtuous contentment of its female possessor, and indeed the unsettling of contentment should be an object of women's education. Browne, naturally enough, concerns himself with the masculine mind.

She reads on: 'he who devotes himself to the care of the insane . . . must live among them; he must be their domestic associate; he ought to join in their pursuits and pastimes; he ought to engage them in conversation during the day, and listen to their soliloquies in the retirement of their cells; he must watch, analyze, grapple with insanity among the insane, and seek for his weapons of aggression in the constitution and dispositions of each individual, and not in general rules or universal specifics.' Well, it is only in the discovery of general rules and universal specifics that the profession of the mad-doctor will come of age, but even so, she thinks, yes. Each mind has its own story, its own road to perdition, and perhaps that story, once imagined, can be retraced. The difficulty, as she and Browne well know, is to order asylums in such a way as to make this possible. The difficulty is to find space among the multiplying madnesses for a narrative of any kind. She finds herself rising to check that the laundry is drying, as if it might be doing anything else.

'Will your great work wait while we take a walk, Dr Moberley Cavendish?' Her hands are gritty with flour and butter, her fingernails unpleasantly caked. Mamma considered pastry unwholesome, especially for young girls, and it was never made at home, but Tom likes it. And there will be no pies for him in Japan.

She tries to smile for him but her eyes fill. Here it is, the beginning of their last evening. From this moment, the minutes will slip away like stitches dropped from a knitting needle. Unravelling, irrecoverable.

'If you are content to dine at a positively dissipated hour, Mr Cavendish. The book says that pastry may profitably be left to rest in the pantry.'

24

He holds out his hand. 'Did you not marry me in hopes of dissipated habits? Come, I have been pent in the office all day and there is a fine fresh wind off the sea.'

She sinks her hands in the basin of cold water, scratches the butter from under each nail, shakes them dry to save having to wash the towel. If she splashes her face too, he will see that she is upset.

'Your apron?'

How could she care about an apron? She makes her mouth smile. 'You don't consider it suitable garb for an evening of gay abandon? Perhaps you are right.'

They take the high path, up the stone stairs from the cottage to Penwerris Terrace where there is another row of sea-captains' houses. The sun is still high and the white stucco fronts are as bright as sheets drying in the sun. Seagulls on ridgepoles and chimneys announce Tom and Ally's progress, the cries circling them from above, and below them the town curls around its slopes, poor people in grey stone at the bottom and rich in white paint at the top. Along here, ornate cast-iron fences restrain bushes of pink-starred fuchsia and tendrils of wisteria from which purple flowers drip like bunches of grapes. Through a window, she glimpses the autumn wallpaper which for a long time she thought Papa had made only for the drawing room at home.

'Ally?'

She turns, startled. When he proposed marriage his voice did not sound so serious. Perhaps, at this very last moment, he is going to say it. Come too. I cannot bear to leave you. Whatever the cost to your career, come with me. I can't, she would say. And yes. Yes.

'I hope—' He stops. 'You know – Ally, I am sure the time will pass quickly once we are accustomed to it. At least we

25

both knew from the beginning that this separation was to come. And you will have your work, it is not as if you will need to seek distraction. Letters take only a few weeks now, did you know that? We will perhaps re-read our letters in fifty years and remember—' His hand tightens on hers. 'Remember all of those years together.'

Her skirt swings over her shoes, over the paving stones, as each foot reaches forward. There are fewer minutes left now than when they left the house, than when they crossed the road. She should say something back, embellish his vignette of their old age.

There is nothing to say. They walk on, above the library and gallery now, and she follows him down the cobbled lane where the men outside the pub watch them pass. One says something about her and the others laugh. Her skirt, she thinks, her skirt made in London for a prosperous professional woman, is too narrow here. They will think it not decent. Or her hair is coming down, or has a seagull soiled her clothes? Tom is waiting at the bottom, his elbow crooked for her hand.

'I'm sorry, Ally, I thought you were with me.'

She takes his arm. 'It doesn't matter. I am.'

For this evening, for this one night. The fresh wind he wanted soothes her face like a cold cloth.

'We'll go up the hill?'

They are heading as usual for Gyllingvase, where he likes to see the ships coming in from the Atlantic. Going blue water, she's heard people say here, going far away, as if the coastal waters were not blue.

'I can climb Jacob's Ladder. It is possible in a skirt.'

The first time he brought her here was a hot afternoon and she remarked that climbing one hundred and twelve stone steps from the town square was an inelegant proceeding. But he enjoys Jacob's Ladder partly because it is wholly unnecessary, an egregious feat of engineering like that of a small boy playing with wooden blocks.

'Very well. We will ascend together.'

There are children playing marbles at the top, and as Ally and Tom reach the group a glass ball comes rolling, dropping, bouncing like a body over a cliff. She hears herself exclaim. It will smash, splinter into tiny shards and its heart of blue will be exposed and broken. The boys stand to watch. There are holes in their trousers and their bare feet are dirty, their hair long and unkempt. The smallest one's mouth hangs open.

'It's too steep, don't try to chase it,' says Tom. 'Here, this should buy you another. Whose is it?'

The child takes the penny but the marble has reached the bottom intact. Spheres, she remembers him saying, are the strongest shape. Joins and edges are always points of weakness.

They come over the brow of the hill to the villas of Florence Terrace, and at last see out over the Atlantic as well as up the estuary's intimate curves. The grand estates, newer than the captains' houses, spread down the hill to the sea, their velvet lawns embroidered with palm trees and flowering bushes. Beyond them are bath chairs and perambulators drawn as if by clockwork along the paved promenade, and beyond that, waves in dark blue and white leaping and reaching, and right at the edge, just where sea at last becomes sky, gathering and hurling themselves into the Manacles. It is a clear day, when you can see the Manacles. Her hand tightens on Tom's sleeve, and suddenly her drowned sister is there in her mind, May's legs bound by her twisting wet skirts and May's hair floating out above her face as she sinks and her mouth opens, surprise or some final speech, *I didn't mean this* or *I love you* or—

'Ally?'

'Sorry, Tom. I'm sorry.'

No crying. He does not need this: weakness, hysteria, nerves, on his last day. He knows her strong. He married a doctor, not a patient. She bites her lips.

'Did you find out how long you will be in Singapore?'

He pats her hand. 'It will depend, I think, on the weather and what speed we make. But probably several days. Penvenick will cover a hotel so I can leave the ship. He said I would be ready enough to walk out by then. And of course I will be able to send letters.'

She nods. Tom stepping out, his jaunty gait under a tropical sky, his feet safe on foreign ground.

'You will like to see the city.'

She imagines herself there too, holding his arm and catching the scents of strange fruits and flowers under a tropical sky. Herself at the rail of a ship watching a new land rising over the horizon, a warm wind on her face.

But he does not ask.

Even the seagulls are sleeping, but through the gap in the curtains he can see that the night is beginning to fade. It is today. His trunk is the shape that stands waiting by the door. Ally lies tightly curled, her back to him as if he is already gone, as if there were no comfort for her. It is a betrayal, this journey. Even though they both knew about their separation before agreeing to marry, even though she has said nothing about wanting him to stay and knows that it would be impossible for Penvenick's plans to change, it is a betrayal. Instead of creeping out into the night, to breathe the dew on the grass and the red roses at the gate and feel Cornwall solid under his feet, he curls around his wife, tucks her into his arms, cradles her breast in his hand and her head against his chest for what may, what very well may, be the last time.

an arrangement of plants and stones

The screens are open a few inches and in the gap is outside, a stripe of leaves and bark and rain between the paper windows which remind him of pages, of the blank expanses of unwritten letters. The leaves, some in red lace as well as a variety of fleshy greens, bounce like struck cymbals as the raindrops hit them. As well as the patter of rain there is the chiming of running water, which must come from the bamboo gutters he noticed earlier, or perhaps there is a fountain out there. He reaches out to open the screen, hesitates. The taut paper looks fragile. The woman, whose name he could not say even if he had heard it clearly, probably set her windows just as she wants them. Who is he, to go around rearranging her house? He puts his eye to the gap instead, a child peering in to a room he is not allowed to enter, a servant at the keyhole. It is – probably – a garden. It must take a human mind and hands to make such an arrangement of plants and stones. His eye measures the spaces between wavering branches and crouching rocks, notes how the curves of the gravel path pull the beholder into the intricacy of green shadows under the bushes. No flowers, or flowerbeds. No straight lines, but a garden nevertheless. He feels a gaze on his back, and she is standing there, in her slippers. He will have to get used to that, to the way these buildings are silent about their occupants' movements. You can see everything at once, if you keep looking, but if you're not looking you won't hear anything until it's too late.

She kneels and bows her head almost to the floor, as if pretending he's one of her idols. His knees creak and his trousers tighten across his thighs as he reciprocates: even if it is incorrect, he hopes that mimicry at least suggests the right intentions. Her hair stays in perfect place. All the women's hair is blue-black, the shade of bad bruises, and it all looks cold to the touch. He straightens up. His knees hurt. They practise these postures, he has read, from infancy, but even so he does not see how a human body can remain so folded without damage. Muscles, bones and vasculature are surely the same everywhere?

She murmurs and sits back on her heels, gestures. Food? Is it a mealtime in Japan? There was a drink that seemed a little like both coffee and tea when he awoke, and a bowl of sticky rice and some kind of clear soup. When the student arrives, he will ask. Tell me from the beginning, he will say. Take me for a savage, for a child raised by wolves, and tell me how to wake and sleep, to empty my bladder and bowels, to bathe. Tell me what to eat and when and how, and in return I will advise you on the building of lighthouses. It does not seem much of a bargain. She smiles at him, rises smoothly to her feet, and leaves, silent as a cat. He has no idea what is happening, but he seems to have succeeded in his present ambition, which is not to give offence. He does not know when the student will arrive; Makoto will call on you tomorrow, he was told. He would like to go out, begin to feel Japan under his feet and smell its air and hear its birdsong and the wind in its leaves. He is hungry. He lowers himself onto one of the square cushions on the floor and takes out Fulham's *Structural Engineering*, his prize copy inscribed by Professor Fulham himself. For now, he must wait.

He waits.

The light in the room has changed by the time she comes back. From behind the split curtain hanging in the doorway, feet and the bottom half of a yellow kimono approach, and then the curtain in his own room's entrance flutters blue and white. He wonders what she has been doing while he read. She carries a tray, black lacquer on the inside with tongue-and-groove boxed corners in polished bamboo on the outside, and in it there are upturned cups and bowls. She sinks to her knees and the tray remains horizontal. She positions it on the table from which he hastily removes Fulham. She speaks, gestures towards the door. There are two empty bowls, or handle-less cups. Makoto?

To Tom's relief, Makoto is wearing a suit, with a bowler hat over his short hair, and as Tom scrambles to his feet Makoto holds out his hand to shake.

'Mr Cavendish. How do you do.'

Makoto bows as they shake, his grasp firm.

'How do you do. Mr Makoto?'

Is Makoto a Christian or surname?

'How was your voyage?'

Just as if we were meeting in London, Tom thinks. Makoto's English has odd stresses and elisions, as if he were singing the words of one song to the tune of another, but it is entirely orthodox.

'I enjoyed it. You are recently returned from England yourself?'

Makoto bows again. 'From Scotland. Ah, you are reading Fulham? I was honoured to meet him.'

31

Foolish to be startled. He knew that Makoto had been in Britain to study.

'He taught me. We correspond. He advised me to come here.'

'He is a great man. I was most honoured.'

Honoured, Tom thinks, a word he encounters repeatedly in all he has read about Japan. Does it always translate the same Japanese words, or do the Japanese have as many refinements of obligation as the Eskimos do of snow? The woman, who has stood like a servant in the corner, steps forward, bows and speaks, and this time Tom knows that he is being asked to sit down and take tea.

this thin slip of land between two coasts

From the bottom of the drive, the Truro Asylum looks almost like one of the larger country residences of English gentlemen. There is a central block with a pillared portico, a wing on each side, and grounds spreading around it down the hill. It is only as she approaches that the bars on the upper windows and then the absence of curtains and drapes begin to suggest that this is not a place of comfort. The front door is not used except when the Inspectors and the Committee are expected. She continues on the gravel path towards the porter at the back. The sky is lowering and she slows down, wanting the rain on her skin and in her clothes before she goes into those halls. Inside, the air is worse than the Chelsea Asylum where she worked as a Visitor after her examinations. Dr Crosswyn says that he stopped noticing the odour a long time ago, but it still assaults her every time. Any of us, all of us, would smell so were we without the means of bathing, too alienated from our own bodies and their needs to anticipate the filling of bladder and bowels and without sufficient attendants to supply clean linen when required. Would you have turned your face from Christ himself, Mamma used to say, as he came from the wilderness mired and sick? Are you such a fine lady that you see your Maker's image only in fresh clothes and perfumed bodies? Mamma could bathe the feet of destitute fallen women and dress the sores of street children but not stroke the hair or kiss the cheeks of her own daughters. And Mamma had no charity for the mad, for those incapable of striving for betterment or profiting from her advice.

The rain begins, a fine drizzle only just heavy enough to fall. Mizzle, Tom called it, and said he'd rather have real rain less often, *actual precipitation or a dry day*, but Ally likes the way the droplets settle and cling to leaves, grass and hair, as if water were forming there rather than falling from the sky, and she likes the way the mizzle veils this thin slip of land between two coasts. Here, the crest of the hill, is one of the places from which one can see both. She slows more. The porter will see her dawdling here and think her – well, will think her without sense to come in from the rain.

There are too many voices in the asylum. Listen to their soliloquies, says Browne, but to do that she would have to be able to give each an audience and a stage. It is not an original thought that the overall effect of the asylum is maddening, that the insane compound each other's insanity. And this, after all, is why her new profession beckons: how might one devise a regime to cure the mind? It is not the taxonomy of madness that intrigues her but the possibility of individual salvation. If some situations are maddening, others must be – ought to be – sanitary. But probably not for two thousand people in the same way at the same time. She sees that the porter is indeed looking out at her and waves instead of ringing the bell.

'Morning, Doctor.' William is one of those people who enjoys calling her 'Doctor.' 'Nice weather for the time of year.'

'The garden needs the rain,' she says. They smile at each other. William is an ex-patient, a man who had nowhere to go after ten years' incarceration, and he is, in Ally's professional opinion, the sanest person on the premises.

He closes the door behind her and selects the largest key from the chain around his neck. 'We had a spot of bother in the night.'

'Oh yes?'

William's 'spot of bother' could mean an attempt at suicide – or murder – or just a bad fit on the epilepsy ward.

'Women's side. Ward Four. Well, I wouldn't be telling you else, would I? Mrs Middleton in a taking again, threw herself down the stairs while they were moving her to the back wards. Mrs Middleton's all right, see, only Nurse Miller broke her collarbone trying to catch her. Bad business.' He leans against his desk beside Ally.

Mrs Middleton, like a good third of the women patients here, is RM, religious melancholy. There is a much higher incidence, says Dr Crosswyn, sipping his glass of wine at lunch, in those areas of the country where Methodism prevails. Temperance, too, seems to be a strong predictor, though more in men than women.

'I can imagine. Where's Nurse Miller now?'

'On the sofa in Matron's room. Dr Crosswyn says she's to go home to her mother soon as she can be moved and stay there till it's quite healed. Full pay, too.'

Ally nods. 'Naturally. A broken collarbone is very painful. But complications are rare. I would expect her to be back with us and fully recovered in six weeks.'

In six weeks Tom will have been in Japan for at least a fortnight. She has read about autumn in Japan, about how people travel to particular hillsides to see particular leaves redden and fall, the opposite of the cherry blossom viewings in the spring. He will be there then too.

'Yes, doctor. You'll find Dr Crosswyn in his office.'

There is the scent of coffee in the corridor, and she

knocks quietly because Agatha tends to scream and drop trays at sudden noises. Agatha is also an ex-patient, paid for her work as a parlour maid and sleeping in a room on the servants' corridor, but she has not left the asylum grounds since she was admitted with mania and delusions as a young girl.

'Ah, Dr Moberley Cavendish. Just in time. Agatha brought a cup for you, didn't you, Agatha? Sit down, won't you.'

Ally takes the green chair to the left of the fireplace, where she can see out across the grounds. The mizzle has thickened and is blowing in sheets between the walled garden and the plum trees. There is no-one out there. Agatha, startled by her arrival, seems to have frozen beside Dr Crosswyn's desk.

'I should think you might put the coffee on this table, Agatha,' Ally says. 'Then I can pour for Dr Crosswyn while he finishes his letter.'

'Yes, ma'am. Thank you, ma'am. I mean Doctor, ma'am.'

'Thank you, Agatha.'

Dr Crosswyn thinks it likely that Nurse Miller's deportment during last night's incident was not as it would have been had he or Matron been present to witness her actions. It is not the first time Miller has been involved in scuffles with patients, often patients who seem to cause little trouble to other nurses. Since it is she and not the patient who was injured, there is no reason to begin a formal investigation, and in any case the taking of witness statements tends to be a demoralising and divisive process for all concerned, but he has made a note in Nurse Miller's file and before she leaves, he will have a serious conversation. Mrs Middleton's case is not intractable, she has previously posed no risk to anyone but herself, and conditions in the back wards are likely to worsen her symptoms.

'Does she regret her actions?' Ally asks.

Dr Crosswyn looks up at her over his coffee. 'It had not occurred to me to ask. You consider it significant?'

'If she is genuinely contrite it is because she knows that Nurse Miller's experience is as real as her own. And that she herself is responsible for what she does and perhaps able at least to imagine herself doing otherwise. Although of course contrition is often taken to excess, especially in women.' And self-awareness, she has often thought, is a marker of sanity but not of happiness.

He nods. 'You had better go and talk to her.'

Ally swallows. In London, Dr Camberwell simply refused her admission to the back wards. No, he said, it is no place, no sight, for a lady. But there are women there, she said. I doubt most of them even know they are women, he said. And I forbid it. Here, she has walked those corridors once. And does not want to do so again.

'Where is Mrs Middleton?'

He passes her a plate of biscuits, shortbread made by an inmate who used to run a tea-shop in Penzance. 'Oh, I had them take her back to Four. I don't think she knows what happened. They're all in a bit of a fluster. I thought you might smooth some feathers?'

She wonders again: is this medicine? Should she not rather be conducting appendectomies, or at the very least attending women in childbirth, poor women who are otherwise left to the care of untrained neighbours and friends, or treated as teaching material for young men?

'Yes, of course.'

'And there are two new admissions, a farmer's wife from the Tehidy estate and a young girl from Mylor. You could examine them?'

*

She goes up to the ward first, the smell intensifying as she climbs the stairs. The walls are painted the same shiny green as the London Women's Hospital. A nurse passes in the corridor above her, and a moment later she hears the banging of pipes that the nurses think the doctors do not know is their code for warning each other that a doctor is coming. Dr Crosswyn says they are not hiding anything very terrible, more probably some untidiness, perhaps tardiness in the making of beds, than any abuse of patients. The asylum is hardly a place to keep secrets. One of the disadvantages of all the locks and keys, in Ally's view, is that their noise makes it impossible to surprise anyone. She opens the door to Ward Four.

As usual, half of the patients turn to stare at her and the other half continue to mutter or sing or stroke their hair as if there is no stir in the air around them, no change in the light. There is Miss Carpenter, who is sometimes Lady Clarinda, although in neither character does she seem to Ally to offer any threat to herself or anyone else. Lady Clarinda sings, mostly in Italian and mostly rather above Miss Carpenter's vocal range. One summer day seven years ago, Lady Clarinda went around Miss Carpenter's village knocking on doors and demanding that her tenants serve her tea and present their household accounts for her approval, and since then both have lived here. And there is Mrs Middleton, who tends to be vocal about her own damnation and the similar fate of those around her, but today is in bed, silent and facing the wall. This turns out to be at least partly because the nurses have put her in a 'closed dress', a stiff garment whose sleeves are sewn into the side-seams and sewn up across the cuff so that the wearer's arms are fastened at her sides and she cannot use her hands. Closed dresses are made by patients in the asylum sewing room. The nurses have also fastened the sheets around her mattress so that she can't sit up; it is against the rules to apply physical restraint on the wards but for some reason the closed dresses don't count and this kind of violence by bed-making is tacitly allowed. With one nurse injured, it is better not to antagonise the others, for Dr Crosswyn is right that the patients are in the end dependent on the tempers of their attendants, and also that the more intelligent and charitable nurses do not choose to work in madhouses.

'Mrs Middleton? How are you this morning?'

There is no response. Ally probably wouldn't feel like making conversation either if she were sewn into a nightdress and fastened down by sheets.

'Nurse? Do you think we might let Mrs Middleton sit up? And have you—' she pauses. Don't provoke them, it is the patients who will suffer for it. 'Has she taken her breakfast?'

The nurse, the fat brown-haired one who is either Smith or White, doesn't turn around and takes her time to finish folding a pillowcase.

'Nurse?'

She puts down the pillowcase, sighs, and turns around, dusting her hands on her apron. 'Yes, Mrs Cavendish?'

Ally swallows. To rise to the bait or accept the insult?

Nurse smiles with her teeth. 'Oh, you like to be called Doctor, of course. Well, Doctor?'

'Has Mrs Middleton eaten anything since yesterday, and have you allowed her to use the commode?'

'I couldn't say, Madam. You see, Madam, we came on duty this morning, didn't we? So it would be the night-nurses you'd be wanting to ask, Madam, only unfortunately one of them's in Matron's room now with a broken shoulder, see?'

Ally finds herself thinking that one would not need to be particularly deranged to push this woman down a flight of stairs. It is more surprising that most nurses are not assaulted by patients than that some are.

39

'Thank you, Nurse. Please get Mrs Middleton up, allow her to use the lavatory and wash her hands and face, dress her in her usual clothes and have her ready on my return in an hour or so. Mrs Middleton, in a little while I shall take you to my office and we will have a talk.'

Mrs Middleton's brindled hair, sewn into a plait, nods on her pillow, and Ally goes to register the new patients.

She starts with the farmer's wife, because the woman is returning to the asylum for the third time and readmissions are easier. Mrs Minhinnet, having been home for two weeks, stood beside her kitchen dresser and, piece by piece, working from the bottom of the dresser towards the top, threw her dinner service across the kitchen. She was stopped, she observes 'before I got to the gravy-boat, which is a shame because it would have smashed nicely'. When Ally asks why she did this, Mrs Minhinnet laughs and then sits with her mouth hanging open. She spat, accurately, at the vicar and doctor whom her husband summoned, and, according to the admission form, 'availed herself of obscene and abusive language'. In her fortnight's liberty, she has also accused her dairy maid of 'fornication' with an elderly neighbour, providing unseemly and improbable detail about the imagined transgression, and waylaid the same neighbour with propositions which he found distressing and distasteful. Mrs Minhinnet, noticing Ally's wedding ring, makes some rather startling suggestions about her marital life. Ally returns her to Ward Two.

The girl from Mylor is more troubling. She sits on the edge of her chair, knees pressed together under a dress too big for her, head bowed, thin hands writhing in her lap. Her nails are bitten to the quick and weeping blood. Ally checks the admission form. Mary. Mary Vincent. Melancholy, delusions and, last night, an attempt to harm herself with a knife, wrested from her hands by her employer before much harm was done. Ally draws up a chair and sits beside her.

'Good morning, Mary. I need to ask you some questions.'

Mary glances up. There is a bruise on her jaw, probably four or five days old, as well as the line of red across her neck.

'Did someone hurt you, Mary?'

Mary shakes her head.

'Your jaw is bruised.'

She shakes her head again.

'I understand that last night you tried to injure yourself?'

Her head drops again and the writhing hands speed up.

'Mary, did you want to hurt yourself?'

Ally thinks she saw a slight shake of the head.

'But you had a knife? Your mistress took a knife from you?'

Mary looks up. 'The carving knife. Master uses it, Sundays. For the joint.'

Rain runs down the window.

'What were you using it for, Mary?'

Mary shrugs and looks away.

'You must have been very unhappy?'

There is no reply.

After a few minutes, Ally sends her to Ward Two. It is not as if there is anywhere else for her to go.

Back up to Four. She can hear Mrs Middleton from the door, the usual rising and falling rhythms of the hell-fire preacher. Mrs Middleton sits on her bed, wearing a shrunken asylum dress on which the ghost of a pink rose pattern is still visible around the seams and hem. Across the ward, Mrs Elsfield, somehow neat even with sagging stockings and a dress that trails on the floor, is listening, her head cocked like that of bird wondering whether to fly away.

'It will be burning and burning forever. Not like when you touch your hand to the range, no, not like when the bath water's too hot. Flames stroking your bare body and the skin blistering and then darkening, crackling, and the flesh underneath turning white like pork and it *won't end*. When they used to burn people at the stake it ended, they died, but you'll be already dead and it will go on and on down all the years, fire eating your face oh yes, and down there too, flames in the dirty places and you deserve every minute down all the years, yes you do—'

It goes on for hours, sometimes days.

'You know,' says Mrs Elsfield, 'I always think, whatever you say to the Established Church, you don't find Anglicans going off like that. I can't say I know what the unforgiveable sin might involve, exactly, but wouldn't you think it's not likely a middle-aged Methodist Cornishwoman has committed it?'

'Skin popping and crackling like logs, like apple logs at Christmas, nice and dry, and then they come with the pincers, iron to tear flesh from bone and you think to die but you won't, there's no rest and no end and it's what you deserve, every moment of it—'

Mrs Elsfield nods. 'It'll be a terrible deathbed, won't it, her thinking she's bound for the bad place and smelling the smoke as she goes. I hope she finds peace at the end, that's all. Don't believe in all this promiscuous praying in the parlour but that's what I ask come Sunday. Bring her peace. All of us, come to that. Wouldn't you like to see the silly thing's face when she sees it at the last, the fields of lilies and the silver sea and St Peter waiting at the gate when all this time—'

Ally almost saw that silver sea once, at Broadstairs when May was still alive.

'Pitchforks stabbing and stabbing, deep in your belly and twisting in your guts and other places too, the places you want, and the pincers ripping at your feet, on down all the years and no end to it.'

'Mrs Middleton,' says Ally. 'Come with me now. Come.'

The dark-haired nurse has paused in her reading of letters. 'Yes, Mrs Middleton. Go have a nice little stroll with Mrs Cavendish. Because that's what happens when you kick a nurse down the stairs, a kind lady comes for a chat. Isn't that so, Mrs Elsfield?'

Ally takes Mrs Middleton's hand and the monologue stops. She finds herself stroking the roughened knuckles. The nurses touch the patients all the time, she knows, pushing them into their places at table, pulling them into the line for the airing courts, getting them into and out of the weekly baths, but how long is it since any of them was stroked or embraced? It is no-one's job to do that, least of all hers.

'She's got three little girls, you know,' says Mrs Elsfield. 'And wasting her whole life in here. And who'll marry them, with their mother off her head? It's no wonder they stay away. That, and you wouldn't want children hearing her, would you, even without they're already weak that way.'

Mrs Elsfield has a group of invisible companions, some of whom are unpleasant, but between times she can seem perfectly rational. At least, Dr Crosswyn says, until she is discharged. Ally might like to consider making a study of such patients, for there are several who appear to recover after a few months in the asylum but relapse within weeks of 'release'.

'Come. We will go to my office, Mrs Middleton. We have things to discuss.'

43

a message in a bottle

The *jinrikisha* man is blue. He's wearing only a loincloth, and his skin, from elbows to neck and down to his knees, is stained with indigo and ornamented with patterns that shine and ripple under his sweat. A giant fish, the curve of its belly looping his spine, the scales etched into his shoulder. A foaming wave, and small red things – flowers? – across his trunk. The man pulls the canopy forward to protect Tom from the sun before they set off. He is older than Tom, and so thin that his bones and musculature under the painting, naked and yet adorned, remind Tom of the drawings in Ally's anatomy books. As the man begins to pull, even the cords fastening muscle to bone stand out, as if the giant fish, the carp, shifts over his skin. Tom has seen tattoos before, initials and hearts, sometimes the name of a ship, the result of voyages so long that men who can't or won't read and write take to a kind of self-mutilation out of boredom. *I was here*, they write in their own blood. *I love her.* He imagines himself taking a needle, a knife, and carving Ally's name on his breast.

The wheels rattle and bounce on the cobbled lane. They need springs, the Japanese, Tom thinks, and more than that they need horses or donkeys or teams of dogs, anything less stark than one man pulling another through the streets. The contraption reminds him of a perambulator in reverse, and although the passenger is in theory master, he feels sometimes like a frustrated child being carried too fast past things he would like to see and too slowly when his blood fizzes with energy and his muscles long to work. There is no reason why another man, an older and poorer man, should move two bodies around the streets. There must – or at least there might – be some inoffensive way of explaining to Makoto that he simply likes to walk. Although more probably anything he might say would be a slight, to Makoto who arranges the jin-rikshas or to the Japanese Department of Public Works that pays for them or even to the Emperor who probably approved the import of the idea from India. In Japan a man cannot sneeze without giving offence. A group of children notice him and run alongside the man, shouting. Foreigner, devil, what a stink.

Next week is meant to be the first day of autumn when, Makoto says, women and country people will assume autumn clothes regardless of the weather. Tom is hotter than he has ever been, hotter, it seems (though cannot logically be) than in Singapore. He fingers the fan Makoto has given him, made of some kind of shiny paper with the fossils of leaves in it. Merely a tool for a job, he thinks, and plenty of men here use fans, but he would feel a fool, a red-haired man being wheeled about in a giant perambulator fanning himself, and anyway the air is so damp that the effort of waving the fan would probably gen-erate more heat than its draft would alleviate. It will be cooler at sea, and when they reach the island they are to stay in a house on the shore. Tom will rise early, he thinks, and perhaps swim before the day's work begins. He imagines the waves tug-ging at his knees, soothing the heat rash behind the joints, slapping around his white belly and then lifting him so he can look back at the land, at Japan, from water that may eventually surge onto the sand at Gyllyngvase. He could launch a message in a bottle: my darling Ally.

They pass the last bridge over the widening river and there are the docks, the buildings without depth under the midday sun, pale stone too bright for English eyes, and the sea a mirror for the white sky.

Kate's baby crying again

'Who is it with you, my dear?'

Ally, despite herself, glances round. 'With me, Mrs Ashton?'

'The cold one. Terrible cold. Shaking with it.'

Her heartbeat lurches. May. No. May is ten years dead. However much Ally has longed for May, whatever joy it would bring to see her on earth again even for a moment, to reach for her wet hair and shivering bones, May is gone. Interred.

They are looking at her. Ally shakes her head. Mrs Ashton suffers constantly from delusions and often speaks to invisible beings.

'There's no-one with me. Though it has turned cold, hasn't it? And the leaves are beginning to turn, I noticed.' Soon be Christmas, she stops herself adding.

Mrs Elsfield stops making her bed. 'Are the blackberries ripe, Dr Cavendish? I mean Mrs Moberley. Whatever you call yourself. Though I must say, calling yourself two different people tends to cause trouble. In my experience. You've met the Lady Clarinda. I'd stop pretending to be a doctor, if I were you. They won't like it.'

Ally nods. 'Not yet, Mrs Elsfield. Just a few beginning to

redden. It will be another two or three weeks, I'd say, and they will need some more sun.'

'She's often with you, isn't she?' Mrs Ashton says. 'The cold one. She has something to tell you.'

Much to tell, Ally thinks, many things unsaid. But May is not here, or anywhere. There is a draught on her neck. Dr Crosswyn says it's impossible to keep the asylum warm in winter and that he will postpone lighting fires in the wards as long as possible. There were incidents with patients and fires last winter.

'Where is Mrs Middleton, Nurse? Dr Crosswyn asked me to visit her.'

Nurse Miller is still at home. Dr Crosswyn must know that the collarbone of a healthy young woman will have knitted some time ago. This is the small mousy one with a Cornish name, Penhallow or Pol-something. She looks up at Ally with her mouth open.

'Nurse?'

Mrs Elsfield shakes what passes for her pillow. Ally sighs: if there is scant money for coal, there will be none for new bedding. 'She's on the pot. Be back in a minute.'

Mrs Ashton stands up and comes towards Ally. 'She shakes with cold. Did she pass outdoors?'

'How are you today, Mrs Ashton? I hope the new medicine is helping with your sleep?'

It will be. No-one could stay awake on that dose.

Mrs Ashton reaches out to touch Ally's arm. Her hands are grimy, a crescent of dirt under each long nail. Ally's arm clenches, but instead of pushing the hand away she makes herself pat it. Mrs Ashton herself is cold. Mrs Ashton has no chance to walk up the hill from the station, or even up the stairs, to make her heart pump and her blood surge. Mrs Ashton doesn't see the fruit ripening in the hedgerows or the ebb and flow of the sea. It is no wonder that someone so deprived should attend more and more to the voices and images of disordered fantasy.

Ally shakes her head. 'Nurse, is there a wrap for Mrs Ashton? We don't want her to take a chill.'

Mrs Ashton laughs. 'I expect we do, you know. It's cheaper that way. And there's Kate's baby crying again.'

Kate – Miss Rawson – doesn't have a baby, but across the ward she is yet again sitting down and pulling at the front of her dress. Nurse Miller used to put Kate Rawson in the closed gown to stop her exposing herself so.

'He'll never thrive, whatever she does.'

It is Mrs Ashton, Ally thinks, who ought to be kept in solitude. The little nurse finds her tongue and tells Kate Rawson to leave her dress alone, for shame, can't she see the doctor's here? Kate looks up, her eyes blank, seeing no doctor.

'She does no harm, nurse,' Ally says.

Mrs Elsfield folds down her top sheet for the fifth time. She gets stuck, sometimes. 'I wouldn't say that, Mrs Cavendish. She's been feeding that child at least three winters now. Time it had some proper food, I'd say.' She pulls the sheet out again.

Mrs Middleton returns, her arm held by another nurse as if she might try to run away between the lavatory and the ward. She is twisting her hands and muttering about Satan. Most of these women, Ally sometimes thinks, wouldn't alter their daily rounds one iota if someone left all the doors wide open. They forgot how to make choices a long time ago. She wonders what she is trying to do, and why. Indulging the mad, says Mamma's voice in her head, wasting your days and the training for which others made sacrifices on the fantasies of the degenerate. Are there not real problems in the world? Did I not teach you to see the crying needs always at your feet?

As she leaves the asylum, there is rain drifting over the north coast, blurring the fields and trees as if someone were breathing on a window. Weather doesn't always cross the peninsula, but she can feel the damp on her face and curling her hair as she hurries down the hill. It won't help Mrs Elsfield's blackberries, and she has still not learnt to heed Tom's advice and impede herself by carrying an umbrella even when the day looks fine, but the cold and wet, the reality of physical sensation, feel salutary. Maybe it would help some of the patients to leave the room where at this very moment they will be lining up ready to go down to the dining room to eat bread and dripping, to go out into the fields and feel the rain and wind on their faces. But the cold water treatment, she recalls, is already in use in some asylums, and it is not kind, not a process over which she or Dr Crosswyn would be willing to preside.

Her skirt is heavy with rain and beginning to cling unpleasantly around her ankles by the time she reaches the station. As she crosses the footbridge, hunger beginning to churn under her ribs, there is a shrieking whistle and then the bridge rumbles under her as if in an earthquake. The London train is coming, and she stands there, out of the way of the worst smoke and steam, to watch. There are few holiday-makers now, and most of the men of business boarding the train are probably going no further than St Austell or at most Plymouth, but some will reach London, where Aunt Mary will be awaiting the tea-tray and Freddie's return from school by the drawing room fire, probably passing the time with a novel rather more colourful than Mrs Gaskell's. If Ally were to appear, even unexpectedly, Aunt Mary would kiss her, fuss over her wet clothes, command a hot bath and the addition of buttered crumpets to the cakes and scones already on the tea-table. The train below her feet won't reach Paddington until late tonight, long after tea has been cleared, dinner served and the servants gone to their beds, but even so the thought of Aunt Mary seems to bring warmth and sustenance. Mary pampered you, Mamma would say. She indulged you with flattery and taught you to share in her shameful extravagance. There is a beggar girl hiding from the railway staff in the shelter of an archway. Ally leaves the bridge as the doors of the London train slam and hurries down to give the girl the shilling she had been keeping to buy saffron cake on the way home. Who is she, to eat cake while others starve for want of bread?

alone on a hillside in Japan

Despite the tightly shuttered windows, despite feeling unable to use his alarm clock in a place where only paper screens divide one sleeper from another, Tom manages to wake early. Kneeling on his futon, feeling with his fingers to edge back the screen and then the shutter to hold his watch to a trickle of grey light in the blacked-out room, he sees that it is five o' clock. If he can move quietly enough, he has an hour and a half to himself after three days of sharing a cabin with Makoto. After three weeks, now, in which there have been periods of a few hours when he cannot see another person but no time at all in which he cannot both hear and be heard. Europeans do not know, he thinks, that there is a form of solitude for each sense, nor what luxury it is to have all five every night. Not, of course, that he does not look forward to sharing his nights with Ally, but it has already occurred to him more than once that a part of the art of marriage must be to learn to see solitude in its double form.

He left his clothes arranged in order on the floor beside him last night, to make this easier. He sits on the edge of the futon to take off his pyjamas, and locates his drawers and the drawstring at the front of his drawers, trousers and their buttons, socks. Undershirt and then shirt. His hand knocks against the screen's wooden strut as he reaches through the sleeve. The heavy breathing on the other side, Makoto's breathing, pauses. He must be sleeping right against the screen. Tom holds his breath and Makoto grunts, settles.

In the porch, shoes back on his feet at last, he can't move the sliding front door. It rocks a little but won't shift and suddenly he wants to kick it, put his big white fist through a paper wall: must it be so hard for a grown man to take a walk before breakfast? He steps back, drops his shoulders. The door is only bolted, an ingenious arrangement that would indeed make it impossible to open from the outside but perfectly straightforward from here. He thinks again about Makoto making the opposite journey, learning that there are other ways of opening and closing doors, of putting food in one's mouth, of urinating and defecating. It is no wonder the Japanese are so keen on European engineering and medicine; the laws of physics and biology seem to be the only constants between nations and even then, Makoto has assured him, in many cases Japanese medicines work well on Japanese bodies. Supporting as much of the door's weight between his fingers as he can lest it squeak or rumble, Tom closes it and finds himself at last alone.

The sun has risen behind the hill, but the forest around the house is still in deep shade, and the grass heavy with dew. Nothing is awake, he thinks, hearing only trees breathing in the wind, and behind them, the slow heartbeat of the Japan Sea, but as he moves away from the house, as the woods close around him, a bird calls above his head, and then another answers. Although he means to walk, even to swim, he stands still as a spy while the forest resumes its conversation: more bird-talk, high in the canopy and at his own height in the undergrowth, something small rustling near at hand and something bigger further away. There is a drift of spice in the morning air, something like cinnamon or nutmeg, and the suggestion of heavy flowers. Lilies or orchids, funeral flowers that don't grow outside in England. The forest floor is blanketed with last year's half-composted leaves, a lattice of fallen branches interwoven with shrubs. Tom picks his way over to a pathway leading inland, uphill.

Threading the trees, the path is barely wide enough for one person and it winds so he can't see more than a few tree trunks ahead. He wanted a vista, somewhere to stand back and take a wider view, but this is like pushing through hundreds of the half-curtains, his gaze repeatedly veiled. Still, someone has made a path so it must lead to something. There may be a summit, an achievement. He speeds up, feels a flush of sweat across his back and tightening in his thighs. Good. The bamboo leans over the path, meets above his head, and dark fronds reach down to brush his face. If it gets much narrower, he thinks, he will have to turn back, but he knows he won't. And then over the drumming of blood in his ears and the hiss of bamboo leaves, he hears a more purposeful sound. There is someone else, or something else, moving on the hillside, something that pushes through vegetation. He stops. He had forgotten that there are bears. We always carry a bell, Makoto said, because bears prefer to avoid humans unless they are starving or the human is near a cub, but they will attack if they are surprised. The creature is getting nearer. He should shout, he supposes, or sing, but the instinct to hide is too strong. Tom freezes, barely breathing, willing his heart itself to beat more softly. The bamboo beside the path ahead bows and waves wildly, and then the bear (or boar, or wolf, or maybe person) stops also. Perhaps it can hear his respiration, his circulation, the seep of sweat in his pores and the shedding of dust from his skin. Perhaps it can smell him. They wait, Tom and the other. They breathe, listen. And then the bamboo flattens and he catches – maybe – a glimpse of a dark flank as the thing lumbers away. He leans on the green canes, breathing loud now and fast, black blood bounding behind his eyes. His vision blurs, but perhaps it was just a monkey, a Japanese macaque, or a badger (are there badgers in Japan?). He is unhurt, anyway, well and strong and alone on a hillside in Japan. After a moment, hearing the birdsong again and the bamboo sighing in the breeze, he continues, as if the creature's turning away were a kind of acceptance, as if it is all right for him to be here now.

The bamboo ends, and now he can see down through the trees, and up through more trees. He crosses the curve of the hill, the sun warm on his shoulders. Steps lead up through the wood, stone steps so high that sometimes he has to brace his hands on his knee to pull himself up. They go on, up out of sight, and he follows although it is really time, high time, he was turning back to the house and Makoto and the day's work.

There are a hundred and five, or maybe four, steps, and over the last few stand wooden arches like the letter *pi*. He comes panting, red faced, into a clearing, and is on top of the hill, looking down over the treetops towards the house whose shutters are now open, and the beach where turquoise waves spread themselves on white sand, and the headland where the waves are darker and bounce glistening against the cliff and from the rocks that now, at low tide, are plain to see, at least by daylight and on a clear day. Stone figures stand around Tom, and in the centre of the clearing is a wooden building with an open veranda. He approaches the sculptures. The further ones are no more than slabs of rock set on end, rounded and smoothed by years of wind and rain, but in this company their curves suggest shoulders, waists. The nearer figures have stone draperies, or perhaps a form of armour, head-dresses shaped like bishops' mitres and snarling, caricature expressions on their stone faces. Someone has tied cloths around the necks of several, apparently at intervals over many months because some are wisps and rags where others are only tattered and faded. It was a considerable act of faith, he thinks, to carry such stones through the forest and up a hundred stairs. He imagines women climbing up here to give scarves and bibs to these idols, priests struggling through winter weather to conduct ceremonies here where the outline of the whole island is laid out. He takes the clean handkerchief from his pocket, one of the ones on which his mother embroidered his initials when he first went to university, bows to one of the scowling gods and knots the linen square firmly around its neck. He resists the urge to back away from their presence as he leaves the temple.

a basket of blackberries

She is trying to decide whether to light the range when someone knocks on the door. With her shawl, she is only a little
cold, nothing a brisk walk wouldn't remedy, and no-one needs
tea when there is good clean water to drink. But the laundry
has been hanging damp in the house for two days, and she has
learnt that on the third day clothes begin to smell of mildew
and by the fourth it is necessary to wash them and begin the
cycle again. She must not use the requirements of efficient
housekeeping to justify or excuse her self-indulgent desire for
the pleasure of warmth. If you had done the laundry earlier
in the week, Mamma would say, if you had not made tiredness
an excuse for procrastination on Tuesday, it could all have
dried outside on Wednesday morning and you would not find
yourself wishing to waste Tom's money on coals now. Oh be
quiet, she thinks. She bores herself, sometimes, with these spi-
rals of guilt and obligation, with the waste of time and effort.
She remembers Aunt Mary telling her that Mamma is a difficult woman, that Ally and Tom's happiness will depend on
Ally's ability to exercise her own judgement rather than defer-
ring to Mamma's ideas. And she has exercised her own

judgement, has she not? She has married Tom, and here she is in Falmouth. Listening to the ravings of madwomen instead of helping those whose need— Whoever it is, he or she is coming round to the back door, over the loose drain-cover in the passage way. The seagull squatting on the roof tiles above announces her. A plump woman in mourning, a stranger.

'Mrs Cavendish?' The woman rests her umbrella against her shoulder and holds out her right hand. She is older than Ally, dark hair brindled with grey tucked under a black straw hat, her black skirt darkened by rain. Her hand is warm and dry. She smiles. 'I am Mrs Cummings.'

Mrs Cummings? Ally's Falmouth acquaintance is so small that it is scarcely possible that she has forgotten someone.

'The vicar's wife. Miss De Rivers suggested that I should call on you, and indeed I have tried several times. You are often from home.'

A charitable visit. She is to be the object of concern. Of Miss De Rivers's concern. She does not usher in Mrs Cummings.

'In that case it is kind of you to persist. I work in Truro most days.' She does not wish to mention the asylum.

Mrs Cummings nods. 'You are a trained nurse, Miss De Rivers tells me.' Rain drips from her umbrella onto Ally's skirt.

'A doctor.' Ally pulls herself together. 'Mrs Cummings, if you wish to shelter from the rain you are most welcome to come in, but whatever Miss De Rivers may have suggested, you need not add me to your doubtless onerous list of parish visits. I am sure you have many more serious demands on your time.'

Mrs Cummings looks away, at the water running along the channel in the slate paving at her feet. 'Indeed, Mrs Cavendish, there is much need in Falmouth and that is part of the reason for my call. It is not my habit to press myself upon those who worship elsewhere. But I wished also to tell you that there are many wives, from all walks of life, living alone in this town while their husbands are away at sea, and therefore many societies and clubs where you would find a warm welcome and much sympathy for your position. Either I or Miss De Rivers would be pleased to furnish you with introductions, should you care for them.'

Ally must look to them like an ordinary woman, like someone who can join a club and find things to say to other people.

'You are kind to think of me, Mrs Cummings. You and Miss De Rivers. But in truth I have no gift for such gatherings, and find my time quite filled by my professional obligations.' She swallows. Here, in Mrs Cummings, is the straight road to the work she once promised Mamma and May that she would do. Here is what her sponsors always expected of her. Welfare work. Healing the poor and helpless. 'But Mrs Cummings, should you ever find in your parish work that there is urgent need for medical assistance, perhaps where there is no means to pay, you may always call upon me.'

Mrs Cummings turns her umbrella. 'Do you mean to say, Mrs Cavendish, that you are really a doctor? That you are qualified to practise? I have read, of course, of women students, but I had not thought – well, it is a surprising idea.'

Ally steps back. She will, she thinks, light the fire after all. And make herself a pot of tea. 'If there is ever need, you may summon me. Good afternoon, Mrs Cummings.'

The rain blows up the river, leaving the air washed under a pale sky. Warmed by Aunt Mary's lapsang souchong, Ally rearranges the clothes on the airer, closes the range and sets out for a walk. Wasting your time in self-indulgence, hisses Mamma. But she has not been sleeping well, she argues, and outdoor exercise would always be the first prescription for insomnia. She takes the basket, in case of blackberries. If she

59

goes out around Pendennis Head, along Invalid's Walk and then right along the coast to Maenporth, by the time she comes home it will be falling dark, the questions about how to use her time solved for another day. She will write to Tom, who will like to hear about the coast and the hedgerows, and maybe also to Annie, to whom she could perhaps confide something of her troubles, of the way Mamma's voice always in her head becomes louder and angrier now she is so much alone. Enough. She will not think of Mamma now, with shadows coalescing around buildings and plants under her very eyes as the sun strengthens, with the tide so high against Flushing pier that the passengers leaving the ferry can step down onto the dock and now with the waves beginning to sparkle. The fields have been ploughed, and the great beech and oak trees above Flushing beach are turning. Autumn is here, the northern hemisphere leaning away from the sun, the first season of Tom's absence, and when those fields are harvested again he will be home. *To every thing there is a season*, she thinks. Ecclesiastes was not one of Mamma's preferred books, but even so Ally's mind supplies more of the verse: *A time to plant, and a time to pluck up that which has been planted ... He hath made everything beautiful in his time.* And although she stopped attending church after May died, there is consolation in the words. Here is beauty in time, in the turning of the trees, the rising and falling of the water, in the slow breathing of this land.

She did not bother to unfasten her hair and brush it all out yesterday. It is not as if anyone sees her on her day off. And now, watching the sweeps of her brush in the mirror, she cannot quite recall why it is necessary to primp oneself before visiting the asylum. The patients, in their arbitrary dress and sewn-up hair, will hardly observe a dishevelled chignon. The nurses' objections to her presence go far beyond any niceties of presentation. Perhaps, she finds herself thinking, the asylum may be a rare place where a person's physical appearance, even a woman's plainness, is truly of no moment. A place where only the mind matters. She shakes her head, and then catches herself in the mirror, head waggling, mouth crammed with hairpins, alone in a silent house and reflecting that a lunatic asylum might offer forms of sanity missing from the wider world. It is not an impossible idea, certainly not an impossible ambition; one might even argue that since the wider world drives some of its citizens to madness, an asylum for their cure should by definition be run on healthier lines than the rest of society. Even so, she thinks, even so. Usually she would make a plait and then tie knots with it until the knobble of hair is short enough to pin up. Her fingers hesitate. No. Today, for the asylum, for the patients, she will do it properly, as Annie taught her.

The post has not yet come. She will still catch her train if she leaves in five minutes, if, for example, she sweeps the kitchen floor now rather than leaving it for her return. If she puts that stocking into the mending basket, and shakes the dust out of Tom's knitted blanket covering the landlord's garish armchair in the sitting room. She takes the blanket out into the garden, an armful of dusty wool that she should have noticed earlier. The mizzle has come back, but between the houses she can still see across the water. Only the Flushing ferry is moving. The sailing boats hang broken-winged on the flat sea. There are many reasons, of course, why a letter would be delayed. She unfurls the blanket, thousands of stitches representing hundreds of hours of Tom's mother's time. It is probable that she thought of all of those reasons the year May died.

*

61

'Let me take your brolly, Doctor,' says William. 'We've maybe had the last of the sunshine now. Be like this till spring.'

Ally shakes her umbrella – Tom's umbrella – over the doorstep before furling it. 'But it's warm enough for the time of year.' Soon be Christmas, she thinks. What on earth will she do for Christmas? Perhaps she will offer to join the patients for dinner. It will be a hard day, for those who remember.

'And your basket, Doctor?'

'Thank you, William, but I'll keep that.' She is suddenly embarrassed. Perhaps this was a foolish idea.

He smiles at her. 'Just so you've not got the keys in it, Doctor.'

She rattles her skirt. 'In my pocket as always.'

All the nurses and even Dr Crosswyn carry keys on a chain around their necks, like some kind of primitive jewellery or medal, a heavy badge of sanity. If Ally were a patient, she thinks, she would not like to speak with people who were forever jangling the keys of her confinement on their bosoms.

She starts with Ward Two, saving Four for later. Mary Vincent, the nurse says, weeps frequently, for no apparent reason. She ate nothing until she was told she must be force-fed and saw another patient undergo the procedure, and now it requires only a reminder of that sight to persuade her to take nourishment. Ally frowns; it is true that there are a very few patients who would apparently starve to death without such treatment, but she sees no-one here in any danger of such an end. What's more of a problem, says the nurse, is that Mary Vincent touches herself, and not only in bed at night either. And her so young! It doesn't help that Mrs Minhinnet talks as she does, the filthiest things the nurse has heard yet and she's been here ten years. God knows where she learnt such things.

'I expect someone taught her. Made her do them, or watch them.'

Ally and the nurse look round. A woman of perhaps forty-five, solidly built, greying hair trying to wave above the sewn-up plait. There are no private conversations on the ward, but most of the patients even here preserve the fiction that what medical staff say to each other is mysteriously incomprehensible or inaudible to those without training.

'Well, really, Margaret. Eavesdropping! I'm sorry, doctor. I'll put her in the corner till we're done. Interrupting like that.'

Ally touches the nurse's arm. 'No. There is no need.'

She turns to the patient. To Margaret. 'Good morning. I am Dr Moberley Cavendish. You are right, of course.'

Margaret holds out her hand, as if they were meeting at a coffee morning. 'Margaret Rudge.'

Not looking at the nurse, Ally shakes hands. 'You know Mrs Minhinnet well?'

Patients' disorders feed on each other but they also adapt to each other, creating an ecology of madness all too easily upset by arrivals and departures.

'We've been on the same ward six months. Can't help but get to know people.'

And in your view, she wants to ask, is Mrs Minhinnet mad or only damaged? Is she, in fact, telling truths that no-one wants to hear? Because if, she sometimes thinks, if all the women in here who speak of indecent things, who recount endlessly obscene acts and unnatural couplings, are speaking from unhappy experience, then their madness may be perfectly reasonable. May be the inevitable response of a healthy mind to things that should not happen. And if that is the case, then the primary problem is not so much with the minds of some women as with the acts of some men. Older men, almost invariably. Men with power.

'And you think someone has hurt her?'

Margaret Rudge shrugs. 'I think someone's hurt all of us, doctor. But not everyone ends up in here.'

Ally eyes Margaret Rudge. She doesn't have time, not today. She'll come back and hear some more.

She suggests keeping the two women as much apart as possible. There is no space to move one of them unless Dr Crosswyn agrees to move someone else, a game of chess that invariably ends by causing at least as much trouble as it solves. As in other branches of medicine, despite one's instincts and best intentions it is often best to do nothing. Perhaps some gentle occupation for Mary Vincent, she suggests, not the laundry and obviously not the kitchen but a little dusting, something to occupy her hands and allow her to feel useful. For Mrs Minhinnet, she thinks, she will ask Dr Crosswyn if there might be a women's garden work group. The farm labour is another matter, but there is surely sufficient precedent for women's cultivation of flowers? She examines a patient with a cough, declines to prescribe for the abdominal pains of a woman who has believed herself in an advanced state of pregnancy for some years, and makes her way up the stairs.

Mrs Ashton is standing in the window, fingering the bars. She turns.

'She is still with you,' she says, her eyes fixed on a point behind Ally. 'She has words for you and she'll follow you until you hear her.'

She is always with me and always gone, Ally thinks. As are all the dead. One does not need to see ghosts, to know that people are haunted.

Mrs Middleton stops rocking on her bed and looks straight at Mrs Ashton. 'You are an evil, wicked woman and the flames of Hell will take you and burn you for all eternity.'

'Good morning,' Ally says. 'Mrs Elsfield, look, I brought

some blackberries for you all. I gathered them on Pendennis Head.'

There is silence. Even Mrs Curnow looks up.

The nurse coughs. 'You've brought a basket of blackberries onto the ward?'

She has made a mistake. She should have checked with Dr Crosswyn, and she should have known it was a mistake because she didn't want him to know.

Ally bites her lip. 'I gathered more than I could eat myself. I thought you would all enjoy some fresh food.'

But it is not her job, not a doctor's job, personally to remedy weaknesses in the asylum's commissariat. Next she will be bringing in pillows and new dresses.

'Very kind of you, Mrs Cavendish, I'm sure.' The nurse doesn't look at her. 'Thank Mrs Cavendish, ladies. I suppose I'd better go find a dish. Only we'll have to take them down to tea, Mrs Cavendish, I can't be serving out fruit up here, and then the other wards'll be wondering why they haven't got blackberries and before you know it – well. You mean well, I dare say.'

The road to Hell, Ally thinks.

'It's a good year, then, for blackberries?' asks Mrs Elsfield. 'Time was, we'd be out after school picking and picking any fine day and the nettles and prickles on our hands. Ate a few, of course, but there were seven of us and never too much to go around, we'd get a proper slap if Mother thought we'd been greedy. Damsons, too, and rosehips to make a jelly for winter coughs. I didn't like the work then but I'd be glad enough to be out in the fields now. Rain and all.'

Mrs Ashton has turned back to window. 'You'll not see another autumn,' she says. 'You'll not leave here but feet first in a wooden box, and that before another harvest's in.'

Stop it, Ally wants to say. Shut up, you vile witch.

'Mrs Elsfield's in fine health.' She puts the basket down on the nurse's table. 'And maybe you will be back home next year, Mrs Elsfield, who knows.'

The nurse, returning, shakes her head. 'Best not, Mrs Cavendish,' she murmurs. 'They sometimes remember things we say, you know.'

Mrs Elsfield comes over to the table. The dress she has this week is cut so wide on the shoulders that the neckline sags open, showing breasts flat as empty socks lying on her ribs. She has to gather the skirt in her hands to walk. Hogarth, thinks Ally, the end of *A Harlot's Progress* when the daring finery falls to rags, the manifest disjunction between a person's appearance and her idea of herself. The clothes make Mrs Elsfield look mad. Mrs Elsfield removes Ally's blue and white gingham cloth from the basket and then takes a handful of blackberries and pushes them all into her mouth. One rolls to the floor where Mrs Middleton stamps on it. Purple juice drips from Mrs Elsfield's face onto the bodice of the dress, already less colourfully stained.

'Stop that now.' The nurse tries to grab Mrs Elsfield's hands. 'I told you to stop it.'

'Greed,' says Mrs Middleton. 'Gluttony and greed.'

But even as she is restrained, Mrs Elsfield reaches for another handful, and when the nurse grasps her wrist she squeezes the berries, the berries Ally picked, so that pips and juice extrude between her swollen knuckles and drop to the floor.

The nurse looks up and meets Ally's gaze. 'There. I told you there'd be trouble. Stirring things up like that.'

a man with whom you're sharing a bathtub

Autumn has come, waves of bronze and red sweeping the wooded hills like a rising tide. It is like wearing tinted spectacles, seeing trees and the carpet of leaves in unnatural shades. He finds himself reaching out to finger individual leaves in colours he has not thought of, crimson and orange, the five-fingered lace of maples. Watching the land from the sea, from the end of the rocky peninsula where he's spent the last three days, Tom has to remind himself that he too, is liable to the changing seasons, that his foreigner's immunity to conversation, to manners and cuisine and laughter, does not extend to the body itself. Japanese rain wets his English skin and Japanese winds chill his English blood.

Makoto pours tea. Curls of steam twine away from the translucent curve of the tea-bowl and rise in a different shape. *Temmoku*, Tom thinks, that kind of pottery with the glassy spots is called temmoku. He will take some home to Ally, although just now he craves a mug, a great workman's mug, full of milky, sugary tea to warm his bones. And a handful of the bannocks Douglass's cook used to make, spread with salt butter and sometimes indented with currants. Makoto offers him a green sweet that will be made of slimy rice dough and sweetened beans.

'Makoto, what did you miss most when you were in Britain?'

Makoto sips his tea, his tapering fingers holding the bowl as if it were an injured bird. 'I was happy to be there.'

Tom bites the sweet, and then remembers that it is a breach of etiquette to bite things this size. Or perhaps that is only sushi; the whole sweet would be quite a mouthful.

'Of course. I mean, I am glad to hear that. As I am to be here. But perhaps after a time you began to wish for rice instead of bread, or fish in place of all our butcher's meat, or your back ached from sitting always in chairs?'

He finds it hard to imagine how anyone's body could find ease in Japanese deportment, and in fact most of the Japanese objections to European furniture seem to pertain to its being immorally comfortable and softening to the Japanese character rather than any claim to convenience.

Makoto gazes at the opening in the *shoji* screen, through which they can see a stripe of glowing forest and sunset sky. 'Miso soup,' he says. 'And of course the baths. We can buy bread for you, you know, once we return to the city. And beef. There are even restaurants.'

But there was nowhere in Aberdeen, Tom thinks, nor even in London, where Makoto and his colleagues could have found miso soup, or taken off their shoes and sat on the floor to drink green tea out of a bowl. He eats the other half of his sweet.

'I like rice and fish,' he says. 'And I'll miss the baths too, when I go home.'

'We'll bathe before dinner? There are separate facilities for ladies here.'

'Of course. I was only surprised, last time.'

One would think – Tom thought – that a people as concerned by modesty and humility as the Japanese would have a strong regard for decency. One would be wrong. Tom knew from his reading that the Japanese bathe communally but he had not, somehow, expected that he himself would arrive at the bath in the last inn to find a naked woman in it, her bundled hair uncurling down her spine. He backed away and did not wash. Things are changing, Makoto says, and now it is rare even in the countryside to find such an arrangement. It was unfortunate, and he hoped that Tom would forgive the offence. Tom was left feeling dirty-minded, and apologetic. It's not, he wants to protest, that women's bodies upset him. It's not that he thinks badly of people whose ideas about modesty and shame are different from those to which he is accustomed. It's not that he doubts his own control (although the possibility of a physical – no, a *physiological* – reaction did cross his mind, as he stood there with only a towel to protect his own – his own conventions). He was just surprised, that's all.

Makoto is already sitting on a wooden stool, scrubbing himself with the seriousness of someone caulking a boat, as if any missed spot would make him sink. Tom takes the next place. There is no-one else present, but a line of wet footprints whose maker is now in the outdoor bath and was probably asking Makoto about the red-haired foreigner. Tom takes the bag of rice bran and begins to scrub as Makoto taught him, some thirty years after he thought he had learnt to wash himself. He is thinner than when he first came to Japan, softened by weeks as a passenger, and for the first time in his life he is glad to be short, but apart from his stature he is about as different from Makoto as a man might be. He recalls the array of human skulls he and Ally saw in the Natural History Museum in London: Negro, Asiatic, Caucasian, American Indian,

Eskimo. The differences between races, Ally said, are no greater than the variations within each race, but they don't show those. Perhaps because of the difficulties of acquisition, he suggested. He wants her. He wants to talk to his wife.

Makoto rinses off his seat and replaces it for the next person. Tom empties a final bucket over his head and follows him outdoors, almost pleased to be so violently recalled to here and now by the cold wind over his wet skin. His feet cringe from the stone steps. Lanterns hung around the bath show two dark heads in the steam, but Tom's need for the water's warmth is far greater than his self-consciousness. For a moment his shocked feet don't recognise heat, and then they tingle and burn. Sitting on the stone edge, he lowers himself in, thighs, buttocks, belly and chest softening, melting into the water. His ribs open, pulling steam and mountain air deep into him, and his arms float in the warmth, fingers opening, breathing, like sea anemones.

He opens his eyes to find Makoto looking at him, at his ginger-furred white torso and his freckles. 'It's good for you? The baths?'

He looks back at Makoto, whose slender shoulders rise from the water, who is somehow clothed in self-possession. 'Very pleasant, thank you.'

The two other faces turn towards them, and one of the men speaks to Makoto. Makoto makes a small bow as part of his response. Imagine bowing, Tom thinks, to a man with whom you're sharing a bathtub. He imagines Makoto, naked, waving his hand, scraping his foot, making a Renaissance courtier's obeisance. The story of the Emperor's new clothes comes to mind; Japanese dignity is so profound that every aspect of business could probably be conducted in the state of nature without anyone betraying a flicker of dismay. He has not, he realises, heard any Japanese jokes. Or at least has not recognised any Japanese jokes. He himself has not laughed in many weeks.

'He asks if you are Dutch,' Makoto says through the steam. 'And he says it is an honour to meet you.'

Tom raises his head, which he has been resting against the side of the bath. Teak, he thinks, but possibly dark bamboo. 'Please tell him I am honoured to be here. Or whatever is appropriate.'

There is more talking and bowing and then the other men leave. They are made like boys, Tom thinks, and move as if their very bones were lighter than those of Europeans. He averts his gaze as they pass, genitals bobbing at eye-height, and then stretches out his legs into the middle of the bath. The water feels chalky, perhaps even oily, between his fingers and toes.

Makoto leans back, looking up to the stars. Their feet touch each other and glide away like fish. In the lamplight, Tom can see the steam curving around Makoto's head and face, haunting the shape of his skull and the hair beginning to fall down over his ears and brow.

'I am due some vacation,' Makoto says. 'Some holiday.'

'You have worked many days without one.' So, Tom supposes, has he, but the idea of being without occupation is not appealing.

'My parents live not so very far from here. On the way back to the city.'

Tom raises his head, pulls his arms back into his body, a more conventional pose. 'You wish to visit them. Of course. I am sure I can return alone.'

Probably. If Makoto hands him over to someone reliable with clear instructions about when and where he is to be delivered.

'I would make every arrangement. Or, if you wish, we

would be most honoured to receive you as our guest. My parents are mere farmers and it is not a fine establishment, but if it would please or interest you to visit they would be very happy. They have a room that is sometimes used for travellers.'

It is almost impossible, Tom has read, for a foreigner to be invited into a Japanese house. To a restaurant, yes, or even a theatre, but it is not the Japanese way to entertain at home. He finds himself lumbering to his feet to bow properly, face down until his hair dips into the bath. Idiot, he thinks, hippopotamus. Makoto smiles, nods, satisfied if also amused.

'Makoto, I thank you. I am greatly—' the word *honoured* is exhausted – 'greatly privileged, greatly moved. Of course, I am delighted to accept.'

He is not sure that the books, proclaiming the impossibility of such an occasion, offer any guidance to its etiquette. He must take a gift, of course, surely an instinctive and universal response, and he knows more about the deployment of footgear and chopsticks than he did. All his speech must go through Makoto in any case, and Makoto is doubtless making translations of intent and convention as well as mere words. He will not be allowed to offend through utterance. But how long, he wonders. Makoto may be owed holiday but Tom is here to work, and the sooner he finishes, the sooner he can return to Ally.

'A few days only,' says Makoto. 'And it is barely a diversion from the road back.'

a doctor does not weep

Ally was woken in the night by an angry wind hurling rain against the window, and this morning the boats are toppling and jerking on their anchors, their masts scribbling at the air. There is no point in taking an umbrella because even if she could hold it in the wind, the rain is horizontal, blowing across the lawn into the limestone wall. As she stoops to lace her boots she sees that the damp patch under the window has metastasized along the skirting board and up the wall, stretching out to join the water seeping under the cornice. One day, she thinks, the whole house will dissolve around her, the granite blocks settling back into the earth from which they came as cement and plaster trickle milkily down the hill to the sea. She doesn't go down to the kitchen, where this process is relatively advanced; Dr Crosswyn will give her coffee and biscuits later and it is not worth the effort and fuel to light the range when she will be out all day.

There are two letters on the mat, the Japanese ink from Tom's pen already blurred and spattered with Cornish rain. She scrabbles for her pocket, crushes them in. The other is not Aunt Mary's stationery; probably from Annie who is staying with a sister about to have a baby. Even in the high-walled garden, she has trouble closing the front door against the wind, and her skirts whirl up around her knees as she wrestles with it. She could stay at home today. It is not as if she were being paid to attend to the asylum. But they will be expecting her, Mrs Middleton and Mrs Elsfield and Mary Vincent, and the state of her clothes when she arrives will be of no moment to them whatsoever. Besides, the nurses need no additional ammunition for accusations of flightiness and unprofessional behaviour. She sees herself at home all day, watching the progress of the damp and trying to study against the sound of wind and rain. She pulls her scarf up over her hat, a pointless gesture towards conventional concerns.

The train comes. Ally takes a corner seat, dries her fingers and pats her face with a damp handkerchief, but her skirts cling about her calves and her shoulders are soaked to the skin. It would be the practical thing to borrow a set of asylum clothes. She will wait, she thinks, until she can take off her coat and scarf to read the letter properly, but she runs her fingers through the drier parts of her hair so they don't damage Tom's paper and takes down a hairpin to open it, just to peep and make sure the first line doesn't say *I write from my hospital bed* or *Please do not worry but.* That's when she sees that the other letter isn't from Annie, or even from Cousin George at Cambridge. It's from Mamma.

The carriage upholstery, the steamed-up windows, the damp coats and dripping hats of the other passengers, tessellate and dissolve. The smell of wet wool and pipe smoke is suddenly nauseating. No. Mamma has not written to her since her marriage, since the last letter telling her that in marrying she destroyed all her own work and threw away the efforts of all who had laboured so hard to support her. Ally's breath comes short, as if there's a great weight pressed on her chest. What can Mamma want with her now? Unless perhaps Papa has been taken sick, or is— She remembers the letter that told her May was dead. *This is the letter I have been hoping not to write, and you not to receive.* She turns Mamma's letter over and opens it.

Mamma wants Ally to return to Manchester. There is no reason, she writes, for Tom to be spending his money renting a house for Ally when there is a room for her in her parents' house. It is not as if Ally had any real position at the asylum, or as if she were doing anything other than dabbling in philanthropy. An opportunity has arisen for a doctor committed to the care of the poor, a doctor willing to minister to those for whom there is no other hope, who must otherwise die like wild animals. Mamma knows that, especially with Tom away and no particular reason to remain in Cornwall, Ally will not harden her heart to such need. She will perhaps recall Dr Henry, who does such great work in the Home and among the people of the slums? Dr Henry, exhausted by so many years of hard service, has become increasingly unwell and eventually agreed to allow the Committee to send him to spend the winter resting on the south coast. A colleague is covering his private practice, and Mamma has assured the Committee that it would be to Ally's benefit to take on his charitable work. The pay is of course not great, but it is something and therefore surely preferable to unpaid labour at the asylum. Mamma hopes also that Ally will not reject an opportunity to pass a season at home. Neither she nor Papa now enjoys quite the perfect health that was once theirs.

Ally looks out of the clear patch someone has rubbed on the window. The letter is not what she feared. Mamma sounds gentler than usual. She acknowledges Ally's expertise, that her work deserves payment. It is an invitation, of sorts, perhaps the nearest thing to a welcome of which Mamma is capable.

She remembers previous returns, all ending in Mamma's anger and Ally's reversion to cowed and nervous adolescence. It takes you days, Aunt Mary once observed, to speak to us again after you have been a night or two with my sister. Maybe it would be different now, maybe there is now room in that house for Ally to be the adult she has become, to take her place on almost equal terms. It is not like Mamma to mention her own health. Does Mamma herself require advice? She cannot remember that Mamma has ever been ill, not once in Ally's whole life. She remembers the private penitence Mamma taught to her daughters, the stones in the shoes as a reminder of sin, the food denied to cure temper and 'hot blood'. The tests of endurance. It is not as if Mamma would have betrayed any bodily discomfort even to her own house-hold. She remembers the candle flame. The night in the cellar. She shifts in her seat. She cannot say even now that she has not had need of everything Mamma taught her.

They are approaching Truro station. A man leaving the compartment stands back for her, gestures that she should go first, so Ally finds her feet, stands, queues in the corridor with her wet skirt clinging to her legs, tugs it free to climb down the steps to the platform. The rain has eased a little, dimpling the puddles rather than pounding out bubbles of air. The beggar girl is there again, blue-tinged hands hugging her legs to keep herself in the shelter of the archway, and a porter looking away, pretending not to see her. Someone should speak to her. Ally bows her head to the wind and sets off up the hill, rain spattering her wet face and clothes.

'My dear girl. You should have waited for the rain to stop. Or at the very least taken a cab from the station.'

Ally can't meet his eyes. 'We had an arrangement. Besides, it may rain for days.'

She has made a fool of herself. She had forgotten that respectable adults take cabs. Dr Crosswyn touches her arm. 'Not like this. I do not expect you to walk a mile in such weather merely to take coffee with me. Promise me at least that next time you will take a cab. We may not at the moment be able to pay you a salary, but I do not ask you to give yourself hypothermia in the asylum's service. My dear, I am quite concerned.'

He ushers her to the fire, into his own chair.

'My skirts will mark the leather,' she says. 'I will stand a little.'

'Your hands are quite blue.' He rests his fingertips on her knuckles a moment.

'It is only peripheral. I am warm from the walk.' I can take care of myself, she thinks, I am neither a child nor a patient. And also *wrap me, warm me, feed me*. Her skirt begins to steam in the fire's heat.

Dr Crosswyn rings the bell for Agatha. 'I will have them bring you some soup. I don't know what we should do about your clothes. Perhaps one of the nurses?'

'I am almost dry already. And I cannot take soup at this hour. Truly, a cup of coffee is all I could want.' She hears herself, bordering on hysteria. She is a fool. And she is hungry.

'You like to be hardy, I see.'

'A certain hardiness is a necessity of our training, is it not?'

A necessity met by Mamma's regime long before Ally arrived in London. A necessity that has left her unable to say, *I am hungry*, or *I am cold*, left her without the first utterances of a child.

There is a soft tap on the door and Agatha edges around it. She looks up at Ally, startled, and then gazes steadfastly at the edge of Dr Crosswyn's fringed rug.

'Agatha. Good morning.' It is Dr Crosswyn's habit, or perhaps gift, to give the impression that every encounter with a patient brightens his day. 'Very well, Dr Moberley Cavendish. We will have coffee, please, Agatha. You won't take a little sponge cake, doctor? No special pleading at all?'

Ally's stomach rumbles. She hears herself speak. 'I thank you, no.'

Ally doesn't want to see Mrs Ashton, doesn't want to hear any more about the cold spirit at her side. She doesn't much want to see Ward Four's nurse. Mary Vincent has managed to give herself a mild concussion running her head into the wall so there is an excuse to start on Two. Although self-indulgence even in such small matters is habit-forming. Ally goes upstairs towards Four, the coffee sour in her stomach, tendrils of newly-dry hair waving about her ears. Tom's letter crackles in her pocket. At least she has it, and him. Even if she does spend the winter with Mamma, in spring Tom will come home and they will live together again. What Mamma calls 'going home' will not be a return to past years. Not least, Ally thinks, because May is gone, and although May has been dead nine years suddenly there is a weight in her throat and heat behind her eyes. A doctor does not weep on the central staircase of the Truro Asylum. Quickly, before a nurse comes and sees her changing her mind between landings, Ally turns back towards Ward Two. It would be helpful to nobody for Mrs Ashton to see what is in Ally's eyes.

the last wolves of Japan

They climb through the woods. From the top of the pass, says Makoto, you will see that the first snow has come on the mountains, and then we will take the old road down onto the plateau. My parents' valley is broad, good soil, but the hills are high and when winter comes it is hard to travel. Leaves fall around them as they walk, Makoto first with a bell to warn bears of their presence. A dinner bell, Tom thinks, but Makoto would not see the joke.

Tom has travelled enough mountain roads here to know that in some districts every house is a farm, and also that all farms are arable. Even so, he finds himself imagining some kind of Japanese barn, probably with ornate gables and – what is he thinking – sliding doors for the animals. A farmyard with hens, for in the absence of meat and milk the Japanese do eat eggs and presumably, though he has not been offered it, chicken. Haystacks, he thinks, the autumn smell of ploughed fields, damp and rich on the cooling air. He and his mother used often to walk out of Harrogate on Sunday afternoons, past hedgerows where hips and berries began to brighten around fields of wheat ruffling like lakes in the wind, and later in the year, after the harvest, he would carry a basket for her and reach high for damsons and crab apples. It is time he wrote to her again.

Makoto has turned to wait for him.

'There is a tea-house on the other side,' he says. 'We can rest a while there.'

Tom stops beside him. There is birdsong, a woodpecker nearby, small creatures busy in the undergrowth. Dead vines drip from a tree sparkling with golden leaves. 'I am not tired. I found myself thinking of home.'

Makoto sets off again. The path winds up through the trees with no summit in sight.

'It is an interesting tea-house. Very old.'

Not the tea ceremony. Makoto took him to a tea-house in the city where he had to sit on his feet for most of the afternoon while a man in an exquisite kimono spent hours making bitter tea in a surprisingly crude grey bowl and Tom, who had hoped to be seduced by the experience as the authors of the books he's read were seduced, felt like a gorilla obliged to attend a ball at Buckingham Palace. Uncomprehending, unclean and finally enraged.

'But perhaps we should rather press on? I am sure your mother is eager to see you, and doubtless will have tea in readiness.'

Makoto glances back, smiles. 'This is a country place. Not the full ceremony, I promise, only a pot of tea and a plate of sweets. But you like the old Japanese houses, yes? This one is nearly three hundred years old. The same building.'

Tom uses the roots of a tree as steps up a steep part, glad that Makoto persuaded him to send most of his luggage back to the city by road and rail.

'The same family?'

'Naturally.'

*

The tea-house is set back from the path, almost overwhelmed by the trees clustering close around it, the ends of their branches meshing over its wooden roof. Fallen leaves lie thick against its wooden walls, as if the forest is slowly taking back its own. The building does not look as if it has been holding off the trees for three centuries, and if Makoto had not been there – not that he can imagine Makoto not being here – Tom would probably have taken it for some kind of hut or shed and walked on. The wooden screens are pushed back so Tom can see in to a bare earth floor with low platforms around the walls and a fire burning in a pit in the middle. He checks the roof again; there is no chimney.

'Here,' says Makoto. 'We keep our boots on, this time.'

There is a pair of stone dogs or wolves, one each side of the doorway. Tom hasn't seen or heard any wolves; the Japanese government has almost finished exterminating them. The bounty for a dead one is more than a year's wages for a rural labourer. He stops to look.

'*Inari*,' says Makoto. 'Foxes.'

Tom nods. He's read about this. 'To keep off evil spirits?'

'Not evil, I think. Difficult. Can one say, tricky?'

'Yes. Mischievous?' Tom suggests.

'Something like that.'

Cornish piskies, Tom thinks, the Hidden People of rural Scotland, the invisible beings who hide the tool you need for the job in hand and finish the end of the flour that was going to do tomorrow's loaf. He strokes the nose of the nearest fox. 'They hide things, perhaps knock over cups or jars?'

'In old stories. Superstitions and women's tales. Come, our host is waiting.'

A figure comes out of the darkness at the back of the tea-house, a white-haired man in a dark tunic and leggings, barely as high as Tom's shoulder but holding himself straight and loose as a boy. Everyone bows, and then the man comes over to Tom and touches his tweed jacket, looks up into his face where, he knows, a bronze stubble is blooming like rust. Just grow a beard on your travels, the ambassador's secretary told him, that's what everyone does, but Tom thinks a ginger beard is more than any Japanese child could be expected to encounter.

'He asks if your jacket is silk,' Makoto says.

'Wool,' says Tom. 'Baa.'

But of course the owner of a Japanese mountain tea-house has never heard a sheep, has not recognised Tom's bleating as different from the other sounds coming out of his mouth.

The old man carries a cast-iron kettle to the fire in one hand and hangs it from a chain suspended from the roof beam. Tom stretches out his legs. It feels odd to sit indoors in his boots and his feet are cramped and hot inside the leather and lacing.

'Is there any thought of introducing sheep here?' he asks Makoto. Most of the upland he has seen is forested, but if railways and mining, if lighthouses and telegraphs, why not sheep?

Makoto shakes his head. 'I have not heard of it. It would hurt our silk manufacture and there is no demand for mutton.'

Tom remembers a story in Brunton's memoir, about a team of European engineers who came upon a cow belonging to a Buddhist monastery on one of the islands. They tried to buy it and were refused on the grounds that foreigners were known to kill and eat such beasts and this was a sacred animal, raised by monks who refuse all harm. The engineers tried harder, offered more money, and eventually gave their word that the cow would be treated with respect and not killed, that they wanted it only for the milk. They drove it over the hill into the next bay and slaughtered it below the tideline before rowing back to their ship with the dinghy full of excellent beef. The Japanese, Brunton complains, lie all the time, often for no reason.

The kettle steams and rumbles. The old man comes forward again, carrying a tray holding a teapot and a plate of the inevitable sweets. There must be a woman somewhere in a back room, pounding and rolling rice dough.

'You are thinking that sheep farming should be tried?' asks Makoto.

Tom shakes his head. The man lifts the kettle from its hook in one hand and fills the teapot. The steam and the scent of green tea rise in the gloom, and Tom is suddenly thirsty.

'No. I know nothing about it. I think the climate may be too hot. And sheep would change your landscape.'

He tries to imagine these hills stripped of their woods, turned to bare heath. There would be no heather or gorse. Of what could Japanese houses be built, without trees?

Makoto nods, watching the old man's hands lifting and pouring. 'We were taken out on the – moors, you say? To see the purple flowers. Very beautiful.'

Tom wants to see Britain from behind Makoto's eyes, to see the strange and unnatural things to which he himself and everyone he knows is forever blind. The bleakness of the moors, where heather ruffles like water under the wind. Farmhouses of grey stone below grey-green hills. The pulsating verdure of a hedgerow in spring, bluebells scribbled purple in the shade of budding trees. The ancient forts and earthworks that form a chain across the uplands of the north.

'It did not look odd to you? Perhaps desolate or bleak?'

'Desolate?' Makoto's tongue still can't quite point the 'l'.

Tom accepts his tea, ducks his head in thanks. 'Er, comfortless, I suppose. Bare and unwelcoming.'

Makoto's back straightens. 'We were most kindly welcomed. Most generously.'

Oh Lord, Tom thinks, it is not possible, even when an Englishman and a Japanese man speak the same language it is not possible to talk.

'As I have been here,' he replies, bowing.

another presence at her shoulder

Ally is running through the woods, thorns snatching at her dress and hands. Although the sun is hot, there are no shadows and blood pounds painfully against her eyeballs and eardrums. She must hurry. She may already be too late. Something snatches at her ankle – a bramble, its barbs deep in her skin – and she tears free, tries to run faster but she's dodging around trees and there isn't a path, she may be lost, may be wasting even more time. Too late, too late, she has failed. A branch whips her face, snags her hair and she hurries on but it's too late, for by the time she stumbles into the clearing May is gone.

She wakes sweaty, tangled in sheets and blankets meant for two. The mizzle has at last cleared and the moon stands bright in the window. May, she thinks, May's grave under this same moon. She sits up. Her hair has come undone and is tangled around her neck, stuck to her hot face. She pulls it back. It is normal to have such dreams, normal for the unguarded mind to resurrect the dead, to re-enact the catastrophe that is so hard to accept. She gets out of bed to straighten the covers and brush her hair at the dresser whose mirror is full of moonlight.

Her own face, swollen with sleep, gazes out into the dark room and there is no shadow, no flicker, of another presence at her shoulder. The hard thing, Ally thinks, plaiting her hair, is not that May is with her, trailing her, peering from behind, but that May is gone from the world. It is not ghosts but absence that is harder to bear. She fastens her braid and closes the curtains, rattling on their iron rail. Perhaps this idea offers some under-standing of Mrs Ashton; perhaps she is simply, childishly, in flight from mortality, fantasising spirits to spare herself the final-ity of death. She should see if Mrs Ashton's admission papers offer some explanation for her disorder.

Ally wakes feeling better, less hollow, as if seeing May even in a bad dream offers some kind of strength. May was never afraid of Mamma. May was able to be angry with Mamma, to refuse her demands and reject her reasoning without the reaction Ally suffers from any attempt at resistance. If you wish to reply, May would say – and goodness knows Mamma has left enough of your letters unanswered over the years – tell her that it is not convenient to you or your husband for you to leave Falmouth this winter. If a person wishes a married woman to pay visits, she should not express such opinions about her marriage as Mamma has done about yours; you need no further reason to decline her invitation. Nineteen-year-old May sniffs. If you want to call it an invitation.

But perhaps this is not what May would say. More proba-bly Ally, like Mrs Ashton, is conjuring the dead in her own image, imputing to a girl nine years buried what she herself knows she cannot say. How can you say such things, Mamma would say, how can you be so hurtful, so selfish? Have you no care for my feelings? Alethea, you run mad. Ally presses her hands over her eyes and sags against the wall. She needs Tom, or Annie, or Aunt Mary, someone whose voice comes from a real face. There are too many voices.

Stop being so theatrical and put your clothes on, says Mamma in her head, there's nobody watching your hysterical tricks.

I don't know why you listen to her, says May, she's driving you mad. Again.

Ally, alone in her bedroom, trying to select her day's clothes, wants to stop and scream until they both – all – fall silent. She's not a madwoman. She's a doctor. She fastens her stockings, her petticoats, her blouse, settles her skirt and goes downstairs. In half an hour, she can leave for the asylum.

She asks William for the key to the record room, and makes her way there directly, before the vortex of patients' needs pulls her in. Along the ground-floor corridor, the great windows open to daylight like a cage, past Dr Crosswyn's office and the parlour to another plain wooden door, stained dark. She has been here before, finding out that Mrs Middleton's belief in her own damnation goes back to her girlhood and was probably shared by her mother, that Mrs Elsfield's husband was a heavy drinker and that the village doctor knew that Mrs Elsfield was often seen in church with a black eye in the days of her marriage. The detail of the admissions forms varies widely; some country doctors have narrative tendencies and others appear to regard the form itself as an impertinence. The files are kept in boxes arranged, unhelpfully, by year of admission, with no particular policy governing those admitted more than once. Ally has never heard of anyone consulting the files except to add the note of a patient's death or discharge to the admission form.

Dust rises as she takes down and returns box after box, beginning nineteen years ago when Mrs Ashton was sixteen, for although the asylum has housed a fourteen-year-old, sixteen is the usual minimum. Her navy skirt is streaked with it and her hands are dry and gritty. How can a locked room where no-one sets foot from one week to the next accumulate so much dust? Sunshine forms and strengthens in the high window, making banners of dancing grey motes. She should hurry; she will be wanted on the ward and is far from sure that what she is doing here can be reckoned part of the treatment of patients. Three more boxes only, or her curiosity will have to await another opportunity.

It is in the second box. Clare Ashton, previously Clare Constance, aged 31 on the summer day of her admission. Facts Indicating Insanity observed by the doctor in Redruth: patient claims to see and converse with the dead and has caused considerable distress to grieving townspeople by insisting that she has 'messages' for them. Inappropriate conduct in church. Patient given to wandering the streets at night in an agitated state. Husband wishes her admission. Family circumstances: patient's two brothers disappeared together aged 10 and 12, believed to have fallen over the cliffs while truanting from school. Patient's mother never believed that they were dead. Patient appeared to recover from this loss as a girl but the present disorder began after a stillbirth in the first year of her marriage. Facts Indicating Insanity observed by Dr Crosswyn: patient appears agitated, speech fast and loud, insists that she sees people in the room where there are none and cannot bear to be contradicted. And then there is the standard form completed by Mr Ashton, asking to be notified in the event of his wife's death.

Ally finds that there are tears in her eyes. Patient's mother never believed that they were dead. At least she and Mamma and Papa had May's body, the rain-scoured funeral, the mourning clothes, and even so she can still hear May's voice. Who among us is not haunted? Who does not walk in the shadow of those who are not here? Our dead are always with us and yet always lost. Only those who die young, she thinks, will not be inhabited by dead voices, by shadowy glimpses of figures long fallen to dust. Ghosts await you in the future if they do not follow you from the past. There is no clear border between insanity and grief, no basis for a limit to the permissible time of mourning. A time to reap, a time to sow, she thinks. Mrs Ashton is caught in the season of grief. Time passes, but there are many purposes under heaven that find no season here.

she has been named in Japan

'There,' says Makoto. 'You can see it now.'

They have been coming down the mountainside for an hour, and as far as Tom can see there is nothing visible now that was not apparent some time ago. It is like the Alps, he has been thinking, although he has not himself seen the Alps. The clustered hamlets, where two-storey houses lean in over cobbled alleys, are like Cornish fishing villages, like St Mawes or Marazion. If he were from Canada, or Egypt or the Sudan, he would still find likenesses. The mind reaches for similitude, making the new in the image of the familiar. He wonders again what Makoto saw in England.

'Which one?' he asks.

Makoto tests his grip on the rocky path and stops, one foot shored on protruding roots and the other in a rock's crevice. He points into the huddle of roofs along the track below.

'The last one on the right. With three maple trees in the garden.'

An ornamental garden for a farm? The maple trees are like red flags between the grey roofs.

Makoto sets off again, sure-footed along the path that Tom

is finding troublesome. There is scrub on the hillside, enough to arrest a tumbling man. It is his dignity and not his limbs at stake.

'My grandfather planted the trees. He made a walking garden, after my father took over the farm.'

'A walking garden?' He wishes Makoto would slow down. But it is natural, to hurry home.

'For walking around. There are paths.'

Tom steals a glance away from his feet and the path, down into the valley, but dare not spare enough attention to pick out a particular garden. He will address the matter of Japanese horticulture later.

'You grandfather is still – still with you?'

Makoto scrambles down a section of loose stones, for once using a branch as a hand-hold. 'The last time I returned was for his funeral. You will meet my grandmother. And of course my mother and father.'

Makoto waits for him as he steps carefully as a girl, not letting go of one branch until the next is within reach.

'Do you have a brother?' Tom asks, reaching firmer ground. The oldest son, presumably, inherits the farm.

'No. A sister, but she is married and lives in another village.' Makoto holds aside a long branch for Tom, pauses. 'And you, you have brothers, sisters?'

How, Tom wonders, have they not already exchanged such information, how after so many weeks do he and Makoto not possess these basic schoolboy facts about each other?

'No. My father died when I was an infant.'

He hears Makoto's inhalation, almost skids as Makoto stops and turns to bow. 'So. I am sorry.'

Tom shakes his head. 'I don't remember him.' He can always hear the other person's unvoiced response to this: but you grew up without a father. But it is a greater loss not to know the dimensions of what you have lost.

They set off again, almost side by side.

'It is hard for your mother, then,' says Makoto. 'To have her only child so far away.'

'She is accustomed to my absence. I have not lived with her since I left school.'

He tries to think what else Makoto should know, what his acquaintances and workmates in England know about him. 'I married only six weeks before leaving England. I rent a small house in a Cornish port called Falmouth. I attended the grammar school in Harrogate, as a scholarship boy, and then took an Engineering degree in Aberdeen. I worked for Mr Douglass for five years and then for Mr Penvenick.'

He glances up. Makoto is smiling, as he has not seen him smile before.

'What is your wife's name, please?'

'Ally,' says Tom. 'Alethea. Dr Alethea Moberley Cavendish.'

It is the first time he has spoken her name aloud since he had dinner with the attaché in Singapore, the first time, he thinks, she has been named in Japan. It is late at night in England and she will be going to bed, climbing under his blankets with her legs bare under the white nightgown that has the buttons down the front.

'Alethea,' says Makoto. It is not an easy name for a Japanese tongue. 'Doctor Alethea. So women become doctors now?'

He nods. 'Not many. There will be more.'

And you, he wants to say, tell me who you are. But he is learning to tread carefully, to be indirect and trust what is not said. It is probable that he and Makoto have an understanding.

the keys around her neck

'Trouble again,' says William, helping her off with her coat. 'Women's side.'

She takes off her scarf. 'Nurse Miller's back?'

'Not yet. Slow-growing collarbone, that one. No, Mary Vincent. Did herself some proper damage, from what I hear.'

Ally's patient. Ally will be responsible if – 'She's not –?'

'No. Sick ward, though. A lot of stitches. Got hold of a knife.'

'I'll go and see Dr Crosswyn straight away.'

William hangs up her scarf and straightens its folds. 'Might be best, Doctor. He's been running about all morning, trying to get to the bottom of it.'

She finds Dr Crosswyn in the kitchens, interviewing the cooks in turn to find out how Mary got the knife. He looks as if he was summoned from his bed, threw on some clothes and has not glanced in the mirror since. The cooks are also trying to prepare the patients' midday dinner, which appears to involve a great many turnips and therefore knives.

'Do you, or do you not, recognise this one?' He holds up a knife that still bears smears of blood. The kitchen maid recoils, glances about her.

'No, sir. That's to say, they're all somewhat the same, sir.'

'But you think it comes from this kitchen?'

The kitchen maid folds her hands over her apron, drops her gaze to the floor. Ally hopes she isn't an ex-patient, or there may be readmissions soon.

'I couldn't say, sir. It's like ours.'

'Which are kept always under lock and key?'

Her hands clench and her eyes slide round towards the Assistant Cook. 'Without we have to use them, sir.'

Dr Crosswyn tips his head back and sighs. 'So you are telling me it may or may not be a knife from this kitchen, and such knives may or may not be locked up at any given moment?'

'I – I couldn't say, sir. Please sir.'

'Go.'

'Dr Crosswyn,' says Ally. 'William told me there has been an incident. Perhaps we might –?'

He nods. 'I am getting nowhere here. Come.'

You know they cannot cook without using knives, she wants to say. You know that blades and fires and needles, irons and bleach and caustic soda, are the fabric of working women's lives?

He hurries ahead of her, forgetting his usual ballet of holding open for her all the doors that must be unlocked and locked again, to his office, where Agatha has left a tray of cooling coffee and biscuits on the table by the fire.

'Please,' he says. 'Sit.'

Dr Crosswyn stands at the window. 'We will have to notify the committee and make an official enquiry.' He does not look at her. He needs a bath, a shave and a comb. 'I hope to God it was no negligence on our part. The committee's views, you know – well, Trelennick's views – are conservative. All patients are lunatics and really I think he believes the safest course

94

would be to keep all of them permanently in straitjackets. I have never known him vote to release anyone.'

'Then they might as well be dead,' Ally hears herself say. But it is true; she has tried not to ask herself whether she would prefer death or the certainty of permanent confinement in the asylum even without a straitjacket. 'And the others must be more reasonable, since we do discharge people.'

He nods. 'Oh, I wouldn't call Trelennick unreasonable. Doubt anyone round here would dare, anyway. Traditional. Speaks his mind. Anyway, he won't like it if Mary Vincent got hold of that knife by – well, by any of the means I can think of, frankly.'

Ally sits forward and pours coffee. Trelennick owns several mines out in West Penwith and finds time also to act as a Justice of the Peace, chairman of Penzance town council and director of the Penzance Hospital Committee as well as of the asylum. Somewhere high up in the building, Mary Vincent's pain throbs and burns. There is no-one more pitiful, more abject, than the failed suicide.

She holds out the biscuits to Dr Crosswyn. 'How is Mary?'

He motions them away. 'The patient?'

She nods.

'I put sixty-eight stitches in her at five o'clock this morning. She missed her femoral artery by a rat's whisker and hit a tendon in the wrist. Should have trouble holding a knife next time.'

'Femoral?'

'She went for the – er – genital region. Among others.' He takes his coffee. 'The committee will say she should have been on the back wards. After all, she was admitted suicidal. You interviewed her, didn't you?'

Ally puts down her coffee, untasted. The cup rattles. 'Weeks ago. She was withdrawn.'

'But she'd had a knife, hadn't she? That was why they brought her in. And then we had to force-feed her. All the signs were there, that's what they'll say. It was a matter of when, not if.'

Ally feels nauseous. 'From the history I could piece together, it seemed she might have been holding the knife in self-defence. She had touched her neck with it but the injury was superficial. There was a suggestion that her employer interfered with her. And she wasn't force-fed, she just saw it happen to someone else and started eating. Which seems rather sane, to me.'

He swallows half the coffee at once. 'Tell that to the committee. As no doubt you will find yourself obliged to do. I hope the knife was clean, that's all. Maybe we should make a new rule, if you're going to leave weapons lying around where patients can get at them, at least sterilise them first.'

'May I go see her? Mary?'

'Go where you like. But you know her temperature will be normal now, even if there is an infection. It's only been six hours.'

She leaves Dr Crosswyn's office and leans against the wall. She has made a mistake. She has made a mistake and now Mary Vincent lies lacerated in the sick ward, losing the use of a hand and facing sepsis. If the committee hold her responsible, she will never work again. Her degree and her prize will count for nothing if she cannot be relied upon to keep healthy patients alive. She will be used as proof that women should not be doctors, that women's sympathies override whatever capacity for judgement they may possess. She should have sent Mary straight to the back wards, the back wards that Ally lacks the nerve even to visit. She sets off, unseeing, along the corridor. Did Mamma raise her to flinch from reality, to put her own fine sensibilities before the needs of others? Did Mamma turn away from the girls bound and filthy in the police cells in Paris, from the suppurating wounds of prostitutes injured, sometimes inventively, by their clients? And yet Ally has spent her time picking blackberries and listening to idle talk about spirits while the women on the back corridor plumb new depths of degradation and misery. She does not send patients there because she has been allowing herself to pretend that it does not exist, as prosperous families pretend that their comfort is not underwritten by the misery and hunger of the poor. No-one who knows what happens in the world, what humans do to humans, has any claim to contentment. The truth, she thinks, the painful, unpalatable truth, is that Mamma is right. Knowledge of the human condition is not compatible with happiness, and the weak choose to be happy. She locks the door of the sick ward behind her and hangs the keys around her neck.

Ally goes from Mary's bedside straight up the stairs to the back ward. She stands under the dormer window at the top of the stairs, trying key after key because this door has two locks and naturally the keys are not labelled. The stairs are too steep for infirm or elderly patients, she thinks, but the patients do not use the stairs because they do not leave the corridor. In a fire – There is a rattling of metal behind the door and a key strikes hers from the other side. The door opens a few inches and a nurse peers around, her face dour. She's taller than Ally.

'Yes?'

Ally straightens her shoulders. 'Good morning, Nurse. I don't think we've met, have we? I'm Doctor Moberley Cavendish.'

She holds out her hand and the nurse pulls the door a little wider.

'I've heard about you. Lady doctors, I don't know. I suppose you want to come in, nose around?'

Ally has to sidle around the door, crushing her skirt against the frame. 'I would like – I will visit the ward, yes.'

There are lady nurses, she thinks, or at least female nurses. There is an odour, and somewhere down the corridor someone shouting and banging. The floorboards are thick with grime.

'We don't allow visitors, see. Not even the Committee come here.' She slams the door behind Ally and begins to lock it again. ''S only patients, here.'

Ally stands tall. Abductors and pimps of young girls tried to set Josephine Butler's clothes on fire and did not succeed in frightening her away from her work; Mamma has endured calumny and innumerable threats without turning from her righteous vocation. The Edinburgh Seven, the first women to achieve medical qualifications in Britain, were assaulted and menaced by their own colleagues and teachers. She will not be threatened by a nurse. Doubtless, says Mamma's voice, the woman is underpaid, overworked and wholly uneducated. Do not fancy yourself better than her because you have had such indulgence and opportunity as she cannot imagine.

'I am a doctor,' Ally says again.

'So you say.' The nurse moves off. The corridor's windows are widely spaced and between them it is dim. The shouting stops but the banging goes on. Ally follows her.

asking strange gods

A 'walking garden' is simply a garden around which one walks, like a maze without the deceit. A gravel path, bordered by moss and lumps of granite, winds from the veranda around a variety of pine and maple trees towards a summer house half-hidden from the main building by foliage. Makoto's grandfather channelled a stream to loop through his garden and dammed it to make a pond over which a willow weeps. There are stepping stones across the pond and two bamboo bridges where the path crosses the stream. Tom guesses he understands how the young Makoto developed an interest in engineering. He makes his way back to the veranda, noticing how the light on the mountains is beginning to change as the afternoon goes on. He is, after all, on almost the same latitude as home.

The screens are pushed back so that the house is part of the garden and the last of the day's sunshine bathes the *tatami* mats. Makoto kneels beside his grandmother, who is sewing something small and red. For the first time, Makoto is wearing Japanese clothes, something like a scaled-down kimono with matching trousers in blue and grey stripes. A man who was not trying to appreciate Japanese culture might be reminded of an English prison uniform. Tom approaches, sits on the edge of the veranda to unfasten his boots, and then pauses. He can't imagine what the old lady, who lived most of her life in Samurai times, must feel about his presence. How would his mother react if he brought home an African savage with a bone in his nose?

Makoto looks up, switches languages and, somehow, indefinably, posture. 'How do you find the garden?'

'Beautiful,' says Tom. 'I do not think even the best British gardeners take such care for visual effect, for depth and detail. We do not understand gardening as a form of art.' The delicacy of the red leaves with the mountain forest behind them, he thinks, the way the bushes are trimmed to echo the shapes of the hills as seen from the path. He is not sure he would have noticed such things two months ago.

Makoto nods. 'It is perhaps different. I used to walk in the Botanic Gardens in Glasgow.' And long for the ones at home, he does not say. He speaks to his grandmother, who glances at Tom quickly, as if appraising something she is about to buy, and then bows her head to him.

'I told her that you like it,' Makoto says. 'She is glad.'

As in Falmouth, the sun drops behind the hill long before nightfall. A servant girl comes out of the stone-floored kitchen that Tom glimpsed on the other side of the entrance hall and closes the screens, first the heavy wooden ones, dark with age, and then the shoji inside. Firelight blooms around the sand-filled pit in the middle of the floor, flickering over the iron pot hanging from a chain and the maid's soft gown as she bustles around a low table. He finds himself wondering what women wear under their kimono, what a man would find if he unwrapped an obi. The girl stands back to check that everything is ready and then hurries back to the kitchen.

There is too much food. Clear soup, of course, and river fish curled in its batter as if it had leapt from the stream into the hot oil. Little bowls of brown cubes. Smaller bowls of wilted leaves and shoots, sitting in dark liquid and scattered with crunchy things. Bowls with upturned saucers over them, which will contain more substances unnameable in English or even Linnaean Latin. Tom folds himself onto the cushion indicated by Makoto and watches as the others settle. Here, it seems, women and men eat together. Makoto's grandmother sinks to her knees as easily as a child at prayer. The firelight plays on the tortoiseshell hairpins rising from her grey chignon, carved into the shapes he has learnt to recognise as representative of cherry blossom to the Japanese mind. Perhaps Ally would like such a thing? But it would not combine well with a hat. Makoto's father, fresh from his bath, has also changed from the working clothes in which he came from the field, and is now in the same striped uniform as Makoto. He bows across the table to Tom, who bows back. The maid comes to light the oil lamps, *okiandon*, flames flickering against the paper so that Tom looks around for water, and arranges them on the floor beside the table. Faces and fabrics blush in the wavering light, bodies fading into the gathering darkness around the fire. The music of voices speaking a language he still can't follow, the purr and crackle of a wood fire, and somewhere, beyond the wooden walls, wind in the mountain forest where under the trees stone idols pass the night wide-eyed and the last wolves of Japan lurk in their dens.

In the morning, he walks in the garden again. He overslept, alone with the shutters closed in the one room at the top of the ladder, and when he came down the maid brought rice and soup for him alone. Makoto seems already to have left the house, and Tom, like a baby whose mother has gone out, has no way of understanding where he has gone or when he will return. The women, even the grandmother, seem to be occupied in the kitchen. He stands on the first stepping stone, seeing that the mountain and the trees are reflected in the smooth water below the summer house. As the objects displayed in houses change with the seasons, so the composition of this garden will change with the inclination of the sun and the variation of the forest around. It is a space for contemplation, he thinks, intended to be conducive to meditation and perhaps even prayer, but Tom has nothing to discuss with the gods and his thoughts are not restful. Winter is coming, he can smell it on the cold morning air, and it is time he was back in the city, drawing up plans and ordering the new lenses so lights can be built in the spring. While he waits for shipments, he can execute De Rivers' commission. He doesn't know how long it might take to make what De Rivers wants, but the sooner the seamstresses start, the sooner they will finish and the sooner he can book his tickets home. It may have been a mistake, coming here, however interesting and atmospheric. Ally will be fine, of course, she is an independent professional woman and her letters show that she is busy enough at the asylum, but even so, he thinks, even so it is not as if she had any acquaintance in Falmouth. It is not as if she had the habit of taking care of herself. The cottage is undeniably damp even when fires are lit, and she may be huddling in that coarse shawl instead of paying for coal. It would have been better to leave her in London with her aunt and uncle, where he first found her. He paces back over the bridge, which seems now a foolish toy for the wasted hours of a grown man. What difference does a garden make, to the progress of humanity? Since he is here, since the day is lost, he will write to Penvenick. And to Ally. He will bring his letter case out here, to the summer house, where he will be neither a nuisance nor a curiosity to the daily household routine.

The air warms as the morning wears on until Tom, sitting in the sun on the steps of the summer house, takes off his jacket and tilts his face to the sky, eyes closed. The sun shines through his blood like last night's flames through the paper lanterns, but there is still an edge in the breeze carrying the dusty scent of falling leaves.

'Cavendish?'

He starts. Makoto. Damn it, they can creep up on a man sitting on a gravel path.

Makoto bows. 'Sorry. I started you. I apologise I was not here when you arose.'

'Startled. You startled me. Not at all. I am sorry I overslept.'

'Startled,' Makoto repeats. Another difficult word. 'I am glad you slept comfortably. I had to pay a visit. You have enjoyed the garden?'

'Very much.'

Makoto bows again. 'You would like to take some luncheon now? And then my mother wishes that I accompany her to the temple. Perhaps it would interest you? It is not far.'

'Of course,' Tom says. 'Thank you.' Because he is a child, to go where he is taken.

The grandmother is kneeling on the veranda with three small human heads on the boards in front of her. Tom stops.

'She makes dolls,' says Makoto at his elbow. 'An old tradition. Would you like to see?'

They are not the kind of dolls one could give to a child, or at least not to an English child. The heads are bone-white, with an eggshell texture. Their eye sockets remind him of something. He fumbles. Of holes, of fretwork. Of the holes either side of a violin's strings.

'Will they have eyes?' he asks, suddenly afraid that there are blinded creatures out there, that Japanese children play with eyeless homunculi.

Makoto glances at him. The grandmother goes on scraping at a teaspoon-sized wooden paddle with what looks like a razor blade. There are tiny feet in an open-mouthed bag beside her.

'Of course. And hair. There is a man in the village who makes very small hair ornaments for her.'

'Miniature,' Tom suggests.

'Miniature. And my grandmother sews clothes for them, kimono and obi.'

Fingers begin to take shape under the blade. Long fingers.

'It is exacting work,' says Tom. 'She is most skilful.'

Makoto says something to the old lady, who folds her scalpel in her hands to bow to Tom. He wonders if De Rivers would like one of the dolls, but he has no idea how he would enquire about making a purchase, and anyway he does not want to return to the city carrying one on his back.

He follows the back of Makoto's mother's red kimono away from the village, along a track between the rice fields. There is sun in the trees again, and on the shoulders of his tweed jacket. He expects another temple like the one he found in the hills, stone gods congregating in a forest clearing.

Where the track enters the woods, there is another of the great wooden *pi*, this time painted red, and then, leading through the trees, another and another, only a few inches above Makoto's head. It is like walking under dancers' raised hands in Oranges and Lemons. Fallen leaves, maple and yellow elongated triangles he doesn't recognise, form a tessellated pattern on the path's blue-grey stones. Tom touches one of the uprights as he passes, but of course it is only painted wood. Makoto looks back.

'They are *torii* gates,' he says. 'Families give them in thanks, or sometimes in memory of the dead.'

Tom nods. Like stained glass windows at home, although there is no sign, yet, of the thing to which these arches are given. To the woods, or the path. Makoto's mother speaks and Makoto replies, nothing Makoto feels any need to translate for Tom. The path becomes cobbled, in readiness, and they go on into the expected clearing. Sunbeams drip through the gaps where leaves have fallen.

'Oh.' There is a flight of stone steps leading up to a wooden building whose openings are screened with latticework. Red banners with black writing on them hang from poles like the state flags of visiting dignitaries. A pair of stone foxes guards the steps. Water trickles into a stone trough under a wooden roof; it must be piped from a spring further up the hill. Tom hangs back while Makoto and his mother rinse their hands and mouths, spitting onto the copper and gold leaves drifting around the sacred clearing.

'May I?' he asks.

Makoto nods. 'Please. If you like it.'

The water is tepid, pleasant on his hands damp from walking under the sun in a tweed jacket. It tastes of nothing. He follows mother and son up the steps and copies them as they clap three times to summon the gods. He asks for Ally to be well and happy, and for a safe return to her. He stands aside, waiting, with the feeling that asking strange gods for these things may have removed them from the realm of workday probability into the category of impossible magic, desperate measures.

she is like you

The fields lie bare to the plough now, and in the hedges the berries shrivel and drop, mouldering under the rotting fingers of hawthorn leaves and dead grass. Rain drifts around the peninsula. It is not cold, not cold enough to light a fire for one person, but the nights lengthen and the rain drips day by day. It is a preparation for the spring, Ally reminds herself. There will be wild flowers, violets and bluebells, which she will take to the asylum whatever the nurses say, and the white cottage will be bright in the sun, but meanwhile there is water seeping from the earth and running down the wall in the kitchen, and a musty smell in the cupboard in the other bedroom led her to find her blue wedding gown spotted with mildew. She can smell mould in the way the house exhales when she opens the door. It's important to keep the windows open, Tom said, even when the fire's lit, but for some days it has been no drier outside than in. One winter, she thinks, Cornwall will simply dissolve and slide back into the sea, perhaps leaving the jagged cliffs of the north coast as a memorial and a hazard to shipping. Probably Atlantis did exist until the north Atlantic rains washed it away. She will write to Annie, who enjoys such whimsy and has been fretting that Ally is falling prey to low spirits and nervous strain at the asylum.

The stationmaster at Perranwell has somehow managed to keep his roses blooming, although each flower hangs heavy with rain and the soil in the flowerbed glistens wet. There is no nightfall these days, only a gradual dimming. Ally gets off the train and feels the saturated sky press low over her head. She thinks of Aunt Mary in London and Annie further along the south coast. Somewhere out there, somewhere upcountry, there will be room to move and breathe between the earth and sky, perhaps even a line of sight to the stars and sun. The solar system is still there, beyond the clouds.

She hurries home, her skirts gathered in her hand away from puddles and mud. Up the hill to the main road, from which she can see the estuary and the boats rocking at anchor, and then down past the taverns of Killigrew Street, brightly lit and leaking music and talk. A door opens and a man comes out with a woman clinging to his arm. A ship must have come in. She turns along Dunstanville, past the captains' houses, where lamplight and firelight glow like beacons in the great bay windows. The curtains have not yet been drawn, and she sees a family gathered around a table where a maid in a white apron brings food, and two doors down a woman stitching at an embroidery frame by the fire. They would not sit so cheerfully, she thinks, if they had seen the back wards. If they knew that tomorrow, Mary Vincent who is not stupid and understands perfectly well what is happening to her, is to be moved to a place where she will spend her days sitting with deranged and incontinent women whose only advantage is that most of them are – probably – too mad to know that they will be there until they die.

When she wakes, her linen pillowcase is soft with moisture and the outside sheet is clammy to the touch. She rests her hand in the dry hollow where she has lain all night and then on Tom's side, chill and damp. She pushes back the covers and stands up, knowing even before drawing the curtains that Falmouth is still swathed in rain. Some drops bead the window and some roll slowly down the glass, drawing trails thin as the finest etching. She watches a droplet roll into another droplet and gather speed, finds herself tracing their progress with her finger on the glass. Come now, Ally tells herself. She makes the bed, entombing the warmth and dryness under heavy blankets, and puts on layers of clothes. Her stockings cling and wrinkle on her legs as if she had just had a bath. This evening, it may be time to light a fire, for the house and for Tom's possessions if not for herself. She remembers the verse on the bedroom wall in Manchester: *Lay not up for yourselves treasures upon earth, where moth and rust doth corrupt.* Even so, even Mamma might agree that the balance between the wastefulness of lighting a fire for one person and the carelessness of allowing cloth to rot and books to moulder is beginning to tip. Or perhaps the books and clothes are merely a specious excuse for self-indulgence, perhaps she imagines their peril worse than it is because she wants a fire. *We have followed too much the devices and desires of our own hearts. There is no health in us.* I do not believe, she thinks. I do not believe.

And at the top of the hill, the rain clears, and she can see that there is white sky raised high over the north coast. Ally pushes back her hood, her vision unblinkered for the first time in days, and feels the wind on her ears and neck. The asylum stands before her on the hill's apex, looking like Janus in two directions. To the south, Truro disappears into the mizzle, the spire of the new cathedral haunting the cloud like pencil under watercolour.

She has spent most of her time on the back wards and not been to Ward Four for a few days. Dr Crosswyn, summoned for a consultation at the hospital, has left a message saying that Mrs Elsfield seems to be failing and Ally should examine her. A medical problem, at least. The kind of call any doctor would make. She makes her way slowly up the stairs, noticing how washed sunlight floods through the high window over the landing and down the wooden stairs. There is dust on the ends of each tread and inside the spindles, and she can see where a patch on the wall has been repainted a slightly different colour. Perhaps it will be a different nurse on duty, someone who hasn't already concluded that Ally is incompetent.

'She is still with you,' says Mrs Ashton. 'Stronger day by day.'

Ally straightens her skirt. 'Good morning, Mrs Ashton. Still sleeping well, I hope?'

'She won't leave, you know. Not until you hear her. Did anyone listen to her while she was among us, I wonder? Was she carrying secrets too heavy for her?'

Aubrey, she thinks. But what May did with Aubrey, with Papa's friend, is on the wall of the Manchester Art Gallery for all to see. Not secret at all. Ally takes a breath. One can see how it would be so effective, the suggestion that the dead had terrible secrets. One would need to pick over the past, reimagine and re-examine the actions of dead hands and the words of a dead tongue, and then, presumably, one would pay a woman who claimed to be able to finish the story.

'Oh, we all have our secrets,' she says. 'The living and the dead.'

The red-haired nurse backs out of the linen closet. 'Oh. Good afternoon, Mrs Cavendish. Sorry, Doctor. Come to see Mrs Elsfield, have you? She's on her bed. Not much a firm hand wouldn't cure, in my view.'

Mrs Ashton looks up. 'She tried that. A firm hand. Didn't you, Nurse?'

The nurse puts down her armful of sheets. 'Now then. We

109

don't like liars on this ward, Mrs Ashton. And you wouldn't want to go upstairs, would you?'

If there are no bruises, Ally thinks, I can do nothing. And one has to pretend to trust the nurses more than the patients or the whole system will collapse.

Mrs Elsfield looks oddly small lying on her bed with the swathes of a dress fallen over her body like a shroud. She lies on her right, facing the wall, and has turned her face into the crook of her arm. Apart from the blackberries, Ally has never seen any sign that Mrs Elsfield is in any way disordered.

'Good morning, Mrs Elsfield. You're not feeling well?'

Mrs Elsfield turns her head, puts her hands over her face and opens her fingers to peek at Ally.

'Mrs Elsfield?'

Mrs Elsfield turns her face back into the mattress. Ally looks around to find Mrs Middleton gazing over her shoulder.

'Poor old dear,' says Mrs Middleton. 'She shouldn't be here, not at this last. And it's the vicar she's needing, not the doctor.'

Ally meets Mrs Middleton's eyes, perhaps for the first time. The first part of her statement is true.

'I'd like to examine her and find out about that,' Ally says. She glances around. There are no screens here, and it seems unlikely that Mrs Elsfield will rise from her bed and accompany Ally to an office or to the sick ward. 'Nurse, would you help me to undress her? Gently.'

Watched by Mrs Middleton, the nurse takes hold of Mrs Elsfield's hand screening her face and tugs. 'Come along now. Don't make this difficult, Maria. Soon be over and done with if you help us.'

Mrs Elsfield curls herself smaller, tighter. Her thin grey plait, sewn at the end, moves on the pillow. The nurse yanks her hand and Mrs Elsfield whimpers and tries to burrow away.

'Leave it,' says Ally. 'It doesn't matter.'

'They have to do as they're told or we'll have no order. Last chance, Maria, or I'm sending for another nurse. Do you want her stripped, doctor, or is it just her chest?'

Mrs Elsfield shrinks again.

'Neither. Please, nurse, stop this.'

'Right. Excuse me.' The nurse pushes in front of Ally and seizes both of Mrs Elsfield's hands, hauls on them. Mrs Elsfield spits and the nurse slaps her.

'Stop it,' says Ally. 'Nurse, stop it.'

She remembers the housekeeper Jenny slapping May, holding her down and slapping her while May fought and shouted and Ally stood, hands behind her back, waiting her turn.

'Now you see what we have to put up with.' The nurse drops Mrs Elsfield, who curls up again like a released spring. She'll never get out now, Ally thinks, but she was never going to get out anyway. 'I'll call another nurse and we'll soon have her ready for you. Not that I couldn't deal with her myself, but we have to keep the rules, don't we?'

'No,' says Ally. 'Leave it. It doesn't matter.'

'It's no trouble. We do this kind of thing all the time. Have to, in this line of work. Stop that now, Maria, you're only making things worse for yourself.'

The others watch while two nurses hold Mrs Elsfield down and open her dress so that Ally, with trembling hands, can listen to her chest. NAD, Ally writes. Nothing abnormal diagnosed.

She's on her way down the stairs to Ward Two when there are running feet along the corridor. The nurse from the sick ward.

She sees Ally. 'Where's Dr Crosswyn?'

'Out,' says Ally. 'At the hospital.'

'You'd better come.'

The nurse opens the door of the sick ward and stands back.

111

There is shouting. Mary Vincent, with blood running down her face and a contusion on her forehead with the white gleam of bone behind it, is struggling with two nurses. Her closed dress is torn at the shoulder. Leave me alone, she shouts, get off me. Stop that, say the nurses, stop that at once. The nurse who came to find Dr Crosswyn goes to their assistance and uses Mary's hair to pull her to the bed. They put her face-down and fasten a strap around her bare white ankles. Mary arches her bound body and tries to fling herself off the bed but they seize her again.

'You don't get out of going upstairs like this, Mary. Thought you could get some more time down here, didn't you? Stop that now.'

'Always been sly, haven't you? Rather be lounging in bed here than on the ward.'

'She's hurt,' says Ally. 'Her head is hurt.'

The corridor nurse looks up. 'Some of them'll try anything. She thinks if she hurts herself she can stay here. Ran herself into the wall.'

Mary howls. The sound makes Ally's scalp crinkle. Stop, she thinks, stop, I can't bear it. The doctor can't bear it.

The other nurse puts her hands on Mary's head, stubby fingers over her eyeballs. Silence. The nurse looks up. 'Often works,' she says to Ally. 'Don't have to press very hard, see, on the eyes.'

Ally bites her lip, closes her own eyes. Fingers pressing on the darkness, and one's arms tied.

'We'll take her up, shall we?' asks the first nurse. 'You'll probably find her more docile after a few hours on her own.'

They are going to put Mary 'in seclusion', in a windowless room on the top corridor where Dr Crosswyn himself has authorised the use of restraints on patients experiencing episodes of unmanageable behaviour. It is therapeutic, he says, for those who have lost all control and find themselves quite at the mercy of destructive mania, to remove all sensory stimulus and all means of destruction. It is not unknown for patients entering such a phase of illness to ask for seclusion.

Mary drags her face around. There may be some traumatic deformity of the frontal bone and her eyes are already blackening. 'No, please. I'll stop, I promise. Please don't send me up there.'

'Pity she didn't think of that earlier, isn't it, doctor? Get the chair, Nurse Crawford. We won't chance any tricks on the stairs.'

They are going to tie her to a chair and carry her up those stairs.

Mary's eyes meet Ally's. 'Please, doctor.'

'Trying to put one over the doctor now, are we?'

So which are you, Alethea? A madwoman or a doctor? Did I not know, did I not warn you from childhood of your nervous weakness, of your propensity to hysteria and unreason? You chose the asylum, Alethea, because you indulge yourself in feeble-mindedness. Because despite all your training and all your so-called qualifications, you are still crazed.

'No,' says Ally. 'No. Nurse, stop this. You are unkind.' Her voice is too loud. All of them, even Mary, fall silent. 'Tell me, nurse, how would you have to feel, to do as Mary does? How bad would it be, in your head, for you to run against the wall until your skull cracks, or to force a knife through your own flesh to the very bone? What would it take, Nurse?'

There are tears on her face. She swallows.

'That is how it is for Mary. That is it. She is like you, and like me. Like all of us. Only more sad.'

She cries, there on the ward. She has not cried for years.

They do not let her go. They take her down to Dr Crosswyn's office, a nurse on each side, where one of them stays with her, watching her, until he comes.

113

a place that would call him across years

Drops of rain gather on the twigs and hang, suspended like icicles, longer than seems possible before gravity plucks. Concentric circles spread in the pond, reaching out until they overlap into miniature overfalls, sometimes tossing a floating leaf just as a small boat would be tossed by wind-over-tide. He has not yet seen a leaf capsize. Another drop gathers and rolls down the central vein of one of the last leaves left on the tree, hangs tantalising from its point. The weight of rain must have some bearing on the fall of each leaf. The drop falls, and an insect supported by the pond's surface tension skids and rocks. He watches the ripples diminish, trying to identify the moment where they become invisible although the shock continues to spread, immeasurably, to the mossy bank, taking shape around the stepping stones and the water lilies. Tom shakes his head. In Japanese terms this may be contemplation, one of the purposes of the summer house. Penvenick would call it time-wasting. As soon as he gets back to the city, he will find out about those silk workshops. De Rivers could have given him a more specific commission: what if he purchases something that seems to him extraordinary and De Rivers does not like it? I bear that risk, De Rivers said, if I do not want it myself I will sell it and as long as you meet my specifications my investment will be sound. But get it right, Tom, and I'll pay you a bonus, enough that that wife of yours can sit by the fire doing fancy-work as long as she likes instead of dragging your name around the county asylum. It's enough to make a man wonder if you should pay a visit yourself, allowing it.

Even at this distance, Tom's buttocks and shoulders clench. But the money is enough, just about. Ally herself is a pragmatist; let him say what he will, she said. It does not hurt me and his money will certainly help. Goodness knows worse things have been said of all of us working for women's liberation and not by people who are offering money either. One of her little smiles flickered out at him: we can use some of De Rivers' payment to offer a small bursary at the Hospital for Women, if you like. His breath catches. Ally.

Enough, he thinks, enough. What is he doing here, gazing at raindrops like an infant left in a crib? He will take a walk. It is wet, but not cold. The path to the shrine went on, winding up through the woods. A very old route, Makoto said. There used to be a monastery up there. He should try to tell someone where he is going, or that he is going, not slip away from his hosts like a thief in the night. He tries to imagine the pantomime, the risk of insult, of giving the impression that he does not intend to return or that he is going in search of something they have failed to offer him. He won't be long, just far enough beyond the temple to see where that path leads.

The forest is loud. Rain hisses on the dying leaves overhead and drips through the bushes at the edges of the track. Bamboo leans whispering at the path's turnings; he remembers the creature he didn't meet on the island, and Makoto telling him a country saying to the effect that it's foolish to fear bears because one within twenty paces will kill you whatever you do and one at any greater distance will run away whatever you do. Bears will be preparing to hibernate now, and hungry. There is no birdsong, no slithering or pattering in the undergrowth. Everything will be sheltering, bright eyes peeping from under leaves and twisted roots, fur spiked with rain and feathers fluffed. Cold water is beginning to seep through the shoulder seams of his jacket, but he's warm enough, walking fast.

He's only beginning to settle into the forest, to the rhythm of his tread and his breathing and the rain, when he comes to the torii gates, their red deeper and brighter than it was yesterday, echoing under the dim greys of a wet wood. He pauses to touch one again, as if physical contact could substitute for under-standing. Each one is raised in prayer, he remembers. They are memorials, or hopes or fears made manifest in wood and left to glow here under the trees. His fingers graze each one as he passes, but as he comes towards the clearing he stops. There is something there, low to the ground and fleet in sinuous move-ment. He freezes. Two of them, feline in their delicacy. He slows his breathing. A fox sitting on the lowest step of the temple, tail curled around its feet, sharp nose turned towards its mate who swirls and leaps in the open space between the water stoup and the building. Dancing, the other fox is dancing, turn-ing fast as a fish back on itself, flowing, red fur rain-dark and the white bib bright. Tom and the fox-wife watch. Fine feet lope, feathery tail brushes the damp air and flickers over the fallen leaves. The dog fox leaps and bends low, waltzes and jumps. And then the dancer sees the intruder. There is a moment's shock and they are gone so fast that for a moment he thinks they have vanished where they stood, vanished into thin air.

He stands a long time, in case they come back, and even-tually makes his way to the step. There is no sign, no token of their presence, no footprints or shed hair.

*

He had planned to return to the summerhouse, to hope that no-one would notice that he'd ever left, but he's too wet not to go straight in to change. He returns the way he set out, through the back gate into the compound. The surface of the pond is still dimpling, circles still spreading, drops still gathering on the overhanging leaves. He can feel wet socks squishing in his shoes as he makes his way along the gravel path, and the water that crept through his jacket is now pasting his shirt sleeves to his arms. He climbs onto the veranda. The screens are open, but not far enough for him to pass through. It seems uncouth, to walk into someone's house. At home he would knock, or at least call as he opened the door. He hesitates, and hears footsteps. Makoto, looking like a willow pattern figure clasping his gown under an umbrella, is coming along the path.

'I am sorry to leave you again. I had a call to pay, and then I was in discussion with my father. I hope you have not been dull.'

Makoto's eyes are hooded, his gaze just below Tom's face.

'Not in the least. I would not have guessed that a summer house would be so beguiling in the rain.'

He finds that he does not want to tell Makoto about his walk.

Makoto nods. 'In such a climate, we must build for wet weather also. But you are very wet!'

As we should build at home, Tom thinks, but who makes a rain garden? We huddle in our dimmed rooms and blinker the grey skies with net curtains. And he is being foolish. There is no possible call for secrecy. In any case, most of the village has probably heard that he passed by.

'Not so very wet. I took a short walk. Mostly I have been admiring your garden.'

Their eyes meet, and slide away.

'Back to the shrine?' Makoto asks, as if he doesn't already know, as if he hasn't already been told that his foreigner has been sneaking around up there in the rain.

'Makoto,' he asks. 'Makoto, just for this evening, do you have a suit of Japanese clothes I could wear? Perhaps you keep one for guests?'

Rain scrabbles on the roof and the fire hisses and shifts. In the kitchen, cups and bowls chime as water pours and the maids' voices rise and fall. What do they talk about, two servants at night in a Japanese mountain village? Makoto's face is burnished by firelight, intent on the charcoal glow. Without looking up, he calls. There is silence in the kitchen and then lamplight from behind the curtain, the shuffle of sock feet over straw. Tom adjusts the cotton gown, feeling, as he has felt all evening, half-dressed, as if he's gone to the office in his nightshirt. He thinks Makoto is asking for sake.

It comes in a stoneware bottle, with two cups.

'Yes?' asks Makoto. No bowing, no invitation.

'Please,' says Tom.

He repeats what Makoto says as well as he can – a toast, probably – and sips. His eyes water. Not sake but some kind of spirits.

'No,' says Makoto. 'Like this.' He tips back his head and tosses the draught. 'Again.'

The firelight dissolves and spins. They are both lying down now, like Roman senators at a feast. Makoto reaches for the bottle and closes his hand on it the second time he tries. Tom holds his hand over his cup, no more, but Makoto pours anyway. The charcoals glow dragon-red and Makoto's legs and feet fade away into the room's night. Tom licks his hand.

'You're so sad, to leave home again?'

Tom hasn't visited his mother since before his marriage, but his last nights there have usually been marked by a guilty sense of freedom, of a duty discharged, like the trickle of outdoor air into a stale room.

Makoto rolls onto his back. 'No. I have asked my parents for something and they have declined.'

He's too drunk to phrase an indirect question. Arranged marriages, they still have arranged marriages in Japan. Often, he's read, the couple hardly meet before the wedding.

'A woman? You want to marry. Or not?'

Makoto sighs. 'No. I want the land. To come home.'

Tom sits up to see Makoto's face. The land? To walk away from his career?

'You want to be a farmer? After all those years of training?'

Firelight plays on Makoto's face, on his closed eyelids.

'Not yet, of course. I have my work. And my father is still strong. But later, yes. This is my home.'

Tom tries to imagine having such a home, a place that would call him across years. It is probably necessary to be born to it, it is probably not something one can buy, even with the figure De Rivers mentioned. He tries to imagine having a father, to tell him what he is allowed to do.

'But your parents perhaps need your salary? Or they are proud of what you have done?' Perhaps they don't see why their son should throw away years of work and turn back on the great stride between a village that strikes Tom as essentially medieval and the Engineering Department in Aberdeen.

Makoto puts his hands behind his head, opens his eyes and stares up at the ceiling. The rain seems to have stopped.

'No. It is the foxes.'

Tom must have misheard. Or Makoto's English is at last succumbing to the drink. The *shochu*. The Japanese, James

Moorhouse observes in *Three Years in the Land of the Rising Sun*, have a child's tolerance for alcohol.

'Foxes?'

Makoto huffs in exasperation. 'We own foxes. We are *kitsunemochi*. It is stupid. A winter's tale for old women.'

Tom lies back. A person, he supposes, could own a fox. 'You mean you farm them? Perhaps for fur?'

'No. No-one does that. No, in the countryside some families are said to be kitsunemochi. It means there are foxes on the land. I should have known. I should not have asked my father.'

'Well, there probably are foxes on the land. I saw some only today.'

Makoto waves his arm, as if swatting a fly. 'Not real foxes. Spirits, perhaps you would say. Not devils but bad.'

'Goblins?' Demons, he thinks, elves, ghosts. It's all the same.

'I have not heard the word. Goblins. Very well. So in each village there is a family who have goblin foxes. And we are that family. And I have annoyed my father by raising the subject again.'

Tom lifts his head to drain his glass again. He is not sure which of them is deranged. 'You have goblin foxes? You, an engineer?'

Makoto sits up and pours again. 'Some of the new railway lines are said to have their own fox spirits. People see trains coming to hit them but when the train is on them there is only a fox.'

'What?' And what are people doing on the railway lines anyway, fox or no fox?

'We have had them since my great-great-grandfather's time. He was adopted into the family, you see, and then inherited and the villagers did not like it. And they said he owned foxes. They cause trouble.'

'Stealing hens?' We must make haste and tell the King, because the sky is falling down.

'No. I told you these are not real foxes. No, they spread lies about people. Gossip. They borrow things and leave them lying around, or they make things break. Sometimes they eat up all the food.'

Gossiping foxes? Tom gives up. 'I saw two foxes earlier,' he says. 'Dancing. The dog fox was dancing for the vixen. At the temple.'

Makoto lies back again. 'At the temple? Don't tell my mother. She'll say you saw – what were they? – golbins?'

'Goblins,' says Tom. 'Though I'm not sure that's right.'

They lie there. It's warm, and the Japanese clothes are very comfortable once you get used to them. Tom thinks about what he doesn't understand.

'Why do the spirit foxes mean you can't come back?'

'They don't. That's what I tell my parents. My father says these stories aren't told in the city, no-one there calls me kitsunemochi, so I should stay there and live my life without these lies. He says they sent me away so I could escape this story. He says he does not wish to hear of this again.'

'Why don't they move somewhere else? Another village?'

Makoto drains his glass. 'They have always been here. And no-one would buy the land because of the foxes. I should not have asked.'

In the morning, Tom thinks, he will try to make sense of this. He will be able to see where the problems are, in the morning.

'Like the stone foxes?' Tom asks. 'At the shrines? I mean, temples?'

Makoto rolls onto his side. His eyes are closing. 'Inari. No. And yes.'

*

They are woken by the maid, pulling back the shutters to fill the room with a blinding white light. Tom groans and rolls over. His head hurts. What is the etiquette for vomiting? He pulls the striped gown closed, although the maid must already have seen his hairy white belly. There are reasons for the buttons on European clothes. She speaks to him, the global things that women with things to do say to men who ought to know better. His neck is stiff and one arm is numb. The maid scolds and clucks. Makoto is lying on his back like an effigy, apparently oblivious to the morning. There are kitchen noises: soon the rest of the family will appear, washed and dressed for breakfast. Tom uses the functioning arm to push himself up and sits there, rubbing his neck. A bath, he needs a bath, but as far as he knows bathing is possible only in the evenings. He stands up and the room tilts. It's a long time since he last drank spirits and he's felt like this only once before, one night in Aberdeen after exams when he stumbled back to his rooms, his disgrace along the way veiled by a freezing fog that seemed sent to slap him awake. He makes his way to the lavatory like someone testing the ice.

When he comes back, at least approximately washed and dressed, Makoto is sitting at the table with his family. There are steaming bowls on the table and the smell of fish and soy on the air. Tom's throat closes and he swallows hard. Makoto doesn't translate his greeting and apologies. He had better wait, he thinks, to ask about the foxes.

four dark twigs

She leans her head on the window, lets the train shake her skull, as it pulls her across England. Cornwall, Devon, Somerset, Wiltshire. It is all the same, all rolling pasture scattered with trees and clumps of stone houses. There is more or less grey cloud and the water flowing through England, hills to coast to cloud and round again, runs in larger or smaller channels. Sometimes someone comes to sit in her compartment and she pulls her wrap up around her face, shakes her head when a woman with knitting asks where she is going and a man with a newspaper flaps and folds it and asks if he can bring her anything from the tea room at Salisbury station. As there are clothes for mourning, so there should be clothes for failure, clothes that mark the wearer's degradation. Gloucestershire, Oxfordshire, Warwickshire. The tracks run along a canal plucked by raindrops. A man and a boy work a lock with sacks wrapped over their heads while a horse grazes at worn grass. Birmingham begins, smoke and red brick. Where money is made, Alethea, there is always misery and suffering beyond the imaginations of so-called respectable citizens. The carriage fills up and she turns in her seat towards the window. The light has dimmed and the brickwork outside is stained with soot and smoke. Staffordshire, where patches of pastoral England pretend to outwear brick chimneys and gouged hillsides. Workers in the Potteries die of the poison glazes they handle for a livelihood. But you have not the excuse of ignorance, Alethea. When you devote yourself to trivial matters instead of saving those who need you and have no other help, you cannot say that you know not what you do. More canals, and ragged children walking beside the horses in the rain. The mortality rate for canal children is relatively low, probably because there is less overcrowding on boats than in the rooms of the urban working class and better sanitation. And because they are not left unattended in infancy while their parents work, although on the other hand they presumably remain uneducated. Mamma is right, England is not a civilised country.

The hills of Derbyshire rise, and in the distance she sees the village where Papa and Aubrey took her and May one summer. She remembers climbing a hill, May and Aubrey jumping from tussock to tussock across a bog, and later herself reading Virgil under a willow tree, refusing ham and plums at lunch because Mamma doubted her self-discipline. In the valley bottoms where rivers fall, grey mills rise like cliffs. Like the asylum. She closes her eyes. In the mills, machinery bangs and roars. Children pull carts of babies through the streets, taking them to be fed by mothers who sacrifice their own moment to eat in doing so. The weight of outrage and unmet need presses down on this country like wet cloud. Burn it all down, wash England away into the sea, and start again.

Stockport, the brick viaduct slashing the valley like oil paint thrown on a watercolour. Rows of terraced houses plough the hillsides and smoke hangs above their tiled roofs, waiting for the rain to wipe it down into the roads and backyards. Nausea thickens at the back of Ally's throat: not long now.

She has to put the trunk down on the wet pavement three times between the omnibus and the front gate. She has hooked Tom's small valise over her forearm. Other families, other parents, would have come to meet her at the station. There is no point in such thoughts. The trunk bangs against her leg as she sets it down to open the gate. The black paint is peeling and the hedge is overgrown. There are weeds in the gravel path and green stains under the gutters on the white sections of half-timbering. Ally looks up to the window of the attic, where she slept the year Mamma said her nightmares were disturbing May, and to Papa's north-facing studio, where he has had larger windows made and a balcony put in over the porch. She stops, her hand on the gate. Even now, she could turn away. And show Mamma a new kind of failure and weakness. She lifts the trunk onto the gravel and closes the gate behind her. It may be different, this time. It is three years since she was last here. Mamma wrote, did she not, that she is sorry to hear of Ally's difficulties at the asylum, that she looks forward to seeing Ally happier in more useful work. She herself is changed. She is a doctor. She lifts the trunk for the last time and approaches the porch.

It is Papa who answers her third ring on the bell, when she is peering through the stained glass of the sidelight and thinking that if there is no-one in, if despite her letter there is no-one in, she will go and sit at the back door to avoid the ignominy of waiting like a stray dog on the front step, in view of the street. He looks through the fanlight before he opens the door, as if he doesn't know who might be there.

'Ally. Darling girl. I didn't know you were coming today. Come in.'

He's wearing his painting smock. It can't be same one, but the ochre smear on the left sleeve looks familiar. She humps the trunk over the step.

'Oh, remember the parquet. Scratches if you breathe on it.'

Ally bows her head. 'Sorry, Papa. We have only painted boards in Cornwall.'

He watches her taking off her coat. Mamma won't like it, and won't like her bustled skirt. Papa is greyer than last time, and his eyebrows have begun to sprout white hairs, but he still carries himself upright and his face is unlined. She hangs her coat in the cupboard, as she always did. A winter cloak that must be Papa's is on May's peg.

'So, you've come back to us?'

'Just for the winter, Papa. To help with Dr Henry's clinic.'

Papa nods. 'Your mother said so. I don't recall that you and Dr Henry were such great friends.'

Mamma used to consult Dr Henry for Ally's nervous troubles. He prescribed blistering and hard work, as a medieval physician might have done, although the rest of his practice appeared to be conducted along approximately modern lines. More than once, Papa simply countermanded Dr Henry's orders. The child will turn into a calf if she eats so many milk puddings.

'He always did good work with the poor. He never spared himself.'

Papa sighs. 'Nor anyone else. Just as you please, Ally. You are surely old enough to do as you will. I was in the studio, my dear, when you arrived, and if you don't mind I'll just go back up. Your Mamma expects to be home this evening, I believe.'

'And Jenny?' she asks. She has been weakly dreading Jenny, who has known her since infancy and has never been taken in by any pretence of strength or competence. Who knows her a useless and foolish thing.

'Oh, Mamma pensioned her off last year. Said she'd had a harder life than my coddled imagination could compass and deserved to pass her last years in comfort. She's living with her sister, I think. Mamma will have the address if you want to visit.'

He hurries up the stairs. She should perhaps have known when he didn't answer her second ring that Papa was painting, not to be disturbed. But I did write, she thinks, I did give them the time of my train.

The towel in the downstairs lavatory is grimy and soft, and there are stains in the WC. She decides not to try to carry the trunk upstairs and risk banging the banister spindles or the treads. She moves quietly, not to disturb Papa. The door of her room, her room and May's, is closed and Ally stands on the landing, her hand on the concentric circles of the door-knob. May's bed. The pillow on which her hair lay spread every morning, however tightly it was plaited at night. When Ally came to change the sheets or make May's bed, there was the scent of May, a powdery drift for which she can now remember only the words. She opens the door, and May's bed is bare and flat, the mattress covered only by a ridged cotton bedspread exactly as it was last time Ally visited. Someone – it can only be Mamma – has left in a glass vase four dark twigs of bronze beech leaves from the tree in the garden. A gesture, a hand lifted in the direction of the cut flowers that would seem to Mamma an intolerable waste of money urgently needed elsewhere. Maybe this time it will be different. On Ally's bed against the opposite wall, there are folded sheets and the same worn green blanket that was always hers. She is, then, expected. She moves the pile to the table where she used to do her homework and begins to make the bed. The text from the gospel of Matthew is still on the wall: *Lay not up for yourselves treasures upon earth.*

The house was always cold, cool even in the height of summer. Ally opens her trunk in the hall and carries up piles of clothes and books until it is light enough for her to take the whole thing. She finds herself putting her possessions back into the trunk instead of the chest of drawers, as if her visit is so short there is no point unpacking. She slides her garnet engagement ring over the first joint of her finger and back down again, making a tiny click in the house's silence as it rejoins her wedding ring. She wants, anyway, to add the trunk bought for her wedding journey to the furniture of her childhood. Things have changed. She blows on her fingers and rubs her hands. It is not as if she will be here in the house very much. The clinic may at least be heated, and she will be too busy to mope. In the street, the trees are shedding their last leaves, and through the branches she can see the other houses. The children across the road, who used to go out in a carriage with their Mamma or accompanied by a nurse to the park, will be grown up now. She remembers them chattering and skipping along the pavement, dressed in clothes of which May was fiercely envious. Next door was a banker and his wife; he used to leave early and return late on foot while she seemed rarely to leave the house, although other rich women called in carriages on Thursday afternoons and a maidservant took a lapdog around the block twice a day. It is not as if she is going to be here, in this house or in this room, enough to learn these patterns again.

Ally presses her cold fingertips to her eyelids until she can feel the chill in her eyeballs. What has happened to Mary Vincent now? She is on the back ward, inevitably, perhaps still in isolation. Not restrained, surely Dr Crosswyn would not authorise such a long period. Although the nurses seem able to use the closed gown at will. In some ways, Ally thinks, it would be a relief to be so tethered and put to bed, to be required to do nothing except remain warm and still for days. That, after all, is the principle of the treatment, inasmuch as there is a principle and it is a treatment. Mamma is right, it will be better for Ally to be stitching cuts and setting bones, treating the contagious diseases of prostitutes and the fevers and infections of slum children.

Darkness is falling. It appears that Papa still resists gaslight. The Briar Rose curtains are faded on the folds and threadbare at the hems. She remembers the curtains new, and Aubrey sitting on May's bed telling her and May about the prince who came to hack his way through a hundred years' growth of thorns to reach the sleeping princess. You stuff their heads with nonsense, said Mamma, as if a woman's life began and ended with romance, as if girls had no souls but only hearts. I won't have it. The next day the black and white text was on the wall. *If thine eye be single, thy whole body shall be full of light.*

Ally eases the door open and closed behind her. Her feet remember where the creaky floorboards are. There is a line of golden light under Papa's door, behind which will be velvet drapes, candles and a log fire. The hall is full of winter dusk, thick around her ankles. The kitchen door handle is sticky to her touch, but inside there is warmth by the range and candles still in the same drawer. Papa might at least permit gaslight in the kitchen, where he hardly sets foot and certainly would not paint. Ally lights the lamp on the table and holds it up. The tiled floor is spattered with food around the range and table, and there are crumbs and hairs in unswept corners of the floor. She carries the lamp to the sink, where there are slimy potato peels piled up and stains on the enamel. She can smell the damp cloth on the draining board. It is clear, at least, what she should do until Mamma's return.

he imagines being a child

The station was much nearer the village than Tom expected, barely two hours' walk down the cobbled track through the forest, and then along the valley bottom over a swooping new bridge and so into a town where a stone school building with glass windows squatted among the wooden houses and shops. No, Makoto said, he did not go to school there but from the age of ten stayed with his mother's brother in another town. The train comes so close, Tom thinks. Any of those villagers who believe in demon foxes and stare at his white skin and red hair as if they had never heard of other nations could walk down here, where there are newspapers in the shops and even milk for sale, and be in the city by dinner time.

There are only two other people in their carriage, one asleep with his head lolling against the window and the other reading at the far end. Tom waits while the train pulls out and the town buildings give way to more forest. Makoto, in the window seat, appears intent on the passage of trees.

Tom clears his throat. 'Makoto? I have been thinking about the foxes. I am puzzled.'

Makoto does not look at him. 'Please, do not trouble yourself. It is a foolish tale. Not worthy of the attention of an educated man.'

There is a house in a clearing, where they must hear the approach and passage of every train loud as thunder.

'But I don't understand. If people worship the fox gods in shrines, why is it an accusation to say that someone is a fox owner?'

'As I said, it is foolishness. Superstition.'

'I am interested, even so.'

'Then you should consult someone who has made a study of such things. I will try to arrange an introduction.'

Makoto takes a book from his bag, not the one he was reading before. Tom gazes out of the window, feeling bruised, remembering the garden in the rain. It is not as if he had asked Makoto to speak of foxes, as if he had behaved like a nosy foreigner. He would never have known about the superstition if Makoto had not volunteered information.

Most of the railway buildings look European, as if a giant little boy from Hamburg or Edinburgh had laid out his train set around the hills and plains of Japan. The porters wear braided jackets and peaked caps as they stand before relief Corinthian columns and arched windows. The engine whistles and blows the same tune as at home, but the street-sellers carry bamboo baskets containing artful arrangements of rice and vegetation and the women shuffle in *geta* and kimono, as if the little boy's sister has added a scattering of dolls from a very different game. Green hills and rice paddies gave way to huddled wooden houses a while ago. Tom wants to turn back.

Makoto lowers his book. 'I will take you to your residence, or you would like to eat first?'

'My residence? I am not returning to the guest house?'

He had been looking forward to it, now he knows how to

131

behave. A little more about how to behave. He wanted to see the woman's kimono approaching below the curtains, and glimpse the courtyard through the paper screens.

Makoto makes eye contact for the first time since Tom came down to breakfast in his tweed suit. 'To stay several weeks? No. Mr Senhouse offered an apartment in his house. You will have a bed, tables and chairs. More comfortable.'

'Oh,' says Tom. And then, 'Thank you.'

Makoto ducks his head. 'It was nothing. I hope you will be content there.'

'Of course. I thank you.'

'Not at all.'

It is as if they have gone right back to the beginning. Perhaps it is rude, to present a man in the morning with what he said the night before. He does not see, anyway, why Makoto should regret merely asking a question of his parents, asking permission, for how else is one to obtain an answer? (Perhaps not, perhaps in Japan there are ways of knowing how a question will be answered before it is asked, in which case the question is merely ritual, though it is increasingly clear that Japanese ritual is not *mere*.) Are fox owners a caste or was the status acquired, and if so, when and by whom? Why did they send you away? Who will inherit the farm, if you stay in the city? He has tried, holding Brunton's book on his lap and gazing out of the window, to think of an English equivalent. One might not wish to marry into a family showing hereditary insanity, but that is a practical concern about the health of resulting children, well supported by science and probably obtaining also in Japan. Most families prefer alliances within their own class but there is no magic involved, no supernatural element. A Catholic, he thinks, marrying a Protestant, an English girl with an Indian man, but it is not the same thing. The shapeshifters and witches left Britain long ago.

The train is slowing, but Makoto has gone back to his book. Tom clears his throat. 'Makoto? Who is Mr Senhouse?'

Makoto's glance slides across Tom to the window. 'A teacher. At the new business college. He is here with his wife and they have a large house.'

Makoto pushes his book into his bag, begins to fasten his coat and scarf. Tom stands up, his breakfast soup and rice still curdled in his stomach. A teacher and his family. He wishes there were a way for Makoto to say what he has done wrong, to say Tom, I think we are good enough friends for me to tell you that I would not have been so confidential without the shochu and that I hope we need never refer to it again. Or Tom, old chap, I know you meant no harm but the way you said goodbye to my family was not quite right. Maybe, it occurs to him, Makoto is saying such things in some way that Tom is unable to intuit. It is not fair, he thinks. He has intended no wrong, no insult.

He thinks hard about his tone of voice, about the rhythm of what he is about to say. 'I enjoyed the guesthouse. It would seem less strange now.'

Makoto stands back to let Tom walk first to the door. 'You will want a place to work. A desk and chair. It is not the custom to spend more than two or three days in such an inn.'

But I want to, he thinks. But the Japanese have been working without desks and chairs since the dawn of time, since Izanagi and Izanami came to a world without form and void. But I will be back to feather-beds and stuffed armchairs, to meat pies and suet puddings, soon enough and for the rest of my life.

There is a sound like horses crossing a bridge as all the clog-wearers on the train walk along the platform. Tom waits for Makoto to join him. He has seen some Europeans' houses that look as if they were imported, foundation to ridgepole, from suburban London. 'Mr Senhouse has a Japanese house?'

133

'The arrangement is made by the Ministry. As the Minister judges best. There is a restaurant near here, if you would like to eat. And then this afternoon I must return to the department.'

'But are you hungry, Makoto?'

'You would like to eat lunch?'

'As you prefer.'

Checkmate, Tom thinks. Tag. You're it.

They end up in a noodle place, where Makoto allows his gaze to linger just a moment on the spots of soup that soon fleck Tom's shirt.

They're crossing the bridge, heading up towards the European quarter which is to become Tom's rightful home, when he sees the obelisk set beside the river, a great stone like the ones raised across Yorkshire by ancient Britons. A flood marker? Some remnant of the people who farmed and fished here never imagining that one day the emperor would bring his court to Tokyo and the city swell around it? He leans forward to ask the jinrikisha man to stop. Makoto in his own jinrikisha may keep going if he wishes. The man drops the traces and watches as Tom clambers awkwardly down. The stone is darker than he has seen here, cut as smoothly as wood, with a script that seems curvier than Japanese swooping down each side. People have stuck pieces of paper in slots on its sides. Wishes, probably, or prayers, like the notes stuck up around altars on street corners as if the gods could read and would engage in correspondence. He touches the stone.

Makoto joins him, does not meet his gaze. 'The stone interests you? They are signs for lost children.'

Tom can feel the relief on his face, relief that Makoto is again sufficiently well disposed to volunteer information. There is, he knows, a Japanese god especially concerned with infants. 'Prayers?'

'No. If you seek a child, or sometimes any person, you leave a letter here, on this side. If you find a lost child, you leave a note here, so the seeker can find. The lost can be returned.'

'Do many children get lost?'

He counts the papers, more for the lost than the found. Ten, fifteen.

'The city is growing week by week. If they leave their own neighbourhood, who would know them?'

'Who cares for the children in the meanwhile?'

Makoto shrugs. 'The finder, perhaps. Or there are special places now.'

Tom remembers the street children in parts of London. Not lost, so far as he knew. Not visibly distressed. Someone probably knew where they were, more or less. No-one, Ally said, was looking for them, nor, very often, looking after them. It is a national sin, she said, that there are children there for anyone's taking, for anyone's pleasure or pain. The dogs of England, she said, are better protected in law than the wives and children. And yet she has married him. Become his wife. She may bear his child. He imagines being a child in limbo, missing and not missed, found and not sought. He lifts his hand again to the stone marker, as if by touch he will learn more than by gazing on what he cannot read.

Makoto touches his arm, friendship – somehow, perhaps – re-established. 'Come. Mr Senhouse expects you, and I must return to the office. But later, if you like, we can take a walk around here. It is a traditional neighbourhood.'

Tom watches Makoto's jinrikisha bowl away. He cranes forward to see past the oiled paper hood and then thinks that any movement on the passenger's part must affect the runner's work. It is probably better to sit back, to tilt the yoke upwards. Unless one is going downhill. Between the hood and the man's back, beginning to sweat through his tunic even in today's cold, Tom can see glimpses of the city, the Imperial Gardens where the leaves have fallen since he was last here, wooden houses with their shutters closed to the cobbled streets, and steam, now, rising from some of the street-sellers' carts. He wants the mountains, the murmuring forest. He thinks maybe he understands why Makoto needs to know that the place is waiting for him in the end. He, too, wants Makoto's grandfather's strolling garden, and he does not want to spend the winter doing a rich man's shopping.

The road ahead slopes upwards, lined on each side by shops where women throng with baskets. There is a lane leading to a temple where red and white banners flutter, and then a wall topped by a tiled roof over which twisted trees reach black fingers. He thinks he may be approaching the European quarter, where there is a church that seems to have come on a magic carpet from Bavaria and a range of architectural follies that must give the people of Tokyo strange ideas about European buildings. They scribble in stone in Europe, like children drawing fancy chimneys and extra staircases because they can. Europeans mistake quantity for quality, filling great rooms with useless objects as if the accumulation of possessions is an object in itself. European acquisitiveness is a compulsion, a disease. He remembers De Rivers' house and shudders; it is not silks and teapots the English should be importing from Japan but houses. Architects, if not engineers. Missionaries, perhaps, to teach us what is worthy of veneration. The Japanese have known for generations to pipe water through cities in a way that keeps sewage apart from drinking water; it is London, the centre of the civilised world, that is rife with typhoid and cholera.

The jinrikisha turns down a lane where wooden houses jostle, and then down another where there is only a high stone wall. There is a gateway, and they stop.

the May Moberley Mother and Infant Welfare Centre

Ally wakes. The gaslight from the road creeps under the curtains as it always did, and across the bare boards. Mamma has removed the carpet on which she and May used to pretend to fly around the world. The blankets pulled around her face smell musty and the sheets are worn so thin that she can feel the coarse wool through them on her arms and feet. She is cold. She feels sticky between her legs and under her arms, still gritty from the journey. It's too late, said Mamma, to be fussing with the range and the copper at this time of night. Cold water is healthful, especially for nervous complaints. Goodnight, Alethea. I am glad to see you home and ready to devote yourself to truly necessary work. But I do not have a nervous complaint, Ally thinks. Not exactly. She straightens her legs and then curls up again when she finds the cold at the bottom of the bed. Mamma is glad to see her. She would not have said that, before. Perhaps it was safe to come home after all. To come to her parents' house.

She pulls the covers up around her shoulders. Next winter, she supposes, she and Tom will be able to curl around each other when the nights are cold. But she does not believe it.

Tom is so far away, and their weeks together now so much shorter than their separation, that he begins to feel like a fiction, their marriage only a story she has told herself to ward off the truth of her failure. He will not come back. Perhaps he never existed, perhaps the truth is that she has been here, asleep among Briar Rose's thorns with the biblical admonition over her head, all along. May's bed lies flat in the darkness and Ally, who thought her grieving for May was long finished, who knew anyway that Mamma was right to say that mourning is a form of self-indulgence which can do nothing for the departed and dishonours their memory by using it as an excuse for morbid idleness, finds herself weeping a little for May.

When she wakes again there is muffled grey light around the window and a cart passing along the road. She has become unused to street noise, in the white cottage where she is woken by seagulls and sometimes by the bells and horns of ships feeling their way by dawn or fog. The house will be colder and damper for her absence, with no-one to watch the spread of cracks in the plaster. What if the ceiling falls while she is so far away? She should not have left it, her house and Tom's and all Tom's things, his books and blankets and clothes, his pots and pans, all their wedding presents from Aunt Mary and Annie and Tom's mother and the framed engravings from Penvenick himself, all succumbing to the creeping damp. She should not have come here. She stands up, bare feet on the bare boards, the cold air from the window and the fireplace and the gaps in the floor reaching up under her nightdress, snatching at her thighs and waist. There is no pot under the bed, so she creeps down the stairs, across the hall where there is mud and grit under her feet and into the lavatory. There is a bad smell that was not there yesterday, and no paper.

Ally prepares breakfast. Mamma goes through the morning's post at the kitchen table. The bread is stale and the butter yellowed and cheesy; Mamma says it is her habit to take only rusks in the morning and that Papa does Ally a rare honour in breakfasting at home. There are no eggs, and no milk with which to make porridge, and no, Mamma does not wish the range to be lit; it is a wasteful practice when all three of them will be out all day. Mamma has said that Ally will be at the clinic by half-past eight.

Papa comes down while Ally is setting the table in the dining room with tarnished silver. She will clean the silver this evening. There is something satisfying about cleaning silver and perhaps once Mamma has seen the difference she will remember how much pleasanter it is, to be clean. Papa is wearing a blue silk scarf over a crimson velvet dressing gown and blowing on his hands.

'Good morning, Ally. You slept well?'

'Good morning, Papa. You come splendid to the breakfast table.'

He touches the scarf. 'Oh, a painting prop. It's really Desdemona's but she doesn't grudge it, not in a house where it's a mortal sin to light a fire in the morning. Do you want to bring a tray up to the studio? I've buckets of coal up there.'

Ally shakes her head. 'We'll eat together.'

'As you like, your first day home. You're looking pretty, Princess Al. The low hair suits you and that's a nice dress.'

Mamma comes in. 'Anyone would look pretty, as you call it, got up in such an outfit after hours primping her hair before the mirror. Such tight lacing will make you ill, Alethea.'

Ally sits down. She remembers the clothes she had when she first went to London, the clothes she wore for the first autumn at medical school, until Aunt Mary intervened. 'I do not think I spend five minutes on my hair, Mamma. And I am afraid that it is still most important for a professional woman to appear smart and prosperous. We are very often taunted with ugliness and unnatural inclinations as it is.'

Mamma shakes her head and pours herself a glass of water. 'And do you think Our Lord did not have to bear worse jibes and insults in His work? Do you think that your poorest patients will think your appeasement of such men worth the money with which they could feed their children for many weeks? You should care more for your soul and less for the opinions of the world, Alethea.'

Our Lord, Ally thinks, was dead by the time he was not much older than I am, and no woman will earn a living by disdaining the opinions of the world. The butter crumbles under her knife and she glances down. Does she look too tightly laced? In fact her stays are, as always, scarcely pulled and gently tied, but she has always been slim and perhaps the effect suggests tight lacing. She has let down her bustle, which was in any case slight, a mere nod to fashion, and the bodice is adorned only by black binding on the grey wool, but maybe the nurses will indeed see a fine lady. She is not sure the brown skirt and coat would be any better and the blue dress is too long to wear in a clinic, especially without a bustle to raise it.

'This is what I have, Mamma. I am sorry if it is unsuitable.'

'I am surprised that you consider such dress a good use of your husband's money, that is all. It is unexpected.'

Papa pushes back his chair. He has taken only one bite of the bread and butter. 'It is pretty. I am out this evening, Elizabeth, and will probably sleep at the office.' He bends to kiss Ally's hair. 'I have an apartment there now, you know. With Jenny gone, Mamma did not like to entertain at home.'

'Goodbye, Papa.'

His footsteps hurry up the stairs and then not into Mamma and Papa's bedroom but to the studio, where he must be sleeping and dressing as well as painting. Ally feels a sudden desire to creep in while he is out, to rifle through the stacked paintings, warm her hands at the ghost of his coal fire and sit in his velvet armchair breathing the smell of oil paint and pipe smoke. The sound of Mamma crunching her rusks rings in the cold air.

'We will need to leave in fifteen minutes, Alethea. Cold water will suffice to wash these plates.'

There is a queue outside the May Moberley Mother and Infant Welfare Centre when Ally and Mamma arrive. Ally catches her breath at May's name carved into the stone plaque; it must be a long time since she has seen it written down, seen the material sign of May. The red-brick walls are already grimed with soot. The breath of the mothers and infants hangs visible around their faces, although there are bare feet on the pavement and bare heads bobbing at their mothers' sides. It is not that there is not poverty like this in Falmouth, but there is not – so far – such cold.

'They need to be warm,' Ally says. 'Whatever else ails them, we must warm them. There is a stove within?'

'But not always fuel,' Mamma says. 'We find our donors more generous around Christmas than in the autumn. And by Christmas it is too late for some of the infants.'

Ally nods. Across all classes, it is safer to be born like the animals in spring, but the seasonal variations in infant mortality are especially stark for the urban poor. Most of the babies now in arms along this pavement will be buried before their first birthdays. Nothing Ally can do within the walls of the May Moberley Welfare Centre will make much difference to this fact. The children need fuel, food and sanitation; those dying for simple lack of medical care are statistically insignificant. And yet the only ones for whom she works. Mamma's is the more useful life, for even if a doctor saves an individual child, the child will continue to live in misery and hunger. It is not primarily medical care that is lacking but the most basic elements of public health. If Ally truly wished her work, her life itself, to be beneficial, she would have taken a different path.

'Besides, Alethea, you surely have the sense to see that sitting them by the fire even for the whole morning serves only to weaken their constitutions. Come, I will introduce you to the nurses.'

Papa, Ally sees immediately, has not been involved in the architecture or interior design of the Centre. The floor is tiled, a chequerboard of black and red, and the windows set so high that only grey sky is visible from the floor. The hall reminds Ally of a municipal bath house, as if one could turn a tap somewhere and fill it with water. A municipal bath house might go some way towards fulfilling the aims of the Centre. Mamma strides ahead of Ally, through the hall and into a corridor painted the same shade of pale green as parts of the asylum and indeed the London Women's Hospital.

'Come along, Alethea. I have a committee meeting in Hulme at ten. Ah, Miss Eastman. I have brought you my daughter. Dr Moberley.'

Moberley Cavendish. She wishes she had simply taken Tom's name, separated herself from Mamma and Papa. Miss Eastman holds herself tall and meets Ally's gaze, a wholly different manner from the asylum nurses. Even Ally recognises the expensive simplicity of Miss Eastman's attire.

'How do you do, Dr Moberley. We are glad of your presence.'

'I am glad to be of service, Miss Eastman.'

Mamma nods. 'If you are done with the civilities, I must make haste. Alethea, if you will want a meal this evening you will perhaps find time to stop at Evans on your way home? I expect to be late.'

One cannot in conscience look at that line of people outside and then blame Mamma for not keeping a servant. Although some of them would doubtless be most grateful for such a position. 'Yes, Mamma.'

'No extravagance, please. I am not your Aunt Mary.'

'No, Mamma.'

Mamma's men's boots are usually quiet enough, but her retreating tread echoes and then fades between the tiled floor and the bare walls. There is more space in Ally's ribcage when Mamma is not there.

'Your Mamma is a tireless worker.' Miss Eastman cocks her head, evaluating Ally. A charitable gentlewoman, Ally thinks, doubtless volunteering her time, and her accent more ladylike than Ally's, the consonants precise and the vowels southern soft.

'She has always been so. Will you show me the consulting rooms?'

There is a clatter from the hall as the doors are opening, and then a scuffle of feet and voices as not water but sound rises up the walls.

'They can hardly be so called. This way, please, Miss Moberley.' She glances to the side. 'That is, Doctor.'

a trusted agent

Mrs Senhouse apologises again for the dinner. It is so hard to explain to Japanese servants what is required.

Tom sets down his fork. The food indeed requires apology. 'Perhaps a Japanese cook would be more competent in preparing Japanese food?'

She wrinkles her nose. 'It is the slimy things one cannot abide. Rice, of course, and clear soup, but I cannot expect Mr Senhouse to do a day's work on such pauper food.'

He thinks of the jinrikisha men, and the men who carried stones up the rocks for the lighthouses, and the men on the mountain farms.

Senhouse is also giving up on what is probably tinned ham cooked in salty brown sauce with some inexplicably gluey vegetable admixture. 'The Japanese constitution is a mystery. Maybe it should be tried in our slums, Cavendish, the rice and pickle diet. Cheap enough.'

'Rice is not so very cheap, at home,' Tom says. 'And the difficulty is often not so much the ingredients as the fuel over which they are to be cooked. It is why the poor do not eat bean soup, as everlastingly suggested by the rich.' Who do not eat it either, Ally likes to point out.

Mrs Senhouse, also, stops toying with the mess on her plate. 'Gracious, Mr Cavendish, you seem to have made quite a study of the subject.'

Outside, beyond the white tablecloth and the placemats and napkins and candelabra, beyond the cushions and anti-macassars on the chaise longue blocking the glass panels that replace the old shoji screens, the last leaf waltzes from the maple tree into the pond, leaving the outline of branches beautiful against the winter sky. At least the Senhouses will not be here long enough to plant roses. At least they may not replace the stepping stones with a spouting dolphin or a piss-ing child. He remembers the leaves floating on dark water in Makoto's grandfather's walking garden.

Back in his room, he sits at the foot of the armchair, on a tatami mat, to re-read the letter from De Rivers that awaited him at the post office. I don't like to use that lamp, Mrs Senhouse said, because it seems nothing more than kindling wrapped around a flame. And then to set it on a straw mat! You will be most careful, Mr Cavendish?

De Rivers has at last deigned to be more specific about Tom's commission, has been corresponding with 'an expert collector recently returned'. There is a part of Kyoto, he writes, devoted since time immemorial to the fabrication of painted and embroidered silks, where it is possible to acquire pieces of extraordinary splendour for remarkably little outlay. De Rivers gathers that the craze in Japan is all now for modern goods and that noble families and even temples are selling off priceless antiquities. It is a moment to delight any speculator, and how much more exciting to one, like himself, who unites the availability of ready money with the opportu-nity of a trusted agent on the ground and the taste to appreciate such objects. *Trusted* is underlined. Tom is to use the sum at his disposal to purchase works in silk especially, but also whatever antique pieces in china, lacquerwork and carving may seem to him likely to constitute both a sound investment and a prized addition to the collection of a connoisseur. De Rivers is aware that these matters are hardly Tom's field, but suggests first that he has been offered sufficient reason to inform himself on such subjects and second that the sum entrusted to Tom should surely suffice for the retention of a native guide, the competence of whom Tom must be capable of assessing.

Tom puts down the letter, De Rivers' clumsy scrawl crawling black in the lamplight. Were it not for this, for his allowing himself to be bought by a rich man, and worse than that for his being swayed by the offer of money into agreeing to work for which he has no qualification or taste, he might even now be writing up his reports, paying calls at the ministry, preparing his final lectures, buying only trinkets for friends and then returning to Falmouth. He knows nothing about silk, or carving or – he looks at the letter again – lacquerwork. And he does not see why samurai heirlooms should cross oceans to take up residence in De Rivers' mausoleum, alongside eviscerated hummingbirds and forms of statuary that are not quite the thing for public display. If indeed there are any samurai heirlooms, for as far as Tom can see, Japanese tastes are so utterly simple that the prizing of merely decorative objects seems improbable. Although he has not been in any samurai homes and seems most unlikely to do so; as he understands the situation, the samurai caste has been dispossessed by the modernising bureaucrats who are responsible for the presence of foreign engineers. Foreign engineers who now seek to take advantage of the fall of noble houses to buy cut-price family treasures. He thinks of Ally in the damp cottage, of what it would mean to her work if he were able to give her a more commodious house and employ a housekeeper to cook and clean for her, and of his mother who has risen early to wash and bake before going out to work in the shop all his life and still has little put by because she spent it all to send him to school. Ally's and Mother's welfare matter more, after all, than the movements of embroidered silk. And in any case, he has signed De Rivers' agreement and must therefore carry out the commission to the best of his ability. It is too late, now, for these thoughts.

Painfully, he straightens his legs, and staggers as he stands up. The Senhouses find the Japanese bathroom in their house 'indecent' and instead have placed tin hip-baths in each room, but it is probably too late to ask the servants to bring hot water and in any case he does not see how a girl could carry sufficient water up the ladder stairs. He removes his tweed jacket, waistcoat, tie, collar and cuffs, shirt, underlinen and sponges himself down at the washstand with cold water and expensively imported coal tar soap. He can see his breath in the air. He puts on his pyjamas and, for the first time since setting foot on Japanese soil, climbs into bed. He thinks of Ally, also lying alone under cold sheets, although of course it is daytime in England. He thinks of the line of buttons on her nightdress, from the white cotton ruffle over the hollows in her collarbones down towards her belly, deep enough that he can push the fabric back over one but not both breasts, cup it in his hand and— He finds his hand cupped, his thumb moving over a nipple that is not there, the other hand reaching as if to gather up the skirts that swathe his wife's legs on the other side of the world.

two women in middle life

Even in the consulting room, the windows are set so high in the walls that if Ally wanted to open one she would have to climb onto a chair. The room is narrower than it is tall, as if the walls are closing in from the sides. She can hear the prickle of rain on the glass but the clinic is – she calculates – at least a mile from the nearest tree so there is no sound of wind. She remembers Cornwall, and the view from the asylum to the north and south coasts, over fields and woods and villages to the edges of the sea. It is still there, she thinks. She will return, will walk again on the headlands above the waves, watching sea-birds dive and flicker among the rocks. She will see a pale sunlight over the water, as if shining through watered silk, and hear the lapping of the Fal at her feet as she looks across the river's mouth to where the trees gather dark on the shore beyond Flushing. It is still there.

She is looking through yesterday's notes. The patients' troubles are much as one would expect: consumption; complications of pregnancy mostly associated with inadequate nutrition, overcrowding and overwork; parasites and fungal infections in the children. Coughs, croup and digestive disturbances. There are a few treatable conditions requiring medical rather than social attention, but for the most part these people need housing, sanitation, food and perhaps prophylactics far more than they need doctoring. I prescribe new pillows and blankets, Ally thinks. I prescribe new houses, with sound walls, proper drainage and tightly fitted windows. I prescribe creamy milk and new-laid eggs. I prescribe a long visit to Aunt Mary. She must cook again for Mamma tonight. She has not dared enquire what Mamma ate before Ally arrived, since it seems now rare indeed for Papa to dine at home. She has been cooking, not, she hopes, in an attempt to gain Mamma's approbation, to curry favour, but simply to care for Mamma as it has occurred to Ally that no-one else does. To offer her a little comfort, a few minutes' solace in a life from which joy was cast out many years ago.

The first night, Ally made a mutton hash. Returning from the clinic too late to make a stew, recalling that Mamma finds the smell of meat grilled or fried objectionable and recalling also Aunt Mary's cook's view that while one must trust one's butcher only a fool buys mince, she bought end of neck. A cheap cut, safe from the imputation of extravagance, but including rather too much connective tissue to be appetising when rapidly cooked. A training in dissection, Ally thought, carrying the seeping paper package through the rainy evening in her string bag, must have uses beyond the operating theatre, although it turned out that Mamma's kitchen knives were too blunt for any kind of surgery. She ended up pulling filaments of iridescent tendon out of the red muscle with her fingernails, surrounded by a litter of bloodied and discarded knives. But the dish ought to meet Mamma's requirements: Mamma considers highly-seasoned foods to be an indulgence of the palate, but regards the purchase of more delicate meats as profligate. The smell of onions, she says, permeates the house, and she tolerates enough such odours in the course of her work to be spared them at home. Ally set some potatoes to boil when she cleaned the knives and the board, and then chopped all together and fried it with a little fresh butter. She cleaned some of the silver and set the table. An hour later, Mamma tasted a mouthful and grimaced; had Alethea imagined she was cooking for a family of miners? Quite apart from the excessive quantity, such greasy concoctions are indigestible and wholly unsuitable for two women in middle life, engaged really in the lightest of work. Alethea having lavished her money and Mamma's fuel, Mamma would attempt to eat it, but please, Alethea, a little more thought next time. It is no wonder, Ally thought, that Papa has given up, that he has left Mamma to her adulterous passion for self-denial, but even so he should not have done so. Promises were made, to love and to honour. If years ago Papa had lit fires in the drawing room instead of in his studio, if he had brought home eggs and cream and ham instead of seeking out restaurants with his friends while Mamma and May and Ally shrove themselves on bean broth and rice pudding, perhaps Mamma could have been different. Perhaps they could all remember May differently, if Papa, if someone, had shown Mamma how to be kind.

The noise of rainfall is drowned by the rush of feet and voices in the atrium. Now, at least, there will be no more time to think until the end of the day. Although then she will need to find something else for Mamma's supper. It is like a game they play, a guessing game, where Mamma must already know the answer to the riddle and teaches Ally by withholding it. What dish is quick to prepare, wholesome and cheap, not rich or greasy, unseasoned and mild to the palate? What garb is neat and respectable, durable and easy to wash, suggestive of professional competence but in no way extravagant or showy? What demeanour shows both respect and self-respect, strength of character and humility— Miss Eastman is at the door, with the first patient, and the beginning of a sequence of problems Ally is trained to address.

She is listening to the crepitations in yet another child's chest when Miss Eastman hurries in. She bends to her stethoscope. A student here would go a long time without hearing the chest sounds considered normal elsewhere in the country. The mother watches from across the room, afraid, uncomprehending. Ally offered to let her listen herself but she doesn't want to touch the instrument. Doesn't want to be here.

'Doctor?'

Ally holds up her hand. Coarse rales. A low fever. The child is emaciated, his skin patched with ringworm. Pus in one eye. He needs meat and fruit and sponge cakes made with fresh eggs, a warm bath, new clothes and weeks of careful nursing in a clean, dry room. For any real chance of reaching his fifth birthday, he needs, in fact, to be a lot less poor.

'Doctor? You're needed.'

No, she thinks, a revolution is needed. Bring Lord Salisbury in here and let him tell me to my face, to the face of this child's mother, that the deserving poor have every opportunity to improve their lot.

'One moment.' What to tell the mother? He's going to die. You're going to lose another child, because you're poor, and there's nothing you can do about it, because you're poor. Sorry.

Miss Eastman stands tall. 'No. Now, Doctor. In the waiting room.'

The girl's been in labour three days. Her father and his friends have carried her through the streets on a door and the howls of her like something not human. She's quiet enough now, but even through the ragged blanket over her distended body Ally can see the contractions grip and ripple. The girl moans, the low bovine noise of the second stage. Several waiting children peer.

'Take her through, please.'

While they lift the door, Ally hurries to scrub her hands. The forceps in her bag, she's thinking, are clean but not sterile. May have to suffice. How long has the girl been pushing? Is the child still alive? Miss Eastman helps the men move the patient onto the table.

'Thank you,' says Miss Eastman. 'Thank you for bringing her. We will do all we can.'

So she, too, has assessed the situation. There is another moan. As the men leave, Miss Eastman pulls back the blanket and pauses.

'I'm Miss Eastman, the nurse, and here is Dr Moberley. We're going to help you. We need to have a look at you now, see how you're doing.'

Miss Eastman turns the girl onto her back, lifts her skirt and gently parts the knees. The patient has no underwear and has not washed in some time. A tuft of dark hair is already visible in the vaginal opening. Ally looks up. The patient's eyes are closed and her mouth slack. In the grimy wrist, the pulse is weak and slow. Three days in labour, and she can't be more than sixteen. The face is thin and pointed, the legs like twigs below the swollen abdomen. And Ally's heart drops, because even in this foreshortened position the thighs are visibly bowed. Rickets. Probable pelvic distortion. Cephalopelvic disproportion: the foetal skull may simply not fit through the patient's pelvic ring. Damn. She rests a hand on the belly while it hardens again. Nurse Eastman, without being asked, passes her the Pinard. She listens and hears the drumming of blood, the march of a different beat within the patient's body. The child, for now, lives. The mother is failing. They have perhaps ten minutes, Ally thinks, maybe fifteen, to work between the beats of those two hearts, to keep all the human music in the room playing. Her and Miss Eastman. Starting now.

The patient is too weak to stay on all fours. Miss Eastman tries to support her while Ally pushes her fingers around the child's head to find the jammed shoulders. They sway the girl back and forth but nothing happens, nothing frees. Ninety seconds gone. Ally sees the map of the pelvis in her head. A mechanical problem. An engineering problem.

'On her back.'

Miss Eastman raises her eyebrows but complies. Ally takes a knee.

'Copy me.'

Miss Eastman takes the other and they push back against the patient's abdomen, extending the sacrum. Ally sees the skull jammed against the pelvic bones, the angles all wrong. Not fundal pressure. She pushes hard on the pubic bone, rocks it. Sometimes the head can spring free but not this time, not now. Another moan and every muscle in the girl's body gripping, tightening, forcing the child deeper into a cave with no way out. Not unless Ally makes the child's head smaller or the mother's pelvis larger. She holds out her hand for the Pinard again and hears the small music slow, almost stop, and reluctantly resume some seconds after the contraction passes. Miss Eastman, her fingers on the patient's wrist, bites her lip, shakes her head and feels for a carotid pulse instead. Five minutes, Ally thinks, five minutes and we'll lose both of them.

'Get the instrument box,' she says.

'Craniotomy?'

Perforate the skull, mash the brain with scissors, crush the bone so the child can be pulled free. She's seen it done.

'No. Symphysiotomy. It's possible to spring the pelvis.'

153

Not a complex procedure. She remembers Dr Burnet. All you need, ladies, is a catheter, a strong scalpel and stronger nerves, and you can manage without the catheter.

'Glass catheter, please, and then a number four scalpel.'

A minute and a half. No time for analgesia. The patient is conscious enough to whimper as the blade goes in.

The child is limp and does not breathe, but the cord is still pulsing, the two hearts still working from one set of lungs, as she passes him to Miss Eastman. There is so much blood that it is hard to assess the mother's trauma. She needs to deliver the placenta, now. Ally ties and cuts the cord, ending the baby's oxygen supply, and works on her patient.

'When you can, Miss Eastman, morphia please.'

Afterwards, Miss Eastman goes back and forth, attending to the mother and child while Ally works through the clinic, her blood singing with elation. The girl, Nellie Tillman, is sore and exhausted but has taken tea and the bread and butter Ally had brought for her own lunch and has fed her new son. The baby, whose first cry wasn't heard until Ally was binding his mother's hips to stabilise the spliced pelvis, has looked at the world and apparently, for now, decided to stay, making underwater movements and turning a strange gaze on the new element, air. His chances of surviving childhood are not good, worsened by his mother's extreme youth and single state. Nellie is not well placed to recover from an obstructed labour, and even after the hospital stay that Miss Eastman has arranged may not avoid infection in Ally's layers of careful stitching. She may never be able to walk far, may find standing at mill or factory work impossibly painful, especially if – especially as – she cannot take several weeks' rest. But even so, Ally thinks while she listens to tubercular chests and weighs children who appear several years younger than their mothers say they are, while she hears a heart murmur that would indicate the avoidance of exertion in a person who had any means of survival without exertion, even so, because of what she did, because of her training and her knowledge, there are two people alive now who were all but dead before lunch.

The rain must have stopped sometime during the afternoon, but the handle wets her gloves as she closes the heavy door of May's Centre and locks it behind her. Puddles gleam in the gaslight. Ally buttons her pocket over her purse and glances behind her as she sets off; this is not a place where she would advise a well-to-do woman to walk alone after dark. She is tired. She remembers the smell of earth and water after rain in Cornwall. Here, there is still smoke on the air and at the back of her throat, and the streetlights show a sky washed brown. It is not reasonable to think in Cornwall that the climate is too damp and the land too wet and in Manchester that there is too much smoke and soot; one must be somewhere. She tugs at her cuffs and walks faster. She could take the omnibus, she thinks, for Mamma need never know and it would mean she could reach the grocer before the shopkeepers are cross because they are about to close and there is only tripe left. It would not be unreasonable, to take the omnibus with such an aim, as it would be from laziness, though it would probably not occur to Mamma to do such a thing. She will walk past the stop, she decides, and take the bus if one comes; Mamma will be angry if there is no supper and only disappointed if she learns that Ally has taken a bus instead of walking. Her throats tightens at the thought of Mamma's anger, and then again in irritation with herself for caring so much. She remembers herself holding the scalpel, herself remembering to protect the urethra, to deliver the child down

155

over the perineum as the seconds flickered away. Herself controlling her patient's bleeding with death at her shoulder as she worked. She should have outgrown the fear of Mamma. But has not.

She rounds the corner. There is a bus. It is not raining so very hard, she thinks. If she has money to spare for bus tickets, it could be given to a hungry family, to any of Mamma's charities, rather than used to spare a healthy and well-fed woman a walk of barely two miles. It is not as if her day's work has been physically demanding. The bus moves off, and Ally quickens her pace through the puddles and the dusk.

The house stands unlit, the gate shadowed by the privet hedge. The sky seems darker here and there is half a moon in the taller beech tree and the suggestion of moonlight on the wet grass. The gate has swollen in the rain and is stiff; her footsteps crash on the gravel path. She fumbles for her key, inside her purse inside her coat pocket, with cold hands, and has to peer to find the keyhole. This is the day's lowest point, she reminds herself, the return to a chill dark house and the need to begin again, to clean and prepare a meal, when it feels as if the day's work is done. There are women all over the city who have been standing in a factory all day and are now returning to the needs of their husbands and children; she has no business complaining of a house that is too large and empty. Leaving the door open for the sake of the light from the street, she feels for the matches in the niche at the bottom of the stairs, a niche where Papa used to keep a great vase painted with peacock feathers and now there is only dust soft under her fingertips. She lights the lantern and then sees that there was a fat letter on the doormat and that she has walked on it, left a wet brown footprint smudging the ink on the front and crossing the pale blue stamp. Japanese Empire, Five Sen, and a white chrysanthemum, her Falmouth address crossed out for redirection. He thinks she is still there, still sleeping in his bed and waking each morning to the sight of his garden. Or at least he did think that, six weeks ago when the letter was posted. Later, she thinks. It is important that there should be food ready when Mamma comes home.

The potatoes are soft to the knife and the cabbage has brightened in the pan. She drains them through the old colander from which one handle has been lost, leaning over the sink to feel the steam curl around her face. She is real, she has a body, hands that feel the pain of the hot pan and cold skin on which steam condenses. She has a letter in her pocket, and a ring on her finger. She saved two lives today. She takes a plate down from the rack where she left it to dry last night and pulls the lid off the flour jar. Liver is to be dredged with seasoned flour before frying, and although Mamma regards seasoning as unnecessary it is Ally's view that omitting this step altogether would have an unappetising result. The flour must be damp and does not pour onto the plate, so Ally shakes the jar and half of it, a good pound of flour, falls in a squared lump and explodes on the floor. She's hardly started to clear it up when she hears Mamma's key in the lock and can only wait, kneeling on the flour in her blue dress, for Mamma to find what she has done.

What possible reason can you find for such behaviour, Alethea? For such waste? Do you not know, can you not think, what demands are made on my time and energies during the day that I should return to this disorder in my own house? I do not know how your husband can bear your carelessness and wasteful habits, it is no wonder he has gone away. I suppose it is asking too much that you should clear up this mess. Do not imagine, Alethea, that your true motives go unseen. Do not imagine that I will wait upon you as the servants in my sister's house have done, as I suppose you must have required your husband to do. Until he left you. Clean the floor, please, Alethea. And then get to your bed. I cannot bear further messing in my kitchen and a night's fasting will do neither of us any harm.

Mamma's skirts, always cut high because of places she goes and the roads and floors she walks, swing above the floor and the kitchen door closes behind her. No slamming, not in this house, no throwing or shouting, no hand raised in anger. Only words.

Words and a candle flame offered on her tenth birthday. Show me how you can bear pain, Alethea. Show me how you can choose to endure.

Lying hands at her sides with her skirts lifted for Mamma and Dr Henry to apply blisters. The best cure for weak nerves, Alethea. Pray refrain from that hysterical gasping.

Before she knows what she is doing she finds herself at the stove, her sleeve rolled back as Mamma once rolled it for her. She lifts one of the lids. She extends her arm. She watches the skin turn red and then white. There is a faint odour of roast meat.

There is not enough pain.

She wants the end now.

She is too old for this.

the length of a dinner party

It is probably as well that he can see only his head and shoulders in the mirror. He suspects that the rest of him looks ridiculous to eyes accustomed to the *kosode* and *hakama*, to the fall of woven cloth cut to the neatness of the male form. He loosens his tie, a garment with no purpose whatsoever. When did British men start to wear bows around their necks?

There is a murmur from the bottom of the stairs where the Senhouses are already waiting for him, he in a black evening suit so much like Tom's that they could have been cut and sewn at the same time from the same cloth. Every man there will be wearing the same thing. She wears a gown with large yellow flowers on a white ground, one of those puffs over her behind and her breasts cantilevered up and pushed together to make a line of cleavage above the tasselled yellow trim around the edge of her bodice. A length of yellow silk lies across the back of the skirt, looped around her elbows as if it had slipped from her shoulders. Her hair, a paler blonde than Ally's, is braided and twisted around her head and small white flowers nestle in the swirls. She's pretty enough, but most of all she looks uncomfortable, artificial.

'You are looking very beautiful this evening, Mrs Senhouse. Your shawl is of local manufacture?'

There are white chrysanthemums embroidered on the silk. Ally might like such a thing, in grey or a light blue.

'Indeed so, Mr Cavendish. There are now several shops where they understand the requirements of European dress.'

Senhouse holds his wife's evening cloak for her. 'Come, Cavendish. The Ambassador values punctuality.'

He is pleased to see that there are no jinrikishas at the gate. He would have thought the evening too cold for Mrs Senhouse to walk, certainly in her finery, but her heeled silk slippers tap a staccato rhythm to her conversation with her husband. He walks behind them. The sky is clear and the stars winter-bright. The stars must have different names here, and maybe the constellations themselves are differently ordered, taking the form of flowers or temples rather than agricultural implements and animals. Until recently, Makoto told him, there was no word for 'animal' in Japanese. Living things were divided into categories of movement. There were creeping things – lizards, woodlice, some small mammals – and flying things, which included butterflies and bats as well as birds. Things that leap and run, and also a category of furred beasts. There is nothing natural, nothing innate, about taxonomies. He wonders what other aspects of being in the world might be wholly different in Japanese. There are, plainly, men and women, but it is less clear that the categories of children and adults are as distinct as at home. Japanese medicine is different and perhaps the very definition of health is questionable. The quick and the dead, ghosts. There are samurai and farmers, a distinction at least until recently much more rigid than its British equivalent. There are fox owners. He thinks of the jinrikisha men, beasts of burden, and the shape-shifting foxes. If the idea of animals is recent, what about the idea of humans?

He almost treads on Mrs Senhouse's skirt. Her face turns to him, white under the hood of her cape.

'And what do you think, Mr Cavendish?'

The pavement is wide enough now for him to walk beside them.

'I beg your pardon?'

'Ah, you were thinking of home, I dare say. We were discussing the possibility of having a Christmas tree, and perhaps giving a dinner. There are several bachelors here, you know, and I do not like to think of them gathering only in some bar or club to mark the birth of Christ.'

'Mrs Senhouse comes of a large family,' says Mr Senhouse. 'She always feels the need for a crowd at Christmastime.'

Christmas. He had forgotten about Christmas. There are – he counts – five weeks yet. Almost six. With a little luck, time for the post. Silk shawls, he thinks, for Ally and Mother, easy to wrap and hard to damage on the way. Perhaps also for Mrs Dunne, since they are likely cheap enough.

'Mrs Senhouse, before I leave for Kyoto could you be so kind as to find a moment to show me the shops of which you spoke? You remind me that I have been remiss in my shopping.'

Her laughter tinkles in the quiet street. They will hear her behind the paper screens, around the firepits and the red lanterns. Foreign laughter.

'You need a gift for your wife. Of course, Mr Cavendish, it will be my pleasure. Tell me, what is her taste, her favourite colours, her complexion?'

The double doors of the ambassador's residence are wide open, and lanterns hanging in the porch send a dancing light down the stone steps. The ambassador is an aficionado of Japanese gardens and has had the box hedges and lavender taken out and replaced with black bamboo which waves and rustles by the path. Tom remembers the temple on the island, and the unseen bear. He follows Mrs Senhouse's cloak up the steps, its beads glistening like raindrops in the lamplight.

There are place cards. Mrs Senhouse says that the ambassador's wife, who is much younger than the ambassador, spends days before each party working on precedent and placement, her task infinitely complicated by the changes of the last twenty years. Sometimes she will be entertaining a prince in whose youth streets were closed so that the populace might not glimpse his face when he walked out, along with an industrialist whose grandfather worked the land, not to mention the European nobility who are visiting Japan in increasing numbers and then itinerant Americans who may be the sons of eminent professors taking a kind of Grand Tour or ne'er-do-wells in permanent exile, or indeed in some cases both. There are always more men than women, partly because the enthusiasm for modernity of the best Japanese families stops short at asking their wives and daughters to dine in public, to dance and speak to foreign men, and partly because of professional men like Tom who travel alone. He must not mind, must not take it personally, if he finds himself seated beside another man. Dear Lady Alexandra has such a time with these things! He does not mind, for the card beside his own says, in Lady Alexandra's own italic hand, Professor William Baxter. Professor of European History at the University of Tokyo, he thinks and the author, if he is not mistaken, of *The Land of Cherry Blossom: Japan in Our Own Time*.

He is among the first to sit down, glad to escape the wife of an American missionary who has a great deal to say on the subject of girls' schools in Japan. At exact intervals down the tables are glass bowls half filled with water, in which float flat pink candles and the heads of miniature water lilies. He won't reach over and stir up a tornado with his soup spoon, see if the candles set the lilies on fire before everything sinks. He watches as a lady further up the table is settled into her chair by a man in a clerical collar. The vicar pulls out a chair, supports the woman's elbow as she approaches the table, eases the chair under her and stands back respectful as she arranges her skirt. He must ask Ally about the puffed up skirts, the way they seem to fold when the wearer sits and open out as she rises. Some kind of concertina arrangement. He counts the silver arrayed on the white damask cloth: soup, entrée, fish, meat and pudding, and a crystal glass for each course. In the Kiso valley, Makoto's family will be sitting by firelight on the floor around a table holding one rice-bowl and one tea-bowl for each person.

A man of about his own age takes the seat on his left. Herr Friedrich Anders, the place card says, and he can see that she started to write 'Freidrich' and caught herself almost in time. Friedrich Anders has a wholly unconvincing blond beard.

'Tom Cavendish,' he says, offering his hand.

Friedrich Anders bows and they shake, awkwardly side-by-side.

'I speak not good English. You have German?'

Tom shakes his head. 'A little French. From school.'

'*Moi aussi. Pas beaucoup.*'

'*Pas beaucoup*,' Tom repeats. '*Un petit peu.*'

They smile foolishly, each, Tom thinks, hoping that Lady Alexandra had the sense to put a German speaker on Friedrich's other side. Tom builds a sentence in his head.

'*Qu'est-ce vous fais* – I mean, *faites* – *ici*? *Je suis* – engineer. *Je fais* – what's the word, sorry – *je fais construire.*'

Herr Anders nods. Communication received. '*Je suis medecin. A l'hopital.*'

Comme ma femme, Tom thinks, but he really doesn't want to

try to have that conversation in French. They both turn over their shoulders to smile a warm welcome at the man coming to sit opposite. *Ja, ich spreche Deutsch. Komme aus Amsterdam. Und Sie, Herr Anders? Von Bremen? Ach so. Meine Schwester—*

Smiling, Tom looks away. The centres of the candles are beginning to hollow around the wicks, making boats of molten wax. By the end of the evening, or eventually, a boat will melt a hole in its own bottom and sink, hissing. Perhaps Lady Alexandra has candles made to the length of a dinner party. When the shipwreck comes, it's time to go home. He's too hot, in his suit with the room so full and the candles and a fire in the stone hearths at each end.

This must be Professor Baxter now, a tall stooped man with an iron-grey beard overflowing his collar. Tom stands, shakes his damp hand. Professor Baxter, he says, *The Land of Cherry Blossom*? I read your book with great pleasure. The professor beams from behind his moustache and bows. We are all doing it now, Tom thinks, on the ship home we will all be bowing to each other. On the ship home. Open sea, and Japan left behind forever. And you, Mr Cavendish, what brings you to these shores?

The menu says *Soupe au Poisson*, but the presence of soy sauce is obvious, and maybe a little ginger. Don't you think they would do better, Professor Baxter murmurs, so close to his ear that he expects to feel the moustache, don't you think they would do better on these occasions to pay a really first-rate Japanese chef to prepare a really first-rate Japanese banquet? I fear we may expect a Japanese rendition of white sauce on the vegetables next, and of course they have no idea and why should they? As soon ask an English cook to make sushi.

Tom turns to him. 'You like Japanese food, then?'

'My dear boy, I would hardly have stayed here so many years if I did not. Or perhaps, having stayed here so many

164

years it is inevitable that I must. And you? You pine for cauliflower in cheese sauce, for dumplings and suet pudding?'

Tom gulps the end of his wine, which really is good. 'Truth to tell, Professor, I dread them.'

'Shake hands, dear boy, shake hands.'

He waits until the meat course – grey, unidentifiable, in brown sauce – to ask about fox owners. It feels dishonourable, as if, having been welcomed to Makoto's home, he has stolen a letter that he now asks the professor to translate. But if Makoto wouldn't tell me, he thinks. Anyway, his interest is general; he wants to know about the stone foxes at the entrances to so many shrines and houses and indeed about the idea of fox owning rather than about Makoto's particular situation. Intellectual curiosity, not nosiness.

Ah, says Professor Baxter, fox owners. You have met such a family in your travels? Tom shrugs: maybe. He has heard of them. Without Japanese, it is difficult to interpret one's experiences, especially in the countryside where everything seems so strange that one soon ceases to place much trust in one's own judgement. The professor nods and puts down his fork. Tom should of course learn Japanese. He is right, there is no getting anywhere without it. Most of the people here in this room live only on the surface of Japan, depending on guides and translators for everything that they know and believe and then writing books about their experiences that merely rehearse what they have been told. If Tom would like to arrange a course of lessons? Ah, he is off to Kyoto. Well, that's the place to go if you care about the old ways. A shame, really, to go there without at least the elements of Japanese, but there we go. He has business there? A commission, Tom says, able to imagine how Professor Baxter might regard collectors of art who have never crossed the English Channel and care

165

nothing for the provenance of their purchases. He refills the professor's glass.

'You were going to tell me about fox owners?'

Professor Baxter nods but takes another mouthful and swallows it, grimacing a little, before he answers. 'Ah yes. Fox owners. Fascinating peasant belief.'

He pushes the grey meat with his fork, making a pattern in the gravy on the plate.

'It always was, by the way. Rather like the myths of European peasantry, werewolves and faery folk and such, tales told around village fires on winter evenings. Some people will tell you the Japanese believe this or that but don't believe them, it's like saying the Germans believe in vampires or the English in headless horses and then expecting professional men and landed gentry to walk in fear of such fantasies.'

Tom cuts a potato. Seeing real foxes dance and wondering about it is not the same thing as believing in headless horses. Any man would think twice, about dancing foxes in a fox temple.

'Has to be said, though, some of the peasants really do believe. I know personally of several cases where people thought to be possessed by foxes were killed by attempts to exorcise them, stabbing and burning to get the devils out. It's not the same, though, to be possessed by foxes and to own them. Important distinction, that one.'

He looks reproachful, as if Tom were a forgetful student. 'People possessed by foxes run quite mad, poor blighters. Run around naked shouting at things that aren't there, lie on the ground frothing at the mouth, that kind of thing. The women will sometimes hurt or threaten their own children in the throes of possession. Those kind of foxes are sent by Inari, by fox gods, but they're not deities themselves. People often get that wrong.'

Tom nods. 'What about the stone foxes? In the temples?'

'Inari. But again, the significance varies. Depends partly if it's a shrine to the fox gods or a house, whether we're warding off goblin or spirit foxes or worshipping the gods, see?'

Tom pushes his wine away. Not particularly clearly, no. There are fox gods, and insanity is called fox possession, but the two facts are not straightforwardly related.

'You mean that in Japan when people go mad they are said to be possessed by foxes?'

He thinks about English foxes, sneaking into henhouses, about rich men galloping around in red coats blowing trumpets. Sometimes he used to see the hunt, as a boy on the loose with his friends on Saturdays and in the summer. He thinks about the talking foxes in children's stories, who know how to trick other animals, how to beguile the foolish into becoming dinner. He used to read to his landlady's daughter in Aberdeen: and the fox said well, Chicken Licken, Henny Penny, Goosey Lucy and Ducky Daddles, come with me and I'll show you the way to the King. English foxes are cunning and clever, not mad.

'Not so simple, dear boy. Some of the behaviour we would call insanity, Japanese villagers attribute to fox possession. It's a way of explaining conduct that doesn't fit the rules. And it can be quite sane, really. Disobeying your mother-in-law, refusing to get up before dawn to cook rice. Young married women have a hell of a time.'

Tom frowns, doesn't see how a person can be sane and insane at the same time. Anyway, Makoto's not possessed. 'And the other kind? Owners rather than the possessed?'

The plates are taken away. The pink candles list drunkenly, won't last the evening, and the edges of the lily petals are beginning to brown.

'Oh, they're less alarming, though most inconvenient.

Some families have foxes, kitsune. It's not always clear if the foxes belong to the house or to the household but in most of the villages such a distinction would be immaterial anyway since families never change abode. Though the presence of foxes can make the land hard to sell. No, not real foxes, dear boy, or at least not visible foxes. Though they say the shadows or reflections are sometimes visible even though the animals themselves aren't. They eat a lot, these goblin foxes. As soon as the rice is ready they rise up through the floor and tuck in, so however much is cooked there's never a good plenty for the family. They can cause terrible trouble, too, stealing from the neighbours and then leaving the stolen goods lying around the house, sometimes taking the form of servants or children and telling tales of goings-on in their own houses and those of the neighbours.'

Professor Baxter settles his elbows on the table, runs his fingers through his beard. He's going to keep talking for a long time.

'The spirit foxes are frightful gossips and sometimes outright liars, and eavesdroppers too, will hang around on someone's veranda until they hear him speak ill of his neighbours and then frisk off in different form to pass it on. Not that they can't be useful, when the fancy takes them, but the problem is they're not human and you can never predict or depend on their fancies. No consistency even in evil-doing. So some fox owners, kitsunemochi, find extraordinary fortune, might become quite rich for no obvious reason, and it might last several generations. But that kind of money's like fairy gold, not to be relied on, liable to disappear into thin air, or sometimes turn to grass, just when you really need it.'

Tom nods, though he's quite lost. Friedrich Anders is also leaning on the table and his blond hair falling over his forehead, deep in red-faced conversation with the Dutchman and the man across from him. The servants are beginning to bring pudding, big bowls of something placed centrally, one between four.

'So they're the village ne'er-do-wells, fox owners?' Tom asks. 'They're the family that always borrows and never lends and their children are always ragged and snot-nosed?' Not that he can see any way that this description fits Makoto's family.

Professor Baxter drains his glass. 'Can be. But then you see even when they do well, that's because of the foxes too. Of course if they do well enough for long enough they can marry anyway, but people are pretty chary of them. You wouldn't want your son to marry a fox owner and you'd only give them your daughter if she really couldn't do better. And the land's not worth much, however good it is. No-one wants to risk owning foxes because it goes on for generations.'

It reminds him of something. *For I the Lord thy God am a jealous God, visiting the iniquity of the fathers upon the children unto the third and fourth generation.* He remembers hearing the verse at school, and all the others about fathers, and wondering what he might unknowingly carry. Foxes, iniquity, red hair, the way the corners of his eyes fold when he laughs. Still, there are worse things, than to have an empty space where a parent should be. Tom leans aside to let the waiter put down the crystal bowl. Something creamy, a fool or syllabub, and a plate of biscuits to go with it. There are dairies now in Tokyo, and a public campaign to persuade the Japanese to drink milk and grow taller.

'Can they ever get rid of the foxes?' he asks. 'Does it ever end?'

'Oh, sometimes they just go away. Not often. And of course you never know when they might come back. Have some of this? You never know, it might be good. They've quite taken to ice cream.'

'There goes the candle,' Tom says. 'Look.'

They watch, the spoon raised in the professor's hand, as the meniscus on the water bowl rises, swells, breaks and the candle takes on water, fills, and sinks. The talking filling the room is too loud for Tom to hear the hiss as the flame goes out.

the gap in the hedge

Papa came home last night, so at least she is not to be alone with Mamma today. Standing in the kitchen, she does not know what to do. She cannot recall that breakfast on Christmas Day used to be any different from usual, but 'usual' used to mean porridge, tea and toast, the lighting of the range and the warming of the pot. Will Mamma want the present usual today, only rusks? Or will she say that Ally seeks to deny her parents even the most sparing recognition of Our Lord's birth? Ally fills the water jug and begins to slice bread. Under the bandage she stole from May's Welfare Centre the broken skin of her forearm throbs and burns, and under her breastbone shame simmers. Behaving like a hysterical young girl at your age. Betraying your training, betraying the title in which you take such unwarranted pride.

The dining room is always dark, now the laurel bushes are starting to grow up into the windows. She begins to set the table, the silver cold in her cold hands. In other houses, she thinks, children are waking to bulging stockings by a crackling fire, and already the smell of roasting meat and plum pudding seeps from the kitchen. Because in those houses the servants have been working since before Ally awoke, and in other houses –

more houses – there is scant heat and no pudding or meat in the children's hope or memory. Ally remembers being called to the fall of one of the children of Aunt Mary's neighbours on Boxing Day and finding the bruises of a beating across the girl's legs and up her back; yes, said the governess, I am afraid she is often a naughty girl. It is not as if ribboned parcels and a tree with candles on it are any guarantee of happiness.

Her stomach skids at the sound of Mamma's key in the door. She should not be so weak, so nervous. I am thirty years old, she thinks, I am a doctor. I did not rise early to attend church because I do not believe a god can be omnipotent and benevolent, because I do not believe in a man born of a virgin, because the whole thing is a collection of stories used for centuries to keep poor, uneducated people poor and uneducated. She goes into the hall to greet Mamma, to begin the day as if this were an ordinarily happy family.

'Good morning, Mamma. Happy Christmas.'

Mamma takes off her hat. 'Good morning. I trust you are refreshed by your long rest?'

Ally feels her fingers tighten on the fork she is still holding. 'I rose at the usual hour, Mamma. I have prepared breakfast.'

'So I would expect. There is no need for that tone, Alethea, I said only that I hope you are well rested.' Mamma goes into the kitchen. 'But I see you have not troubled to light the range.'

I am a bird in a net, Ally thinks. I am a madwoman in a closed dress. I cannot do this. I must leave here. 'I am sorry, Mamma. I will do it now.'

Mamma sighs. 'I will do it. At least that way we know there will be no waste of matches.'

She takes a cup of tea and a plate of buttered toast up to Papa. He is sitting up in bed with a blanket wrapped around his shoulders, reading what would appear to be a novel.

'Thank you, Princess Al. And happy Christmas! She's let you light a fire, has she? Maybe I'll come down.'

She sets the tray on the bedside table, beside Papa's water glass and spectacles. 'Mamma was chilled when she came in from church. Will you join us, Papa? I have made a steak pudding for lunch. With oysters.'

She dared not buy a joint of beef, even with her own money. Tom's own money. But she hoped Papa would enjoy the oysters.

'In a while, Princess Al. You are getting as bad as your mother. Let me drink my tea in peace, on Christmas morning.'

Papa remaining in bed, Mamma takes to the drawing room with a pile of letters to answer. The morning services today will be overrun with ill-disciplined children, but she intends to attend Evensong at five and she expects Ally to accompany her. Meanwhile, since Ally appears to have nothing better to do, she might clean the pantry. Mamma has had more pressing matters to which to attend for some weeks. She closes the door behind her. Ally wanders into the kitchen, cold even in her wool shawl with the range lit. She has been growing thinner here. She must clean the pantry. Hot soapy water and clean rags. While there is hot water, she will clean the lavatory properly and wash the floors. There will be plenty of time while the puddings steam. She does not know if Mamma has noticed the puddings. You take us for railway labourers, Alethea. Did you not think a lighter dish more fitting for those of such sedentary habits? I did not believe I had brought you up to be always thinking of your stomach in this way. Papa used to invite Aubrey for Christmas lunch, and Aubrey used to bring a plum pudding already steamed by his daily housekeeper and a box of candied fruits for Ally and May. Such sugary trash as only infantile or vitiated appetites could stomach, to rot the teeth and ruin the digestion for more wholesome fare. Mamma, May said in their bedroom later, would have the whole world live on bread and water if she could. Mamma cannot be content while another person is happy. I am afraid my sister is just such a difficult woman as our mother was, says Aunt Mary, and living with her must be a test of anyone's health and strength. I do not wonder she considers you fragile. But May was not fragile, Ally thinks, May was strong. So strong she went away and drowned.

Ally is still standing in the kitchen.

Hot soapy water, she thinks. The pantry. The lavatory and the puddings.

I do not know how you can bear to stand about in that manner, Alethea, idling your time away when there is such work to be done!

The clock ticks. A coal falls in the range.

What, you will not exert yourself even now?

Dearest Ally, says Aunt Mary, it is sad that you who brave such opposition from the most powerful men in your profession yet quail at Elizabeth's reproaches. Can you find no strength to brook her, darling? Are you yet so frightened?

There is ringing in her ears, like the reverberation of a distant bell. Like an alarm.

Gracious me, Al, says May, you're such a coward. Just tell her she can't have a prize-winning doctor clean her pantry on Christmas Day and go do something else. Eat something.

You're being ridiculous, no wonder she calls you crazy. It's a game you play, both of you, following your own mad rules. You let her hurt you, Al. You like it. You keep coming back.

As if not inheriting those rules, not playing that game, did May any good in the end.

The bell is louder, filling her head, an emergency behind her eyes and in her mouth and ears and nose.

She finds herself upstairs, pushing a few clothes and her medical books into Tom's valise, and then creeping down again, past the closed door behind which Papa reads in bed and the closed door behind which Mamma writes her letters. She finds herself easing the handle of the front door and then leaving it ajar because that way there is no sound and by the time they realise she's left the door open she won't be there any more. She finds herself balancing on the edge of the bottom step to make a long stretch to the flowerbed, swinging the valise to help her leap over the gravel to the soil. The gap in the hedge is visible from the drawing room and she stands on the flowerbed for a while. If Mamma sees her now, sees her running away, if Mamma chases her and catches her – she cannot stand here in the soil.

You are being ridiculous. What extraordinary conduct is this, Alethea? Where, pray, do you think you are going? Today of all days?

She's not the police, Al, and you've committed no crime. She doesn't own you, you know.

You know you will always have a home here in London with us, Ally. I know something of what it must be like to be

175

brought up by Elizabeth. We shared a room, you know, until she married.

She begins to shake. She has left her gloves hanging from the rack over the range, where Mamma will see that they have silk linings and were expensive. But there is Tom's letter in her pocket. *Dearest Ally, it sometimes seems that I miss you more every day because there is so much here that would interest you and that we would enjoy discussing.* Mamma will be looking at her letters, not out of the window, and the winter jasmine is growing up over the window sill anyway. She ducks and runs, banging the valise on her leg.

Her breathing is loud in her head. There's no-one else out, no traffic or footfalls and she would be easily seen, easily found. She takes the first turning, to get off Mamma and Papa's road, to be out of sight of anyone standing at the gate. Her skirt tangles around her legs, catches around her knees. The beech trees stand bare overhead.

The park, they won't look in the park and there are places to hide. But she should get away, she should go as far and as fast as she can. And not be seen.

The park is locked. Not back past the house, go the other way.

The other way leads to the shops, the church and the library, where there will be people who will see her.

No, not today. Today the people are all in their houses.

Keep moving, she thinks, go somewhere, you are not five minutes from the house and they may come looking any moment.

She hurries again, away from the park and away from the house. She feels like a mouse crossing a road, like a goldfish beside whose pond a heron has just landed. The main road, silent and bare. As if everyone has died instead of someone being born.

She crosses it to be under the trees on the other side.

She crosses back to avoid passing a bay window where people sit around a candle-lit table.

What are Mamma and Papa doing now? She left the puddings steaming, the pan will steam dry and burn. If she went back now, could she get into the house, back to the kitchen, without them knowing that she had left?

But she has not cleaned the pantry. Mamma will be angry, angrier than she can bear. She has never hidden before, never fled.

She trips on the valise and almost falls.

Quick now, hurry.

I cannot believe that you are too scared even to run away, says May. Honestly, you and Mamma almost deserve each other sometimes.

She has nowhere to go.

As the sun goes down, she finds herself around the back of the station. Her skirt is wet to the knees, Tom's valise spattered with mud. She draws into the corner as the lamplighter comes by, the first person she has noticed in some hours.

If the station is lit, there may be a train.

If the station is lit, they will look for her there.

And what of it, says May, they cannot arrest you, a respectable married woman, for leaving your parents' house.

They can call me mad, Ally replies, they can have me committed to the asylum.

The patient, who has a long history of hysteria perhaps exacerbated by an unfortunate attempt at higher education, appeared disordered in her dress and manner and displayed symptoms of great confusion and distress. Her parents, both well-known and respected citizens of Manchester, attested that she had given up a position in Cornwall because of nervous trouble but had not made the recovery hoped for while in their care.

You will always have a home with us, says Aunt Mary again. We will keep your room just as it has been these last years.

She turns back down a side street where there are no lights and checks all around before kneeling on the pavement to open the valise. She takes out a black silk scarf meant for Mamma's Christmas present.

Alethea, it troubles me that you waste your money on such fripperies in my name; you could surely have guessed that I would rather, far rather, you gave what you deign to spare from the purchase of your own finery to feed those who starve at our very door.

She pushes back her hood and arranges the scarf over her hat, as a veil. As long as they are not already waiting for her at the ticket office, as long as there is a train – any train, the milk train – the station master will remember only a woman in scrabbled together mourning who had been urgently summoned even as the pudding was lit.

unto us a boy is born

He would have liked to travel yesterday. It is not that he longed, as some of Mrs Senhouse's other guests obviously did, for an English Christmas. It is not that he felt the tug of home any more that day than any other, for he and Ally have not yet had a Christmas together and there have been many years when it has not been practical for him to return to Harrogate for the day. Mother will go to the neighbours with whom she often takes Sunday dinner and Ally, he fears, has returned to her parents in Manchester. So it is not as if there is anything to miss, as if he is aware of an empty place at a table on the other side of the globe. Even so, since there is not Christmas here and since he is not among friends, it would have been more seemly to continue with life as usual, to take trains and fulfil professional appointments and postpone celebration for the Japanese feast days, of which there is hardly a shortage. There is something pathetic in the child-like craving for presents and sweets, in the drunken singing of songs about the holly and the ivy and the ox and the ass. He saw the pity in Makoto's eyes when the Japanese guests joined them for English tea and crumbling slabs of plum cake. He would have preferred to have been spared the occasion.

He has a copy of *The Times* from six weeks ago, pressed on him by Senhouse this morning. Take it, Cavendish, for the Ambassador promised me first read of his next copy. We need to try to stay up to date, you know. Believe me it's a frightful shock when you get home if you haven't. It doesn't do, you know, to let oneself lose interest. At the Royal Albert Hall the Choral Society performed *Judas Maccabeus*, the orchestra being swelled for the occasion by the band of the Coldstream Guards. On Regent Street there was a zither concert by the zitherist to HRH the Princess of Wales. The London Orphan Asylum must urgently plead for help in maintaining the 550 orphans currently in their care. On the 29th of October, at Langham Lodge, Barnes, the wife of Rev. Henry Hayman, prematurely of a daughter, who survived her birth but a short time. They are leaving Osaka and there is snow on the ground, at first only a sifting, stones dark through grains of ice, and then more, a covering moulding itself to the shape of the land as a sheet rests over a body. Each tree bears its own ghost in snow, and the blades of Japanese flora, of bamboo and reeds, etch themselves black and vertical. On the 5th of Sept, at Rosslyn House, Double Bay, Sydney, NSW, the wife of Charles Telford, of a boy. *Unto us a boy is born*, he thinks, nearly three months ago. A letter from Australia to London, the printing of *The Times*, the diplomatic bag from London to Tokyo and the child already smiling, grasping. Charles Telford proud in the knowledge that his name and the way his hair grows over his ears will stay in the world when he is dead and buried. His iniquities, Tom thinks, passed down unto the third and fourth generation. Ally does not want a family. One child, she said, if you wish it very much; I would not deny you fatherhood. But not until we can keep a nurse. At first he thought she feared to give birth, had seen too many women die in the course of delivery to approach such an event herself, but it's not that. It's something to do with his mother-in-law, whom he has not met, who opposed their marriage, and with whom his wife is now living. Mamma is a difficult woman, she said when he pressed her. I cannot be certain that I would make a better mother than I have had. Mrs Dunne took him aside one day; Tom, no good comes of interfering relatives, but I must tell you to be wary of your mother-in-law. She is my sister and has reasons for being as she is but it is not good for Ally and you should keep her away. He shakes his head at the Christmas snow. He liked to think of Ally in Falmouth.

He opens the newspaper. Liverpool to Bombay via the canal, first class steamers fitted expressly for the trade, surgeon and stewardesses carried. The New Zealand Shipping Company will dispatch the following ships for Auckland, Canterbury, Otago and Wellington. Those wishing to take passage should address themselves immediately to the Company's offices. He should book his own passage home. Change at Singapore for Falmouth, and one day he will come on deck to see the Wolf Rock light and then, if the morning is clear, the Lizard peninsula rising over the horizon grey and veiled in mist. There will be bluebells under the oak trees on Pendennis Head and the gorse flaming yellow across the peninsula, wild garlic along the hedgerows and cow parsley bobbing amid long grass. No. It is like trying to raise an appetite when suffering sea-sickness, or trying – he recalls one night in Aberdeen, the only such occasion – to raise desire when there is only shame and distaste. He does not want daffodils and lambs. He wants to be here as spring turns to summer, wants to see the rice paddies green and growing, the orchids creeping in the woods as rain falls and the sun strengthens week by week. He wouldn't mind seeing the cherry blossom, and especially seeing the people seeing the cherry blossom. He folds up *The Times* and leaves it on the seat beside him. Let it ride the rails; it is a waste to spend in reading any time that could be used in committing to memory the mountains of Japan.

Snow has been swept from the platform, but more is falling outside the canopy, flakes drifting to the ground like leaves. He feels rising excitement: a new place, new snow, new work. The porters are unloading luggage from the last van and he takes his wooden token and Makoto's note from his pocket. Show this paper to anyone in a railway uniform, Makoto said, and he will explain to the jinrikisha man. I trust you will find your lodging satisfactory. Professor Baxter asked me to retain Tatsuo as your guide; he will come and find you in the morning. Tom nods, bows his thanks for the return of his trunk and holds out Makoto's note. It is like being the hero of a fairy tale, travelling alone in Japan. When you meet a man in a peaked cap, give him this paper and you will be conducted to a place where you may pass the night. Give him this carved wooden amulet and he will give you your books.

Darkness is falling as they leave the station, Tom in one jinrikisha and his trunk in another. Red lanterns float under the awnings of shops and restaurants and the streets are busy with men and umbrellas. There are fewer European suits than in Osaka and Tokyo, and less noise. He feels as if he's inside one of De Rivers' glass domes, inside a snow globe, where banners with Japanese lettering hang over the silent streets and figures enfolded in silk glide across small stone bridges. He doesn't want it to end.

asylum

Condensation drips from the wooden handle at the end of the lavatory chain, carved to the likeness of a pine cone and once compared by Freddie to something more obviously relevant to its purpose. Her knees rise from water turned green by Aunt Mary's bath salts, and she inhales lime-scented steam. She tips back her head and feels the heat reaching through her skull and her ears. Her arms float. She could dissolve into this water, dissolve and wash away. *Cleanse us of our sins, we beseech thee.* There would be nothing left.

'Ally? You haven't fainted in there?'

'I'm here, Aunt Mary. I'm sorry, of course the rest of you need the bathroom. I'll be out in a moment.'

She sits up and everything drains black. Postural drop caused by lack of food and exacerbated by the vasodilation consequent upon a hot bath. She leans her head forward between her knees so her forehead and hair dip again.

'No-one needs anything and if they do they can use the downstairs lavatory. But you should take some food. There's a tray in your room.'

She sits up again, more carefully. Her ears ring but in a

moment she can try to stand. 'You're too kind, Aunt Mary. I don't need a tray. Really. Please, don't go to any trouble for me. I don't need it.'

She hears Aunt Mary sniff. 'Less trouble than having you faint in the drawing room, my dear. I'm leaving a dressing gown outside the door and we'll give that dress to Fanny to be washed.'

No, she thinks, no, no-one is to do anything for me. I cannot bear it, you must not treat me so. Hysteria. Eat and rest first. Why did you come here, if not to be cared for, to be fed and bathed and clothed like an infant? Weak, you are weak and useless as a little child. She stands on the bath mat. She has indeed lost flesh, the bones in her feet clear to see. The towel lies over the mahogany rail. Take it and dry yourself, she thinks. Come now, dry your body. Another drip falls from the pine cone. Dry yourself.

'Gracious me, Ally, I thought you had gone up to bed. What are you doing here, darling?'

She is standing on the upstairs landing, beside the bathroom door, because it is the height of laziness and self-indulgence for a healthy woman to take to her bed in the middle of the day, because she is plainly assuming illness as a means of securing to herself that attention for which she appears to feel an incessant craving, and because at the same time she cannot go into the drawing room in a dressing gown several inches too short and in any case if she is going to be unwell it is better to take quietly to her bed rather than displaying herself on the sofa in a blatant bid for sympathy and concern.

'Come, let me take you to your bed. I must cable to Elizabeth and Alfred, darling, just to let them know where you are. And then I think I will call Dr Stratton.'

Ally looks at Aunt Mary. Elizabeth and Alfred, Mamma

and Papa. She finds herself weeping. 'No, Aunt Mary, please. Don't tell Mamma. Please. She will be so angry. You can't think how angry. Please, I can't bear it.' Fool. Weak-willed, hysterical fool. She swallows. 'And not Dr Stratton. Aunt Mary, I'm so ashamed. I could never practise again.'

Aunt Mary puts her arms around Ally. Ally is stiff. 'Perhaps it is better if she doesn't see you today. Promise me that you will eat and rest, and I won't call her until tomorrow. But darling, I must tell Elizabeth that you are safe. They must be in great distress. You left no note, no explanation?'

She shakes her head. 'It wasn't – I didn't plan to leave. I just couldn't clean the pantry. I couldn't move. I couldn't do it.'

Aunt Mary strokes her wet hair, which is dripping into the frills of the dressing gown. She wants Tom, wants him to hold her.

No, he must not see her like this, must not know that he is married to such a worthless thing.

'Shh, Ally. Shh. Very well. What if I cable to Mrs Lewis and have her send a message to say that she has heard that you are safely lodged?'

Then Mrs Lewis will know what has happened, and Professor Lewis will know that she is weak and foolish, that she cannot even cover part of a practice for a few measly weeks.

'No. I don't want anyone to know.'

'They may have called the police. And what if your Papa should appear at the door looking for you?'

'No. No. I don't know what to do.'

Aunt Mary begins to lead her down the hall. 'Well, I do, my dear, and so you must allow me to do it.'

Aunt Mary takes her up the stairs to her own room, where she lived for all the time she was becoming a doctor. Years that now seem to have peeled away, to have been erased by Mamma. Years that she has allowed Mamma to erase. The room smells as it always did of the jasmine-scented soap on the washstand and the coal fire burning in the grate. Aunt Mary draws down the sheets for her. Outside, behind the bare plane trees, the sky is dull and heavy with rain.

'I don't need a fire, Aunt Mary. Don't waste the coal.'

'Shh. Get into bed, Ally. Or I must call Dr Stratton.'

Ally obeys. Aunt Mary beats the pillows and props them against the headboard.

'Now, sit up and eat your breakfast.' Aunt Mary places the tray on the bedside table and removes its silver dome. The smell of bacon mingles with the jasmine, and there is a pot of coffee. Ally remembers the bread and water at Mamma's house. She does not deserve this, the fine china and linen napkin, the white toast in a silver toast rack and the butter pat and marmalade bowl. She looks up at Aunt Mary. Aunt Mary meets her eyes, and then begins to spread butter for her, to pour coffee and cream.

'Eat it, darling. And then I'm going to bring my embroidery and sit with you while you rest – I want the fire even if you don't – and then we'll talk. You can come down to supper if I think you're strong enough, there's no-one coming tonight and a relief after last week I can tell you. Fourteen to dinner on Wednesday! I could see in Cook's eyes she was thinking of giving notice but you know how James loves to entertain. The boys will be so happy to see you. And Annie's home for Christmas, did her letter reach you? You'd maybe rather consult her than Dr Stratton.'

Salt butter, bitter marmalade, crisp toast flood Ally's tongue and the coffee seems to enter her bloodstream. Aunt Mary stands by the window. Her hair has greyed since the summer, but she is wearing a new dress in royal blue damask trimmed with silver braid. Aunt Mary's love of clothes has always been somehow cheering, an assertion of the value of aesthetic pleasure that has little to do with personal vanity. Her dresses are flags for beauty.

'That's it, darling. You'll soon feel better for some nice food. You didn't eat at all yesterday?'

Ally tries to remember. Yesterday. She lit the kitchen range but she doesn't remember eating anything herself. 'I don't think so.'

Aunt Mary nods. 'You've got very thin. I never understood why Elizabeth doesn't waste away. Alfred of course takes his meals elsewhere now?'

Ally bites her lips. 'Mm.'

'Poor Ally. I'll stop talking to you about it. Finish your toast, darling. More coffee?'

Aunt Mary stays until Ally has eaten all that is comfortable, and then takes the tray herself. Ally lolls against the pillows, tries not to hear Mamma. *Sating yourself in idle luxury when there is such suffering as even you would be ashamed to behold not five minutes from where you lie lazing.*

The fire crackles and there are hoof beats down the street, getting louder. The cart rattles past and then fades. A man's voice in the hall – George – and the front door opens and closes. Her neck is stiff and she adjusts the pillow. How long since she was ill, since she lay in bed excused from ordinary life? This day only, she thinks, it would be too easy to become an invalid, to lie here and perhaps pass the days with novels or a little fancy-work. Mamma is quite right, ladies take to the sofa as gentlemen to the club, because it is a place where nothing is asked, where we are fed and coddled like babies at the breast and allowed to slide unknowing into damnation. Like some babies at the breast, some fortunate few. She remembers having measles as a child, before she and May started school. There is nothing wrong with Alethea except that she would rather mope by the fire than learn her lessons. If you are unwell, Alethea, please go to your room; you are scarcely a fit sight for the drawing room with those eruptions on your face. You vomited because you took too much water; did I not tell you that moderation is particularly important in cases of fever? And then one night Mamma came to her with a covered bowl, an egg custard made by her own hand. Here, Alethea, now that the fever is passed you should take some food. You must get strong and fit again.

And she has seen Mamma at other bedsides, tending to women in the acute abdominal pain that characterises the progress of certain inflammations to which prostitution makes them especially prone, sitting up at night with a girl brought in from the street in the late stages of both tuberculosis and pregnancy. Mamma will sooner read the Bible to someone in pain than administer analgesia, but she chooses genuinely consoling passages, and as far as Ally can tell Mamma believes them. *Our soul is escaped as a bird out of the snare of the fowlers: the snare is broken, and we are escaped. Our help is in the name of the Lord, who made Heaven and Earth. He that keepeth thee will not slumber.* Sleep now in peace, Mamma murmured, did not our Lord himself take Mary Magdalene into his keeping? Mamma is not wicked, or without love. Only without love for Ally. Ally finds herself crying again.

A light tread on the stairs, Aunt Mary coming back. She taps on the door as she opens it, and comes in with her workbox in her hands.

'Poor Ally. Do you want to tell me all about it, or not yet?'

She shakes her head. 'Not yet, Aunt Mary. But thank you, truly thank you, for taking me in like this.'

'Nonsense, darling. It is what any aunt, any friend would do.'

Aunt Mary settles herself in the rocking chair with her box

on the occasional table. Ally, who has no interest in fancy-work or embroidery, has always admired the workbox for its miniature drawers and folding trays, the neatness of the shiny wood and silver fittings. There are holes for thimbles to nest and a needle holder in the shape of a furled umbrella. Aunt Mary takes out a piece of cross-stitch in a circular wooden frame and wets a length of red silk in her mouth.

'Lie down, Ally. Try to sleep. You can rest now. I've told the servants that no-one is to be admitted and that I am not at home to anyone at all.'

Ally pulls the pillows down into the bed and curls up. Refuge, she thinks. Asylum.

there's no-one here

He is woken by bells. No, by one bell, one sound. The note reverberates through the wooden walls and the floor, through the thin futon and around his ribs, his sternum. He rolls onto his back and waits for the next one. There. The echoes hum through the ground, through his shoulder blades and spine, and then the voices come, a low chant. A temple, he thinks, or a shrine, because there is meant to be a difference, now, between Shinto and Buddhism. Divide and conquer, probably. Didn't lots of samurai retire to monasteries?

Once again, the room lies calm and empty around him. He puts his hands behind his head and opens out his shoulders. It is perfectly possible to sleep very well on a futon but some postures result in stiffness; one should learn to lie straight. There is one banner showing four Japanese characters hanging on the wall in the alcove, with one green vase containing one sprig of bamboo beneath it. His trunk is downstairs, because he saw no reason to try to wrestle it up the narrow open-tread staircase, and his clothes are downstairs also, beside the wooden bathtub which he found last night full of boiling hot water and covered with a wooden lid. He had to leave it to cool while he ate the tray of food he found on the low table in the main room, accompanied by green tea from a lidded jug which was also disconcertingly hot, the person who made it surely still close at hand. It is like coming to the little house in the fairy-tale forest and finding supper on the table and candles lit, as if sometime this morning he should expect a visit from his fairy godmother. Or someone else, the rightful owner.

He sits up and tugs on the shutters, which were already closed when he arrived. They slide back to show paper screens set with small glass panels at the eye height of a person sitting on the floor, but there are outer shutters which are also closed. Three layers: why not just build a wall? But he knows why not. It is so that in summer one can open the whole building and live almost outdoors, using the shoji screens for shade or to keep out insects, or using the inner shutters for darkness without stuffiness and then the outer ones only to secure the house at need and for winter insulation. He tries to imagine Cornish houses so arranged, how different things would be. There must be some essential difference about the Japanese mind, or at least some moment very early in the human story, thousands of years ago, when what seems obvious to the rest of the world became strange and barbaric here. And vice versa.

Cold air, smelling of the snow outside, seeps around the outer shutter. The urge to lie down again and wrap the quilt around his shoulders wrestles with his curiosity about the world out there, a new city waiting behind the shutters to be explored. Besides, he does not know when the provider of hot baths and meals on trays will return. He takes a deep breath of winter morning, pushes the quilt onto the floor and climbs gingerly down the dim stairs.

The stove has been lit. There is a folded blue quilt beside it that was not there last night, and in the bathroom his clothes have also been folded – perfectly folded, along the seams and then at exact right-angles – and left in a stack on a wooden ledge low in the wall. Someone has been handling his drawers, his undershirt. Shivering in his pyjamas, he walks the house. It's among the smallest self-contained dwellings he's seen and no-one could possibly be concealed here, not even a tiny Japanese fairy godmother, but even so he pushes back the screen separating the four-mat room from the entrance way and checks the cupboard in the wall between the bathroom and the main room and then, idiotically, behind the bath and behind the curtain screening the street door. There's no-one here, unless he's missing something obvious, some door that looks like a wall (the sliding bookcase, he thinks, the fake panelling and the hidden trap door). Some of the more important Japanese houses, Professor Baxter told him, do have secret rooms, bare so that there are no hiding places for eavesdroppers or assassins, and positioned to make spying or ambush almost impossible. Tom grins to himself, remembering a complicated game he used to play with William Vickers who lived down the road and shared his taste for the cheaper and more exciting kind of boys' stories. Perhaps presently he will be summoned to the secret chamber and entrusted with his quest. Meanwhile, he will dress by the stove and see if anyone brings him breakfast, and then if Mr Tatsuo appears to take him out.

Aunt Mary rings the bell for tea

For perhaps the first time in her life, Ally has nothing to do. After breakfast, Uncle James leaves for the office. No rest for the wicked, he says, kissing Aunt Mary, and he will be home for afternoon tea, but it is perfectly plain that after three days of Christmas there is a lift in his step as he sets off. Dear James, says Aunt Mary, he does love to entertain but he has always less stamina for company than he expects. Don't be silly, darling, you're not company, we've both missed you these last six months. But I can't stay, Ally thinks, this isn't a permanent arrangement. I can't sit by your fire and eat your delicacies until Tom comes home. George goes out to walk with a college friend living nearby – a glorious day, Mamma, and we've hardly left the house since Midnight Mass, sure you won't come, Cousin Al? She's not going anywhere, said Aunt Mary, not yet. Anyway, Annie's coming later. Ally can go into the gardens with Annie if she feels like it. And then Aunt Mary herself went down to the kitchen for her daily confabulations with the cook.

Ally, left in the morning room, wanders into the bay and stands in the window. There are new drapes since the summer, thick velvet that will be troublesome to keep clean, in the shade of kingfisher blue that Aunt Mary loves to have in her clothes, and behind them swags of white muslin that will probably need laundering every week in winter with the fire burning all day and the fogs outside. Next door's housemaid is scrubbing the steps of their porch, steam wavering above her bucket of water and rising from her breath as she works. A carriage passes, and two men in dark suits walk briskly towards the station. Across the road, the railings around the garden in the middle of the square have been repainted. A nurse with a perambulator and a child of two or three at her side is unlocking the garden gate. Ally turns away. You must rest, says Aunt Mary, but there is nothing restful about idleness. Mamma's voice mutters in her head: are you then wholly abandoned to self-indulgence, Alethea? You have seen fit to excuse yourself all justification of your existence in this vale of tears? She stops herself putting her hands over her ears. Nothing in this room needs doing. There is no disorder, nothing to address. She begins to align the spines of the books on the shelf along the long wall, mostly Uncle James's collection of voyages and travel writing. One or two are out of alphabetical sequence and can be replaced, but it doesn't take long. She strokes Aunt Mary's ferns on the plant stand, but there are no brown leaves and their soil is moist. George is right, it is a nice day outside. Annie won't be here for another hour at least; perhaps she will take a walk in the park. Frittering away your time, says Mamma, casting around for ways of passing your very life. For shame, Alethea, for shame.

She can't concentrate on the novel Aunt Mary has put into her hands, something about three sisters living in a small town in Scotland. The middle sister, Aunt Mary says, is terribly clever and a great supporter of women's suffrage and things like that, and the book always makes her think of Ally. It makes Ally think of doing something else. It is not five minutes since she last looked at the clock. It is too hot beside the fire anyway. She puts the book down on the side table and walks to the window.

'Dear Al. You have never learnt to rest yourself.'

Aunt Mary is settled in her usual chair, with her feet crossed on a needlepoint footstool of her own making, writing a letter on paper that rests on a padded tray balanced on the chair's arm. The impedimenta of idleness, Mamma would say. Ally thinks that she should write to Tom, but she is too ashamed of herself, would not know where to start. *Dearest Tom, I am with Aunt Mary once again because I found myself incapable of the work I had undertaken to do. Because I allowed my difficulties with Mamma to make me break my word and leave the most desperate and needy patients without any hope of medical attention until the spring. Because in the name of personal troubles I betrayed my profession.* What will Miss Eastman be thinking now, having reached the Welfare Centre and found that Ally has not returned from the Christmas holiday? What will Mamma tell her? The breakfast kedgeree and coffee churn in Ally's stomach. She has abandoned two posts, two sets of patients, in the last month. Who would write her a reference now?

Aunt Mary sets aside her letter. 'There now. I expect this will be Annie at the door.'

Ally had not heard the bell, but there are voices in the hall and then Annie blows in before Fanny has time to announce her. A grey skirt, bustled and swagged, and a cream blouse with lace at the collar. Her hair somehow different.

'Ally! It is such a joy to see you again. And up! I thought you might be in bed.'

Aunt Mary comes to kiss Annie. 'How are you, my dear? A happy Christmas? She should be in bed, but she is very naughty about resting.'

Ally stands up. She had forgotten that Annie likes to kiss on arrival and departure. 'I am glad to see you too. And really, I have slept. I am not unwell. I feel no need to lie in a bed.'

Aunt Mary and Annie exchange glances. What on earth did Aunt Mary write in the note that summoned Annie? *Ally has run mad. Ally is in the grip of a nervous crisis.* What might be called a touch of hysterical tendency in a young girl bears a more sinister name in a woman over thirty.

'Good,' says Annie. 'It is an excellent sign. But later, Ally, perhaps after we have taken a walk, you will allow me to examine you? For I gather you have had a shock and I see that you have lost flesh. You are a little pale, darling, and – forgive me – look tired even if you don't feel it.'

Ally returns to her chair, since it appears that the promised walk is not immediate. She is like an eager dog, following everyone who moves towards the door. Aunt Mary waves Annie to the sofa.

Aunt Mary and Annie speak of Christmas, of Annie's sisters, of the boys. Of Annie's mother's difficulty in replacing her cook. Of a play that both of them have considered seeing but not seen. Outside, the sun moves across the sky. In Manchester, Mamma tends to her fallen women, persuades her subscribers to give just a little more. In Truro, Dr Crosswyn visits the wards, writes letters, makes notes, reasons with the committee. Aunt Mary and Annie speak of a book that Annie cannot recommend. The sky turns pink and Aunt Mary rings the bell for tea.

a pattern of butterflies

A blade held between two fingers opens the silk like skin, lifts away the white shape as a surgeon might raise a tumour. Tom finds himself craning to see the flesh underneath but of course there is only the cutting board.

Tatsuo leans over his shoulder. 'Now the dyeing. Very beautiful.'

There is a wooden tray full of steaming blue liquid on the bench under the window. The craftsman carries the breadth of silk tenderly, over both arms, and lowers a portion of it into the dye. Bright blue, *azure*, laps at the grey, and then the cloth is lifted and draped over a rack so that the blue drips into a tray without crossing the grey. The man's hands are blue and his fingers calloused.

'So. It stays to dry.'

Tom nods. There are several kimono in process here, brought as lengths – tatami-sized lengths, he thinks, as if one's whole life is measured in the same units – from the weaving shop across the lane. Two garments hang from horizontal poles on the wall, as if crucified, finished and awaiting collection. Spring kimono, Tatsuo translated. Irises grow from a pool of purple at the hem of one, lilies from pale pink on the other. The kimono is an artist's canvas, its uniformity of shape and size freeing the painter from any consideration of the wearer's body. Woman as picture frame. Would Ally find it better or worse than the corset and bustle? He thinks of the paintings he saw in Alfred Moberley's London exhibition, Ally and yet not Ally. It is odd to have a wife on whose undressed body any man may gaze on the walls of the Royal Academy. Perhaps she would like a kimono, not one of these which are far beyond his means and anyway intended to be worn by the richest of women on the rarest occasions, but one like his fairy godmother Makiko's.

'You wish to see the sewing? The – embroidery?' A difficult word for the Japanese tongue.

'Please.' Tom bows.

He wants to see everything. He is a child at Christmas, wide-eyed and without discrimination. Tatsuo leads him up a wooden ladder so that his head emerges on the level of the floor where men sit on their folded legs around a kimono length stretched on a wooden frame. He tries to return their bows before he has found his feet and they regard him gravely for a moment before turning again to their stitching. One hand above the stretched silk, one below it, working together, the right knowing perfectly the actions of the left. The outlines of a pattern of butterflies and grasses are filling with silk in yellow, blue and green and the needles flutter above the work.

'A special commission,' Tatsuo murmurs. 'A great geisha.'

Tom feels himself tensing. Geisha. Not *exactly* prostitutes, he's heard. Hardly patrons of the arts. Although there are four men at work, there has been no visible expansion of the colours since he first looked.

'How long does it take?' he asks.

'The whole or the – the embroidering?'

'Say the whole.'

'To spin, to weave, to dye, to embroider, to sew? Many months. Half a year.'

Good God. They need factories. Mechanised spinners and looms, sewing machines. Mass production. You could make hundreds in a couple of days. If they can build trains and lighthouses, why on earth do they still have old men working wooden looms with their hands and feet? It is medieval. And what does it cost, he thinks, what are these men paid and what is the price of the silk and what does the geisha pay at the end? He is here, after all, as a possible customer. There must be a way of asking. He has never bought a work of art before.

They retreat down the ladder, Tatsuo facing forward with one hand on the rails, Tom backwards, feeling with each foot for the step below and painfully aware of his large European behind progressing through the mid-air of the room beneath. The director, dressed in loose black trousers and tunic with white insignia on the shoulder and back, awaits Tom's descent. As Tom adjusts his jacket and his dignity, the director bows and speaks. He is offering tea, Tom realises. He nods and bows back.

'*Arigato*,' he says. '*Domo arigato*.' He can feel the grin spreading across his face.

The three men sit cross-legged around a black lacquer table facing the workshop's courtyard garden. A charcoal falls in the stove behind Tom and he can feel its heat in his back and shoulders; one advantage of sitting on the floor is that one is at the height of the fire. The screens are open far enough to show a stripe of snow on grey stones, the white shading to grey with the curve of each rock, and the black twigs of a pine tree also bearing their own ghosts in snow. Tom accepts a translucent bowl of green tea, noticing the single frond of pine painted grey on its ridged white side. The accompanying sweet, the same colour as the tea, echoes the shape of the cones on the tree.

'Arigato,' he says again. Thank you. He forgets about the transaction, about the shopping.

When they leave – arigato, *sayonara* – it is snowing again in the cobbled street, and the mountains have vanished behind the clouds. Two women walk under umbrellas, their geta silenced by the snow on the ground. The curved roofs are white, only their curved ridgepoles and gable ends dark against the paper sky, and the blue and white banners hang motionless in the still air. He finds himself holding his breath, as if to stop time, to make it forever now, here.

Aubade in Yellow

There is a fog outside, wrapped so thickly through the branches of the plane tree that she can't see the ground or the people who are probably walking along the pavement, so thickly that she could be high in a tower, with many storeys of Aunt Mary's carpets and hearths between her and the world. She has been rocking the chair as she reads and the blanket over her lap has slipped down; she pulls it back up to her waist, noticing the new silk edging. Ally is reading Browne again, reflecting on his suggestion that some 'lunatics' are simply not capable of functioning outside the asylum although apparently sane within it. The appearance of sanity in such cases, he argues, depends upon the protection afforded by the asylum and ends with that protection: these are the patients who relapse repeatedly on discharge, only to satisfy all conditions of release almost immediately on readmission. Browne does not suggest, nor, apparently, seek a solution to this conundrum. These patients are simply people who should live in lunatic asylums. But what, Ally thinks, if there is something in the environment to which they return that drives them back to madness, that reawakens the intolerable voices in their minds? It is hardly a new idea that certain situations induce insanity. That being told repeatedly over many months that one is mad will make one so, for the person who believes herself to be insane must be insane. A medical version of the Cretan paradox: all lunatics are deluded and I am a lunatic; is it possible that what I say about myself is true? It is not these games of words that will cure hurt minds.

She begins to rock again, the book still open on her lap. She returns to her original question: what of those whose home situations are maddening, so maddening that a lunatic asylum appears by comparison a sane and healthful place? It is a possibility that does not seem to have occurred to Browne: it is not that some people's minds are so fragile that they require the permanent protection of an institution but that some people's homes are crazier than institutions for the mad. Some households do not tolerate sanity. Perhaps such an understanding of domestic life is exactly what a woman brings to medicine. Ally sighs. It is an idea unlikely to be well received by the medical profession and indeed by the general public, especially when presented by a woman doctor. An unnatural, undomesticated being, very probably subject to mental instability herself, for why else would a woman declare herself unsatisfied by her own family life and seek to usurp the masculine role? It is axiomatic that a woman with a professional life cannot speak of domestic happiness. It is almost lunchtime. Ally sets aside her blanket, checks her hair in the mirror and goes downstairs.

Aunt Mary is in the hall, also looking at herself in the mirror. Ally sees Aunt Mary's reflected face change to the guilty expression of the person surprised in the act of self-regard.

'You are still beautiful, Aunt Mary.'

Aunt Mary shakes her head. Seen from above, there is more grey.

'I was never that. And I'm not wearing so badly, but then why should I? I'm not out all hours and all weathers, living on bread and water like Elizabeth. I wasn't contemplating mortality, darling, only wondering if this lovely green is a little trying to a winter complexion. What do you think?'

Ally comes down the remaining stairs and shakes her head. Through the fanlight over the front door, she sees the fog eddy and re-gather. 'Ask Uncle James. Or Annie.'

Aunt Mary turns away from the mirror. 'He said he'd be home to lunch today, but with this fog, I don't know whether to wait. You know how he likes us to lunch together. But there's rice with the chicken, it won't improve with keeping and Cook will be cross.'

Ally smiles at her. 'Well, are you more afraid of your cook or your husband?'

'Cook. Without a doubt. Do you know how hard it is to replace a good cook? Let's go in and eat.'

Ally and Aunt Mary have almost finished their chicken and rice when they hear the front door open and close. Uncle James comes in, droplets of fog clinging to his beard.

'Sorry to be late, dearest. The post came just as I was leaving. The fog, you know. Lunch smells delicious, is that paprika and mushrooms in the sauce?'

Uncle James is more interested in food than anyone Ally knows, except perhaps Aubrey. Maybe there is something in the discriminating eye of the artist connected to a similar exactitude about the palate. Paprika and mushrooms. She remembers the mutton hash, the rusks.

'I believe so, yes.'

'Splendid.'

Fanny comes in, but Uncle James waves her away and begins to eat. 'Wine, Ally?'

She shakes her head. She takes a glass in the evening, sometimes, when Uncle James is especially persuasive.

'Suit yourself. It's a good bottle.'

Aunt Mary accepts half a glass. Their eyes meet and they lift their glasses to each other, husband and wife, Uncle James's eyebrows raised a fraction of an inch, remembering something that makes Aunt Mary blush and suppress a smile. Still, at their age, friends and lovers.

Uncle James is still smiling at Aunt Mary. 'Ally, are you busy this afternoon?'

The kind of question best answered with caution. 'I was planning to study. Why?'

'Three new paintings came in. Aubrey West.' He and Aunt Mary exchange more sober glances; they must have talked about this. 'We thought you might like to see them. Well, see one of them again in particular. Before it disappears back into private hands.'

She knows, of course, that there are images of herself and her sister on walls, in houses, around the country and even, now, in America. She knows that her face, versions of her face, and versions of May's face watch over other people's meals and parties and solitary moments, drift in other people's dreams and memories. She has no picture of May.

'May?' she asks. 'You have one of Aubrey's paintings of May, in your office now?'

He sips his wine. 'Yes.'

Aunt Mary leans forward. 'We weren't sure whether to tell you, darling. Whether it would upset you, when you have been so recently troubled. But we thought – James thought – that the auction is next week and there is no knowing when you might be able to see it again. We thought you should choose. But you know that it is quite up to you. It will make no difference to anyone else, no difference whatsoever, and you must do just as you think will be best for you. But we thought you

204

should decide for yourself. And I will accompany you if you like me to, and not if you don't.'

Ally puts down her knife and fork. The chicken was too rich, rises in her stomach.

'I don't know. I don't know what I should do.'

No, she thinks, no, she does not want to see May, whose voice and step flit through her dreams, whose words mock and goad, who has been dead and gone and taunting her – no, that is not fair – almost these ten years.

'Which one is it? Which painting?'

Uncle James takes more rice. '*Aubade in Yellow*. 1873.'

'Oh.'

May was twelve. Ally was busy with her schoolwork, still, then hoping to go to Edinburgh, because the Edinburgh Seven were working their way through the medical syllabus there and the university had not yet moved to close the loophole that had allowed women to take examinations. It was the worst year for her attacks of hysteria, and also therefore the worst year for Mamma's attempts to cure her of nervous weakness by blistering, early rising and constant domestic chores. Hysteria, Alethea, is an outward symptom of under-occupation and unfettered self-regard. She was not even sharing May's room for much of the year, since Mamma feared that Ally's bad dreams and early rising would disturb her sister's rest. May was always good at spending a great deal of time at the houses of other girls from the school, and often managed to elicit Papa's permission for outings with Aubrey without seeming to consult Mamma at all; it is not entirely surprising that Ally has only a vague memory of this painting. Aubade, dawn. Did May spend a night with Aubrey?

Fanny comes to clear the plates. 'You're finished, Miss Ally?'

She's given up trying to devise something for Fanny to call her. 'Yes, thank you, Fanny.'

Aunt Mary shakes her head. 'You must try to eat more, darling. Or at this rate we'll have to have all your dresses altered and Tom will come home and find you quite wasted away.'

He wants her strong. Really, Alethea, says Mamma in her head. If you had wished to honour your sister you would have fulfilled your obligations to her Welfare Centre; this gadding around to see paintings is mere self-indulgence, luxuriating in your own sorrow and the attention it brings you.

Stop it. Stop it. She must stop allowing Mamma to live in her head.

'Yes, please. I would like to see the painting.'

There is apple snow to follow the chicken, and then Uncle James toys with the end of the Christmas stilton and water biscuits. The cheese is crumbling on its special plate, the edges turning brown as if it were a dying leaf, and the heat of the fire crackling behind Aunt Mary's chair lifts the smell across the room, somehow familiar but associated with work, with the Women's Hospital. Decomposition, she thinks. It smells of mortality.

'Would you excuse me, Aunt Mary.'

They look up as she hurries from the room. They will think her flighty, unstable. Perhaps that she should not see the painting after all. She stops in the hall, where the draught creeping under the front door brings chill and the grey breath of the fog that presses against the glass panels and the fanlight. She wants to stay in her white room in the attic, safe with her rocking chair and her books. She stands at the bottom of the stairs. Apart from a couple of walks in the park, she has barely left the house since she arrived from Manchester. Regardless of Aubrey's picture, she thinks, she should accompany Uncle James for the air and exercise. Or perhaps Mamma's voice is right, perhaps the wish to go out is a foolish yearning for diversion and distraction, for the attention of others. Ally catches sight of herself in the mirror, pale and wide-eyed. Stop this. The question of whether to walk out this afternoon does not merit such alarm. Why don't you just do what you wish to do, enquires May's voice. It will be much simpler that way and actually, Al, nobody else cares. Study when you get back. Or not; it's not as if you have more examinations. Or even as if you haven't read that book before. In fact, it's not really studying at all, is it, Al?

The eyes in the mirror dilate. All that is required is the strength of mind not to listen, to remember that May is dead and Mamma far away and that their voices are phantasms. But there is no arguing with the distant and the dead, she thinks. There is no possibility of winning. One must live with their voices.

Aubrey used to like fog. And rain, so long as he could sit somewhere dry to paint, and snow. Twilight and candlelight. There would probably have been more aubades if he had been less certain that early rising was a bourgeois habit. Are there more paintings of sunset than sunrise because painters disdain the early hours of office workers and professional men? This fog is still so thick that she can see it stroking the pillars of next door's portico, rubbing against the gaslamps and trailing along the iron railings of the square's garden. Uncle James crooks his elbow and she takes it. She has not walked on a man's arm since Tom left.

'You are sure you are up to the walk on such a day? We could find a cab.'

There are tiny beads of water forming on the fibres of her wool coat, miniature as insects.

'I doubt we could, Uncle James. But in any case I like to walk, and I have been too much indoors.'

'You must tell me the moment you begin to tire, or to chill.'

If she had been Uncle James's daughter, if she could have had Aunt Mary for her mother and grown up here—

'You are too kind to me.'

'Nonsense, my dear. I should say rather that others have not been kind enough.'

He squeezes her hand. It is, she is fairly sure, the first time he has spoken even implicitly of Mamma and Papa to her. He cannot have met them above two or three times. Uncle James grew up in Kent, where his parents died within a month of each other a few years ago. Mother did not want to go on without my father, Uncle James said. She died of grief.

The carriages have their lamps lit, but even so she can hear the horses before the lights come through the fog. She thinks of the ships in the estuary at home, creeping upriver with ears strained for all the notes in the symphony: ships' bells and foghorns, waves on the rocks and further inland the rustle of trees or church bells chiming the hour. She remembers saying to Tom that in some ways Japan looks like Britain on a map, both archipelagic nations off the northern coasts of their continents, both moated by intricate coastlines and rocky seas. There will be fogs there too, and peril for those who go down to the sea in ships. When he leaves, there will still be weeks and oceans to cross, fogs and storms and the rocky shores of three continents. She shivers.

There is a fire in the stone hearth in the hall of Uncle James's office, sending a flickering orange light across the marble chessboard floor. One of RDS's paintings hangs over the mantel, from what Papa used to call his Tennyson phase, all long-haired maidens and knights on horseback. Papa used to tease RDS about the weight of the armour in relation to the size of the horses.

'May I take your coat, or will you keep it on while you warm up?'

She feels as if she'll never warm up, as if the fog has got into her blood and bones. She should have walked faster. She should not have allowed herself to lose the habit of outdoor exercise. Somewhere in this building, behind one of these doors, is May's face. Uncle James stands back, gestures for her to precede him into his office and it's there, on the easel. She hears her own intake of breath.

But of course it's not May's face, not the face she can no longer recall. And she has seen the painting before, in Aubrey's studio at one of the last parties she attended there. The dawn light streams through a bay window she doesn't recognise, not Aubrey's rooms or her parents' house, onto a daffodil-yellow sofa where a young girl lies asleep, her blonde hair tumbled across a pale green cushion and her bare arms and legs flung out from under a yellow drape. The swirl of sunlight and hair are roughly painted, and the painter has given his exact attention not to the girl's sleeping face but to the white straps crossing her collarbones and bisecting the shadowed curve of her shoulders. He's made the viewer want to push the straps off.

'Where was it painted?' she demands.

'I don't know. I can write to West and ask. Or of course you could.'

She last wrote to thank him for his wedding present, an exquisitely framed design for a fan that showed the beginning of Aubrey's interest in Japanese objects but also invoked the submarine shapes of waves, weeds and shells in a way that Ally found hard to forgive. It is in a chest in the attic in Cornwall, well wrapped but inevitably not fully protected from the damp. She does not want to write to him again, especially not to suggest the old tenderness about him and May.

'It doesn't matter.'

Papa would say, the painting is an object of beauty. It is

about lines and curves, light and dark, colour. Just think about colour, Ally! Only the philistine mind goes running to names and places. She looks again, notices the way the damask pattern on the window's curtains changes where the sunlight grazes it, notices the daring composition in which the curtains, the sofa and the window frame a sky which occupies half the picture but is empty and pale, only the source of the light flowing into the painted room. Papa is right; May is only part of the furniture here, another object on which light falls. She cannot remember ever seeing a painting of a sleeping man.

'Would you like to see the others?' asks Uncle James. 'There are two more recent ones.'

No, she thinks. But Uncle James is already lifting the *Aubade* off the easel and uncovering another of the paintings stacked against the wall.

'There.' He whisks off the blanket with a flourish. '*Harmony in Red*. Isn't it extraordinary?'

It's the same sofa. The same yellow. Despite the title, there's little red. And the girl is about the same age, but this time she lies propped against the sofa's arm, her head back to expose a slim white throat and raised collarbones, one arm lying along the sofa's back and the other hanging at her side, as if she's sated and tumbled. Dark hair is falling out of a low chignon, and she seems to be wearing a nightdress or dressing gown, some pale froth of skirt thrown back over her legs and apparently held down by a swathe of red silk. A red fan lies discarded by her feet, and there appear to be items of clothing scattered on the floor. The light is dim; evening or lamplight.

'Beautiful. He's going from strength to strength at the moment. Astonishing work. And beginning to find favour, you know. He'll get a lot for this.'

Ally swallows. 'Who is she?'

'Who? Oh, the model? Someone's daughter. He's very taken with her. She's the subject of the other one as well. But look at the composition, the shape of the skirts and the sofa.'

'Yes,' she says. 'They are very striking.'

Uncle James wants to take her to a tea room on the way home. Aunt Mary will like it, he says, to think that she has had a treat, and she still looks cold; he is worried that she will take a chill if she does not have something hot before they walk back. She remembers tea rooms with Aubrey, his manifest pleasure in icing and whipped cream and the ceremonies of teapots, cake stands and doilies. She does not want to go back, to cross the carpet under the gaze of ladies in hats, to sit stiff-backed awaiting the services of thin girls in black dresses and lace aprons all for a cup of tea and a bun. Uncle James is too kind, she says, but unless he himself has a particular wish for a tea room she would rather go home. But the cold, he says. But he would like to give her tea. She does not say that he will be giving her the tea wherever she has it, that her food and drink and shelter come from him as they did for many years. She would like to take tea with Aunt Mary, she says. She bites her lip.

He glances down. 'Of course, Ally. I dare say you will want to talk to her about your sister.' He squeezes her arm. 'I should have thought of it that way. And I will take you both to tea another day, perhaps when you go to the sales.'

She has no intention of going to the sales. Unless, of course, Aunt Mary should want a companion; with no work to do, she has no longer any reason to avoid such outings.

'Thank you, Uncle James.'

'Nonsense, my dear. Let's take you home.'

Uncle James, who rarely takes tea himself, sees her in through the front door and then leaves for his club. As if she were a child, as if she had not for many years lived in this house and made her own way to the hospital and around London at all seasons and hours. After all, she still has her door key. Aunt Mary tries to help Ally take off her coat and bustles her back to the fireside. Here again, the same velvet under her behind, her feet in the same place on the carpet. Her fingers begin to tingle in the warmth. She needs to go somewhere, do something. She does not know how Aunt Mary bears her narrow round, the endless ceremonies of meals and dressing and passing the time in between. She has forgotten how to tolerate kindness, she thinks. Only cruelty feels real. Aunt Mary crosses her feet on her footstool and takes up her embroidery.

'And so you saw the painting?'

Ally nods. 'I had seen it before. I'd forgotten. It's very beautiful. An excellent composition.'

Aunt Mary looks up from her stitching. 'Oh yes, I dare say.' The needle begins to flash again, etching a green line in the space between her lap and her face. 'And the subject?'

Ally looks away, not into the flames in the grate but out of the window, where the fog may be thinning a little and a cart rumbles in the street. 'The subject is sleeping. She could be anyone, any girl with hair to match the sofa.'

The thread tautens, dives, tautens. 'Is that how it was, Ally? Hair to match the sofa?'

Ally shrugs. 'We knew that, Aunt Mary. We lent our bodies to Papa and Aubrey as others lent props and costumes. That was all.'

But we did not choose it, she thinks. Our bodies, our images, were taken because we were in no position to give, because children do not, in the end, own themselves. We were posing for Papa and Aubrey almost before we understood how to keep still. How to obey, how to hold our limbs as we were asked to do, how to see our bodies as if we did not inhabit them.

'I understand he has a new model now. Mr Casey's daughter. Rebecca, I think. I hear he takes her to tea every Wednesday.'

There is a slight sound as the needle punctures the stretched canvas, as the thread glides through the hole.

Ally swallows. 'He used to take May to tea. Well, and me.' Until I got too old, she thinks. Until I was becoming a woman. And when May was becoming a woman, when he didn't want to paint her or take her clothes off and photograph her any more, he sent her off to drown in Scotland. No, this is not fair. Aubrey's last painting of May shows some teasing appreciation of her maturing body, of the curve of her behind and the rounding of her thighs, and no-one could have known how the Scottish journey would end. It was an accident. Blaming Aubrey is a way of making meaning, of believing that May died because someone intended it rather than because people die at all times for no reason. May died because a storm came up and she was there, as many have before her and will again. And Aubrey gave May an extraordinary silk shawl on her last night at home, a wildly extravagant present to a young girl. He had not lost interest in her.

Aunt Mary holds her embroidery to the fading light from the window. 'I dare say it is all quite harmless.'

It is a question. The fog dims against the glass; soon the lamp-lighters will come and Fanny will close the curtains and light the gas before she brings the tea-tray. A coal falls in the fire.

'I cannot say, Aunt Mary.'

There was harm. Harm was done. She leans forward to hold her chilled hands to the fire, to feel the blood bloom against constricted vessels.

a knife like a shard of light

He dreams again of falling. He leans as he has often done on the parapet, taking pleasure in the explosion of waves against the stone tower a hundred feet below. The Atlantic hammers on the granite blocks and foam leaps high, but under his feet the structure stands firm. He looks down and then something happens, something breaks, and there is time to feel falling, to know his own end, to regret, before—

He wakes always now a few minutes before the gong sounds and the chanting begins. He lies breathless, sweaty, but knows that in a moment his bones will ring in darkness with the morning prayer. He remembers the foxes again; a more superstitious person, a Japanese person, might imagine that they haunted him, that they had crept along in his shadow, when his clumsy foreign gaze was distracted, and glided now low through the house by night, shaping his dreams. If spirit foxes can travel by train, will they also board the ship with him?

The sound comes.

The air and the earth reverberate. The voices rise. Somewhere very near, over a wall or behind a gate, there are men who spend their lives in beauty, shaven-headed boys growing up in the service of silence. And he is not dead. He has not fallen, not yet, and there is another day beginning. As always, he lies still while the sound pulses through his ribs and his skull, and then he sits up, hugs his knees in the dark. Behind the shutters, the sky will be paling; another day closer to leaving Japan.

Makiko must have just slipped back to the main house, because he burns his fingers on the teapot and steam rises when he lifts the saucer-lid of the cup of miso soup. Cubes of tofu bob above the green seaweed and in the other bowl his rice is topped with a fried egg. He tucks his feet under his knees and edges forward to the table, pours tea and sips his soup while the tea cools. He is glad to be without witnesses while he eats an egg with chopsticks. He should write to Ally, try to tell her about Kyoto in the snow, about days that begin with ringing in the dark and with green tea in a grey bowl. He must take home some green tea but he knows it won't taste the same on the other side of the globe. He might write to Makoto: *I must thank you again for your hospitality and for the privilege of your introduction to this beautiful country. I hope the new bridge progresses?* He should write also to his mother, and probably to De Rivers who will like to have a description of the workshops where his acquisitions, his silks and his inlaid wood, are being made. *Beautiful girls bow over their work as delicate fingers coax gold thread through the bright satin.* But it is men, so far, who do this work, men with stooped shoulders and hands stained and calloused by years of stitching and dyeing.

Tatsuo is taking him to a market today, a place where second-hand goods are sold. De Rivers wants a chest or a cupboard, something he can use to hold the carved toggles and medicine boxes Tom is to buy. None of your modern rubbish, he says. Something really old. Something that was sitting under one of those curved roofs when the country was still closed, something that belonged to one of those samurai lords with two swords and a topknot. Tom has already explained, more than once, that ancient Japanese furniture is a contradiction in terms, but it's not what De Rivers wants to hear. I hope you do not mean to suggest that the inducement you have been offered for this work is insufficient, and look forward to hearing that my orders have been fulfilled. Tom is not without hope that he may find a chest, and understands exactly why someone would want to fill it with the toggles meant to fasten a purse to the wearer's clothing. Although he has noticed an almost complete absence of personal mannerisms, of fidgeting, in the Japanese, the toggles seem conceived for fiddling and stroking, for touching as a man might finger his keys or the small change in his pocket. They are palm-sized, made always of cool and shiny wood or ivory, and shaped as amulets or familiars, small animals or homuncules, occasionally lucky beans or fruit. As Japanese men assume Western garb, there is less call for such devices. He has so far refrained from buying anything for himself, not wanting a part in De Rivers' greed, not wanting to behave as if Japan is something that can be bought and taken home in the hold of a ship, but there is great attraction in the idea of walking the streets of Falmouth and London, sitting in his chair at home, with a *netsuke* in his pocket. Since he must indeed return.

The soup has cooled while he did his best with the egg. He tries to drink it, but the lukewarm salty fluid reminds him too much of having a cold. He pours more tea and sips: it has brewed too long and turned bitter. Tatsuo should be here in a moment, but he will start his letters while he waits. No point in sitting idle in an empty house.

The sky has cleared, and sits like a blue bowl upturned over the mountains ringing the city. Black cobbles are beginning to show through the snow like rocks breaking the surface of a pond, but the swooping roofs and tiled walls are still quilted white. As they walk, the sun comes over the mountaintop, plain and swift as the turning tide, and before his eyes shadows form and strengthen on the ground and the ice crystals begin to sparkle in the snow. He screws up his eyes; it is too bright.

At first the streets were quiet, shutters still closed and only a few men hurrying, collars turned high and footsteps muffled by snow, their wraps blots of indigo in a black and white scene. Now there are pairs of women under the paper umbrellas and the occasional bundled child holding its mother's hand, and then squealing and two small boys conducting a snowball fight across the street, getting in the way of an elderly woman shuffling cautiously down the middle where the snow is thin. He has not seen much play, he thinks, or at least not much of what can be recognised as childhood.

'Tatsuo?' he asks. 'Do the children play sports here? Ball games, races?'

Tatsuo checks his pace. 'It is a new thing in the schools. They make exercises, to build strength.'

Of course, sword-fighting, wrestling, the traditional ways that must be upheld in the face of change. 'But for fun?' he asks. 'For pleasure?'

Tatsuo shakes his head, uncomprehending or perhaps pushed beyond what he can explain in English. Tom misses Makoto.

There are more people, and then more again, and they turn a corner and the street ends in stairs running up to a great gateway, its canopy seeming heavier than the wooden poles could support. Those immense roofs are hollow, he knows, and lighter than they look, but even so in an earthquake one would not want—

'Through here, please,' says Tatsuo.

'Here? Isn't this a temple?'

Tatsuo bows. 'Buddhist temple. Yes. This way, please.'

Everyone is going this way. Tom joins the crowd, behind a family with an infant riding in a pouch on the mother's back and two older children walking either side of their father, holding the man's hands and looking up into his face as he speaks to them. He does not remember his own father, cannot conjure a memory even when his mother insists that he must recall the stories his father used to tell him and the songs his father taught him to sing. His mother does not speak of his father's death. It was quick, she said once. He went fast. Tom has always assumed, been allowed to assume, that it was an illness, a fever, that took his father. The Japanese father rests his hand on his son's head as they walk.

The gravelled courtyard between the gateway and the temple building is filled with canopied stalls, around which people cluster like rooks to trees. Tom turns to Tatsuo. The moneylenders in the temple, he thinks. Are Buddhist monks not sworn to poverty? Stones that are probably statues loom over the throng from square plinths.

'This way, please. There is someone you meet.'

He glimpses pots set out on the tables, tea sets and sake cups. Above another stall, a purple kimono patterned with silver fish is raised in the sunshine and a blue one lies at its feet. There are painted scrolls, a mass of the indecipherable, and then what he triumphantly identifies as hair ornaments, the sort that waver like antenna above the lacquered perfection of blue-black hair. Absolutely not a gift for Ally, whose soft mouse hair is forever slipping over her neck and ears, escaping her plait and spreading across her pillow as she sleeps. He remembers it in his fingers, the warmth of her head in its roughness. He remembers lifting it to bring his lips to her neck. He will write to her about the hair ornaments. Light flashes from another stall, straight lines of iron and steel. Blades; swords and knives. He pauses, his gaze drawn to the edges in the cold sun. Wasn't it only samurai who were allowed swords? He wonders where these have been, what hands wielded them. So sharp, Professor Baxter said, that you'd never know your head had been cut off. So sharp it wouldn't hurt until later. A shiver traces his spine; bring on the modern age, he thinks. Hail progress.

Tatsuo is waiting for him. 'All right? Here. Look. *Kiyumizu* ware. Very beautiful.'

Tom approaches. Rice bowls, if they are meant for any purpose, although it is hard to imagine anything so delicate subject to heat and spoons and chopsticks. A leaf pattern reminds him of the crimson and gold on the floor of the mountain forest, winter bamboo is almost black against the bone-white china, the blossoms' pink is so pale that at first he does not see it. A seasonal set.

'These,' Tatsuo says.

Not the rice bowls, obviously, on reflection, too useful for De Rivers' interest, but a teapot and a set of bowls, thin as snail shells, grass-green and gilt. He bends to look: overlapping green bamboo, jewelled with bright birds and butterflies barely the size of a raindrop. The paintbrush must comprise no more than half a dozen bristles.

The stallholder says something. 'You may touch.'

They don't invite touch. It is their fragility that is remarkable, the evidence that something so brittle and thin, so fine in its miniaturism, remains capable of physical integrity from one hour to the next. He buys them, for De Rivers, and has them sent to the house. He buys three fans, and a parasol on which chrysanthemums seem to have fallen like rain. A lacquer tray, deep and shiny as still water, across which golden birds fly, and a matching box with tiny drawers that would hold stamps or, just about, cuff links. Then he goes back to the sword-seller and buys a knife, probably for himself, a knife like a shard of light against his thumb.

the lilies of the field

The first snowdrops are in bud in the Square's garden, a cluster sheltered in the rockery on a south-facing rise. There are leaf-buds swelling on twigs and birdsong in the air. In Cornwall, probably, there are already camellias and even the first daffodils, and still Ally is in London. Still she has done nothing. Aunt Mary does not understand, even Annie does not understand, that there is nothing restful in idleness. She reads, calling it 'work', and she walks, calling it 'exercise'. She reads badly, distracted by the flight of a bird past the window, by the wind in the trees, the passage of carts and carriages, and when she looks back at the book she cannot remember the last five pages. The hours pass more and more slowly and the days faster and faster. Life could slip away, she thinks. In a few weeks there will be bluebells under these trees. She could find herself forty and then fifty, hiding between her qualifications the truth that she is no more than any other superfluous woman eating at the table and lodging under the roof of whichever man finds himself burdened by family obligation to support her. Ally closes her eyes and tries to draw a deep breath of the air, to catch, despite the smoke of a million coal fires, the exhalation of things growing and stirring in the earth. Tom will be home before they die again.

She turns back towards the house. She must do something, get something done. She has been speaking of writing a paper, perhaps something for the new *British Journal of Asylum Medicine*, but the truth is that so far she has not even a title, only the vague idea that there is a widely recognised category of patients who appear to pass their entire adult lives recovering when confined and relapsing upon release. She wonders if anyone has tried to invent at least a temporary refuge from both the madhouse and the mad home, a compromise between an institution and a family. A place where people chose to be, not a place of confinement. A convent, an Oxford college, only with a less formal hierarchy, without vows. A place of healing, for those who know where to go afterwards, but perhaps also a permanent abode without the stigma of an asylum for those whose need for a sanctuary will not pass. And if asylum medicine is beginning to concern itself with treatment as well as containment, it is time to learn what makes people sane as well as what makes them mad. Mad-doctors must question their assumption that sanity is obvious, requiring no study. There are few settings less appropriate for scientific experiment than a county asylum, where the variables are beyond anyone's control, but a smaller setting, with a few carefully selected patients ... An institution where the damage of homes, of domestic life, can be undone, or at least healed. A place where the shape of sanity might emerge. It's an idea, not an essay, and claiming to be thinking about writing hardly qualifies as work. She needs a job, a position with set hours and a salary. She needs time to pass without having to push every minute up a hill.

Really, Alethea, you dare to complain of inactivity when you know the deadly overwork of your fellow beings, treated

as no more than beasts of burden to keep the looms and spinners working? You who have witnessed children sick and dying
because their fathers have no work can yet bemoan your own
boredom?

Oh, stop. Go away. She finds herself sometimes wishing
Mamma dead, going even so far as to imagine poison or, more
satisfactorily, a knife to the heart, blood spreading like spilt
milk across the floor, but increasingly she is just tired of
Mamma. Bored by her. Tom's latest letter says that Japanese
peasants believe that the symptoms of madness result from
possession by demonic foxes. It is in some ways an appealing
idea, to blame the foxes, to imagine demons in one's head. But
she must not make Mamma into a demon, nor allow herself
to fall prey to any form of superstition. The clock downstairs
whirs as it does before striking. It is almost time for tea.

She opens the door to hear laughter from the drawing
room, and to see Annie's coat and hat on the stand. Annie
must be back from Bath, where she has been covering the
absence of another doctor at the Lying-In Hospital. Annie has
always liked the slow chattiness of Obstetrics, the narratives
sustained over weeks and months and the frequent happy end-
ings. Annie doesn't worry that female obstetricians are just
glorified midwives, their acceptance a way of making sure that
women doctors don't threaten the central expertise of men.
Naturally a woman doctor will be especially suited to the crises
of women's lives, Annie says, and anyway if one obtains a
family's trust at the birth of the first child one is almost guar-
anteed the role of their primary physician; it is an excellent
beginning to a practice of one's own. But Annie does not seem
to want a practice.

Ally hangs up her coat beside Annie's and rubs her cold
hands.

'Ally?' calls Aunt Mary.

The door opens and there is Annie, all shiny hair and blue gown and skin that looks powdered whether it is or not. She kisses Ally's cheek; the drift of floral scent and the brush of warm lips on a cold face.

'Ally! How are you?'

Annie stands back and looks Ally up and down, sees her three-year-old skirt and jacket showing signs of wear, her blouse with its dated frilled collar.

'I'm well, Annie. And you?'

'Tired. I don't wonder Dr Kerry went away for a month. But there were some good cases. Triplets, Al, can you believe? The smallest one a good four pounds, and all doing well.'

She's studying Ally as she speaks.

'The poor mother,' Ally says.

Annie holds out her hand, inviting Ally in. 'She came through it nicely. The tea's just made. And there are crumpets.'

Aunt Mary, nursing a cup of tea on a saucer in her lap, a gilt-edged plate holding a slice of sponge cake on the occasional table beside her chair, smiles up at Ally. 'There you are. A nice walk? It's getting chilly out there.'

Ally sometimes thinks Aunt Mary and Annie would get along beautifully without her. Buttered crumpets to ward off an early nightfall.

She sits down. 'There are snowdrops. In the square.'

Annie pours a cup of tea and hands it to her, remembering lemon-not-milk and no sugar. 'They were out in Brighton. And there are palm trees! From certain angles one could think oneself in France.'

Annie and her family have been to France several times, to the Normandy coast in summer and once to Paris, where Annie's father offered each of his daughters an evening gown from an atelier of which even Ally has heard.

'There are palm trees in Falmouth,' Ally says. She cups her hands around the porcelain tea cup and lets the heat sear her fingers. 'I think I know what you mean, Annie. It doesn't feel quite like England either, not until you notice the red-brick houses behind the bougainvillea. And it's so far away. Further than France.'

She remembers flowers like scarlet irises that grow in the corner of the stone wall and the garden path, the profusion of the fuchsia's magenta bells cascading through cast-iron fences along the terraces high on the hill, and beyond the town gorse flaming along the cliff tops and upland heath. She remembers the woods that in a few weeks will be dusted and then blanketed with bluebells. The bluebells are quite startling, said Tom, and when you see them you will know that I am on my way home. She sips her tea, feels the heat trace her oesophagus. She needs to go back, she thinks. It will be better there.

'When you and Tom are settled again, may I come and visit?' asks Annie. 'Cornwall always sounds so romantic.'

She and Annie could walk on the coast path while Tom is out at work. In summer, they could picnic on the rocks of Castle Beach and perhaps take the train to St Ives where Annie would enjoy the cobbled lanes and the ancient chapel on the hilltop.

'It can rain for weeks. And some of those picturesque fishermen are desperately poor. But I'd love you to visit, Annie, truly.'

She will return to Falmouth, and the summer will come again and the sea sparkle in the early mornings. She has not thought properly of Tom, of his body and his smile, for a long time. She must write to him, now he is settled in Kyoto, and describe the snowdrops and the news of George's success at Cambridge. For the first time in weeks, she thinks of the globe, of Tom there on the other side of it. There is snow in Kyoto still, but the days are lengthening as they are here and the skies are blue over the white mountains. She turns the ring on her left hand, which fits better than it did a few weeks ago. *With this ring, I thee wed. With my body, I thee worship.* Really, Alethea, are you fallen so far as to find justification in your marital relations?

'Are you quite well, Ally?'

Aunt Mary sets down her cup and lifts her feet from her footstool. 'I believe I forgot to ask Mrs Hayfield about the soufflé. Do excuse me, girls.'

Girls no more, Ally thinks. They watch Aunt Mary's upright back, her bustled green skirt, cross the room.

Annie sits forward. 'Ally? You looked suddenly pained.'

Ally closes her eyes. Annie won't question her sanity, won't send her to the asylum. Probably.

'It is Mamma's voice. Her remarks. It's not an auditory hallucination, I don't imagine that her voice makes sound, but she is always in my thoughts. Questioning my motives. I cannot decide to go for a walk without reflecting that perhaps it is an act of self-indulgence to fritter away my time so, or then to remain at home without reproaching myself for idleness. If I do not eat I think that perhaps I am seeking attention and excuse for inactivity by remaining weakened and thin, but if I enjoy Aunt Mary's table I am guilty of sensual indulgence. And I cannot tell any longer which thoughts are mine and which hers.' Which reason and which madness, or whether it is her own ideas or Mamma's that represent a rational mind.

Annie reaches for Ally's hand and then thinks better of it, but Ally wouldn't mind, not just now. 'She is a terrible woman.'

Ally shakes her head. 'No, Annie. She is capable of great kindness and endless, selfless work for the good of those who receive nothing from anyone else. She has given her whole life to the untiring service of the most degraded women and looked for nothing, no gratitude or appreciation, in return.'

'I know. But it seems that the cost of such dedication has been paid by you and May, and your Papa.'

Ally's throat hurts. 'No. No, we must not say that. That a woman must choose between her work and her family obligations. That she must devote herself first and always to her husband and children. No-one says that of men. She has a right to her work.'

Annie shrugs. 'To be sure. But also an obligation to her children, and indeed the obligation that we all share: to be kind to each other. There is no exemption, short of insanity, from kindness. Tell me, Ally, do you intend a large family?'

'No. You know that.'

'If you have a child, will you employ a nurse?'

'You know that too. But Annie, our work is paid. It allows for the employment of nurses. And May and I had Jenny, and then went to school. Mamma was not neglectful.'

Not yet, it isn't paid. Not in Ally's case.

'Oh, Al. She was negligent. At best, negligent. Whatever her virtues elsewhere. It isn't the point, the politics of women's pay. Tell me more about hearing her voice.'

But it is the point, Ally thinks. Annie is able to say otherwise only because her domestic life is easy, because her parents appear to live without recrimination. There is no separation between what Annie calls the politics of women's pay and the formation of women's minds. Mamma was trained to philanthropy, not to a professional life. Mamma was taught to set no price or value on her own time and effort, to understand her own labours merely as the justification of her existence. *The labourer is worthy of her hire*, Ally thinks, though she wishes her mind would not produce a Biblical text as the last word on any given subject. It is not as if Mamma's own girlhood equipped her with the opportunities she made sure to give to Ally and May. It is not as if Mamma had the choices, or indeed the Dutch rubber device, available to Ally. Mamma also is a creature of circumstance, of history and location, as are we all. Mamma works, Ally sees, because she does not believe that she deserves to live. Mamma justifies herself by work. And so does Ally. There must be better metaphors for life than money, than numbers. Consider the lilies of the field, Mamma. How they grow, they toil not, neither do they spin.

'Her voice is disabling. It makes any action impossible. If I read, I am guilty of indolence but if I do not read I reveal the trivial mind she always feared for me. If I take tea with Aunt Mary I am indulging in gossip and gluttony but if I keep to my room it is because I wish to draw attention to myself. I think I need something to do. Some work, something real. I have too much time for self-reflection and self-questioning.'

And you believe, Alethea, that you should work not for the good of others but because it will be of benefit to you? For amusement, for diversion from the burdens of leisure? Think then of all those women laboured to exhaustion and looking only to death for release and say again that you want work as a rest from self-reflection.

It doesn't matter, she thinks. It doesn't matter why I work, if the work is in itself useful. It doesn't really matter whether I take a walk out of boredom with the comfort of the fireside or because physical exercise is healthful; there is no recording angel, Mamma, noting each cup of tea not taken, each skirt patched and dragged out another season. Denying myself butter on my bread, even if I go out that very morning and give the butter to the nearest soup kitchen, will do nothing to alter the fate of all the children of this country born and yet to be born into grinding poverty. For that one would need a different kind of change, a revolution. For that one would need to turn the nation upside down, and perhaps that is what Mamma should be doing, if the hungry are to be fed, the children of the masses educated and the stain of poverty wiped from the land. But that is not what Mamma wants. As the nurses could not bear to see that the mad are just like us, only sadder, so Mamma cannot bear to see that the poor are just like us, only poorer.

'Ally?'

Ally meets Annie's eyes. Dear Annie, who is able to accept her manifest blessings without opening an existential account, and to do the work to which she is called without holding a running trial in her head.

'I was thinking about Mamma, and my patients in the asylum. I was thinking that everything could be different.'

Annie reaches towards her again. 'Many things could be different. But Ally, are you sure you want to stay in mad-doctoring? Forgive me, but it does not always seem perhaps the best line for you. To be so constantly exposed to such distress, to pass your days among those who – well—'

'Those who hear voices?' Ally asks. 'Those who cannot tell their own minds, who cannot walk but cannot be still, cannot work and cannot bear idleness?'

Annie gasps. 'No, Ally. Please. I did not say that. Dear Al. I did not.'

Ally looks up at her. 'And you did not think it? Come, Annie. Do you think I have not questioned my own reason? I found myself hiding in the bushes in the park on Christmas Day for fear of my parents' pursuit. I wept in the corridors of the asylum and shouted at the nurses that we are all more like the patients than we know. A mind can be aware of its own danger. I have perhaps not been mad but we cannot say that I have been without the symptoms of a deranged mind.'

And I hurt myself, she thinks, I remembered that only pain

228

sings louder in my head than Mamma's voice. I remembered that sometimes the pain I cause myself can eclipse the harm she does to me. But also that I hurt myself for her, because I do as she wishes and she wishes me harm.

This time Annie takes her hand. 'Very few of us reach the ends of our lives without times of derangement. Through grief, or rage, or encounters with the spite or ill-will of others. I did visit the asylum, you know, last summer after you said it was every physician's obligation to know what they are like. The saddest cases were not the most mad. There were those to whom delusion would be a blessed release, who were tormented by the knowledge of their own damaged intellects. But you did leave. You came here, and now you are better, I think? It was a breakdown of the sort to which fine minds are subject.'

Ally squeezes the hand.

If she were to be confined, she thinks, Annie would still visit her.

If she were to be discharged, Aunt Mary would still take her in.

There are people who like her whether she walks or reads, takes tea or stays upstairs. They do not love her for her work, or for her prize, but for herself. She cannot see why but she can see that it is true.

'I dare say they didn't show you the back wards?' she asks.

'I am ashamed to say I didn't ask. I wanted to get out. The smell, and all those locks. I couldn't work in such a place. I like to be with women having babies, and I'll keep working in the lying-in hospitals but I like it when they have flowers in their rooms afterwards and a good fire and everyone happy that they are doing well.'

'And when they don't do well? Or the babies die?'

Annie looks down at their linked hands. 'Then I do my best.

229

I try to say the right words and I go home and tell Papa what happened. Sometimes he tells me his cases too.' She looks up. 'Papa and Henry have asked if I would join their practice. Henry says if they cannot beat women doctors they must join them.'

Henry is Annie's brother-in-law, Ally remembers. He used to work at St Michael's hospital and never liked the idea of women doctors.

'You will accept?'

Annie nods. 'I can keep on living at home. No worries about house-keeping or anything. I will be quite free to work. And of course to go to the theatre and see my friends. I have spent quite enough nights in boarding houses and hospital bedrooms.'

And what when your parents die, Ally thinks. What when there is no longer anyone to look after you, to see to the laundry and the cooking, the cleaning and the chimney-sweeping and the paying of bills so that you can attend the rich of West London in their pleasant homes and go to the opera in the evenings? But then Annie, probably, will move in with her sister and brother-in-law and be welcome there. Envy is corrosive. Annie is her friend. And Annie has chosen – several times – not to marry, to remain unentangled, to depend as she so easily does upon her family and her friends for company and affection. *If therefore thine eye be single, thy whole body shall be full of light.* We make our choices and then we live with them, but nothing that we can choose exonerates us from the need for kindness. Ally draws a deep breath.

'I'm very happy for you,' she says. 'It is just right. A perfect plan. Your Papa must be delighted.'

Annie sits back, nods. 'He is pleased. And Mamma is glad that she will not lose all her daughters. Well, I mean—'

Annie has remembered May, the other kind of loss.

'I know, Annie. It's all right. She deserves contentment, your Mamma.'

'Don't think like that. Deserving. No-one deserves loss. It's a kind of religious melancholy, Ally, can't you see it? You believe yourself damned, and you despair, and then you chastise yourself for despairing and sink further. And if you feel a little better you condemn yourself for pride and luxury. A classic case. You'll never win.'

She can hear Aunt Mary on the stairs. Religious melancholy. Patients who swing from believing themselves unpardonable, which is the sin of despair and leads to eternal damnation, to believing themselves saved, which is the sin of pride and leads to eternal damnation. Then they despair again because they are damned again. Annie has said this, things like this, to her before, but for the first time Ally thinks she understands. We cannot achieve justification by works. We cannot earn our lives, our place on the green earth. Life is a gift and not a contract. According to Annie.

Aunt Mary puts her head around the door. 'Annie, I hope you will stay to dinner? There's no-one coming, we don't dress.'

Annie stands up. 'I would be delighted, but Mamma is expecting me. She has guests and I promised to help. Thank you for the lovely tea.'

Ally helps Annie to put on her coat, watches Annie's face in the mirror as she wraps her scarf and pins her hat. For the first time, Ally returns Annie's embrace as she leaves, and the two women hold each other in the hall, Annie's hat brushing Ally's cheek, as in the fanlight the clouds drift past the moon.

gold flakes float in lacquer

His hand reaches towards the box. The silk wrapping-cloth, the *furoshiki*, has fallen back like a discarded gown around the gleaming curves.

The man bows and lifts the box to his touch. Only Tom's fingertips graze the lacquer, the gold. It is as if one could touch warm ice. In the grey winter light filtering through the paper screens, the golden leaves, the freckled fruits and the plump birds, pheasants or partridges, seem lit from within, glow like candle flames. *On the fifth day of Christmas*. The black background gleams deep as a winter lake.

'*Kodaiji maki-e*,' murmurs Tatsuo at his elbow. '*Nashiji*. Apple – no – pear skin. Gold flakes float in lacquer. I think the fruit is called persimmon?'

Tom withdraws his hand. 'Suspended,' he says. 'Suspended in the lacquer.'

Tatsuo bows. 'Is two hundred years old. Very beautiful.'

Tom cannot take his gaze from it, the bronze speckles in the golden persimmons, the way the birds' breasts and necks echo the curves of the fruit and then the contrast between the trailing away of the feathered tails and the firmness of heads and wings, all shining gold. He imagines Ally's face if he were to bring her such a thing, undress it on the table in the white cottage's window.

The shopkeeper lifts the lid, disclosing a lacquered interior fitted out as if by a fine ship's carpenter with fretwork and tiny drawers. A workbox, Tom wonders, a jewellery case? A toolbox for some exquisite and miniature craft? But one would not want to store blades and points under such a finish. The man speaks and Tatsuo translates.

'For scent. And the paint of a woman, her face.' He mimes someone painting eyebrows on a shaven forehead and a layer of white on Asian skin.

Tom nods. 'But not for use, surely?'

Tatsuo shrugs. 'Two hundred years past, perhaps.'

'Where does it come from?' It is not a question he likes to ask. He would prefer these objects anonymous, unencumbered by past lives.

Tatsuo speaks again with the shopkeeper and then turns to Tom. 'As usual. There are debts. Money owing, and misfortune. They must sell some things. Old things.'

There is no good reason, Tom has decided, why these stories should be sad. Let the old order, feudalism founded as always on violence, pass away. What rational British man could mourn the end of the samurais' absolute regime, especially given the largely peaceful end of a three-hundred-year reign of terror? If it is now possible for men like Makoto and Tatsuo to learn English, to stand in the presence of their hereditary oppressors and gain power and wealth through knowledge and intelligent work, who could argue that the aristocrats' fall is any loss at all to Japan? And if those who once throve on the labour of others are now reduced to selling their gold lacquer cosmetics boxes to buy rice, who should grieve? Let them learn to labour like other men. Let them learn from

233

their artisans to take pride in good work well done. He remembers a painter saying when Tom looked for his signature that either the quality of the work tells the artist's name or he should be ashamed to associate himself with it. Wolf Rock, he thinks, Skerryvore. No-one needs to sign a lighthouse. But still he feels as if he is filching something, betraying someone, as he listens to Tatsuo's delicate translation of his delicate inquiry about the price of the box. For whatever it costs, it is travelling back to Falmouth with him.

Miss Gillingham's mirror

'Ally? Are you ready?'

Ally puts down her book and stands up. She cannot see what other preparation might be thought necessary. 'Coming, Aunt Mary.'

Aunt Mary's Christmas present to Ally was a breadth of tweed, heathered blue and grey, and the promise that Aunt Mary's dressmaker would make it into a new walking suit. Good tailoring makes anyone feel better, Aunt Mary said, and whatever Elizabeth has to say about trivial minds I notice that most of these New Women have nice clothes. Call it armour if you prefer, Ally, but let me do this for you. Ally remembers Aunt Mary going through the contents of Ally's trunk when she first arrived in London, nineteen and dressed in Mamma's made-over cast-offs and men's boots. Aunt Mary's right about the armour, but Ally's been invalided out of whatever war is being fought. If you are to be interviewed for a position, says Aunt Mary, you will give a better account of yourself in a decent suit. True enough, but Ally has failed, so far, to identify any position for which she would be a plausible candidate. A qualified lady doctor with no experience of paid employment and recent nervous illness seeks professional employment in West Cornwall. Did I not tell you so, Alethea? Did I not warn you of just such an outcome?

Aunt Mary judges the outing grand enough for her new hat, a triumph of form over function whose effect reminds Ally of the hummingbirds in Mr De Rivers' Falmouth house. She looks up as Ally comes down the stairs.

'There you are. I am looking forward to seeing how Miss Gillingham has managed. And James has booked us a table at Quincy's for lunch afterwards.'

Ally fastens her coat and opens the door for Aunt Mary.

'Thank you. You and Uncle James.'

Aunt Mary pats her hand. 'Not at all, my dear, not at all. Here, your hair is coming down.'

Ally stands obedient, hunched, the doorknob in her hand, while Aunt Mary reaches up to replace her hairpins. It's sunny outside, and there are leaf-buds on the branches of chestnut trees bounced by a boisterous wind. The snowdrops in the square are visible from the doorstep.

'That's better.'

They set off, Ally checking her stride to match Aunt Mary's unhurried progress. Aunt Mary looks smaller out of doors. It is not her natural habitat.

'Will we walk all the way, Aunt Mary? It is such a nice morning.'

'All the way to Markham Street? It must be miles!'

Aunt Mary suddenly reminds her of May.

'Perhaps as much as two miles, although I doubt it very much.'

'No, my dear. We will sit down on the bus and very probably take a perfectly comfortable cab home.'

*

Ally is startled by her own appearance in Miss Gillingham's mirror. The tweed is a stronger colour than she, raised by Mamma and accustomed to echo the sober garb of men, would usually choose, a royal blue only just short of Aunt Mary's own favourite peacock palette, and there are flecks of purple as well as grey in it. Almost too strong, she thinks, gazing at herself, almost overwhelming her pale skin, her light brown hair, her blue eyes. And then realises that this thought means that she does know what suits her, that she does have an instinct for her own aesthetic value. Grey matches her eyes, but must not be darker than her hair. Pink and brown make her look dip-dyed, the same colour all over. Green, perhaps, but no stronger than the colour of pears or her pallor will appear unhealthy. Papa's trademark sage colour would be becoming if she could stand it. It is not entirely Mamma's fault that Ally looked shapeless and unkempt all her girlhood; particular attention is required to make a tall pale woman with light hair appear to advantage and it is not attention that Ally herself usually cares to pay. But this suit – if she could wear such a thing every day – . Annie, she thinks, likes clothes, and so does Mrs Butler herself. Aubrey, come to that, or Street; most artists embrace pretentions or particularities of dress. One does not solve the problem of beauty by denouncing it. The new suit murmurs of men's tailoring, the jacket double-breasted and trimmed only with frogging, the skirt cut trim and plain with the suggestion of a bustle at the back, and it fits Ally perfectly, shows that though tall and slim she does have a bosom, a waist. Flaunting yourself in the guise of our poor women of the streets, hisses Mamma, betraying everything I gave you. Ally smooths her hands over her hips, turns and looks back over her shoulder to see her three-quarter profile at full length. Aunt Mary is quite right; so attired, she will indeed give a better account of herself. Looking at her own clothes laid over the chair, she doesn't want to take off the tweed suit, to go back into the world in worn and dated grey, but Miss Gillingham needs to finish the hem and sew the buttons where at the moment Ally is pinned into the waistband and jacket. Next week, Miss Gillingham promises, best leave it till Tuesday to be safe.

Back in her room among the treetops, stayed with sole in cream sauce and then orange pudding ordered for her by Uncle James, Ally looks through the notes she's made of her rather arbitrary reading these last few weeks. How is sanity defined? The mad reside in homes, asylums, institutions. Are families or madhouses more likely to take, or make, a person's mind? There is no research on the capacity for recovery of lunatics confined permanently at home, nor indeed much reliable information about their numbers. If a person can be driven to madness, by what means is she to be driven back to sanity? A place of healing, she thinks, a place of healing and hope for the future as well as a distaste for the past. It is not the first time such ideas have been voiced, but it is, so far as she knows, the first time a doctor has suggested that part of the work of an institution could be to undo the work of the family, that there are sick households as well as sick individuals. Households that can't allow or sustain sanity. She thinks of her patients: Mary Vincent, hurt by her master; Mrs Elsfield, reverting in her old age to the blows and harsh words of her long-dead mother; Mrs Ashton, haunted by perverted grief for her lost brothers. She remembers Margaret Rudge saying that everyone has been hurt but not everyone ends up in the asylum. What distinguishes those who survive their harm from those found to be mad? There are undoubtedly cases of organic brain disease, but there is also a great deal of damage, often passed down from parent to child like Tom's Japanese foxes. Ally gazes out into the branches, on whose winter lines

238

the first leaf-buds are beginning to form. The sky is white, neutral, and from the street below the sounds of activity drift, people going places, moving things, working and coming home. The profession needs a definition of sanity, or needs at least a discussion about the definition of sanity, about the boundaries of grief and rage and pain. The profession needs someone to say that some domestic homes, some families, produce madness not by hereditary organic disorder but by a *modus operandi* that requires the insanity of one or more members. That families can be dangerous. She pushes back the hair from her face, picks up her pen and begins to write. She has things to say, and it is not as if her professional life has anything left to lose.

the fox *inro*

The snow has melted. This morning, every roof and twig dripped as if the whole city had become one of the slow fountains in a courtyard garden and every step left a footprint as if stamped in grey ink, on cobbles now only furred with collapsing crystals of white. All morning he and Tatsuo have walked to the tinkle and sluice of water in bamboo pipes and gutters, purling through the drains and streams, and still he can see through the open screens drips falling from the eaves both here and across the street.

The shop's screen doors are pushed back so the box he's being shown lies in cold sunlight, and whatever heat is generated by the *hibachi* beside the counter does not reach Tom. He wriggles his toes inside his boots. He pulls his fingers out of his gloves' fingers and balls them in his fists.

'Spring, summer, autumn, winter,' says Tatsuo. He steps back so that Tom can see.

Four *inro* lie in a wooden box. Indentations have been carved in the polished *hinoki* for each of them to nest, and their curves rise in a way that reminds Tom of women lying on their backs, bellies and breasts mounded. Four different shapes: a cylinder, gold inlay on black lacquer; a disk with frisking animals – foxes? – carved in red lacquer; a rounded oblong whose corners beg a finger's touch, embellished with pregnant bronze gourds, and a green-and-gold shape like a spinning top or a censer. Each of them has a plaited cord through it, because inro, he has been told, were the Japanese version of pockets, boxes to tie around the waist holding whatever small things a rich man might want during the day, originally seals but later paper prayers or amulets and then medicines or even playing cards. The toggles, netsuke, were used to secure inro to the belt, and each inro has a netsuke umbilically attached: a curled up fox, just the size to nestle in a man's palm. A gourd with a stalk whose hairs are visible in what looks like ivory. A magnolia bud, blousy and peeling, and a tassel for the spinning top, carved so finely that each strand of the plied silk is plain. It crosses his mind to wonder what De Rivers is going to do with such objects, already redundant even in Kyoto, but at the same time his hand is reaching out and he knows the answer. De Rivers is going to possess them. Tom removes his gloves and stuffs them in his pocket.

'May I?' he asks.

The seller lifts the red one from the case with reverent fingers. Tom places it in the palm of his left hand and lets his right index and middle fingers trace the carved foxes. Three weave around each other, the lines of tails and backs and pointed noses making one sweeping curve, and there is another small one sitting, head cocked, nose raised, under the shoulder of the inro. It is perfection, he thinks, the angle of their ears, the quizzical cast of their faces. How can a person carve four perfect foxes on a rounded and hollow shape smaller than his pocketbook? How could another person bear to use such a thing, to have it hanging at his side where it will get knocked and scratched and wet? It would be different, life would be different, if one walked through one's days with a perfect object always at one's side. He lets the fox netsuke crawl into his hand and nestle there.

The dealer holds out his hand for Tom to return the fox inro. Tom gasps. The dealer is breaking it up, sliding it apart. It's made in sections, of course. Not a box but a stack of boxes, held together by the cord through the sides, although there's not a trace of the join, not to the eye or the fingertip, when the five segments are closed, and the inside is as perfectly finished, as smooth and gleaming, as the outside. The merchant turns the pieces through the grey winter light so the inro leans, articulated, and then in one movement of his fingers reassembles it into the solid object Tom was handling. He wants it back, but the man picks up the next one, the spinning top, blows a speck of dust from it and passes it to Tom. The gourds are cold to the touch but the bronze looks warm and the big-bellied shapes, the size of the top joint of Tom's clumsy reddened finger, hold a golden light.

As dusk falls, he comes home. No need, he has persuaded Tatsuo, to escort him back to the house every day, and Tatsuo, who has mentioned a father once and friends twice, seems happy enough to return to the real world, where he doesn't have to try to imagine how Japan might look to a man from somewhere else, where he doesn't have to keep explaining how the paper is made to be waterproof or why some married women still blacken their teeth or what is the point of carving carrots into the shape of miniature carp. Where he doesn't have to assist in the abduction of his country's heirlooms. Tom pushes his hands deep into his pockets and lets his shoulders hunch to close the draught around his neck, but he doesn't hurry. Nightfall is not as slow here as at home, but there is a twilight while people move around the city, from work to home, from the shops to the kitchen, from school back to mother. The raised wooden geta come into their own now, for Tom's trouser cuffs are soaked in the slush and his boots beginning to leak. Two schoolgirls clatter past him, giggling behind their fingers as their split skirts flutter in the wind. Lights flicker and glow behind the window-screens, and the smell of cooking, of soy sauce and miso and fish, begins to drift into the street. Behind each of these wooden screens will be a family gathering around a hibachi, sitting close under the quilt laid over the stove while they share the news of the day, and in the background the bustle of women preparing food. Baths will be heating, and the man of the house changing from European or work clothes into the *yukata* in which he'll spend the evening. There is singing in one house, and children's laughter from another. And later, later they will roll out their futons and lie down together, man and wife and the afterthought of the stove's heat still charcoal-scented in the air, warm enough that quilts can be thrown back, kimono opened, whatever is underneath eased away by gentle hands. He wants Ally.

Except for the red lettering on some of the white paper lanterns still hanging under the awnings of restaurants, the colours are gone by the time he reaches his own street corner, the city blocked in shades of dark. He slides open the front door, steps in, and shoulders it shut behind him. The house closes around him, dark and still, holding him like a heart under its ribs. No-one will see him, there will be no more speech, until Tatsuo calls tomorrow morning.

the key in her coat pocket

Spring advances hour by hour as the train moves south and west. In the park yesterday, there was only the first suggestion of green on the trees, infant leaf-buds still curled tight on the lindens and clenched fingers of furred grey on the horse-chestnuts, the wind still sharp about her ears. In Wiltshire she sees the first bare field dusted with grass-green, surveyed by a scarecrow and a boy with a rattle. In Somerset there are lambs leggy and bounding, grouping together on a rise like schoolgirls to watch the train pass, and the shadows of clouds scudding across the Levels from which the spring floods are receding, leaving the land damp and black and simmering with life. Devon: the kind of Englishness she had not believed until she saw it, thatched cottages whose garden greens, hedge-dark and lawn-bright, are already flecked with daffodil yellow and lily white. Almost, she thinks, almost one can see the cream and eggs on a gingham cloth on the kitchen table. Almost one can smell the lavender scented sheets on the beds and the polish on the wooden furniture made to last. And she thinks, as she always will in the face of comfort or pleasure, of the children in every way stunted by malnutrition and cold in the back streets of Manchester. But one must either devote oneself to total revolution, forsaking all else, or find ways of seeing happiness and beauty without grudge. These are both possible courses of action: she persuaded Annie – in a gloriously unsuitable hat – to accompany her to a lecture on Socialism last week, but for now she has other occupation, ambitions easier to achieve than social justice. She glances across to the compartment's other occupant, a man who boarded the train at Reading and has been asleep since Castle Cary. His mouth has fallen open and his head, wobbly as a new-born's, settled at last against the partition at an angle that will cause him pain for the rest of the day. She feels in her bag for Dr Crosswyn's letter, which she has been carrying as a kind of talisman, a passport that offers, after such a long period of limbo, justification for her presence, or at least, if justification is not required, permission to call herself a doctor again.

She unfolds the letter. *I meant to write earlier to congratulate you on the publication of your excellent paper,* he writes, *but the delay means that I now also make a proposition on which I hope you will look favourably if you are still at liberty and intending to return to this part of the country. Partly as a result of your essay and the attention it has received, I have been able to persuade the Committee to open a Female Convalescent Home, to be established in Flushing where the patients will have opportunity to enjoy and indeed rehearse the amenities of Falmouth while remaining visible and, one might say, secure on the outskirts of a village.* Crosswyn does not say so, but he is thinking that Falmouth town offers too many means of escape from exactly the normal life to which the patients are to be returned. Ships bound for blue water, bars, an endless procession of sailors with money in their pockets and fire in their bellies. The stone walls of the docks, dropping fifty feet into cold water, and the dark cliffs on Pendennis Point and over Castle Beach. Mineshafts hidden in the woods under brambles and bluebells, trains rounding a winding track twice an hour until well after dusk, and enough people lost or wandering, in the wrong county or country or continent, that no-one notices another stranger. But there's one road to Flushing village, a settlement mostly of those who have made their money and retreated from Falmouth to live in peaceful gentility, and Crosswyn's right that Flushing is a better place to relearn the ways of respectable sanity. *We require a Medical Director and I am delighted that the Committee authorises me to make haste to offer you the position. I do not doubt that you have received several offers since the publication of your essay but I venture to hope that your connections in this county may favour us.* Whether Ally is the best person to teach these ways is, as neither Annie nor Aunt Mary could resist suggesting, a different matter. Are you quite sure such a position will really suit you, darling? Only you have made such progress with your health this spring, we would not like to see you unwell again as you were at Christmas. It is my work, she told Aunt Mary. It is what I do, thinking about madness. And it was not my work at the asylum that made me ill. Aunt Mary did not point out that if Ally had not had to leave the asylum she would not have been in Manchester in the first place. Annie was more direct: Al, it's the last place you should be. Come and work with me. Join our practice. Deliver some babies. Set the children's broken bones, visit their mumps and measles and see their mothers through bronchitis in the winter. Look after the neurasthenic girls if you really must. Let some kindly man prepare farmers' wives to go back to their kitchens and servant girls back to their work. Ally remembered Mary Vincent and shook her head. No, Annie, thank you. Of course I will miss you greatly but my life is in Cornwall now and I have chosen my work. Who better to help such patients than someone who has strayed near their path herself? And we all, really, have personal reasons for what we do, however we dress our desires and motivations in the language of our profession. You keep happy families happy and I attend sick minds. Come and visit, if you want to see how I do.

The line runs beside the River Exe, flowing wide and fast. Fir trees mass, protecting a gentleman's residence of the last century from the noise of the train and passengers' curious gaze. The gentleman's lawns, punctuated by flights of shallow stone steps and bits of statuary, roll down to the river, where he has a Palladian boathouse and swans. Ally tucks the letter back into her bag. The edges of Exeter begin, and the grey stone cathedral raised high over the redbrick terraces and tiled roofs. She will go back to Truro Cathedral, she thinks, and see how it is coming along. It is a rare thing, to see a cathedral built.

There is another letter in her bag, one written a few days ago amid the business of packing and preparation and not posted. It is better, she decided, to maintain contact with Mamma and Papa, for them to know her address. Otherwise they become monsters in her head, wolves and ogres from whom she must hide as prey from a predator. They are not gods, not embodiments of power, but haunted beings like herself. She does not wish to be prey. She does not wish to go in fear. *Dear Mamma and Papa, I write to tell you that I am returning to Cornwall to take up a salaried position as Medical Director of the Truro Asylum Female Convalescent home.* She devoted some thought, some uncertainty, to 'salaried.' See, Mamma, I have paid work at last, I am independent of you and of the scholarship committee and of Uncle James and even, since it concerns you, of my husband. See, Mamma, the world judges me worth the air I breathe, the food I eat, the roof under which I shelter. But these proofs suggest that Ally accepts Mamma's logic, that even now she hopes to appease. She wants both to triumph over Mamma according to Mamma's own rules and to deny

Mamma's understanding of the world. It is one of the reasons why the letter has not been posted. *I am sorry for the distress and inconvenience at Christmastime.* No, don't apologise. Mamma will hear an acceptance of culpability rather than the wish that things had been different, that Ally had been braver earlier. *I do not expect that we will meet again soon* (don't come, don't come to get me, not by word or thought or deed) *but when we do* (don't be angry with me, don't read this letter as further evidence of my madness) *I hope it will be under happier circumstances* (I hope that if I avoid you for long enough you will learn to treat me as a civilised adult. I hope that you believe in my good will – even I have little reason for it – because if you do not believe me good-willed you continue to know me mad and bad). It is hopeless. There are things that should be said, but no way of saying them, no form of words that does not require, or even contain, instant contradiction. No form of words that does not say that Ally is deranged or dishonest or both. The train whistles, shrieks and halts on Platform Four at Exeter.

It is the next few miles Ally likes best, where the line runs under the red cliffs and sometimes waves breaking against the sea-wall send spray splattering against the carriage windows. The sea, again, at last. The waves are brisk and white, sparkling under the sun, the water a rough tumbled blue, and out to sea a backwards-leaning ship scrawls a horizontal line of smoke across the spring sky. Despite her brief intimation of May's hair drifting on the water as her body sinks, despite the way May's skirts and petticoats swell and rise about her dead face in Ally's mind, she feels herself steady at the sight of the open sea like a bird settling onto a current of air, gliding open-winged at last between water and sky.

The branch line train is waiting at Truro and she crosses the platform with everyone else, glancing down the line to the guard's van to make sure her trunk is being moved. She unwinds the scarf she tied as the train stopped, her body schooled to expect outside to be cold. It's not cold. Even the wind has spring on its breath, green growth and soft rain. She draws a deep breath before climbing into the Falmouth train.

From the window she sees the cattle-market, and behind it the hill leading to the asylum. In a few days she will go back there, up the lane and along the drive to the portico, to the double front door and the tiled hall, greeting William, who has seen madness and sanity and treated them just the same. She will go back to Ward Four, and see if Mrs Elsfield has made it through the winter. Could Dr Crosswyn be persuaded to regard Mrs Elsfield as curable? (Is it possible, or desirable, to cure Mrs Elsfield of the asylum, and is it necessary to count her invisible companions manifestations of madness?) Smoke rising from the great tower at Bissoe mine, and the land scarred and scoured orange and brown, tunnelled and churned and flooded with strange green water, and then the Methodist church at Perranwell, its spire reaching as if to exceed the enfolding valley. Gorse in yellow bloom. Kissing's in fashion, Tom liked to say, when the gorse is in bloom. Perranwell Station, and a large woman with a basket waiting under the clock, the station-master in piped jacket and peaked cap straight-backed as if on parade. The train jerks, and is off again. Open fields, woodland – daffodils – and then the viaduct above Penryn, the road and the grand stone buildings cascading down to the estuary. Blue water again, the tide so high that the boats moored to the groyne at Flushing are almost at the windows of their owners' houses.

Here, then, and now: homecoming. The lightening of her very bones, the slowing of her dancing heart as the air of this place fills her lungs and her blood. The wind off the sea, the watery colours of a summer night in the far west where nightfall is postponed almost until morning. It is home, she thinks. This is where all shall be well, although she knows it is not true, that there is no such place on earth and that particular difficulties await her in this return. She arranges for the trunk to be delivered, calm as if she is just an off-season visitor, here for a week's sea air or sketching while the hotels are cheap. She walks, not the shortest route but the one that takes her down Killigrew Street, past Jacob's Ladder and home along Dunstanville where the ships rest at their buoys with folded sails and the water mirrors the hillside, the rocks and trees. The Greenbank Hotel, last and first night's rest on land, in England, for professional men going blue water, to America and Australia, to Jamaica and Ceylon and Singapore. There are daffodils under the monkey-puzzle tree in the captain's garden, tulips growing out of the stone urns by the neighbour's wrought iron gate. And the turn up the stone-flagged ope, under the limestone archway to the white cottage, the air now heavy with falling dusk and the house waiting, behind the pink-blooming camellia bushes and the ancient holly tree. The key in her coat pocket, where it has been all winter.

reaching out to touch her palm

The dreams came again. A shipwreck, this time, and Tom guilty of leaving before the end, taking a place in a lifeboat while there were still passengers, women, screaming on the deck. Cold water smacked his head, filled his ear, and he struggled and clung, seeing from the peaks of the waves the masts broken off like fallen trees, knowing the depth under his senseless feet, knowing how far there is to sink. He wakes in darkness, before the chanting and the gong, and lies in the silence, feeling the house too small around him. In England it will be lunchtime, broad daylight and time to get back to work for the afternoon. In England Ally will be sitting over the end of lunch with Aunt Mary, the end of last night's pudding – apple pie, perhaps, or marmalade dumpling – still on the table while Aunt Mary speaks of the last concert or party and Ally thinks about the frailties of the human mind or the limits of charity. It is no longer terribly cold. He pushes back the quilt and walks through the dark to the top of the stairs, finds the first polished wooden step with his foot and the rail with his hand. Downstairs is in darkness, as always except in the middle of the day, and he goes down the stone step to the front door, the bare earth of the entrance hall soft and dry underfoot, and pushes the door open far enough to see out. Dawn is near, the eastern sky pale, and the air damp with dew and the smell of spring. He reaches for his coat and shoes and steps out into the street.

There are three people out already, hurrying hunched – to work so early? To buy breakfast? He closes the door behind him. It's still too dark to tell what the weather will be, but the sky feels low and the cobbles are greased with dew. The three people are going north, which is also the way to the hills where it would be no more than eccentric to head for an early morning walk. He might see the sunrise from a mountainside above Kyoto, the sort of thing regularly recorded by the writers of artistic travel books. He loses sight of the first of his neighbours but the other two turn right at the crossroads and pass the lamp-maker's studio and the grocer, both still shuttered and dark. They disappear between two houses, and when Tom reaches the gap he sees a high stone arch, a gateway fringed by bamboo black in the dim light. He advances and stands in the shadows, the bamboo waving at shoulder height. What is he doing here, standing in an alley with his pyjamas under his coat and his feet bare inside his shoes? Go home, he thinks, go home and take a bath and begin this day again. And then red lanterns bob across the courtyard in the front of him and he sees faces and robes streaming to the temple. The gong sounds as the sun rises and he stands still, neither here or there, like a leper watching the divine service through a hole in the wall.

When he returns to the house he knows as soon as he opens the door that Makiko is there, that there is another being breathing and moving within his walls. She comes from the kitchen to the hallway, her face full of question. *What are you doing? Have you been out all night?* She's wearing the grey kimono with the white birds around the hem and back.

'I went for a walk,' he says.

She bows.

'To see the sunrise. Though it's too cloudy, really. I should try again another day.'

She murmurs something – *yes, it's dull today* or *it's good to start the day with a walk* – and bows again, gestures him in to the house.

'Tatsuo's taking me to see a silk workshop today. They make embroidered hangings, mostly for temples but apparently the Emperor himself has bought some. He gave one as a gift to President Hayes.'

He should stop. Makiko looks worried. A curved tortoise-shell ornament holds up her shining hair and the collar of her kimono has tilted back to frame the curve of her neck. He thinks she is the daughter-in-law of the family whose annex is this house, but she may be an unmarried sister or even a serving girl. He cannot pretend he has not wondered, has not looked for a Japanese equivalent of the wedding ring.

'Tatsuo-san?' she asks.

He bows. 'Yes, Tatsuo-san. He's taking me out today.'

She bites her lip. He must stop. She will think there is an emergency, that he requires Tatsuo to be summoned immediately.

'If I can order some hangings from this place, maybe three or four, I've more or less fulfilled my commission. At the end of the week I'll be able to go to Yokohama and arrange my passage home.'

She raises a hand, a gesture that in Europe might mean *I give up* or *please stop talking* and he finds himself reaching out to touch her palm, to feel the warmth of her skin, the lines in her hand. He pulls his arm back and bows deeply, hiding his face, hoping she thinks the half-salute was some foreign sign of respect. Of honour. When he stands up he nods to her and goes to kneel at the table where she has set out breakfast for him. He sits still enough to hear her footsteps on the tatami mat and the sliding of the door as she returns to her own quarters where her own family waits for her to serve breakfast.

Rose Tree House

She takes her morning tea, made with Aunt Mary's smoky leaves still dry in their tin, into the garden and sits on the doorstep with the door open behind her and the house, she hopes, inhaling the sea air and exhaling the winter's damp. Even the sheets left on the bed are mildewed, and the curtains mottled and frayed where they have rested all winter against the cold glass. Before Tom comes, she must arrange for painting and new curtains and the washing of blankets and quilts. She will herself hang the carpets and cushions over the washing line and beat them with a carpet-beater that she will buy, a chore offering a satisfying combination of violence and housewifely virtue. She will write to Aunt Mary for advice about the curtains: nothing of Papa's design, and nothing too dark. White is not practical, but perhaps a very pale grey with white sprigs or fleur-de-lys. Ally prefers small geometric patterns to Papa's botanical outbursts. Maybe if Aunt Mary chooses fabrics she will be persuaded to come and see the results.

It is too cold, really, to sit out here, and it will be some time before the sun touches the camellia blossoms and opens the daisies in the grass. She cups her hands around the cooling tea. Seagulls wheel and cry overhead, and there are two grey chicks on the ridgepole of Greenbank House, open-mouthed with need and severely ignored by the sentinel on the chimney. Until they woke her at dawn, she had forgotten this, the gulls' lives played out in three dimensions above and around the town, birth and courting and death, hunger and aggression and the ceaseless proclamations echoing over the roofs. *Behold the fowls of the air: for they sow not, neither do they reap.* There is nothing for breakfast.

This is the first time she has taken the boat. She and Tom walked around the estuary to Flushing in the summer, stopping to picnic in a glade of beech trees where the leaves were already beginning to turn and drift into the lapping waves. Tom played at building towers and then walls of pebbles. Every dry-stone waller, he said, understands the basic principles of engineering, every shepherd who builds a sheepfold and fisherman who makes a dock. Every mother who knits a jumper, she asked, but he didn't need to tell her that knitting offers no challenge to gravity. Well, he said, it is not knitting but what is a corset if not a cantilever? In three months' time he will be home.

She reaches the quay and buys a ticket from a man who calls her 'me lover'. She has often stood on the pier before, but never climbed down the stone steps to the water where the boat approaches. It is like descending into a basement, one's head at the waist- and then knee-height of the people left behind. The tide is low and under the pier the waves hiss and echo. Seaweed hangs limp against the pilings and she glimpses fish nosing in the shadows. Those are pearls that were his eyes. She allows the boatman to help her into the boat, tugged on its ropes by each wave. She folds herself into a corner of the stern, glad that her gloves cover her whitening knuckles. Dozens of people do this every day, and the water is dense with boats and sailors doubtless competent in a rescue. She looks up at the sunlit trees on the opposite shore and then back over the town. A new perspective. Falmouth appears to advantage from the water, the windows of its white terraces sparkling and the palm trees bowing over gardens and public greens. A flag flies from the square tower of King Charles the Martyr, the Quaker Meeting House is raised high above the taverns and the synagogue broods on the hill. Sun flashes from the windows of the school on St Clare's Terrace and Ally wonders if there are children inside looking out at the water, imagining themselves in her place and waiting for the day they can leave the schoolroom and follow their fathers out onto the high seas. Or their mothers into kitchens and bars, into lives shadowed by waiting and wondering, and fearing in some cases the day the husband and father comes home and in others the day he doesn't. As the boatman pulls away from the pier, across the water and over the one part of the estuary open to the sea, Ally keeps her eyes on her new home.

Dr Crosswyn sent her the address: Rose Tree House, Mylor Church Lane, but even after she's found Mylor Church Lane with the help of an old man sitting on the pier, she can't find the house. On one side the wooded hillside rises, impenetrable as a fairy-tale forest, and on the other imposing gateways announce the bloated follies inhabited by Falmouth's richest men, the church-sized houses adorned with pickings from the boneyard of European architecture, turrets and watchtowers, onion domes and balconies. Doric columns support gothic arches and stone crenellations erupt out of red-brick bay windows. No-one, surely would choose such a thing for a convalescent home, even if the asylum could buy a building of grandeur. The coals, she thinks, the plumbing, the servants required to fetch and carry. It is the committee's intention that the residents will act as the Home's cooks and housekeepers, this being judged an excellent training for their discharge. But here? She checks her letter again. In a few minutes she will be late. He said the house was in the village. She must have come too far.

She has turned back when she hears hooves. A pony and trap comes around the corner. Dr Crosswyn waves. It is the first time she has seen him outdoors and it is strange, somehow, to see him in a hat, holding the reins, as if like the patients he might be expected to exist only within the walls of the asylum. She approaches the carriage, staying well back from the horse. Dr Crosswyn leans out to offer his hand.

'Please do climb up. See, there is plenty of room. How are you, my dear? How does it suit you, to be back in Cornwall?'

His gaze runs from the toes of her boots up the blue suit to the hat she chose from Aunt Mary's milliner. Madwomen are usually but not invariably dishevelled or eccentric in their dress as mad men, interestingly, are not.

'I am well, Dr Crosswyn. Quite recovered. And it is a great pleasure to be back.'

He nods and flaps the reins, which makes the horse set off again. 'That is good news. And Mr Cavendish will be home later in the spring, I understand?'

From whom, she wonders. Dr Crosswyn lives in Truro, not Falmouth, and it seems unlikely that there is any indirect connection between Penvenick and the asylum. 'I hope so, yes.'

'Splendid.'

She had missed Rose Tree House because the name and the gatepost itself is hidden by brambles and ivy. The driveway is so narrow that thorns and branches squeak along the side of Dr Crosswyn's carriage and the wheels jerk and bump.

'We could walk,' Ally suggests. 'Your paintwork.'

He clucks to the horse. 'One could go nowhere around here if one worried about paintwork. But even so I will have someone tend the drive. We want the patients to have visitors, family and friends. I thought perhaps an At Home once a week, let them practise tea and entertaining and so forth?'

Let them practice grape-scissors and egg-spoons, the correct number of minutes to converse while wearing a hat. Some are to be returned to the world as ladies and others as servants. Dr Crosswyn is unmarried and it begins to seem possible that his ideas about the lives of women are uncertain. 'I am sure something of the kind would be helpful,' she says.

The drive ends in a gravel circle overgrown with moss, with a broken stone urn in its centre. Trees press in, screening the sea which flickers between trunks and through branches.

'Here. What do you think?'

The house is modern, no more than fifty years old, but quite free of its neighbours' pretentions. Whitewashed, square, two-storied, sash windows flanking a brick porch. It looks like a transplanted vicarage, like the house of a country professional man, a village doctor or small-town lawyer. Comfortable and sufficient. And for all the garden could belong to Sleeping Beauty, the whitewash is new and the white paint fresh on the window frames and front door.

'It looks neat and comfortable.'

Show me inside, she thinks, give me the keys.

The front door grounds on a bristly new doormat in the hall. The wooden floor is newly polished, the smell hanging in the air with new paint and soap. The walls are distempered the colour of cheese or clotted cream. Primrose, Papa would say. The rooms are empty, volatile with possibility. Ally peers into the reception rooms each side of the front door and passes down the hall, past the stairs and into the kitchen. A white-tiled floor (anything dropped will shatter), white-painted cupboards, a double Belfast sink almost big enough to bathe in. She remembers the operating theatre, the women draped and recumbent on the table like artists' models. She remembers the spread legs, the blood.

She swallows. 'Perhaps a picture or two in here? Or some colour on the walls?'

He looks surprised. 'I read that white was preferable for kitchens. Easier to clean.'

Ally moves to the window. The back garden is an overgrown clearing, a tangle of tall grass and brambles into which the woods lean. 'Yes. But women spend a great many hours in the kitchen.'

'Just as you say. We thought, the committee thought, we would grant you a certain sum to spend as you think best. There is furniture already on order, and pots and pans and so on. Household linen. Matron saw to it.'

I could have done that, Ally thinks. But Dr Crosswyn, the committee, have remembered that she is here as a doctor and not as a woman. 'Thank you.'

There is moss growing over the slate path from the back door into the clearing, and some kind of fruit tree smothered by thorns and ivy.

'Dr Crosswyn? Do you think we might have gardening tools for the women? The exercise and fresh air, you know.' And perhaps a sense of efficacy, the simple reward of seeing that the work of one's hands makes change.

His eyebrows rise. 'It is usually the men who do such work. At the asylum.'

'But many of the women – some of them, anyway – will be accustomed to farm work, will they not? And others perhaps to flower-gardens.' A crowd of rooks rises from one of the taller trees. 'Besides, the outdoor work – the outdoor exercise –

260

would perhaps counteract the tendency to agoraphobia so often found.'

Besides, there is nothing about the possession of breasts and a womb that changes a person's interest in trees and sky.

'I think we will begin in a more traditional manner. We are seeking to return the patients to ordinary life, Dr Moberley Cavendish, not to send them out discontented with their lot.'

But what if it is a choice between discontent and madness? What when discontent is the sane response to one's ordinary life?

'Of course, Dr Crosswyn. As the committee wishes.'

Only part of the money for this house comes from the asylum, the rest being raised by private subscription. And it is unlikely, most unlikely, that the rural gentry and mining magnates who contribute to such schemes will wish to think of women digging the land, unearthing their dissatisfaction.

'We will send in a working party. Before the women arrive. I do not say that once the ground is dug and planted there is any reason why they should not tend some flowers. Roses, perhaps. Next year, spring bulbs. And matron has ordered two sewing machines and I believe some supplies for knitting and such.'

Let them work, she thinks, let them learn. There are machines now and factories for the manufacture of dresses and stockings; let women employ their brains rather than frittering their time in the painstaking making of objects of inferior quality and superior cost to those that can be purchased by the gross. She says nothing.

'Many of them will be accustomed to such work, my dear. They will take comfort in it. They are not scholars and do not wish to be, and nor would such a wish profit them or their families.'

She hears what he tells her: your own solution to the problem of female discontent is the height of idiosyncrasy and it is the test of your professionalism that you recognise your patients' difference from yourself. A doctor must not make her patients in her own image just as she must not come to see them as her negative. It is what Mamma could not do, to understand that each person's head contains a world as convincing and probably as verifiable as her own. Who am I, she thinks, to take away the embroidery frames and paintbrushes of women who have already lost what cannot be enumerated? Who am I, to appoint myself the arbiter of reality?

She bows her head. 'You are right, Dr Crosswyn. I thank you.'

hortus conclusus

They walk down the wide street that runs beside the river, a straight line ruled against the water's curves. The snow has melted from the hills to the east, but the trees are still bare, the temple roofs stark on the mountainside. The school of small boats under the bridge reminds him of the Falmouth oyster boats, the crowd of shapes on the pale water like moths on a paper lantern. The hall of display, Tatsuo says, is right beside the Imperial Palace, on ground where until very recently it had been unthinkable that a foreign foot, or even a Japanese commoner's foot, should tread. It is one of the changes, now the Imperial Court is gone to Tokyo. After one thousand years.

'That sounds sad,' says Tom. He wonders how long it will take him, when he goes home, to resume the habit of asking direct questions. Tatsuo does not reply.

The imperial trees are visible long before the Imperial Palace, their bare limbs reaching into the sky, breaking and smudging the grid of streets and walls, and then in the distance, scored across the end of the road he sees a high wall confining the Imperial Park. The walled garden, *hortus conclusus*. For the last millennium people must have been walking past that wall and imagining on the other side rare flowers and scented paths, fluting streams and still waters, and sometimes the passage of a holy being. A thousand years of violence and oppression, he reminds himself. A thousand years of ignorance and poverty for the many and the constant presence of swords for the few.

Tatsuo's feet pause as they pass through the great gate, as if his muscles and bones recognise the enormity of his transgression. Like passing behind the altar of a cathedral, Tom wonders, or handling the crown of England, but he can quite easily imagine himself doing either of these things given an unobserved opportunity. Where are England's sacred places? Tatsuo fixes his gaze on the ground, avoiding the sight of a park that wouldn't, really, be out of place in London. The broad gravel paths are not unlike the Rotten Row. There are mown lawns, green again, and beds of rich earth around towering trees. The two men come out at a broad arc of white gravel surrounding a slanting stone wall, and only the swooping red roofs announce that this is Japan. Hyde Park and Kensington Gardens: potentates and rulers, parks and palaces. Tatsuo, face averted, sheers down a narrower path between the trees, and leads Tom through wooden palings to a long low building whose great roof seems to crush it almost into the earth. There is no-one in what appears to be a sentry-box below the veranda, no intimation of eyes watching from the peep-holes on the first floor.

'This is it? The exhibition hall?'

Tatsuo nods, gestures him on. 'Please.'

And there are people inside, small clusters of them murmuring reverentially and pausing as if making the tour of a cathedral, as if at the crusader's tattered banner, the bishop and his wimpled wife in recumbent effigy. But they are not worshipping stone. All the screens dividing this mansion house have been pushed back, making a great hall whose diffuse light and panelled floor remind Tom of a barn or a water tower, some structure meant more as a container than a dwelling. Spaced at intervals along the wall like the Stations of the Cross are what he takes at first for unframed paintings, perhaps scrolls, depicting the usual Japanese landscapes, mountains without perspective and waterfalls and figures in kimono on hump-backed bridges. He already has a dozen such things for De Rivers.

And then he sees the cranes, first as five white shapes glowing like moons in the dim and filtered daylight. He approaches and finds himself before some kind of painting or drawing of five long-legged birds wading under overhanging wisteria. He has seen flowers like that, dripping the full height of the trees in a mountain forest, and he has seen cranes bowing and dipping, their white wings raised like the arms of a dancer about to begin. The five cranes are sociable, like a Japanese family preening and teasing in the bath. One is drawn up to its full height to peer down at the others busy at their toilette, and another leans in, neck outstretched so that the black markings on its silver plumage draw Tom's gaze across the darkness at the picture's centre and towards the arched breasts and glossy wings of its companions. Behind them, the wisteria blossoms fall like streams of water and it's not paint, he realises, but silk, the filament of each feather drawn in stitches smaller than a mouse's hair.

The craftsmen see the world differently, see the shapes of flowers and feathers and blades of grass built up from the tiniest elements – flickers – of light and colour. Such a mind must look at a bowl of tea, and see not only each brushstroke on the bowl's glaze but the fall of light on each rising particle of steam. Not only each brick in a bridge or lighthouse but the speckles of grit in the clay, almost the currents of pressure and gravity coursing through each grain of cement. How could one endure a world seen in such detail, how could a mind hold the flight path of each mote of dust? He steps nearer to marvel at the stitching, at the eyes and fingers of the makers, the shading finer and more subtle than that of any bird, the light in the silk more mineral than animal. He had not thought that art could exceed its own subject. He wants to tell Ally, to hear her healer's voice reply that there is no point in any other kind.

birdsong near at hand

She is not, she reminds herself, the first person to come back, to climb this hill knowing what waits at the top. She has been studying the numbers: it is very rare for a patient to be discharged well and to proceed to a life of good health and domestic or financial sufficiency. Approximately half of inmates will die without ever leaving the asylum, and of the other half many will return within three years of discharge.

She is almost at the top of the hill and the building rises before her, square and solid as it has always been. Behind those highest windows, she thinks, tucked under that roof. The back wards. Contained in a space that is only, after all, air and stone. It is not there where she will find the future occupants of Rose Tree House, and she does the women of that place no particular service merely by remembering them. Better, perhaps, to forget, better to be forgotten than to exist only as the epitome of degradation in the minds of others. Nonetheless, she remembers. Mary Vincent.

She is breathing high in her chest with the climb, the unaccustomed muscles in her thighs complaining. The exercise will do her nothing but good, but even so she pauses and turns to look back. The gorse burns again with yellow, and in the fields the gashes of winter's mud are healing. She watches the shadow of a cloud approach across the hillside and stands under the momentary dimming. A few breaths, a few heartbeats, and the sun brightens again on her face as the shadow drifts on, over the field and down towards the town. Out to sea too there is a slow turning of the sky, white clouds trailing shadows of dullness over bright water and the wind following in rushes and sudden darts, stroking the wrong way. In the hedge there is rustling and then birdsong near at hand. Come, she thinks. It is time.

William comes out from behind his table to shake her hand, holding it in both of his. He has aged over the winter, is beginning to lose height. A whole life here. A childhood in which he did not know what was waiting. The familiar smell drifts down the stairs and the tiles spread again at her feet.

'I am glad to be back, William. It is good to see you again too.'

He pats her hand. 'They're waiting for you. We've put you in the parlour for today. And you're to join Dr Crosswyn for coffee at eleven. Cook's made biscuits special.'

She would have liked a freer hand, but the committee has drawn up a list of patients for her to interview. Rose Tree House will take three 'parlour boarders', whose expenses are partially or wholly met by their families, and three 'kitchen boarders' who will work for food, board and – at Ally's urgent representation – a sum of money sufficient to allow them to dress themselves and purchase an occasional ribbon or picture paper. It would be cheaper to clothe them from the asylum, said Trelennick. It would be cheaper, Ally said, if they learnt to dress respectably and did not return to the asylum. Dr Crosswyn coughed: I think that what Dr Moberley Cavendish means is that the patients are to be taught prudence and thrift in the management of small sums, to prove themselves able to master the weakness for finery that can take such outlandish forms when the female mind is unsettled. I think Dr Moberley Cavendish is of the view that we cannot confidently say that a woman is sane until we have seen the dress of her choice. He stopped her later: I am sorry, my dear, I hope you can forgive me. But you know that a certain guile is required for committee-work, that it is better to have the committee make the right decision than trouble ourselves with their reasons for deciding. She did not remind him that she has heard him say the same thing about the management of patients.

There are at this moment 408 female inmates in the asylum, sixteen of them awaiting her judgement. Not those who have already passed the discharge board, because it would be challenging the judgement of the committee to admit them to Rose Tree House. Not those who have been readmitted more than once, whose troubles are categorised as 'chronic.' She is to interview women who have recently failed a discharge hearing for reasons that the committee believes likely to be addressed by a period of residence at Rose Tree House. The committee does not note its reasons for this or, as far as Ally can tell, any other decision it makes. Do not question them, says Dr Crosswyn. There are other ways, my dear, when there is something in which one believes very much, and if you are to make the splendid career I hope for you then you must allow me to show you some of them. It is enough, for now, that we have Rose Tree House and that the principle of your involvement in admissions has been accepted; let us prove it a success and then we may begin to seek more influence over the selection of inmates. I beg your pardon, of boarders. She knew, of course, that Mary Vincent's name would not be on the list, but at least Margaret Rudge is there.

She has passed through the parlour only once before, when she first looked around the asylum. It is a bigger room than a person can comfortably occupy, the size of two of the wards above, and tiled like the hall in a chequerboard pattern with a border in encaustic. They have lit a fire under the granite hearth, but it does not reach half way up the fireplace and dwindles in the sunlight coming through the tall windows. Still, it is a token of goodwill, of generosity, to give her a fire in March. They have set a heavy table before the fire, the sort of table on which one might confidently put to sea, and an armchair for her and what looks like a piano stool for the patient. A hard-backed chair near the door for a nurse. Ally checks the clock on the mantelpiece; she has five minutes yet. She cannot move the table but she pulls the chair out from behind it and carries the stool across so that they can sit together at the fireside. After all, she is meant to be testing the suitability of these patients for reintroduction to domestic life. She dusts down the armchair and arranges herself in a pos-ture neither too officious nor too casual. She must avoid any appearance of anxiety.

When the fourth candidate and her escorting nurse leave, the clock shows ten to eleven. It is reasonable, then, not to see another woman before coffee. She looks round the door and tells the nurse watching the patients who have spent their morn-ing sitting in the corridor that she will see the next one in forty minutes. You might take them into the garden for an airing, Nurse. It is a fresh spring day. She knows that the nurse will do no such thing. Closing the door behind her, she tries not to know that the nurse will be wondering what she is doing alone in here, that the nurse will be counting each moment of her empty soli-tude and holding it against her. Other people, other doctors, would not be feeling the pressure of the nurse's thoughts through the wall. She has only recently been able to put into words the observation that people who grew up in households without fear lack awareness of others' feelings, and that this lack makes their lives easier. More sane. She pokes the fire. But her

270

ability to hear other people's feelings is one of her strengths as a doctor, another incidental advantage of Mamma's training. She wanders to the window and leans into its recess. Rooks wheel from the bare elms, white sunlight on their black wings, and the hedges around the formal garden flinch from a gust of wind. The necessary questions were plain by the time she addressed the second woman, Charlotte something. A pale and almost unnaturally pointed face under dark hair streaked with grey, admitted two years ago for melancholia and suicidal intentions following the death of a young son. After she failed three discharge boards her husband, a local solicitor, began to make a nuisance of himself. Do you wish to move to a convalescent home, Ally asked. What would you yourself do to promote your recovery? Do you wish to return to your home and family? Charlotte's answers were not convincing, but Ally has at least understood what she needs to know. Not only, *do you want to leave the asylum* but *do you want to get better* and *if so, how?* It was not evident during her hospital training but it is plain in other kinds of practice: one should not take it for granted that the patient longs for what others consider perfect health. She will not use one of her precious places merely to placate someone's husband. Dr Crosswyn is right, they must begin with patients who will bring success. It is time for coffee.

His office is unchanged, even the pile of books on the desk exactly as it was four months ago. Agatha is unchanged, wearing the same black dress and white apron and carrying the same tray with the same air of alarm. The caraway seed biscuits could have come from the same baking as those she was offered in November. Time runs differently in closed institutions. She thinks about all the different times in the heads of the patients and the staff, those who live partly in some half-imagined era of childhood or early marriage and also in the repetitive present of the asylum. Those caught in a past moment of loss, obliged to encounter again the fresh agony of grief with every waking. Those whose memories themselves are lost, and live in an unnavigable present without the stars of fear and hope. She does not know how the Medical Director might order the passage of time at Rose Tree House, but it will be important that there is enough routine that no-one needs to devote thought to when to eat breakfast and not so much routine that the days become interchangeable. Sanity, she thinks, may be partly the ability to tolerate the passage of time.

He is speaking of the winter, of the coal used and the incidence of bronchial illness.

'What became of Mary Vincent, Dr Crosswyn?'

He stops. Looks at her.

'I'm sorry. She has been on my mind.'

'Evidently so. Still on the back ward, I'm afraid. I did pay a visit a couple of weeks back. She's deteriorated. Episodes of mania, a lot of raving, obscene allegations. In and out of seclusion. Most unlikely to come back down, I'd say.'

Ally puts down her cup. Coffee splashes into the saucer. 'No-one ever does, do they? Come back down?'

Stop, she thinks. There are limits to what can be done, who can be helped, and she is not behaving well. Not behaving professionally, not like a medical man.

'It is very rare.'

Has there been a single case, she wants to ask. Has it ever happened that a person has been allowed to return to wards with lavatories, with sheets and pillows, to enter the dining room rather than having buckets of congealed stew or porridge carried up the stairs when the kitchen maids find time? Has this institution ever returned an inmate's humanity after taking it away? She takes a bite of the biscuit balanced on the edge of her saucer and says nothing.

a man in the act of leaving

They have come already packed into wooden crates, nailed shut to exclude fingers eager for the touch of silk, a face that wants the soft shining colours lifted to the cheek. Even the inro and the netsuke come in boxes stitched into wadded cotton swaddling, cocooned against gaze and touch. He would like at least to see the treasures while they are in his possession, to greet them one by one and say goodbye. It will be like travelling with eggs or seeds, or perhaps with a pregnant woman, knowing that there is something deep inside capable of changing everything.

He kneels beside the crates with luggage labels and a pot of paste and brush that Makiko brought without being asked. He sniffs at the paste, probably made from rice like everything else. He waits for it to dry, runs his hands over the nearest crate as if they might palpate or somehow intuit the contents. White butterflies on blue silk, each life-sized wing supplied by life-sized veins in cobweb grey. Pink cherry blossoms only just visible, barely suggested, on a pale ground, their brown branches a geometric counterpoint to the froth of flowers. There is a saucer of ink and a finer brush on the tray: Thomas Cavendish, c/o Penvenick & Co., Falmouth.

There. His knees are stiff and he stands up. The screens are open a few inches, admitting a bar of sunlight in which the rough fibres of the tatami mat stand out. He holds his hand in the beam, feeling the sun's warmth and watching his shadow fingers. There have been days lately when it would have been little surprise to find that he no longer cast a shadow, when he could have questioned his own existence. He sees his own spirit haunting the little house, a shadeless and silent presence here long after he has crossed the seas and embraced his wife once more. His own trunks sit on the other side of the room, already locked and corded. A few trinkets as gifts, a kimono for Ally that he realised later might remind her too much of one of her father's designs (but the colours are hers and the shop, beside the new hospital, made him impatient to show her the juxtaposition of ancient and modern). No chrysalis here, only what any man, any man of modest means and limited inter-est in such things, might bring. He rubs his knees. He may as well go out, not a last walk because he has still two days, two days of living from his valise and trying not to hear the clock's tick in every step he takes, but perhaps the first of the last walks. He is already a ghost, a man in the act of leaving. He sits on the wooden ledge in the earth-floored entrance and puts on his shoes, slides open the street door and bolts it behind him. In three days' time, these small acts will be mem-ories. The stones under his feet now, the shuttered windows of this alley, the forested hills rising at the end of the street, will be only in his mind.

He does not want to go home.

He keeps walking, down the street, past the pickle shop and the sweet shop whose owner returns his bow, along the canal with a wooden bridge for each house. Cherry trees make an avenue down to the river, not yet blossoming but in tight-fin-gered green bud. Small birds flutter in their branches.

He does not want to go home. He does not know his wife, not really, not any more. He remembers her breasts in his hands and the smoothness of her back, remembers the satisfaction of entering her at last and then again and again those weeks after the wedding, but any woman has breasts and a back and a place to enter. Makiko, for example, under her *obi* and her kimono. The woman passing him right now, with the shuffling gait as if her legs could hardly part and blue-black hair bound up as if it could never fall between naked shoulder blades. Horrible, he thinks, it is a horrible thought to find in his head. He remembers Ally talking about medicine and poverty, about the injustices of women's lives. He remembers her cooking in his kitchen. He does not quite remember why they are married.

He comes to the river and turns upstream, past the boats where the fishermen's cormorants wait tethered and on to where the willows trailing idle fingers in the stream are green again. He will continue up the hillside, under the red torii arches to the temple where he will stay awhile, watch the shadows move in the priests' garden and the reflections of trees ripple and blur on the water as if perception itself were to waver.

burning boats

Dr Crosswyn has advertised for a matron-housekeeper, but until she is appointed Ally has agreed to sleep at Rose Tree House, taking the opportunity to have the white cottage replastered and repainted. She has chosen an attic room for herself, smaller than those shared by the parlour boarders, from which she can see through the treetops to the sea.

She went to bed leaving the curtains open, for the pleasure of knowing that the moon shone on the waves and the stars circled the sky while she slept. Her hair has come loose in the night and tangled itself at the back of her neck. She sits up and scoops it out of the way. The first grey threads are appearing; if Tom were not already on his way back he might return to find her visibly older. A woman of a certain age. She may very well be half-way through her life, and to what end? What account can she give, what has been learnt? Behind the headland at St Mawes, the sun is rising, the eastern sky flaming and the path of open water, the Carrick Roads, printed with reflected hill and dawn. *Red sky in the morning*.

There is that of which a reasonable person might be proud. It is not nothing, it cannot be dismissed as hysteria or nervous imagining, to pass the examinations and qualify as a doctor. It is not nothing to win the prize, to graduate top in the year. It is not nothing for a woman to publish a paper in the *British Journal of Asylum Medicine*. She kneels up and leans over the window sill, inhaling the March breeze coming through the trees. There is still a faint odour of paint. The rooks are on the wing, swirling like leaves around their tree. And what then? Is it enough for a life, to pass examinations, to win a prize? To assist in the saving of a few lives, and perhaps in the loss of others? To discover kindness, to discover that kindness is the only thing that matters. A late discovery, but then she grew up in a house without it. No, for Aubrey was kind. With whatever motivation, he was kind, to her and to May. We are not judged by the sum of our life's work, she thinks, as if we were hands in a factory valued only for what we produce. Our labour and our moral worth are not the same thing, for what price kindness? Charity, *caritas*. A word for caring, not for the payment of a tax or tithe. It is, she thinks, from Aunt Mary that she learnt caritas, Aunt Mary and Uncle James and Annie and Annie's family, all of whom dress in silks and keep a good table. Not all the words belong to Mamma. It will not matter, in the end, whether she has discharged Mamma's voice from her head or not, whether she has been freed from those who haunt her or goes to her death still shadowed. It will matter that she has been kind, and that she has done the work to which she is called and trained. *And though I bestow all my goods to feed the poor, and though I give my body to be burned, and have not charity, I am nothing.* St Paul, no friend to women. A spectre from the past, or a corrective to Mamma, who despite a life devoted to charitable work has not charity in this sense? One can have charity with voices still in one's head. The things that matter in the end do not depend on a healthy mind or a healthy body, neither on faith nor on hope. Goodness, she thinks, is not denied to the mad.

The first ship of the morning is rounding Pendennis Point, leaning on the wind as it enters home water. All our ghosts, Ally thinks, could pass the other way across the waves, all the voices that torment us here could gather and take wing out to sea. She sees them in her mind's eye, a host of angry spirits crossing the water and dissolving in the light of the rising sun, Mamma and May evaporating like the dew on the grass below to trouble her no more.

She had thought to be up first, to take her ease in the garden for a quarter of an hour before supervising the preparation of breakfast, but the key is already in the front door. It took some time to persuade Dr Crosswyn to support her over this: naturally the doors must be locked at night, but she wants the patients to know that it is ingress, not egress, that is prevented. That they are safe from intruders and may leave at will or on a whim. They have been locked up long enough. And what do I say to the committee when someone goes missing, or worse, he said. It was not easy, you know, to persuade everyone of the need for Rose Tree House. It is a significant expense. It has been said that even if you are able to discharge everyone permanently cured after three months it will be no cheaper than keeping them in asylum for the term of their natural lives. Then we can tell them, Ally said, that it will be cheaper still if the patients disappear; tell them that we keep the key by the door at night for fear of fire. The newspapers of the last week have been full of the inquests consequent upon a midnight fire at an asylum in Staffordshire, where all the internal as well as external doors were locked.

She should have put on a coat, but it is such a pleasure to be outside without being muffled and fastened into thick layers that the chill is not unpleasant. And the day will warm as the sun rises. The garden is still in shade but the top of the house is patterned with tree-shadows. Ally closes her eyes and takes a slow breath: sea, dew, the smell of new growth in the earth.

'Doctor?'

It is Mrs Rudge, wearing a large ticking apron over a worn blue dress and carrying a trowel.

'It's all right for me to be out here, isn't it Doctor? Only I didn't mean anything wrong. It's good to plant in the mornings. My husband always used to say. And you said we could sow seeds. We're already late, see, with the sweet peas.'

'It's fine, Mrs Rudge. That's why the key was by the door, so you can go out if you want to. Sweet peas are scented, aren't they? They'll be nice to put on the table in the summer.'

Mrs Rudge is still looking at her, expectant or anxious.

'Plant away. I'll make sure someone calls you for breakfast.'

'Yes, Doctor. Thank you, Doctor.'

She watches Mrs Rudge walk away and crouch over the soil. At the very least, it will be good for the women to be outside again, to have sun on their faces and wind in their hair. Mrs Rudge sits back on her heels.

'Excuse me, Doctor, may I ask something?'

Ally walks towards her. 'Of course. Mrs Rudge, you don't need to ask permission to ask a question.'

'Sorry, Doctor.' Mrs Rudge picks up the trowel again. Her hands are too pale, as white as fish-flesh.

'What was it? Your question?'

'Oh.' Mrs Rudge spoons up earth. She has half a dozen small earthenware plant pots from somewhere, each already lined with a layer of leaf compost. She puts the trowel down again and looks at the black smears on her fingers. 'It was only – well – some of us were saying, maybe there could be hens here. They'd eat the kitchen scraps, you see, and we'd have the eggs and a chicken for the pot now and again. But I daresay it's a foolish scheme.'

Not foolish, Ally thinks. Just not the kind of thing that would have occurred to her, to a city doctor. 'It sounds very sensible, Mrs Rudge. You are accustomed to caring for hens?'

'Four of us are, Doctor. We were just saying how you get to think they have characters, like.'

Ally nods. 'I'll have to consult Dr Crosswyn. I can't see why not.'

Leaving Mrs Rudge to her tilling, she wanders down towards the trees, stepping over twisting roots and fallen branches. The cost of a henhouse, she thinks. The committee won't like that. And how much does one pay for a hen, or four hens or however many will be required? And the killing. She who has opened a human rib-cage and removed a human heart, she who has weighed the heart and dissected it on a wooden bench, who has seen women exsanguinate in the operating theatre, she does not think she could take a living bird, feel its feathers warm under her hand, and lift a cleaver – no. And it is probably not the kind of thing one should permit patients to do. But that part of proceedings is some way in the future, and presumably one could employ someone with expertise. Another cost for the committee, the hen-killer's fee. Foxes might come. Tom's Japanese foxes, taking up residence, declaring themselves guardian spirits and pillaging the hen-house, although she doubts the people of Flushing need goblin foxes to justify their certainty that the mad are different from themselves.

She comes out of the trees onto the beach and picks her way over the grey stones, smoothed and rounded by the sea. The tide is rising, licking at the dry stones and falling back leaving them shining and purple in their grey. She stands on the tide line, the seaweed a broad scribble of olive-green oil paint and fine strokes in red pen-and-ink. Tom has seen seals here. She remembers her vision of the departing ghosts. We should have a ceremony, she thinks, use our sewing materials to make effigies of those who haunt our minds, and push them out to sea in burning boats.

She finds a dry rock and sits on it. Margaret Rudge was admitted nine months ago, mostly as a result of evidence given by her sister-in-law about a nervous decline resulting from Mrs Rudge's belief that her husband was unsuitably involved with a neighbour. Mrs Rudge had been found more than once wandering the village weeping and drunk, and the sister-in-law had taken over the care of her house and family some weeks earlier after finding the youngest children alone beside an open fire. Her admission papers state that the village doctor had several times observed her 'in a state of disorder' and 'plainly unfit for the charge of young children'. She has given no trouble whatsoever at the asylum, and falls, therefore, into Ally's category of patients whose insanity is likely to be caused, or at least triggered, by circumstance and environment. (Or, of course, some would say, patients who never were insane, but there are far fewer of these than the popular press would have its readers believe. It is in no-one's interest to spend public funds confining capable citizens.) Ally is keeping detailed notes, for of course the problem is that it is not significantly easier to change an individual's social and family situation than it would be to change her heredity. There are no control groups in this experiment. And it is almost breakfast time.

A door inside the house bangs as she opens the front door. Open windows, a breathing house. There's no-one in the dining or sitting rooms, only sunlight on new paint and daffodils in glass vases, and voices from the kitchen. The two parlour-boarders, who might quite properly wait in the dining room to be served, sit at the deal table in the middle of the kitchen, one spooning marmalade into a bowl and the other folding napkins. One of the kitchen boarders is putting eggs into egg cups, where their sea-shell shine lifts immediately into steam, and the other makes toast with more concentrated attention than Ally has seen paid to some surgical procedures.

'Good morning,' Ally says. 'It's a beautiful day outside.'

They look up at her, as if she's said something that breaks the rules. Mrs Henning's hands stop moving marmalade and then her face clears, as if she's remembered a lost word.

'Good morning, Doctor. You had a fine morning for your walk.'

Ally smiles at her. 'The bluebells will soon be out in the wood. More than enough for us to gather a few bunches.'

This is how you build sanity. You speak of flowers and the weather. You put marmalade in pretty bowls and eggs into egg cups, and time has passed and nothing bad has happened, making it seem possible that more time will pass without bad things. Mrs Curnow places the last napkin on her stack, damask that Aunt Mary found cheap and thought might cheer the table at Rose Tree House. I don't say that nice table linen cures madness, she wrote, but the proper domestic appointments have doubtless a role in staying troubled minds. Aunt Mary would know.

'When my daughters visit I can take them there,' Mrs Curnow says. She has not seen her daughters since her admission two years ago, shortly after the birth of the second.

'You can take a picnic,' Ally promises.

She looks at the railway clock between the windows: there are few rules at Rose Tree House, but any community requires regulation and everyone has agreed to rise by seven and to attend breakfast at a quarter to eight, lunch at one, tea at half-past four and supper at half-past seven. Middle-class arrangements, several degrees west of the asylum's boarding school and hospital regime whose daily aim is to return all patients to their beds at a nursery hour.

Mrs Henning clears her throat. 'I believe Frances is having some difficulties, Doctor. She is – we are – unused to – well, to our own clothes.'

Frances Gunner arrived only two days ago. Has she forgotten how to dress herself?

'Please continue with your breakfast,' Ally says. 'Miss Mason has taken such care with the toast, you should eat it hot.'

Miss Mason turns round to smile as Ally hurries upstairs.

Miss Gunner is sitting on her bed, still in her nightgown, with her hands over her face and Emma Trennick standing beside her. Miss Trennick starts, her face alarmed.

'I'm sorry, Doctor. I didn't mean to be late. I know the rules. I didn't mean it.'

Ally remembers herself once apologising to Tom in similar terms. I know the importance of your time, please believe that I never meant to waste your afternoon in this way. I am so very sorry.

'It is nothing, Miss Trennick. Of course there will be times when your judgement tells you that the usual rules do not apply. But now I have come and you should join the others at breakfast.'

She stands at the window while Miss Trennick's footsteps pass down the stairs, giving Miss Gunner a moment to compose herself, to adjust to the change of presences. The sun is bright on the water now, a sharp white light behind the trees' branches where last year's rooks' nests float like winter fruit. She turns back. The room is tidy, Miss Trennick's bed already made with perfectly folded corners and the candle placed in the centre of a white linen cloth on the chest of drawers. It is restful, a room without paintings on the walls, scattered with tree-shadows.

'Miss Gunner, it is breakfast time. You should dress and come down now.'

Ally decided at the beginning that she would use the women's titles, as the nurses in the asylum do not. Miss Gunner's fingers clench over her face.

'Mrs Henning said there was a trouble with your clothes?'

A muffled sound. Ally crosses to the clothes folded on Miss Gunner's bedside chair. She does not handle them – they are not hers to handle – but they appear clean if worn and frayed around the seams. The women leave the asylum in the clothes in which they entered.

'You know that soon you will have a little money. You may save a few weeks and then buy yourself a new dress.'

'I don't know,' says Miss Gunner. 'I don't know what to wear. See? I don't know. I don't know how you decide.'

Miss Gunner has been in the asylum for five years, since she was twenty-two. Her admission papers say that she interrupted a divine service to accuse the vicar of obscene acts, and persisted in recounting her allegations in coarse words quite outside her usual character. Since then, the written records state only that she spent two weeks on the hospital ward in the typhoid epidemic the summer after her admission and that the following year she was attacked by another patient and required stitches in her arm. Ally has not suggested to anyone that if Miss Gunner's accusations are true then there is no basis for questioning her sanity, but the possibility that they are – and the fact that sometime in the last five years Miss Gunner stopped pointing out the possibility – is one of Ally's reasons for accepting her at Rose Tree House. She sits down beside her.

'Some days it is strangely hard to decide,' she says. 'The practical solution is to set out your clothes for the morning when you go to bed. Otherwise, you will need to consider what clothes you have and which is the most suitable, or least unsuitable, for your day's activities.'

Miss Gunner puts her hands in her lap and twists them. 'I've only the two dresses. It's just – I'm sorry, Doctor.'

Ally wonders if she should add another rule: in the interests of their recuperation, boarders are forbidden to apologise.

'Well, today you will be taking a walk and perhaps writing a letter or working a little in the garden.'

Miss Gunner's hands pause in their twining. 'I'm no good at writing. May I sew? I heard something about us sewing.'

Ally resists the desire to pat Miss Gunner's shoulder. 'If the sewing supplies come you may. I expected them yesterday but you know how the post is around here.'

Miss Gunner nods, though it's unlikely that the unreliability of the Cornish post has been high among her concerns.

'So if one of your dresses is an evening gown or your Sunday best, you should wear the other one. Otherwise wear the one you like better. Change at lunchtime if you feel like it. And we will see you at the breakfast table in ten minutes.'

On the stairs, she thinks, there could be a painting. But not one of Papa's. One of the new French city paintings, to remind everyone that there are places where people dine at tables set out on the pavement and dance whirling by candle-light, where couples lean on bridges under starry skies. She finds herself smiling. Some of Degas's dancers, admired by Aubrey and scorned by Papa, or one of Mr Whistler's new Parisian paintings, would do very well. And when the mad-women had had enough of looking at it she could sell it and buy a henhouse. The smell of toast and coffee drifts down the hall and Ally is hungry.

a ship of fools

He stays on deck long after everyone else has gone, back to their cabins to prepare for dinner or to the library to bag the newest books. It takes a long time to leave Japan from here, much longer than to leave England from Cornwall, and there are still islands and whole mountains, even beaches, occupying much of the foreground as the sun goes down. The intermission, the time between places, will begin soon enough and for now he wants to see Japan from this last point of view. He may, after all, return one day: life is long and journeys shorter every year. He may bring Ally. Ahead of the ship, a swathe of sea glints orange and the lowest clouds are sharp-edged, lit from behind. It is unlikely that Japan will have much further call for foreign engineers; in fact he can imagine that in not many years the traffic in expertise will be going the other way, but perhaps if there is need, if something goes wrong with the lights ... Although it has been his job to make sure that nothing goes wrong with the lights. At the moment when his circle on the planet turns away from the sun, a white flash begins on the tip of the fading headland. He counts the beats.

'Tom Cavendish! I heard you were finished in Kyoto.

Saying a fond farewell, are you? You'll be back, don't worry. I remember doing the same thing myself, younger than you, thinking I was going back to a job in the City and I'd never get further than France for the rest of my days, but of course I wanted to and so I did and here I am, dear boy, here I am.'

The light flashes again. Yes, one of his. One of Penvenick's.

'Professor Baxter! What a pleasure to have you on board. But whatever calls you west? Were you not determined to live and die here?'

The professor shrugs. His beard is perhaps even more luxuriant than at New Year. 'Slings and arrows of outrageous fortune. My father died – don't be sorry, dear boy, he was almost ninety, a blessed release, not least I dare say for my sister with whom he had lived for some years – and since my daughter is to be married this summer my wife is adamant, *adamant*, that I should return while the estate is settled. Worried my sister will get my share, I don't doubt, but she says Helena longs to have me walk her down the aisle. I'd rather expect her to write and tell me herself if that were the case, wouldn't you? Foolishness, anyway, it's the man at the altar you want to worry about, not the one at the door.'

'A wife and daughter? I had no idea.'

There are rumours – more than rumours – about Professor Baxter and a Japanese lady who is said to have two half-European children. Bad enough, Tom thinks, without a wife at home, for such children are rejected by the Japanese and never taken home when European men reach the end of their Far Eastern residence. To bring another being into the world condemned to such a half-life from the moment of birth!

'No more you did. Jane and I do best with the Pacific between us, have done for years. A perfectly civilized arrangement, no questions asked – by either side, I might add, Jane has her freedom too – and no hard feelings.'

Yes, marriages do end, break and founder. And if one were going to run away and begin again, one would of course return to Japan, to a wooden house beside a canal where the mountains meet the city in the east of Kyoto. And it would be sensible for a European with a certain expertise then to seek a position at the university, to teach, for example, engineering. And to make every effort to learn Japanese, to speak and sit and eat the Japanese way. To return to a mountain village when there is a holiday, to take the train to visit a friend in Tokyo. If one were to begin again.

'May I ask, how old is your daughter?'

The professor comes to stand beside him at the rail. 'Ask away, dear boy. She must be – let me see – oh, twenty-three, I think. Or four. It's been a long time. Are you going to ask to see a photograph?'

Tom shakes his head. 'Only if you wish to show me one.'

Why would he want to see a photograph of a woman he has never met? The professor fumbles his pocket and pulls out a wallet, from which he extracts a small square of card.

'Here. Pretty enough, I dare say.'

The picture is so small and faded that it's hard to perceive much more than a small white woman in a large dark dress. Her hair is darker than Ally's and the dress fussier than anything Ally would wear. He passes it back.

'A charming young lady. You approve of the match?'

Professor Baxter pushes the photograph back into the wallet and stands on tiptoe to stuff the wallet back into his pocket.

'Never met the chap, of course. My wife likes him and I can't say that promises well.'

Baxter's face is blurring in the fading light. 'If you're going to change for dinner, Cavendish, you'd better look sharp. The cook's French, did you know? So we can postpone the dumplings and suet pudding a few more weeks yet. Do you want me to get you onto the Captain's table, exert a little pull? There're a couple of very fine young ladies dining there.'

Tom shakes his head. 'Don't waste your pull on my account, Professor. Fine young ladies were never my line. And they – or their mammas – would doubtless prefer you to bring someone more eligible.'

'I am disappointed. But just as you like, dear boy. There will be plenty of time to talk between here and Singapore.'

The professor cocks his head, almost, Tom thinks, crooks his elbow as if to escort him away, waiting for Tom to do as he is told and go below to put on a dinner jacket. Tom looks ahead and stays where he is. He wants to see Japan slip over the horizon much more than he wants to sit at a table in a hot room with eleven strangers. There is no rule that says a man must dine, is there? Heaven knows there will be time enough to contend with fine young ladies and their mammas. The crests of the waves are beginning to shine white against the grey sea, and their sound comforts him; Kyoto, after all, is perhaps too far inland for a maritime man. He remembers pausing on the bridges, as everyone pauses on the bridges, to look up river towards the mountains and see the weather coming down the valley. He remembers the cormorants on the fishing boats, and the herons wading, the morning and evening parades of umbrellas and parasols over the parapets.

'Have a pleasant evening, Tom.'

He nods. 'And you, Professor.'

He stays at the railing until nightfall is complete and a piano and a woman's voice join the hubbub from the dining room below. They must have passed a headland, for the ship begins to lift and sway under him. He plants his feet a little further apart and finds the rhythm. Ah, there. It is like breathing. He feels his body calm and settle to the motion, which will carry him, now, all the way home. Back to Ally, to his marriage bed. Away from

289

here. Light flares as the door behind him opens and he turns to see a man helping a woman – a lady – over the mantel.

'Good evening,' Tom says.

She clings to her companion's arm as if at risk of blowing away. 'Oh, see all the stars! Starlight on the sea – who could object to the motion when there is such a sight?'

There may be six weeks of this, six weeks stuck on a ship of fools returning him inexorably to a country he no longer likes and a marriage he cannot quite remember. Tom tips his hat and retires to his cabin.

He is too hungry to sleep deeply, but lies feeling the ship's movement, the Pacific Ocean's movement, in his body, feeling his blood rise and fall with the sea, his muscles and bones and brain rocked on the surface of the water. The berth is too narrow for him to stretch out his arms as he has become accustomed to do on a futon, so he lies on his back, hands folded behind his head. How many other human souls, he wonders, are now afloat on this ocean, between eastern Asia and the west coasts of the Americas? On the other side of this sea there is daylight and somewhere in the middle, sunrise. Passenger ships, fishing vessels, traders. Canoes with outriggers around the islands, Chinese junks, the coastal bark boats of American Indians. Thousands. Tens of thousands, rocked by the same water. He turns over. At any given moment, what proportion of humanity is at sea? *They that go down to the sea in ships, that do business in great waters.* How does it go? *They reel to and fro, and stagger like a drunken man.* He always used to like that bit, that drunk men haven't changed in however many thousand years. *He bringeth them out of their distresses. He maketh the storm a calm.* He wonders, again, how intelligent adults, informed by experience as well as education, manage to believe these pleasant words. As late as the last century, some people argued that building lighthouses was an offence against divine providence, that it was impertinent to attempt to forestall the will of God as revealed by wind and weather. As, indeed, those of similar mind have argued against the development of abdominal surgery: if the Lord has seen fit to place a tumour in a belly, what right have doctors to interfere? He must remember to tell Ally this connection in his next letter, something they have in common. He sleeps, rousing through the night to breathe an unfamiliar air and see an unfamiliar darkness, to the insistence of hunger, to the waves whose mood will one moment change.

In the morning, Japan is still on the horizon, a low bulk that on a duller day could be taken for cloud. A fleet of white birds darts over the waves and out of sight. The sea moves slowly, as if gelatinous. And there is the smell of bread. He has not smelt baking bread for months. He remembers the ambassador's wife's performance of despair: they brew beer, she said, so they can't pretend not to know about yeast. I had my maid show him with her own hands but they're all the same, aren't they, they just don't want to learn. He follows the scent along the deck. The sails are barely holding their shapes, but it is, after all, only just after sunrise. And anyway, he reminds himself, impatience is even more pointless than usual on a long sea voyage. Wind and weather, time and tide. They that do business in great waters. It is for the captain to decide when to use the engine, and meanwhile Tom will enjoy the quiet and the clean air. Baking would be undetectable with a coal-fired engine roaring. He peers into the galley, where a cook whose appearance does not belie his rumoured Frenchness is stirring a pot and two Chinese boys are chopping things with big knives. It is true that he never quite came to terms with the Japanese breakfast, with soup and rice and salt fish on a parched morning tongue, even if it is no different from coffee and salt bacon. Toast, he thinks. And just possibly butter?

Marmalade, anyway. He should have provisioned himself better for this voyage. Pickled plums, or something. Japanese cuisine offers little but dried fish to the traveller. Perhaps he should not have scorned the European offerings of the shops in Yokohama, the imported beef extract, cocoa and condensed milk. Perhaps, indeed, such things should be part of Japanese modernisation. Tools of empire: it's much harder to outwit invaders who bring their own supplies. He checks his watch and wanders back along the deck. He's not used to having nothing to do.

He waits four minutes after half-past seven, not wishing to behave like a dog waiting for the butcher's door to open. There's a seating plan at the door, and someone already at his table, sitting with her back to the room where she can see out of the window. A perfectly straight back, dropped shoulders and a swirl of black hair piled on the back of her head, making her neck look almost too thin for its function. And she's wearing deep mourning. Doubtless certain conventions should obtain, but he's too hungry to reflect on the etiquette of breakfasting alone with an unknown young lady; if she doesn't want to be alone with a man she shouldn't have come to breakfast without a companion. He bows and wishes her a good morning before taking a seat on the other side of the table. Steam rises from her coffee cup.

'Good morning. Coffee?'

He nods and then rises to help her because she's using both hands to lift the coffee pot and he can see the tendons standing out in her wrists.

'Please don't trouble.'

He pours himself coffee, allows her to pass the cream jug. She looks up as if she expects him to say something.

'It's good to smell coffee again,' he says, although it isn't, particularly, and he likes Japanese tea.

292

She looks down at her hands. No rings: she must have lost a parent rather than a husband, and anyway looks barely old enough to be married. 'We were able to buy it quite easily in Kobe.'

Now what? 'You were living there?' he ventures.

'Indeed so.'

He looks around for the waiter, who can hardly be unduly occupied. Her rudeness, he thinks, or at least her evident desire not to talk to him, excuses further effort. He smells bacon. The ship has begun to sway along again, and outside the waves are lifting. She is saying something.

'I beg your pardon?'

She sighs, as if he should have been listening better. 'You have been in Yokohama?' She looks him up and down. 'Some kind of trade?'

He raises a hand to the waiter standing in the kitchen doorway. 'Engineer. And I was travelling around.'

The waiter is coming over.

'You were not at table yesterday.'

'I was on deck and missed dinner.'

The waiter hands Tom a menu.

'Porridge, please,' he says. 'And then toast and eggs. Scrambled, if I may.'

He should, of course, have made sure that the lady had placed her order first. He looks at her.

'Fruit, please.'

The waiter bows and leaves.

'You are sensible to take fruit now,' he says. 'I daresay we will be longing for fresh food before Singapore.'

She shrugs. 'It is my habit. I cannot bear a heavy breakfast.'

I cannot bear a snob, he thinks, and sees with relief an older woman making her way to the table. He will be eating with these people three times a day for several weeks.

birds and butterflies

The cottage will soon look better. She of all people should know that one cannot make a thing more beautiful without damaging it. Dust-blankets shroud the furniture, piled in the centre of the room, and the workmen have left the prints of their boots on the floor. She touches the wall where she has painted squares of possible colours, a daffodil-yellow that is probably too bright and a blue that is too cold. She can't hear Papa's voice in her head the way she hears Mamma's, which means that she can't imagine what he might approve. Dark colours. Murk. Tangled foliage, as if the only mode for the mind's eye were botanical. What if there were an anatomical wallpaper, a design of capillaries and veins, the blue-white curve of tendons and the bloom of red muscle? Her fingertips come dusty from the wall. White, she will have it all painted white, and if Tom has a fancy for something else, paint is cheap enough.

She goes upstairs, glances into Tom's study which she is keeping just as he left it, and stands in his bedroom. In their bedroom. There is still a faint smell of damp, and the swollen sash squawks as she wrestles it up an inch or two. There are daffodils bobbing under the apple tree in the top garden and a fuzz of new green things that are probably weeds. She turns back the blanket and feels the sheet for damp. She remembers her nightgown tossed to the floor here, his hands on her body in this bed, but the memory is not quite real, has been worn out by reiteration. She and Tom will do that again, here. If he has a safe passage home. And if not, well, if not things will change less. She was feeling better, she thinks, at Rose Tree House, and now she is back in Tom's cottage anxiety rises again in her chest. It is not fair to blame Tom. A domestic environment is uneasy for many women. She should leave a note for the painter and get back to Rose Tree House, where she has promised to oversee the setting up of the sewing machine which arrived yesterday. Not that she has ever used a sewing machine.

They open the boxes in the room Ally had imagined being used as a drawing room, for reading and talking and taking tea around the fire.

Mrs Rudge eyes the furniture. 'We'll need space for piecing, you see, Doctor. Most use a table but I've always found the floor's easier, specially with dresses and such, just so's you don't mind crawling around a bit but I don't think any of us'll be choosy.'

Miss Gunner laughs. 'What, stand on our dignity?'

Ally remembers herself crouching on Mamma's kitchen floor. 'You have it back,' she says. 'Your dignity. You can piece on the dining table if you like. Or I dare say we could find another table to put in here.'

The machine came in a wooden crate, from which Mrs Rudge has levered the nails. Miss Gunner and Miss Trennick hold the crate while Ally and Mrs Rudge ease the contraption forward and stand it on the floor. It looks like part of a train, Ally thinks, or like a spare bit of the ornate ironwork that anchors the roof of Euston station, and she likes its shiny blackness, likes the fact that although it is made for women to use it has been decorated with gold scrolls and curlicues instead of coloured flowers. Its ebony cogs mesh, dangerous to fingers, and the needle gleams under the coil of hooks and spindles. The turning handle is cold to the touch.

'May I open it?' Mrs Rudge has reached into the crate and is holding a green box. 'I think it has extra parts.'

'Of course.'

There are implements Ally couldn't name, whose purpose she can't guess, precisely made in bright steel.

'Look, for shirring. And this is for piping, so we can make it to match. And this must be for smocking. I've never seen one before. Well, I suppose I wouldn't have done, would I, if they're new.'

Mrs Henning excuses herself and slips away.

What else, Ally wonders, have they missed? She should order back numbers of the *Quarterly Review* and the *Englishwoman's Journal*, perhaps also the *Gentleman's Magazine*. Wars have begun and ended. The Married Women's Property Act has come into being, the age of consent changed.

'Do you know how to do that?' Miss Trennick asks. 'How to make piping with a machine?'

Mrs Rudge shrugs. 'I used to. Used to work for Miss Whitney in Redruth. Before—' she stops.

Before. The women will need words for this, ways of bridging the lost years.

'Before you were unwell,' Ally says.

Mrs Rudge meets her gaze. 'Yes. Before I was – unwell. Before I was unwell I worked for a dressmaker. And I made piping.'

'Did you enjoy the work?' Ally asks.

Mrs Rudge reaches out to stroke the sewing machine, tests

the point of the needle with her fingertip. She doesn't look up. 'Sometimes. Sometimes I did.'

Mrs Henning returns carrying folded off-white cotton. 'Here, Margaret. Try it out on this.'

'Your petticoat?'

'That big packet yesterday was from my husband. New clothes. Well, old clothes, but ones I haven't been wearing. Not since. Take it, I won't wear it again.'

Since you were unwell, Ally thinks. Let us make this an illness, from which you have recovered. Mrs Rudge shakes out the petticoat and they see faded stains, a rent and worn seams. Ally's own underclothes have always tended towards this state – what is the point in concerning oneself with garments by definition unseen? – but she can imagine the pleasure with which another woman, a more particular woman, might dispose of such a thing. She brings a chair so Mrs Rudge can sit up to the machine. Miss Trennick produces red thread from one of the workboxes provided by the matron of the asylum and they all gather around to watch Mrs Rudge wrap the thread around loops and spindles, whirl the handle to wind a spool that fits under the needle and then begin to sew. She makes fine tucks and then shirring around the petticoat's soiled hem, narrow stitches and broad. She embroiders Charlotte Henning's name across the front breadth in a looping script and then snips the threads and begins an area of cross-hatching that turns into smocking when she pulls the stitches. She holds it out, laughing.

'There. You could still wear it if you want, only you'd know you had all sorts going on underneath. Anyone else?'

There's a silence. Miss Trennick looks up. 'Could you do a butterfly? I mean, if we're allowed?'

They glance at Ally. Are they behaving like sane people, is this acceptable? Women who for several years have taken clothes from a communal pile once a week. Why should they be ordinary?

'Or birds,' Ally suggests. 'The outlines are quite easy. Though maybe not freehand with a sewing machine.'

'Reckon I can do it,' Mrs Rudge says. And she can: by teatime all the petticoats have red letters and flowers, birds and butterflies and for Ally a cylinder meant to represent her stethoscope and an attempt at a doctor's bag. It occurs to Ally only as she folds the petticoat back into her drawer to wonder what Tom will think.

a gentleman's taste

He finds a book on Japanese folklore in the library, on a shelf otherwise crowded with the pious hopes and more pious memories of English missionaries to various parts of East Asia. He wonders if there is any propensity for reciprocal journeys, if there are villages in India where people sell home-made sweets and chutneys to raise money to send priests to Europe in order to save other people from the delusions of Christianity. What would have happened if he had sought enlightenment at the temple with the gongs, if he had knelt at the curtained altar? He flips through *A Light in the East* and *Three Years Among the Ainu Heathen* and decides that whatever he might learn about Japan from a more attentive reading would be too dearly bought. He signs out the folklore book and takes it up to the deck, where the wind is a little fresh for comfort and the waves are cresting white.

There is a whole chapter about fox possession and fox worship. There is a new asylum in Tokyo, the author says, where more than half the patients believe themselves possessed and a good number of the others imagine themselves gifted with magical powers of exorcism. It is not a situation calculated to result in the cure of either group. The author himself has witnessed a village woman in the grip of such a delusion, who after many days of sitting silently with her face to the wall, refusing to respond even to the approaches of her own children, turned one day in rage and attacked her mother-in-law, only to allege the next day that it was not she but a demon fox in her form guilty of the assault. More commonly, however, foxes take human form to waylay solitary travellers, or sometimes to call late at night on those who live alone. One of the author's village acquaintances, a man who had attended college in the city, once answered the door to a man asking help for his companion taken sick on the road. The friend followed his visitor by moonlight through the woods to where a man lay moaning and half-conscious at the roadside. Between them, they brought the man back to the village and settled him on a futon at the fireside. The writer's friend cared for his guests and did not himself retire to bed until sunrise, but when he woke a couple of hours later there was nobody there but a single gold coin on the futon where the sick man had slept. So the friend returned to the roadside where he found only the prints of foxes, and knew that he had entertained the fox gods unaware. And then there is another story from the same village ... The light is bright on Tom's face and he wrinkles his eyes to scan the horizon, to see the ship still at the centre of the circle of sea and sky and the sun half-way between zenith and the edge of the ocean. Almost four o' clock, almost time for tea; one eats, on a ship, to mark the passing of time, because there is no place to go or from which to return and each transit of the cream jug, each turn of the cake-stand, is a step in the dance of the long afternoon.

'Good afternoon, Mr Cavendish.'

The black-haired Louisa Davis under a black straw hat, her freckles her only colour against white skin and black dress. He puts down the book and pushes himself out of the low deckchair. 'Miss Davis.'

'You have found something to read? I thought the library unlikely to suit a gentleman's taste.'

'I doubt that I have a gentleman's taste, Miss Davis.'

She picks up his book. 'Ah, yes. Mr Marston. He relied, you know, much more than he admits upon a translator whose English was far from perfect. And you know how these people will invent something rather than say that they do not know.'

'These people, Miss Davis?'

She opens the book. 'Translators. Guides. Native informants. Of course in Japanese there are ways of communicating ignorance without saying "I do not know" but in English it invariably sounds like lying.'

Her skirt balloons in a gust of wind but she does not clutch as another woman would.

'You speak Japanese, then?'

She flicks through the book. 'Well enough.' She glances up. 'You are surprised?'

He shrugs. Miss Davis's father was a missionary and the family have been in Japan for three years. They are now, according to her mother, returning to England more or less destitute to live with Mrs Davis's brother. It is not Tom's understanding of destitution that travels on such a liner.

'Envious, perhaps.'

'I had no special teaching. I learnt as anyone might learn, by persistent application.'

'I congratulate you.'

She closes the book. 'I was able to help my father. It is hard for a foreign man to address Japanese women.'

'But you were able to do it? To preach in Japanese?'

He imagines her, white-skinned and blue-eyed, on a podium before an audience of women kneeling in kimono. Why would they come?

'When I was called. Yes.'

From the dining room, the gong sounds.

'I suppose you do not take tea?' she asks. Most days, he doesn't.

'I think I will.'

He does not offer his arm, but holds doors. Mrs Davis smiles up at him as he pulls back Miss Davis's chair. There are three tiers on the cake-stand: sandwiches, scones and fruit cake, piled on doilies that remind him of Ally's Aunt Mary.

'There you are, Louisa. It was not too windy, then, out there?'

Miss Davis turns her tea cup so that the handle points the correct way. 'No, Mamma.'

Silence falls. There are chairs at the table for an American man who has been teaching at a business college and his English wife, and for a Japanese man who says little and appears to find the food unappealing, but it is unlikely that they will come now.

Mrs Davis pours tea for Tom and her daughter. Miss Davis takes a sandwich. There is silence. She takes a neat bite. Her mother wields a cake-fork. He shifts in his chair. More silence. He will make them speak, he thinks, he will go on talking until Miss Davis's self-containment is breached.

'I saw some dolphins earlier,' Tom says. 'Playing in the bow wave.'

Miss Davis sips her tea, holding the cup the Japanese way, in both hands.

Mrs Davis is gazing out of the window.

'Only a small school. I always like to see dolphins. To be reminded that the water is full of life.'

Miss Davis takes another bite of her sandwich.

'And that we find the same creatures the world over. That voyaging is not merely an unnatural human propensity. Who knows how far a whale might travel?''

Mrs Davis slowly turns her head, as if hearing a faint sound from far away. He will keep going, he thinks, until one of them says something. He will see how inane they allow him to become before they are shamed into speech.

'It is surprising, isn't it, that in the art of such a seafaring nation as Japan marine life is so little represented. Considering the attention paid to all kinds of foliage. I have seen even mushrooms most precisely represented.' His lips tighten to stop himself smiling as this monologue drifts towards non-sense. Miss Davis touches her fingertips to her napkin. He remembers finding bits of a tea set along the beach at Porth Leven the week after a bad storm, picking up a blue-and-white cup missing only a part of the handle and turning it over to read *Atlantic Line Sophia* painted on the bottom. 'Although I do have among my collection a netsuke in the form of a dolphin. Made of walnut wood, I believe.'

Miss Davis sets down her cup. 'You have been making a col-lection, then, of Japanese art work?'

She sounds disbelieving, as if he's claiming to be a circus acrobat or a dress designer.

'Fulfilling a commission only. I do not claim to be a con-noisseur, but I have enjoyed what little I have been able to learn.'

'Really.' She splits her scone. 'And what did you buy, Mr Cavendish, for this commission?'

He thinks about the treasures in their crates somewhere below his feet, about the netsuke curled and sleeping, the pale green bowls in their nests of straw, the furled silks. He chooses the one whose untimely exposure he minds least, the selection of which he is most certain. Anything sold at the Annual Exhibition is an unquestionable choice.

'There is a silk hanging. Representing deer in an autumn wood. I suppose you had many opportunities to admire the changing trees, but I found the colours quite remarkable, beyond anything I have seen in England. This piece is gold-coloured but somehow quite natural-seeming at the same time, with dark branches and the crimson maple leaves, and under the tree a doe and a fawn. Woven, in this case, but I have also some embroideries.'

She has put a lot of strawberry jam on her scone. 'And you were told, perhaps, that this came from the household of a samurai warrior, where it has been venerated these hundred years and more?'

Her mother murmurs something, some restraint or protest.

'No. It is new. Only the skills are old, such as we have not in Europe.'

She smiles and then dabs her lips with her napkin, as if to cover the smile. 'I thought as much. I am afraid you will find, Mr Cavendish, that the Japanese learnt the arts of these hang-ings, as you call them, from the French within the last twenty years. It is like your lighthouses, you know: they perceive a need, or perhaps a market, and bend their energies to learn-ing. These "hangings" are made only for Europeans, using methods picked up in Lyon by young men sent for the pur-pose. They learn our arts, you know, as well as our sciences, and render them back to us. You could as soon say that the Japanese railways are built to an ancient tradition. May I help you to cake, Mr Cavendish? You are not eating.'

He pushes his plate away. 'As you remarked, it is not my habit to take tea.' Under the black hat, her hair is slipping down. He finds himself imagining how a bruise would look on the white skin between her collarbone and the neckline of her black dress, how it would bloom red, and then dark grey, as if she were smudged with coal, and over days turn purple, green and yellow, a stain of colour on her photographic black-and-white. In any case, Tom has fulfilled his commission, and he believes De Rivers will like the golden deer wherever the weaver learnt his trade.

'We are perhaps beginning an era where a great many of our more interesting endeavours will result from international exchange of one kind or another,' he says. 'Although I cannot think of an instance where Europeans have learnt a new technology or branch of science from another continent.'

'You think all things come of us, and of our own do they give us?'

It takes such sacrilege to rouse Mrs Davis. 'Louisa, please. Do not use those words so lightly.'

'I did not mean them lightly, Mamma. Only to suggest that Mr Cavendish seems to see his own kind as the creators of the world as we know it.'

He is confused; is it not she who has just told him that what he thought to be authentically Japanese is in fact a European fabrication?

'*As we know it*,' he says. 'Perhaps the difficulty is not with the world and its creators but with our knowledge. Or at least, with my knowledge. I do not doubt that there are original Japanese arts and sciences, but it is easy to believe that I have not succeeded in apprehending them. I came here, after all, to assist in the building of lighthouses, and that I believe I have done to the satisfaction of all concerned.'

She nods. 'A pleasing outcome indeed, then, Mr Cavendish.'

He looks at her, but her eyes are downcast. Quite apart from the loss of her father, he thinks, she is a very unhappy woman. It is no wonder she is not married.

As soon as tea is over, he goes in search of the professor. The smoking room first, he thinks, for it has become rather as he imagines a gentleman's club to be, a place of stale air, leather armchairs and prints hung too high to be of anything other than symbolic value. Drinks, he hears, are served at all hours of the day. He does not go there, and nor do the women.

Professor Baxter is asleep in a red armchair with a book open on his lap and his head lolling in the corner of the chair's winged back. On the table beside him is a glass of something brown and clear. His mouth is open red and wet, a gash or an indecency in the shabby refinement of this room. It is the mouth that makes Tom wake him, coughing theatrically from one pace behind the chair. The professor shifts, swats at a non-existent fly and then snores once as his head falls back. His mouth opens again. His teeth are flecked with brown and there is a string of saliva between his lips.

'Ah, Professor Baxter, there you are!'

He snorts, starts and sits up, blinking.

'I am so sorry. I didn't realise you were resting. Please, excuse me.'

'What? What? Ah, Tom Cavendish. Dear me. I must have dropped off. And what was I reading?' He turns over the book. 'Dickens. I fear then that my dozing says little for my literary judgement. Only do you know, I hadn't read it for years, not since I was a boy, and I thought: I remember reading that and I liked it, let's try again. It's not as if the library is full of temptation. Do sit down.'

Tom sits. '*Bleak House* is slow at the beginning,' he says. 'I'm sure the last two thirds would keep you awake.'

'Let us say so, dear boy.' He picks up his glass and sniffs it. 'No point in wasting it, is there? Care for one yourself?'

Tom shakes his head. 'After dinner, perhaps. Professor, may I ask you about something?'

'Naturally. Anything in the world. I am at your disposal.'

The professor sits up and smooths his hair, takes on before Tom's eyes the air of a man of authority.

'I bought some hangings, embroidery on silk, as part of my commission.'

The professor nods. 'Very popular with collectors. Some exquisite work. Quite remarkable.'

'Miss Davis says they're not Japanese. Well, that the Japanese make them in mimicry of the French. That they learnt to do it by sending men to Europe.'

'Does she? A learned young lady. Prefer them pretty, myself.'

'I am a little – a little concerned.'

'Concerned? Why? You fear that your patron will scorn your offerings in the belief that he could buy the same thing in any department store in Paris? Dear boy, the best Japanese things are quite extraordinary. Far beyond anything made in Europe. Surely you can see for yourself, the design as well as the execution, startling. Where did you get them?'

'A place my guide told me, out in the hills. They make things for the Imperial Palace. I thought that meant something.'

The professor leans over to pat his hand. 'I should say it does. Is this Nakayama? Well then. You could not have done better. And perhaps you feel able to mention the sum?'

Red-faced, gaze averted, Tom mentions it.

'You did very well, dear boy, very well indeed. They are not street-sellers to be fleeced or haggled as if their work were fruit at the end of a hot day. I knew the old man, you know, when he first came to Europe. Met him in London. He'd been in Macclesfield at the silk mills. Tiny little chap but he knew what he was doing all right. Miss Davis is right, the hangings are not an old Japanese tradition, any more than the railway lines or the vaccination are old Japanese traditions. But if we limited ourselves to old traditions, you and I would still be painting ourselves blue and living in mud huts. They've been weaving and embroidering silks since we were crawling in the mud, just not hanging them on the walls. Prize beauty where you find it, dear boy, that's my advice. If a thing's well done it's well done, wherever the chap's father learnt to do it.'

He watches Tom for a moment. 'Do you want to have them lift your boxes, let me have a look, put your mind at rest? I'll tell you, if it's Nakayama work you'll sell it easy as whistling if your man doesn't like the look of it.'

Tom shakes his head. 'It's his anyway. Bought with his money. It would be easier in some ways if the risk were mine.'

'Well then, he can sell it. Do you want to show me?'

Outside, nothing is different: sea and sky, waves and wind.

'I thank you but no. They are all wrapped and nailed into their crates. It's not as if I can do anything about it now whatever you say.'

'You have insurance?'

'I do and Mr De Rivers does. For more than I spent.'

'Leave it all be, then. And don't worry. Here, I'll get you a drink.'

Later, he walks the deck. There is moonlight and a light wind and the surge of the ship under his feet, and the waves black and silver under the stars. He does not know why he is troubled. Of course everyone on a ship is by definition literally disturbed, but there is something more than the daily discomfort of the transitory state. He remembers the imaginary bruise on Miss Davis' breast. He remembers Nakayama, the white buildings against the winter-forested hillside and the drift of clouds down the mountain valley and then the shock of the boiling dyes, pink and red and steaming hot, the man holding up the silk now dripping as if with blood. He walks a long time, as the ship and the sea turn under his feet towards the morning stars.

the path of Odysseus

She meets the postman at the gate and opens the letter there, standing on the path with the seagulls crying around her and the wind jostling the last faded petals off the camellias. Odd to have flowers that die in the spring. She can't read the postmark – Kyoto still or Yokohama? She's torn the chrysanthemum stamp in her haste.

He's coming home.

The letter shakes in her hand, as if this were a shock, as if she hadn't believed herself married and her husband yet walking the earth. She holds it in both hands. Five weeks ago. Five weeks ago he was leaving Kyoto. The holly trees arch in the wind like angry cats. He may be here, opening this gate, in two weeks. She must prepare the house. She must make sure his things are just as he left them, that the place is perfectly clean and tidy, all signs of the plasterers and painters gone. What if he dislikes the curtains, if he is angry that she did not take care of the old ones, allowed them to moulder in the damp? She must cook for him. He likes pies. Her pastry is not reliably good – maybe she could ask Molly to make some extra? He need not know, she need not tell him that it is the work of another woman's hands. And her body, she thinks, her breathing accelerating, she is still thin, and her hair noticeably greyer than when he left; what if he does not like this, if he regrets – if he would prefer – And her commitment to Rose Tree House, which means that it will be hard for her to cook before he comes home each day. What if he objects, if he does not like her to be out so much? You must take a housekeeper, Aunt Mary would say. It is time to have a servant. She remembers Jenny and shivers: someone to watch, and judge. Someone to know the stains on her underwear and her fancy for ginger biscuits, to read her letters when she is not there and to see how long she does not mend her clothes. Someone watching for every failure. No. Why should she jeopardise her newfound peace so that Tom doesn't have to eat her cooking? She has stood still for so long that a thrush hops across the grass by her skirt; she will miss the boat.

She sees it leave from the quay as she hurries down Dunstanville. She can see the trees around Rose Tree House and the mansions above it from here, but not the building itself. There is no reason why anything should have gone wrong, no reason why her lateness should cause any distress. She has half an hour, now, before the next ferry. She finds herself turning aside into the Prince Albert Garden, her feet following the path around the palm trees and the pink-flowering cactus, down the slimy stone steps to the beach. She's visible from across the estuary here, from Flushing, but it's also a place of concealment, under the old stone groyne. There is sea-glass among the pebbles, bits of broken china worn smooth as stone, and beer bottles and fishing-line more recently given to the sea. She sits on a rock and looks down the Carrick Roads, out to the open sea. Tom is there, somewhere, perhaps already in the Mediterranean, passing the sands of the Holy Land, maybe with Cyprus a shadow on the horizon.

The path of Odysseus, the wine-dark sea. Papa had wanted to name her after Penelope but Mamma was right, if not accurate, in objecting that there are more uses for a woman's life than undoing her knitting. There is not, Ally thinks, a great deal of difference between Sisyphus' curse and Penelope's salvation, only that what is torture for a man is meant to be fulfilment for a woman. She sees a small white form among the wet stones by her feet and stoops to pick it up. A china figurine, a female shape that has lost its arms and had the detail of its garb and facial features worn away by sands and sea. The curls of hair gathered high on the head are still visible, and the line of a tunic across the breast, a costume such as Ally once wore to model for Papa's Proserpina. She dusts off the sand with her fingertips and slips the figure into her pocket. Across the water, the ferry is leaving Flushing. She makes her way back up the steps towards the quay.

things he can barely name

He stands at the rail again, staring at the horizon which is still empty. He woke early and lay sweating under the sheets until the weight of inactivity became impossible. The brief flurry of dressing over, he paced the deck until he could no longer pretend not to know every knot in every plank. He toyed with breakfast, the eggs now pallid and tasteless, the sun already too hot for coffee to have any appeal and Louisa Davis as usual absent from the table. There is nothing to do. The women, he thinks, are accustomed to it; they sew, read, walk the deck, write letters, attend the meals served with the regularity and ceremony of monastic offices. They dress for dinner, spend time arranging their hair. It does not appear very different from their routines on land, Ally's Aunt Mary and Mrs Senhouse and doubtless English gentlewomen across India all keeping to the same timetable. Or perhaps more of them than one thinks are like Louisa, bored and angry and prowling. Their eyes have not met, they have scarcely spoken at the table, for the last two days.

Waves slap lazily against the hull below his feet. There must be life down there, something happening, a submarine world of fish and weed, a landscape of rock and valley. But for a man used to working, to looking back on a day or an hour and seeing what he has done, a passenger's life is vexatious. To sit, to be served, to read books that would be pleasurable as an evening's recreation but cannot substitute for the satisfactions of hard work done well: he is no fine gentleman to tolerate such weeks. To reflect on what has been done, and what should not have been done. It is not as if he planned what has happened, not as if he intended to do wrong. He paces. He tries not to count the days until they will probably reach harbour, wind and weather permitting. He wonders why he, who passed the voyage out contentedly enough in reading about Japan, watching the sea and conversing with others eastward bound for similar reasons, should suffer such discontent now. Perhaps the presences that dogged his final days in Kyoto are with him still, provoking unease and a state of pointless yearning. For the marriage he left, for Japan, for birds and flowers and fruit more beautiful than the real thing, for things he can barely name and certainly cannot have. For Louisa, or for Ally. He shakes his head, as if yearning were an insect whining around his ears, and then he hears whimpering and snuffling, a sound that reminds him of puppies. There is no dog on board, surely.

He turns around and squints along the ship, up into the sun. Not a dog, but on the deck above, up under the mast, a sailor – a boy scarcely old enough to be a sailor – sits rocking with his head on his knees.

'Hey,' Tom calls. 'Hey, are you ill? You need help?'

He remembers the stories the sailors in Scotland used to tell about young boys on ships, the acts they must suffer. The boy rocks and keens. There is no passenger access to that deck. Tom glances around, gets a foot onto the handle of the door into the corridor and pulls himself up by the railing above. Sweat pulses as he catches his breath. It is the most exercise he has had in days. The boy looks up as Tom moves towards him.

313

Dark hair, too long and falling into his eyes, pale face. He rubs his nose from side to side on the back of his hand.

'What? What do you want?'

At least he speaks English. An accent Tom hasn't heard before, southern.

'Are you hurt?' Tom asks. 'Can I help you?'

The boy grins. There are still tears on his face. He pushes back his hair and then holds out his other arm for Tom to see.

'Knew it'd hurt. See?'

On the back of the forearm, where a down of dark hair is beginning to push, the skin is swollen and red, as if scalded, and in the centre of the burn is a scribble of blue and green and red.

Tom reaches towards it. 'What have you done?'

'Don't touch. Bloody sore and all. 'S a dragon, see? Almost finished.' The boy licks his lip. 'You can't do 'em all at once. No-one could stand the pain.'

'Someone on board does this?'

The boy touches his arm with a fingertip and grimaces. 'Koni done it for me.'

'Koni?'

'Chinaman. AB.'

Able Seaman. Tom has seen several sailors who would fit such a description. He leans over the boy's arm and sees that there is indeed a dragon, a winged serpent whose scaly head reaches towards the wrist while its tail curves towards the pale tenderness of his inside arm. He cannot be older than about fourteen. Tom remembers the *betto*, the blue-skinned jinrikisha man. He pushes up his sleeve. He thinks of pain, throbbing through the hot night, of having a real sensation as his constant companion. He thinks of the risk of infection, and of healing as the ship makes its slow way west.

'Do you think he would do one for me?'

his children's children

The sky is clear on this side of the peninsula. It's the first time, he thinks, he's seen the sun since the *Endellion* entered the channel ten days ago, and it's already low over the sea. Out there is Scilly, the Wolf Rock, and then Spain, Africa, the Atlantic gathering and swirling towards the equator. But even in his mind he can't fly as far as Japan from here.

Ally's hand lifts and falls again, as if she thought better of reaching towards him. He puts his arm around her, hears her intake of breath and sees her glance at the driver. As if they were not man and wife. He pulls her in to him. She adjusts her hat.

'You are thinking of lighthouses,' she says. 'Of Bishop Rock, and Wolf?'

'Yes. And that everything is different here. I had always thought it a nonsense when people say that the light in one place is distinctive, but it is true that the sun shines differently and the very air seems to have another composition.'

Ally's gloved hand pats his. 'No. The mechanisms of respiration are just the same. But Cornwall is unlike anywhere.'

'You have learnt to love it. While I was away.'

She looks out. In the back of the trap, they are just high enough to see over some of the hedges, across stony fields and down to the shimmering sea. He has been to Penzance often enough but this is the first time he has taken this road, along Mount's Bay and over the hill to – what is the village called again? Perran-something. As they all are.

'Perhaps. I am not sure, about loving a place.'

She does not have many places, he thinks. Manchester is a trap from which she has escaped, London, or at least her aunt and uncle's part of London, only her foster-home. Now that De Rivers has paid him he can give her a home of her own. If she wants one. Not Florence Terrace, quite, but somewhere large enough for a servant and a child or two. He sits back and takes a slow breath: damp earth, wild garlic, sea wind. And homes must be made, not given.

There are mine-workings on both sides of the road, and the chapel dwarfed by mining towers better built of larger stones. The towers will outlive the churches, will stand above the low-lying fields when the damp in the walls and the roof timbers has undone all the cottages and the jerry-built miners' terraces have fallen like dominos. His mind's eye strains for the future, for what will happen when all the tin has been taken away, how this place will appear to the eyes of his children's children. If any. It is another conversation they are not having. They turn right, towards the sea. Perranuthoe, he remembers. You didn't take a honeymoon, Penvenick said, and a friend of mine has a small house, nothing much but it happens to be between tenants just now. I'm giving you a week's holiday and here are the keys. My wife reminded me, even in an established marriage it's hard when a man returns from a long trip. But my wife, Tom said, she has her own professional commitments. The new convalescent home. Penvenick had already arranged things with Crosswyn. The road narrows, gorse and grasses brushing the sides of the trap and the seat pitching and bucking over ruts and potholes. Ally turns to him in alarm and he shouts to the driver. We will walk, he says, take the luggage on and we will walk from here.

Perranuthoe is not a village, barely even a hamlet. Three farm houses and a few fishermen's cottages, a new school-house with the bricks – bricks, here? – still sharp and red between the granite cornerstones. And here it is, with their valises and the box of food outside the door, another unfamiliar house where there will be another unfamiliar bed in which he will wake to the unfamiliar light of another day. The last in the row of cottages, with only a field between the front windows and the sea. It's smaller than the white house in Falmouth and has thinner walls, probably colder and the wind will come straight off the open sea. Come, he tells himself, Penvenick has seen enough homecomings and knows what he is about. Tom takes the key from his pocket and opens the door for his wife.

They step straight into the front room, where a fire has already been lit for them. The floor is flagstones, but there is a hooked rug before the hearth where two deep armchairs await them, and a carved wall-cupboard of antique appearance hanging from the whitewashed wall below the stairs.

'There's water laid on,' Ally calls from the room on the other side of the warped wooden door. 'I wasn't expecting that.'

And she would, he thinks, she would happily have carried it from the well herself twice a day, as if she were a medieval peasant. The stone flags continue across the kitchen, where there is an oak dresser against one wall, an old wooden table with a bench at each side, an iron stove and a white sink with one brass tap.

'No bathroom,' he says.

She looks up from the range. 'Most people manage without, you know.'

He hears what she is not saying: most of the population is without bathrooms and apparently capable of happiness. But in Japan, he thinks, in Japan there were bathtubs made of polished wood filled every day and bags of bran to scrub away the dirt, all poured away in daily absolution. De Rivers' payment has been generous, beyond the terms agreed, but if he ever finds himself truly rich he will bring the carpenter from Makoto's village and have a Japanese house built in England. Or perhaps simply move to Japan. If Ally will come too.

She comes to him, raises her arms as if to put them around his neck and then pauses and lets her hands return to her sides. She does sometimes want to touch him.

'No,' he says. 'Don't stop. You can hold me, Al. I've come back.'

He has come back. Here he is. He waits for her to move, to embrace him. Penvenick was right, he thinks, here, here in this house, they will surely find their way back to each other as they have not, so far, been able to do at home. She is still standing there, as if she can't decide what to do.

the space between them

Ally is unpacking the box of food provided by Penvenick, or, more probably, by Penvenick's housekeeper. Such a woman, she fears, will not have imagined Ally's incompetence in the kitchen, will have ordered on the assumption that cooking is a universal feminine skill. There may be rabbits to be skinned or flour and yeast to be turned into bread. She kneels at the dresser and moves the two pans, the four plates and four bowls, to one side. From the other room she hears Tom rustle and cough. She is beginning to think that the – the awkwardness, the constraint – between them is not going to clear like a morning mist, that time itself will not heal their harm. Good: on the top of the crate there is a large loaf of brown bread and a box containing a dozen eggs. A pound of butter and, thank you, Mr Penvenick, a boiled ham. Ham and eggs, ham sandwiches. Milk, tea, sugar. A bunch of leeks, easy enough to cook. Potatoes, onions. A whole plum cake! And at the bottom, a china jar of potted shrimps. She will need to buy some more bread from somewhere during the week. Probably one of the farms will sell milk. Fruit, she thinks, we should have some fruit, but at least fruit is not an omission she can be expected to repair by kitchen work. She sits back on her heels. There must be more to do in the kitchen, there is always more to do in a kitchen. She closes the cupboard and stands up. She could wash and chop some leeks, ready to cook later. It is past teatime; perhaps Tom would like a cup of tea and a slice of the cake. She hasn't found a teapot. She moves towards the sink and touches its cold white edge, briefly reminded of laboratories and the dissection room at the Women's Hospital. Outside the window, a hawk hangs in the sky over the gorse. In ten days, she will be back at Rose Tree House, where there is real work for her.

'Ally? Would you like to take a walk?'

The shadows out there are long and the light pink.

'Of course. Unless you would like me to make tea? There is a cake.'

'It's nearly sunset. Let's go out.'

He helps her into her coat, holds the door for her and locks it behind them. The grass bows as the wind off the sea flaps her skirts and tugs at her hat. The field between the cottages and the sea has been ploughed and lines of green are forming on the dark earth. Behind it is the silver sea, and then the reddening sky. West, America. There are no ships.

Tom offers his arm and she takes it, a sign of willingness. She should say something about the house, about Penvenick's kindness.

'There is a boiled ham,' she says. 'It will make the cooking much easier.'

He nods. 'I like ham.'

They walk back down to the road, which appears to run over the edge of the rocks into the sea. She steals a glance at him, at the line of his jaw and the red hair under his hat.

'And potted shrimps.'

He is looking at the horizon, at the waves in the gap where

320

the road falls onto the beach. 'That's good. Here, let me help you.'

The rocks are partly worn and partly cut into steps leading down to a mass of grey boulders. I will never be able to climb over those, she thinks, not in this skirt and these shoes, but beyond them waves are curling onto the sand. There is sand on the steps and she slips and grabs his arm, feeling the popping of stitches in her skirt.

'Careful,' he says. 'Would you rather go back?'

No, she thinks, she would rather stop and kilt up this ridiculous tight skirt, and there is nobody but him to see if she did and even if there were it is not as if farm labourers are likely to faint at the sight of a woman's ankle.

'I can manage,' she says. 'Thank you.'

But she almost falls twice before they reach the sand. Hobbling yourself in the name of vanity, Mamma would say, trussing up your limbs at the dictate of fashion. Are you quite lost to all sense? She imagines Mamma and May coming back across the sea, finding her undefended here. He braces himself and takes both her hands as she slithers off the last rock. She is too old for this physical comedy, she thinks, too old and too tall.

'There. And no Louisa Musgrove about it.'

'Louisa Musgrove?' She brushes down her skirt.

'A character in a novel. One you would perhaps enjoy.'

She shakes her head. 'I have not time or patience for novels, Tom.'

Not since Mrs Gaskell, before she was unwell. He must know she is not that kind of woman. He should have known it since the day they met.

'I know. But that is not to say you would not enjoy one.'

From here, they can see the castle on St Michael's Mount, and some of the causeway over to Marazion. It is one of those buildings that is not quite real, a turreted palace drifting between the sea and the sky. Perhaps they will make a trip there, later in the week, walk across the causeway and picnic by the church at the foot of the hill. She lifts her face to the wind, closes her eyes to see the sun red through her eyelids. She should not have agreed to this, a week of time-wasting just when she is most needed at Rose Tree House, just when the women are beginning to trust her and each other. She will not be there if a reply comes from Mrs Rudge's children, or when Mrs Curnow goes out on day leave with her husband. She can't think why Dr Crosswyn was so insistent. Unless he has some change or scheme in mind best accomplished in her absence, unless the committee has made some condition that he knows she would resist.

He comes to her side. 'Did you read anything new? While I was away?'

She doesn't open her eyes. 'No. Only medical books.' She must try harder. She must not shut him out, must not allow herself for a moment to admit the possibility that his questions might be foolish. She should tell him that she read his Gaskell, and did not find it unpleasant. 'And you? You wrote to me about the travel books.'

She took off her gloves to come down the rocks and the touch of his fingers on her bare hand makes her start.

'I wanted to learn all I could. I think some of those books are much more accurate than others. It's hard, without reading Japanese.'

His hand is warmer than hers, and larger. Maybe every day they should touch a little more, hands and then forearms and then upper arms, faces, shoulders, chests and bellies. In one week—

'But the ship's library was mostly novels. I began with Richardson but after Singapore I'm afraid my tastes declined sadly.'

She lets her fingers tighten on his. 'There is little to do on a ship, I dare say. Especially for a man used to action.'

He lifts her hand and pats it. 'My time could have been better spent. They were strange days.'

'You were between lands,' she says.

The fire has gone out when they return to the house and shade is gathering in the corners of the rooms. She stands rubbing her chilled hands and watching while he kneels at the grate rebuilding the fire. She should light the candle lantern and find a bedroom candlestick before it is too dark, she should carve the ham and cook some eggs. His match grates and flares and the newspaper kindling flames out and then the log begins to hiss and glow.

'There. Shall I light the range too, or will we have a cold supper?'

She blows into her hands. 'Tea, at least.'

He stands up. 'Why don't you sit here and get warm? I know how to make tea, you know. And how would you like your eggs?'

She holds her hands to the fire, where flames are steadying around the log. 'I don't like to sit idle, Tom. We'll do it together.'

They bring their plates back into the front room and eat from their laps. Tom tells her Japanese tales, as if by talking he can fill the space between them, as if there are stories that will reach across months and oceans apart, bridging madness and despair. He tells her about temples with gardens spread about them, about beds of gravel raked every morning into the semblance of wind-rippled ponds. He tells her about red leaves blowing into a canal, and about roof tiles each embossed with a chrysanthemum pattern, and she does not know why he tells these things, what is the purpose of informing her about foliage and waterways she will never see. Later, when first she and then he have washed at the kitchen sink and climbed the steep stairs carrying a wavering candle, later when they have blown out those candles and lain a few moments side-by-side in an unfamiliar bed in the dark, he reaches for her again and again she feels her body tighten and tense, her shoulders lift and her belly clench and she turns away from him. She thinks of Rose Tree House, of her white room there and the women resting below her, their minds healing in her care. This is not the answer, she thinks. There is no optimism in the propagation of family life. She has found a way to live and it does not involve the institution of marriage. It does not, it turns out, involve Tom. She lies on her side, facing the wall, feeling the lumps in the mattress under her ribs and thigh and the rough grain of the pillow under her cheek in the dark. The air is cold and smells of candle-smoke. It does not seem to take him very long to fall asleep.

anything that matters

At sea he woke early for solitude, to have the deck and sometimes the library to himself for an hour or so before the other
passengers appeared. And because twice, after she'd stopped
speaking to him at the table, Louisa Davis came to find him
there. Now he wakes, he thinks, because of the dawn, because
of the seagulls, because while he is asleep he does not know
where he is. The west-facing bedroom is still dim, full up with
a submarine light strained by curtains whose green he didn't
notice last night. The wall a foot from his face is roughly
painted, uneven as the face of the moon. He lies still so she
doesn't sense his consciousness, tries to breathe slowly so his
body, his heartbeat and the growth of his hair, doesn't signal
to hers that there's somebody here now. She does not love him,
he thinks. It is all gone, whatever it was, and he cannot tell her
anything that matters. Would it help, he wonders, could he get
back to where they were last year, if he turned now, if he
reached over her sleeping shoulder to unbutton the nightdress,
if with his foot he pushed up its frilled hem until his hand
could touch her thigh? If he rolled her over and before she was
fully awake, before she could object, held her wrists and

silenced her mouth with kisses? Would it be a relief to her simply to capitulate, is it the courtesies of negotiation and not the act itself of which they are no longer capable? He remembers Louisa, whose white flesh was indeed tender as ripe fruit, who dropped one layer of black clothing after another to the floor of his cabin and rejoiced when at last he understood his role, when he was not gentle. He remembers her.

He reaches around to touch the fox under his nightshirt. He has not told Ally about his tattoo. He had thought that she would find it, and he would explain. He had imagined her fingers and her mouth travelling over it, and himself telling the story of the dancing dog fox and the blue-skinned betto and the boy on the ship. And not telling another tale, which she does not need to know. Naturally there is awkwardness after so many months apart. Naturally they must learn to be together again. They have both been busy, absorbed in their work, both solitary and free. It is not as if she has spent the time embroidering handkerchiefs and ticking off the days of his absence.

She does not love him.

His shoes sit neatly together beside the bed, and on the chair his clothes lie folded.

He edges from under the sheets, not to cause a draught or a chill to disturb her. He does not know these floorboards, sidles tentatively as a man fearing quicksand. By the door he looks back. She is on her side, just as she went to sleep, with her arms pressed over her breast and her hands tucked under her chin, her knees raised so that her feet and her behind form one rise of the blankets. She's pulled the sheets tight around her shoulders. He can't really see her face, but her hair has spread across the pillow again. He bites his lip and goes downstairs, treading on the outsides of the steps where creaks are least likely.

He opens the curtains. The room smells of woodsmoke and the grate is full of ash, will have to be swept before another fire

326

can be lit. He will need to bring in more logs. One thing at a time, and the day will pass, and then another day and at last they will return to Falmouth and the daily distractions of work. He should have taken his clothes from the chair upstairs. He puts his coat over his pyjamas, unlocks the door and steps out barefoot into the morning. Wet grass closes around his ankles.

The sky is hanging low over the peninsula, the horizon that called to him yesterday absent as the sun behind the clouds. They will have to go out and walk anyway, he thinks, they cannot pass the day in that house. He should have brought some work, the journals he missed in Japan, the beginnings of a paper he might deliver to the Polytechnic Institute and then perhaps the Society of Engineers. He had imagined, somehow, that being here, being with Ally, would constitute occupation. He cannot now recall how he thought they would pass so many hours. He crosses the grass, treading dandelions underfoot, and picks his way along the track to the beach. He will walk on the sand, let the waves come from Africa wash his earthbound feet, but when he comes to the bluff he sees that the tide is so high that there is no beach and the sand is under a man's height of water and sullen grey waves. He clambers across the rocks and sits there, listening to the crash and hiss, trying to remember if it sounds the same as in Japan. There was sand the colour of a white man's skin and palm trees black against the sky. His pyjamas cling around his ankles. It does not matter what he has done.

She does not love him.

there are no birds

She does not know what has woken her. It must be late, she should not have slept so long, he will think she is in the habit of lying long in bed. She turns to find herself alone, because she has overslept, because hardworking people began the day hours ago. He should have woken her. Before he went away he woke her with his hands and his lips half an hour before his alarm clock rang. She pushes back the blankets and swings her feet to the cold floor. The chill reaches up under the flimsy lace-trimmed nightgown she bought with her first month's salary. Flaunting yourself, she thinks, aping the younger and prettier woman you never were. She cannot do this. She can work, she thinks, she can be a doctor, she can write articles and perhaps eventually a monograph, but she cannot be someone's wife, not any more. She has made herself ridiculous, a woman with bony feet and greying hair got up like a young bride, and in her foolishness she has brought no other nightdress. But she will cut off the lace at the hem and neck this day, and save it for the women at Rose Tree House. Mrs Rudge will find a use for it. She plucks at the frilled wrists and feels her stomach curl with embarrassment. Pride and self-flattery bring their own certain punishment. The house does not feel as if there is another person in it, but even so she closes the bedroom door and moves fast in case he should come up the stairs and catch her undressed, the sternal bones where a cleavage should be and her pelvis sharp where true women have soft roundedness. She pulls on her drawers under the nightgown and casts it off only when her chemise is laid out ready on the bed. Corset, petticoat, stockings, blouse, skirt, jacket. It is hard to raise her arms in the jacket but she doesn't brush her hair until she's fully dressed, armoured. A woman reaches an age when her aspiration in dressing should be only to look respectable. At least she has still her work. She hopes all is well at Rose Tree House, that Miss Trennick has been spared further nightmares and especially that Mrs Curnow, who is still very easily alarmed, is finding it easier to make small daily decisions. She hopes the seeds are still growing and that there have been no further difficulties with the sewing machine. She should be there, she thinks. The new housekeeper is a kind and sensible woman, in whom Ally senses some past experience of the unsettled mind, but Dr Crosswyn has lent his senior nurse for the week and she is unaccustomed, probably unsympathetic, to the newly-formed ways of Rose Tree. She won't care for the women, Ally thinks, she won't help them to care for them-selves, she will speak harshly and weeks of their work will be undone. She pins up her hair and goes downstairs.

Tom is not there, and last night's dishes still where he insisted that she leave them on the table. At least, then, it is clear what to do first. She sets water to heat while she goes down the garden path. The floor is not as clean as it might be, especially around the stove; she will wash it when she has done the dishes, and she will sweep the grate and perhaps also clean the bannisters, which are sticky to the touch. The fear has come back, she thinks. She is behaving as if Tom were

Mamma, and she longs to return to the madwomen who do not judge and find her wanting, or even to Annie and Aunt Mary. She does not want to be married, not like this. She does not want to be a wife.

Although as far as she can tell he ate no breakfast, he seems to have little interest in the potted shrimps. She toasted the bread laboriously as a gesture towards cooking, towards an effort to please, but he has let it go cold.

'Would you like something else? I'm afraid there's not much choice but I can maybe go down to the farm.'

He pushes his plate away. 'No, Ally. I'm not fussy, you know that.'

She toys with her own lunch. She is hungry and the shrimps are a treat, but it seems uncouth or even heartless to tuck in while he denies himself.

'You are perhaps still missing the Japanese food?' He says he liked it, that he came to understand subtleties of texture that simply don't appear in English cooking, although nothing about his descriptions makes it sound appetising. Raw fish and cold rice and a broth made from fermented beans, how does a race subsist on that? And how should she, should England, compete with what does not appear in English cooking? He does not wish to be here either, she thinks. We have made a mistake.

She stands up. 'Tea, then. I'll boil the kettle.'

He looks up. 'I can do it. Finish your lunch.'

'It's no trouble.'

When she comes back he has picked up the newspaper he bought in Penzance yesterday.

She looks at her shrimps. 'Is there bad news?'

He stays behind the paper. 'Isn't there always?'

The wind rushes over the grass outside. A seagull ululates,

a chorus repeated from overhead. He puts down the paper, as if lowering a standard, begins to speak and stops.

'What is it?' she asks.

'The news seems so provincial. As if no-one here knows that there are oceans and continents and other ways of understanding everything.'

'You are reading the *Western Morning Herald*,' she points out. 'But I think we do know those things, Tom. Especially here. I hear more languages on the streets of Falmouth than I did in London. It's just that those aren't truths you can live with, really, the suffering and conflict of all the beings everywhere on earth. You can't – you can't hold everyone in your mind at once, it's too much. Like the idea of death. It silences thought.'

Mamma cannot for a moment forget the suffering of the world and since she cannot solve it, she cannot have peace. And at the asylum, she wants to say, at the asylum I knew people who saw the skull in every face and the approach of darkness in every heartbeat and they weren't wrong but they weren't well. But he doesn't want to know about the madwomen and she doesn't want him to think she's suggesting that his thoughts are like madness.

'It's more like the idea of life,' he says. 'There is so much to learn.'

But not here, she thinks. Not in the life together that they are supposed to be resurrecting. 'The water must be boiling by now. I'll make the tea.'

He says there is a path around the headland to Prussia Cove. He says he likes to feel the rain on his face. He says Prussia Cove is the scene of a dramatic wreck, and that for a long time a family of smugglers held the village as a private fiefdom. She looks at him pacing the floor as she has not seen him pace before; he is different now.

She swallows. She must not insinuate herself where she is not wanted, must not cling and clutch a man who wishes to be free, but nor must she give him to believe that she does not wish for his company, that she prefers a warm fireside to her husband's conversation. 'I could come too. If you like. But of course if you wish to be alone I understand, I have letters to write.'

He turns back towards the staircase. 'Come if you want to, Alethea. Just as you prefer.'

No, she wants to say, as you prefer; I have still dignity enough to want only where I am wanted. He is not Mamma. She steels herself. 'I prefer to be with you. As long as I do not intrude.'

He stops. 'Good. Come too. But you'll get wet.'

She shrugs. 'My skin is no more permeable than yours. As long as we keep moving we'll keep warm.'

He does not want her, she thinks. He would, on balance, rather she were not there.

At first they follow the track between the fields. The rain is only mizzle, just heavy enough to fall, beading the leaves in the hedge and the taller grasses with drops too small to run. Gorse flowers seem to glow, almost to pulsate, against the grey and green of land and sky, and on her right the sea and clouds merge. There is no birdsong, but the hawk hovers again on the hill. Before they have passed the beach he is walking ten paces ahead, although she has no difficulty keeping up. She has angered him somehow, has done something to annoy: perhaps he did not want her to come, or objects to her late rising or to the meagre lunch. He did not like to come back and find her washing the floor, he has never liked to see housework. There is no shame, she thinks, in any task done well, and does not he himself insist on cleaning his own shoes and emptying the pot under the bed? Perhaps he will like the slices of plum cake she has brought to eat at Prussia Cove. She must think of something to ask him, something he will like to talk about. She hurries to catch up. Her skirt is already mired and clinging about her ankles. It is too late. What marriage, what friendship, was ever saved by small talk?

She reaches to take his arm and thinks better of it. Don't cling, don't need. 'Tom? What was your favourite of the things you brought back?'

He has spoken much of the places, of houses without walls and gardens without flowerbeds, but very little about his acquisitions.

He checks his pace and glances back at her. 'For De Rivers, you mean? Or my own things?'

She just wants him to talk to her. 'Either. The object you liked best.'

He walks on. They climb a stone stile and the path, free now of the fields, slopes down towards a deep inlet. He is not going to answer her.

'I tried not to like them. Or at least only to admire, because I knew they were not mine. It's a different thing, buying for another person. I did not much like that aspect of it. I had not thought, you see, that buying such things – well, works of art, I suppose one should call them – would be so unlike buying bricks or steel.'

She nods. 'Uncle James says most people buy art the way they choose a wife.' Without thinking, Uncle James adds, but she does not say that.

'Perhaps it felt a little like choosing another man's wife. There were so many beautiful things.'

In the inlet, below the short cliffs, waves buckle and swish, unable to run and break between the narrow walls.

'So there was not one in particular, one more memorable

beauty?' She should stop. She knows that he does not want to answer.

He looks out to sea. There are folded seagulls bobbing on the waves. 'Yes. There was one.'

She says nothing. Behind him, where he can't see, she pulls up her skirts to climb over a rock. The path ahead rises now, up onto the headland. He is saying something but he's several paces ahead and facing out into the wind. Something about the Imperial Palace. She catches up.

'A kind of trade fair, with stalls. Someone from Nakayama. They're famous, they made the hangings for the new palace in Tokyo. They were all extraordinary but there was one – cranes, and wisteria. You can't imagine the fineness of the embroidery. Inconceivable, that someone would spend such time and energy sewing a feather.'

He is an engineer, she thinks. It is the process that fascinates him.

'And it was beautiful?'

He walks on, ahead again. 'Of course.'

'And De Rivers appreciates it?'

'I didn't buy it, Al. I told myself it was too big, and so costly I dare not spend another man's money so.'

'But?'

He looks back at her. 'Oh, I don't know. It was very expensive. If De Rivers hadn't wanted it I doubt it could have been sold here for more than I would have paid. But I didn't want him to have it, I think. It belonged in Japan.'

It feels like a confession. The one that mattered belongs in Japan, and is still there, and also here in his mind. They reach the top of the headland, from which St Michael's Mount is just visible through the rain, disembodied and floating above the bay. And she understands that there will be no outing there, no basket unpacked onto a gingham cloth under the

334

trees. They will not sit together on the grass and see their shadows lengthen and merge in the afternoon sun until the tide turns and it is time to go home. They will not find each other at last in the whitewashed room when darkness has fallen. Not this time.

the tender slowness of a northern dusk

The tide is coming up the estuary. Moored boats lift and bump as their keels feel water once more around them, and the light in the air shifts as waves cover the mud. The groynes at Flushing stand bare, the stonework of Dutch hands three hundred years dead exhibited for admiration. The seagull on the wall outside Tom's window looks around, makes one tart remark and takes wing. Soon the fishing boats will be in.

Penvenick peers around Tom's door. 'I'm off home now, Tom. What are you working on?'

Ink has dripped from his uplifted pen onto the blotting paper. 'Just the letters about the apparatus for Red Rock.'

Penvenick opens the door fully. He became stooped and drawn while Tom was in Japan. Tom wonders when his son last saw him, if he knows how age has come upon the man.

'Taking you a good while.'

Tom dips the pen again. 'I'll stay till they're done.'

Penvenick sighs. 'There's no great urgency. Mrs – Dr Cavendish will be wanting you home.'

Tom keeps his head down. 'She's over at the convalescent home.'

'Thought they had a housekeeper for the nights?'

'Ally had to dismiss her. Not suitable.'

'So your wife stays every night?'

Tom looks up. Penvenick already knows. He writes the first line of the address. 'Most nights, yes. She won't be wanting me home.'

Penvenick pats Tom's shoulder and then draws back. 'I'm sorry to hear that, Tom. Truly sorry.'

What is he supposed to say? Thank you? It is nothing? It is not nothing. He has – they have – failed. He has not learnt to be a husband, has not sufficiently studied what husbands do. He assumed it would be obvious, matrimony. He assumed that love and good will would be enough, and he was wrong. He waits while Penvenick shuffles away and then writes the next line of the address. At least now the old man knows, he can volunteer for the Scilly job without having to give explanations. He dips the pen again.

There is still sunlight lying on the hill above Flushing when he leaves the office. From here, he cannot see even the rooflines of the palaces above Rose Tree House, only the sky above where Ally is and the sea before her. It will be easier to think of their separation in Scilly, from which England itself is only occasionally visible on the horizon. It would be easier still if he returned to Japan. A perfectly civilized arrangement. Not yet. The boats are all afloat now, bobbing and swaying companionable as sheep in a field, and the stillness that precedes sunset is settling on the water. He did not see this in Japan, the tender slowness of a northern dusk. He would need to go further: Aomori, Hakodate, Sapporo, the high forest places of the Ainu, who worship bears by taming them and nurturing them, calling them Brother until one day it is time to put the honoured creature to a slow death. The seagulls wheel and call over his head. He will walk out to the sea before he goes home.

There are flowers blooming in all the gardens, bright colours and variegated shapes foaming over walls and dripping from trees and fences. The terraced houses are painted pink, blue, green, as if by children newly entranced by the power of colour. Along Dunstanville, couples saunter, the women garish in aniline dyed skirts, laughing and chattering loud as ravens. He remembers beds of gravel raked into patterns that wove tapestries of shade under black branches and crimson leaves. He remembers Makiko's grey and white bird kimono, her neat gait as she knelt and rose. He has passed the captains' houses and is almost at Ludgate House. He finds himself on the doorstep, ringing the bell.

'Good evening.'

He remembers the maid from last time, an elderly woman, tall and thin in her black and white, her hair scraped back under a lace cap.

'I'm not expected,' he says. 'I'm Thomas Cavendish. I brought all the things – the hangings, the netsuke – from Japan?'

She waits, the door still in her hand. The house is so big, he thinks, the panelling so deep and the brocade curtains so heavy, that he would not hear if there were a whole dinner party going on in there. He feels dampness under his arms.

'And I was just wondering – well, I was thinking, perhaps if it's not an inconvenience I would so very much like to see them again. In their places. Now Mr De Rivers has had time to – to arrange them.'

She looks him up and down. 'Mr and Miss De Rivers are at table, sir.'

Inside are all the treasures, the foxes on the inro, the blossoms on the tea-bowls, the golden persimmons floating on the lacquerwork tray. And not the cranes, which are still there, still under the imperial roof in Kyoto.

'Perhaps I might return?'

A door opens, a shaft of light across the dim hall behind her.

'Who is it, Ellen?' De Rivers approaches, napkin in hand. 'Tom Cavendish! Good evening.'

Tom shifts. What is he doing, why is he here? He has completed his commission and been generously rewarded.

'It's nothing, Mr De Rivers. Only I was passing, and thinking of Japan, and I found myself here wondering how the – the consignment looks in its new home. Foolishness, I'm afraid. I apologise for interrupting your evening.'

De Rivers watches a cart pass down the hill behind Tom. 'Not tonight, Mr Cavendish. Come back on – let me see – Wednesday. After dinner, if you please, but I dare say we can raise a supper for you.'

'Thank you.' Tom feels his face flush. He is, after all, always was, just a hired hand. A flunkey. He has no idea what hour is meant by after dinner and before supper. 'Er, what time should I come, please? Only, I have business obligations, you understand.'

De Rivers is turning away, impatient for the next course. 'Penvenick does work you hard. Nine o' clock?'

'Thank you. Until then.'

Tom steps back onto the pavement with his fists balled. Wherever he goes, whatever he builds, however he might learn to conduct himself in a Japanese tea room or among the boys on a ship, he will never know the codes of the rich. Even Mr and Mrs Dunne serve suppers only after evenings of dancing or at the theatre. How can a man be dining – he checks his watch – at eight and require feeding again an hour later? He continues down the hill, into town and away from the white cottage. Babies go longer between meals, he thinks, than bloated rich men. At least on a passenger ship there is the excuse of boredom. He is past the quay before his face begins to cool in the breeze picking up on the water.

the darkness at the top of
a cloudless sky

Mrs Curnow's trunk stands at the bottom of the stairs. The
front door is propped open with a grey oval stone, and the
tin trunk bathes in sun like a rock on the beach. There are
scuffs on the floorboards now, and a dent in the wall where
the door-handle hits it. The hall smells of the bluebells in a
jam jar on the windowsill, and as Ally comes down the stairs
she can hear the thump and roll of Miss Mason kneading
dough in the kitchen and the hens squabbling in the back-
yard.

Mrs Curnow is going home. Her husband has agreed to
send the girls to stay with his mother for a fortnight and Mrs
Curnow's sister is coming to stay so that she won't be alone
during the day when Mr Curnow is at work. She will be 'on
probation', as if madness were a crime and sanity as provi-
sional as moral reform, and at the end of her probation she
will have to prove her sanity in an interview with the committee. How will you keep yourself well, they like to ask. What
will you do if you feel yourself weakening again? Do you consider yourself wholly cured? *Yes* means that the patient has
unrealistic ideas and lacks self-knowledge, *no* means that she is

still unwell. Ally stops in the kitchen to greet Miss Mason and then steps out into the morning.

The trees, now in full bright leaf, rise tall as churches around the garden, and the air is loud with their whispers. Even now, near eleven, half the garden lies under shifting shadows, and at first it is hard to see clearly across the sunshine to the two women bending in the shade at the far end.

'Mrs Curnow?'

They both straighten up, hands on hips. Mrs Curnow's hair has come loose and her face is flushed. She will need to look tidier for the committee. They are weeding the new vegetable bed, both able to distinguish the nurtured from the unwelcome green shoots as Ally cannot.

Mrs Rudge gestures towards the basket at her feet. 'I'm keeping the chickweed for the hens. And there's plenty of it.'

Mrs Curnow wipes her forehead with the back of her hand, smearing mud. 'I'm not wanted already? He hasn't come early?'

'No,' says Ally. 'But it is probably time to come in and get ready. You will want to wash your hands and face.' And it was not a good idea to weed the garden in the costume in which you propose to travel, she thinks, but it is too late for that.

'Of course. Margaret, you won't mind if I go in now? And you'll come and say goodbye, won't you, before I go?'

'We all will, I'm sure. The first one. You'd best go make yourself pretty.'

They watch as Mrs Curnow hurries towards the house. The grass is still long and rough, harbouring snails which are also given to the hens, but gradually the garden is being tamed. Dr Crosswyn himself spent some time in personal combat with the brambles, and set up a highly irregular arrangement by which the gardener of the cottage hospital came to dig beds and build a henhouse in exchange for Ally's attendance on the women's ward one Saturday. Mrs Rudge turns back to her work. Her children have not replied to the letter, and her husband shows no interest in assisting in her discharge. And Tom, Ally thinks, Tom has made no approach either, shown no desire for her return.

'These are the marrows?' Ally asks. 'It is hard to imagine that they will get so big. The growth must be almost visible in the summer.'

'Aye. But they're not much use when they're let get too big. Taste of nothing much and liable to fall into a heap when you cook them. We'll eat these small and tender. Maybe with the wild garlic, if it holds on long enough.'

Because they will both be here, still, Ally and Mrs Rudge, when the marrows are small, and when they are large, when summer nights flit over the garden and when the leaves begin to turn and fall again.

'That sounds good. And this one is the chickweed?'

Ally stoops and pulls a few stalks, trying to tug gently so the roots slide out of the soil instead of breaking off. She does not like the hens, with their ancient scaly feet and unblinking hostile eyes, but she is glad that they are there, an audible counterpoint to the work of living together.

The house is resting, full of sunlight and shadows and the smell of flowers. Under its cloth in the kitchen, Miss Mason's bread respires, grows, exhales the smell of yeast at work, of bacteria multiplying and grain lifting towards the sun's warmth. Dust dances in the banners of light hanging across the hall, and the breeze from the sea comes across the stones and the trees to stir the curtains with an idle hand. Ally listens. Miss Gunner and Miss Trennick have gone across the water to help at a church coffee morning organised by the vicar's wife. I think you are so brave, she said to Ally, taking on such responsibility. I wonder you are not afraid to sleep there all alone! Anything we can do to help, of course – I do not sleep there alone, Ally replied. There are seven of us, and if you wish to help it would be most kind of you to invite our residents to participate in the Ladies' Programme. Several of them have considerable experience of such matters and would doubtless be of assistance to you.

Water trickles: Miss Mason in the bathroom, easing flour from under her fingernails and from the creases in her hands. Mrs Henning still prefers, or feels obliged, to spend time in her bedroom rather than taking possession of the sitting room, and she is probably up there trying to finish the handkerchief she has been embroidering for Mrs Curnow. A drawer closes overhead: Mrs Curnow checking again that she has left nothing behind. Another one opens. The repeated checking is not reassuring, and Mrs Curnow's apparent inability to recognise and control the checking less reassuring still. Mr Curnow should be here any moment. Ally hurries up the stairs.

Mrs Curnow is kneeling at her bureau with an open drawer in her hand. There is still mud on her face. She, Ally and Mrs Rudge all verified the bureau's emptiness yesterday.

Ally kneels beside her and touches her arm. 'You know that if anything were to be left behind we would send it on to you. You can lose nothing.'

Mrs Curnow closes the drawer and puts her hand on another one. 'I know. It's just – I worry. I don't want him thinking I can't be trusted to pack. To know my own things.'

'Yes. But also, you don't want those around you to think that you do not know your own mind and doubt your own actions. It is a hard thing to prove oneself well, Mrs Curnow, and it is not foolish to be anxious. Come.'

Ally stands up and holds out a hand to help Mrs Curnow, who has been kneeling on the wooden floor for some time. Mrs Curnow lumbers to her feet. Ally leads her to window, from which they can see the trees sparkling with sunlight and the sea glimmering behind them and the darkness at the top of a cloudless sky.

'It will be a difficulty for some time that your family and friends will be watching you for signs of distress and anxiety, and watching more closely if they see such signs, because naturally you will be anxious about being watched, especially if you fear losing your liberty. If you are indeed well, and if your friends indeed value you most when you are well and happy, the passage of time is likely to ease the circle of surveillance and fear. Otherwise, I can tell you only that when in doubt a woman is more likely to be criticised for action than for inaction, for speech rather than silence.' If a woman in most situations wishes to be considered sane, she should conduct herself in the way best calculated to drive any reasonable adult to distraction. This is probably an exaggeration, and anyway not a useful thing to tell Mrs Curnow, already tangled and trapped in self-surveillance.

'There. I hear wheels. Come, we will talk to your husband. He must be your friend in this matter.'

They give Mr Curnow lunch, as if his wife has been staying with friends instead of detained as being of unsound mind. Ally takes her accustomed place at the head of the table and seats him on her right, where the master of a house would put an honoured lady guest. Miss Mason sets out silver and china with unusual precision. Mrs Rudge speaks of vegetable gardening, Miss Mason of the warm weather and its probable effect on the harvest. Mrs Henning, in between carrying in the stew and taking out the plates, discloses opinions on the Irish Question more insistent than the occasion justifies, but Ally is able to draw out Mr Curnow's consequent account of meeting an Irishman in a Plymouth hotel when Mrs Henning fetches the currant pudding. Ally fills bowls and passes cream.

They gather at the door to watch Mr and Mrs Curnow leave. Mrs Curnow needs to play her part, Ally thinks, she needs to be well, or the first evidence from Rose Tree House will be failure. Mrs Curnow turns around in her seat and waves her new handkerchief until the wheels bump away between the banks of cow parsley and buttercups that sway and dance along the lane.

at this time in Kyoto

The window is sequinned with rain, and beyond it clouds huddle low over the town. He will write this next letter, and then speak to Penvenick about the Scilly job before Joseph Kidd recognises a chance to put himself forward. It would be better for Penvenick to have Tom, the senior man, in charge, for even if he insists on overseeing the design himself his faith in Tom should save him several rough crossings and hard going on the clifftop. The islands themselves will be pleasant enough, this time of year, but the sea is still the Atlantic Ocean, unpredictable and bad-tempered even when the shore breathes the fragrance of gorse and the berries soak up sunshine in the hedgerows. It would be good to be there. Not to be here. He signs his name and presses the blotting paper over the letter. As he peels it back he remembers the movements of the maker of paper fans, the careful unveiling of filigree birds and foliage.

Tom leaves the office earlier than he has been doing, to have time to wash and change at home before appearing again on the doorstep at Ludgate House. It is dull again today, the pavement oiled not quite with rain but with water settling from the air. The tide is rising, the estuary dark and sullen. He fastens his jacket and steps briskly through the mizzle. He does not know what he was thinking, to turn up unannounced like that. He does not know why he is going back today, except that he said he would and it would perhaps be more embarrassing, having asked for an invitation, to change his mind and send apologies than simply to go through with the thing. But you went, Ally would say, because you wanted to visit your things, because you miss them and you hope that seeing them in their new place will reconcile you to yours, and perhaps your instinct will prove correct; in any case the visit does no harm. Or at least that is what she might have said had she anything to say to him still. He looks across the water, to where the low grey sky is snagged and tangled in the tops of the trees on the hill. She will be inside, probably, sitting at her fireside with the madwomen whose companionship she finds preferable to his own. She will be reading or writing, in passionate communion with the minds of people who are not there. Ally, it occurs to him, finds it easier to be with people who are not there, or not all there. She likes people mad, or dead, or far away. Scilly may not be far enough.

The cottage smells of damp again. He pushes hard against the front door to close it behind him and throws his jacket over the bannisters. There is a letter, a London postmark and a scrawled handwriting he doesn't recognise. Ally meant well, he knows, with the white paint and pale curtains, intended a new beginning purified from carpets thick with the dust of departed tenants and previous owners, from the condensed exhalations of everyone who has lived here in three hundred years. The plaster and paint may be evidence that she did not know until he came back that she no longer wishes to be his wife, but he misses the brown floral patterns, the mismatched chairs, a setting in which he was wholly unselfconscious. All this white, he thinks, this emptiness, it makes him feel like a performer, as if some propitiation is required for blotting it with one's presence as a boy spoils a garden of new-fallen snow. He still has the letter in his hand.

It's from Annie Forrest. *Please forgive my writing like this out of the blue, an unwarrantable interference, and I find myself wishing to add, please burn this letter, but you will know best and I will, after all, say nothing that I would not say to her. I have heard of your separation from Ally and I could not let things rest.* She thinks he doesn't understand. She thinks he hasn't tried hard enough, and she's right, this is an unwarrantable interference. *I imagine that when you were in Japan you were always trying to guess what people wanted and what they meant, trying to guess how you might appear in their eyes? Hoping that by rigorous observation you might be able to avoid giving offence? This idea of mine is a compliment, Tom. Many men, even if they travel, never live like this even for half an hour of their lives. But if it was like that for you, if you were watchful and hesitant from first waking until sleep, then you know how it is to be a woman and especially to be a woman entering a profession. We are always strangers in a strange land. I think Ally is like that all the time, hunted and cunning, because she has had no safe place, no home. She is now and has always been afraid of her mother. Her Aunt Mary and Uncle James love her but they don't understand why she is a doctor and she has always known that she doesn't know which fork to use or what should not be said in mixed company or among ladies with their gloves on. I think Rose Tree House may be the first place where she doesn't have to guess or see herself through another person's eyes, and that's why she doesn't want to be anywhere else.*

Who is Annie, he thinks, to tell him about the mind of his own wife, to write from London about a marriage she does not know? He puts the letter down on the windowsill, stares out into the garden where the greens darken and creep in the heavy light. Annie does know Ally, he cannot deny that. She has known Ally much longer than he has. Hunted and

348

cunning. He remembers a fox glimpsed once early in the morning in the rolling fields outside Harrogate, running so fast it seemed to move straight as an arrow over rich ploughed land only dusted with green, and then a few minutes later the inundation of the dogs and the reverberation of hooves in the ground under his feet, where seeds were unfurling in the darkness and sharp-nosed creatures beginning to sense spring. That way, he wanted to tell the men in their red coats, that way back to the river, not up the hill. But the hounds were on the scent and the hunters knew where they were going. He remembers the dance of the temple fox, the fierce joy.

He goes down to the basement and lights the fire he set in the stove this morning, to make hot water for a wash. At this time in Kyoto, all across town men are making their way home in the knowledge that a wooden tub of scented water has been prepared against their return, clean clothes laid out in square folds. Even the less fortunate, even, for example, a foreigner who might arrive there with no position awaiting, a man who might come to make his fortune, have the bath houses at their disposal. He touches the copper, only beginning to warm. It would not be the same, of course. It would be foolhardy to pretend that Makoto, Tatsuo, Makiko would welcome him without the state imprimatur by which even his unofficial activities were marked. Mrs Senhouse was often passing remarks about the disgraceful proceedings of foreign drifters and the embarrassment they caused to respectable expatriates. No. Better to stay here, to justify Penvenick's confidence and hope, in due course, to reap the natural reward. He will go to Scilly. He puts his hand to the copper again. The water is warm enough now.

The tall servant opens the door wider this time, and takes Tom's coat, hat and umbrella. Mr De Rivers is expecting him this evening, she says pointedly. The candles in the hall have not been lit, but in the drawing room the lamps are bright and there is still enough light reflecting off the sea for Tom to see the newspaper held before De Rivers' face. And that there are no Japanese hangings on the walls.

De Rivers lowers the paper but he does not get up. 'Tom Cavendish. Well, well. Here you are. Please, sit down.'

Tom sits, and then finds that he is low in a delicate little chair. A woman's chair.

'I'll ring for some supper for you.'

He is, then, to be fed like an indigent, as if he had come in search of a free meal. 'Please don't trouble. Unless you are taking something yourself.'

De Rivers leans forward and touches the bell. 'No trouble. Not to me. I told them you'd want something. Just dined, myself.'

Tom glances around the room. It may be a new glass case, in the dimness beside the door, but the embroideries, the kimono, the three great vases, are certainly not here, and there is not room in the case for one quarter of what he brought. The maid opens the door and is told to bring a tray for our visitor. Not the lacquerwork persimmons, he thinks, let them not be putting hot dishes on the golden fruit. Although much of the point of lacquer is its strength; he himself was encouraged to scratch and bang. But did not.

'Now then, Tom. I hope things are settling down, now you're home? Back at work, and so on?'

Tom nods. 'Thank you, yes. I believe I was able to do useful work in Japan. Although I had hoped to see an earthquake – just a small one, of course, but sufficient to test the apparatus. It is an interesting challenge.'

'And Mrs Cavendish? I hear that she has not been idle in your absence. A new madhouse in Flushing, of all places. Ruffled some feathers, I can tell you that.'

Tom feels himself flush again. Makoto should come, he

thinks, and teach etiquette. 'It is a convalescent home. The residents are not mad.'

De Rivers sniffs. 'Mad enough to have been confined in the asylum. It's news to me a person can be madder than that. Anyway, your wife's well?'

Although Tom has never known Ally to be ill, she seems, he realises, in better health than he has seen her before. In her acceptance of their separation she has achieved something, a new bearing or manner.

'She is, yes.' He looks around again. 'The embroideries – the silk hangings—'

'Just what I wanted,' says De Rivers. 'I told you so. And you accepted your fee.'

Tom leans forward, his face hot. 'No. It's not that. Not the money.'

'No? Because I think anyone would agree that I have been generous.'

Tom wishes he could throw handfuls of notes onto the floor. Take it, he thinks, take the money. Ally doesn't want a house anyway. 'Indeed so. But you do not display the objects? You do not wish them constantly before your eyes?'

De Rivers sits back. 'I cannot display everything, Tom. Even in such a house as this. Everything you brought me has been added to my collection, I assure you. Properly stored. I take care of my things, I promise you that. Properly catalogued as well, and not every collector does that, not by a long chalk.'

There are footsteps, and the maid knocks and backs through the door, the tray in her hands. Tom rises and takes it from her. In the glass cases, false eyes glimmer with candlelight and dark fur merges with the dusk. Of course a man who likes the company of dead animals will not value the work of Japanese craftsmen. Tom feels sick. There is a small tureen of soup on the tray, with a ladle and a white bowl with a red and gold rim, and something under a white cloth. He returns to De Rivers. There is nowhere to put a tray. He stands.

'Well, put it down, Tom. Here.'

De Rivers throws yesterday's *Times* on the floor and pushes the occasional table with his foot. The tray sticks precariously over both ends. Tom centres the tureen, to make it more stable. He serves himself soup, and the smell rises in the cold room like the smell of seasickness on a ship's deck. He pushes the spoon around.

'So they are in boxes still? The fans, the tea set. The netsuke? They are very small, surely easy to display. Although of course they should not be parted from the inro.'

De Rivers frowns. 'Eat up, it will get cold. You mean those toggle things? Charming little objects, aren't they. Hard to imagine grown men going round with toys hanging round their waists. All quite safe in my storerooms. I didn't get where I am by carelessness, I assure you.'

'No,' Tom says. 'Naturally not.'

He cannot eat the soup. Across the water, the harbour lights at St Mawes flicker and take hold of the darkness, and the first flashes from St Anthony Head scythe the dusk.

She has brought him low, he thinks. There is nothing left. He will cross the water to Rose Tree House and ask her to start again from the beginning. Ally, his wife.

352

a life's work

Although it is the middle of the afternoon, equidistant from the daily offices of lunch and tea, Ally leaves the women in the house and garden and makes her way through the trees to the beach. Tom is gone from her now, she thinks. He has not come to find her, has not objected to her leaving, and there is a pain, a hollowness, in her chest. A pain, she thinks, caused by metaphor, since the correct understanding of anatomy would suggest that sadness should make its bodily manifestations in the head, in the wormy grey matter of the brain rather than the doors and chambers of the heart. The trees' bark is a darker black, the leaves a brighter green, for the pulsating heat of the afternoon, as if today everything is more vivid, clearer to the eye, than usual. The doors of perception, she thinks, the chambers of the human heart. *In my Father's house are many mansions.* We cannot speak even of anatomy without metaphor.

A seagull calls from the rocks ahead and the scent of pine needles hangs in the still air. She thinks of the women behind her, living for now in the shelter of Rose Tree House, between the institution of the asylum and the institution of marriage. So many of women's griefs, she thinks, begin in marriage, in the expectation of a *happily ever after* set into perpetual motion by romance. It is not in romance, nor even sex, that we find the human purpose, but in good work faithfully done. In kindness, which finds sexual expression less often than one might hope, and in endurance. If there is happiness for her in the world, she will find it in the faith of those who never abandoned her, with Annie and Aunt Mary and, in a different way, with her patients and her colleagues. It is they who have sustained her, who caught her when she fell. She lifts her face to the dappled light, breathes in trees and sea. It is here that she will find her peace, in friendship, in the companionship of women and the satisfaction of the labour of mind and heart and hands. In the work of healing and in this place, in the green shade and along the tideline of West Cornwall where she first saw in her mind's eye her taunting spirits crossing the water, first imagined her final parting from those who had so long haunted her mind.

She follows the path worn around the brambles by the feet of madwomen and comes out onto the beach, where the grey rocks reflect the white heat of the sky and the sea surges and spangles. It is a pity that all this analysis, all this understanding, does nothing for the causes and little for the symptoms of our pain, gives us only ways of thinking, ways of saying what cannot be borne. Goblin foxes, ghosts, and also the invisible sickness of what we call the mind: they are all stories, illness itself only a metaphor for what can befall the spirit. Ally steps across the granite, the same stone, probably, that makes the white cottage sitting empty across the water. The seaweed is pale and dry under the sun, the mussel shells closed tight until the cold tide rises over them again. She clambers over the last rocks until waves wash at her feet, lifts her face to the sun and closes her eyes to see the redness of her living blood, the motes in her own eyes. It is not metaphor alone, she thinks, that can save us, but also the act of living, of continuing to be with each other in the world. It is a life's work, to watch the beating of the human heart, to name what we are doing and yet be able to do it.

She hears a footfall on the stones and opens her eyes. Tom is there, coming out from under the trees, crossing the beach to find her in her own place, in her right mind.

Epilogue

Home

The trees on the shore are ten years nearer the sky, and the gulls who cried Tom's return have fallen into the sea, feathers washed from flesh and flesh from bone, beaks and claws sand-sifted in the weeds and wash of the seabed. Rocks are water-worn, tide and current carved in granite as the sea rubs at the edges of the land, erases the outlines of our archipelago.

The boy runs. Small brown birds flee the bushes before him and a blue-gleaming magpie scolds from above. Sticks crack, leaves rustle. He runs on tiptoe over the ants but does not try to save them all; boys run and ants die, other ants lift their corpses and hurry on. He brushes a fly from the pale hair on his arm and runs on, leaps across the rocks and out onto the sand. There is a rock pool here where sea anemones curl tight as fists, where spider-sized crabs rush for crevices too small for his fingers. The afternoon sun has filled the rock with heat and he lies face down, feels the warmth soak through his shorts and shirt, through his skin and bone, the stone ancient under his cheek. He rolls over and offers himself to the sky full of white light.

Tree-shades lean over the tea-house. The first of the afternoon's returning rooks crosses the sunlight, and under the bushes creatures of dusk begin to stir and nose. Sometimes she comes at this hour. Tom tidies the tea set, fills the bamboo caddy. He picks a stray leaf from the edge of a tatami mat and returns it to the outdoors. Sometimes, she comes here now.

The sea-sanded stone has rubbed paint from the door and begun to finger the wood beneath, disclosing rings of growth. Boots and shoes have ground soil, sand, leaf-mould, dust, the droppings of rabbits and chickens and the carapaces of insects into the painted floor. Coats hanging on the wall have somehow left their winter shadows under the empty pegs. Ally leaves the door open behind her. She doesn't notice the annoyance of the crow on the lawn who abandons a fallen plum because of her passage, nor the scurry of the vole under the rose bush by the gate. Sometimes at this hour she finds him in the garden.

Tom and Ally walk together through the trees to the beach. There they find Laurence half-asleep by the rock pool, the day cooling around him. They dust him down, the boy, and take him back to the house where tea waits on the table and Ally's patients gather as evening light from over the water fills the house.

They take him home.

Acknowledgements

I am deeply grateful to the Authors' Foundation for a grant that allowed me to make several trips to Japan. I could not have written this book without their support.

Llewelyn Thomas and the staff of Walk Japan put together an excellent itinerary of Tom's places for me, and Jamie Dwyer was a superb guide on my first Japanese tour.

On my second trip, I stayed in Nakayama House, Higashiyama, Kyoto, where Amy made me very welcome and went far beyond the call of duty in arranging one-to-one classes in traditional arts and crafts. The staff at the Museum of Traditional Crafts in Kyoto answered many questions with great patience and allowed me to sit writing for hours in their beautiful space.

Most of what I know about late nineteenth-century Japan began with the study day at the Ashmolean Museum held in November 2012 to mark the opening of the 'Threads of Silk and Gold' exhibition of Meiji-era textiles. Dr Clare Pollard, the curator of Japanese art at the Ashmolean, spent hours sharing her expertise and did me the great favour of commenting on a full draft. She gave me access to archival material in Oxford and Kyoto and introduced me to Mr Mori and Eri Matsumoto of the Kawashima Selkon Textile Company in Kyoto. Mr Mori and Ms Matsumoto devoted an afternoon to showing me the company's past and present craftsmanship, some of whose qualities I hope are reflected in this book.

Joyce Seaman, also at the Ashmolean, helped me with the archival work and sent copies of nineteenth-century collectors' photos that remained above my desk as I wrote.

In Cornwall, I am deeply obliged to the staff of the Cornwall County Record Office in Truro, who catalogued the handwritten nineteenth-century records of the Bodmin Asylum especially so I could read them. Once again, I thank Katy Lazenby at the Falmouth Bookseller for finding books I needed before I knew I needed them.

I thank my colleagues and students in the Writing Programme at the University of Warwick for their support and conversation.

I am grateful again to Dr Sharon Dixon for many conversations about women and medicine and for sound advice about aspects of Ally's practice. Thank you to Sinead Mooney, for reading a full draft and helping me through an impasse.

All errors of fact or probability remain, as ever, my own.

At Granta, I thank Max Porter for his wisdom and his patience, Anne Meadows for having the courage of her convictions and everyone for being so pleasant to work with. Amber Dowell is the best copy-editor a fussy writer could imagine. Thank you to Anna Webber at United Agents for all that she does.

BODIES OF LIGHT

'Wise and tender' *Financial Times*

'I loved and admired *Bodies of Light*. Right from the
first page, it's fair to say I was quite mesmerised.
This is such a good novel' Margaret Forster

Sisters Ally and May Moberley grow up in
Victorian Manchester, surrounded by their father's
decadent paintings and dominated by their austere,
evangelical mother. While May poses for the artists in her
father's circle, Ally devotes herself to her mother's ambitions,
working hard to join the first generation of female doctors.
But soon bitterness and tragedy divide the family, and
Ally leaves home to escape the subtle terrors of her
childhood and begin a new life in London.

Bodies of Light is a profound and provocative
book about family. It is a gripping story told
with rare precision and tenderness.

'Moss's third novel confirms the richness of her concerns ...
[A] tremendously talented writer' *Guardian*

'Concise and powerful ... [it] ends with you
wanting more' *Independent on Sunday*

'Thought-provoking and illuminating' *Daily Mail*

COLD EARTH

'Moss is such a master at evoking suspense . . .
a rich treat' Jane Smiley, *Guardian*

'Full of burial pits, strange happenings
and the cries of the dead . . . an apocalyptic take
on *Lord of the Flies* meets *The Secret History*' *Metro*

On the west coast of Greenland, a team of six
archaeologists has assembled to unearth traces of the lost
Viking settlements. But while they settle into uneasy
domesticity, camping between the ruined farmstead and the
burnt-out chapel, there is news of a pandemic back home. As
the Arctic winter approaches, their communications with the
outside world fall away. Utterly gripping, *Cold Earth* is an
exceptional and haunting first novel about the possibility
of survival and the traces we leave behind.

'An unnerving, ambitious debut . . . utterly absorbing and –
appropriately enough – very chilling' *Daily Mail*

'A thought-provoking, suspenseful work that leaves
the reader in no doubt about the fragility of the human
condition: not just of the individual struggling to survive a
hostile environment, but of a species that is changing its
home planet in potentially deadly ways' *Observer*

'Moss's stark writing delivers stinging splashes
of cold water. Every element of the novel is
distilled for purity of purpose' *The Times*

NIGHT WAKING

'Moss writes marvellously (and often hilariously) about the clash between career and motherhood' *The Times*

'Highly enjoyable' *Daily Telegraph*

Anna Bennett hasn't slept in months. Overwhelmed by the needs of her two young boys and opposed on principle to domesticity, Anna is a historian struggling to write without a room of her own. Stranded on a Hebridean island where her husband is researching the puffins, Anna's work changes when her son finds a baby's skeleton buried in the garden. As an investigation begins, Anna must confront the island's past while finding a way to live with the competing demands of the present.

'Tartly humourous, sad and clever' *Sunday Times*

'A brilliantly observed comedy of twenty-first century manners ... a tightly plotted mystery that keeps the reader wondering, and hoping, until the final page' *Financial Times*

'The trials of family life are comically and stylishly depicted ... [an] original and accomplished novel' *Daily Mail*

'I read *Night Waking* with avid enjoyment and no small amount of recognition' Maggie O'Farrell, *Scotsman*

Also by Sarah Moss and available from Granta Books
www.granta.com

GHOST WALL

LONGLISTED FOR THE WOMEN'S PRIZE FOR FICTION

SHORTLISTED FOR THE RSL ONDAATJE PRIZE

'I love this book . . . Put your life on hold while you finish it'
Maggie O'Farrell

'This book ratcheted the breath out of me so skilfully that as soon
as I'd finished, the only thing I wanted was to read it again'
Jessie Burton, author of *The Miniaturist*

Seventeen-year-old Silvie is on a camp in rural Northumberland with
her father and a group of scholars, led by an archaeologist with an
interest in Iron Age sacrifice. As Silvie glimpses new freedoms with
the students, her relationship with her father deteriorates, until the
haunting rites of the past begin to bleed into the present.

'An instant classic' Emma Donoghue, author of *Room*

'Grabs you by the guts and never lets go. Dazzling'
Elizabeth Day, author of *The Party*